*heliо*graphica

AS A RESULT OF THE HELIOGRAPHICA SUSTAINABILITY

PROGRAM, 10 CENTS FROM THE PROCEEDS OF

THIS BOOK WILL BE DONATED TO ENVIRONMENTAL

CAUSES THAT SUPPORT FOREST PRESERVATION AND

ENVIRONMENTAL EDUCATION FOR CHILDREN.

Under a Spell

A Novel
By Samantha Adaggio

*helio*graphica

Under a Spell
Copyright© 2004 by Samantha Adaggio

*helio*graphica

For information:
Heliographica
2261 Market St., #504
San Francisco, CA 94114
www.heliographica.com

Library of Congress Catalog Number: 2005923629
ISBN 1-933037-25-3

Printed in the United States of America

No part of this book may be reproduced or transmitted in any form or by any means, graphic, electronic or mechanical, including photocopying, recording, typing, or by any information storage retrieval system, without the permission of the publisher.

Under a Spell

For my soul mate

*"What if you slept, and what if in your sleep you dreamed,
and what if in your dream you went to heaven,
and there you plucked a strange and beautiful flower,
and what if, when you awoke, you held that flower in your hand?
Ah, what then?"*

—Samuel Taylor Coleridge,
Biographia Literaria (1817)

Contents

	Acknowledgments	
Introduction	Half of the Puzzle	1
Chapter 1	March 17th, St. Patrick's Day	3
Chapter 2	March 19th, Aladdin	8
Chapter 3	March 20th, The Conference	21
Chapter 4	March 20th, Grant	29
Chapter 5	March 20th, Mason	35
Chapter 6	March 20th, Club Utopia	41
Chapter 7	March 20th, Phantom	46
Chapter 8	March 21st, Red Flag	56
Chapter 9	March 21st, Serendipity	59
Chapter 10	March 21st, Tournament of Kings	64
Chapter 11	March 22nd, Big Sky	79
Chapter 12	March 22nd, Sydney	90
Chapter 13	March 22nd, The Call	92
Chapter 14	March 22nd, Fate	99
Chapter 15	March 23rd, The Coin	103
Chapter 16	March 23rd, The Stars	105
Chapter 17	March 23rd, Her Gift	112
Chapter 18	March 24th, Lady's Day	118
Chapter 19	Journeys of the Soul	121
Chapter 20	Epiphanies	128
Chapter 21	Her Book	142
Chapter 22	After Las Vegas	149
Chapter 23	The Impossible Wish	165
Chapter 24	The Larchers	177
Chapter 25	Bewitching Hours	188
Chapter 26	Ad Infinitum	192
Chapter 27	Her Personal Collection	203
Chapter 28	Heaven on Earth	217
Chapter 29	Valentine's Day	230
Chapter 30	The Masquerade Ball	234
Chapter 31	Journey Home	236
	Author's Note	

Acknowledgments

My loving thanks to my family and all my friends, whose colorful personalities gave life to the memorable characters in this book. You all know who you are.

To my military technical advisors, especially Major Joe "Hooter" Feheley, you have my heartfelt thanks for allowing the readers and me to *step to the jet* with you.

To my editors, especially Ron Hein, thank you for making sense of it all.

To the staff of Heliographica, especially Jacob LeWinter, Melton Cartes and Sheila Kappeler, you're a great team to have.

To my advanced readers and many reviewers, especially John Flores and Marilyn Monkelbaan, you have my applause for your insights.

To Dr. Kathryn Vullo, I am truly grateful for the pearls.

And, saving the best for last, to my better half Vincent Lawyer, thank you for having faith in me against all odds. I love you even more because of your infinite patience, understanding, and unconditional love through it all, especially through the darkest of spells.

Introduction

Half of the Puzzle

"Ask your question in secret. Relax, open your mind, and focus. Focus on the question and any other people involved."

Mercedes closed her eyes and in her mind she asked, *What does true love have in store for me?*

Madame Claire, a psychic and cartomancer, expertly shuffled the cards. She wore red acrylic nails, each embellished with tiny rhinestone moons and stars. Her dangling earrings reflected the light of the scented candles. The room smelled sweet with lavender.

"Please cut the deck with the question in your mind."

Mercedes did as she was told.

Madame Claire dealt six cards on the left in the pattern of a cross and followed it with four cards on the right. After a moment of meditation, she looked intently at the cards.

Slowly she lifted her head and locked her deep-set, ebony eyes with Mercedes', who felt a sudden uneasiness with her gaze. Drawn across Madame Claire's middle-aged face was a hint of something ancient, wisdom-filled, and mysterious.

"You must go through great pain and tremendous suffering in the name of true love. You will never have to worry about material comfort. Your strength lies within your spirit, which will prevail, even at the very darkest hours. You will always be content, but because of freewill, the happiness you desire will elude you all your life. Numbers and primary colors are very significant in your life, just as double occurrences are. Parallel lives will cross, old souls will reunite. Same names, same circumstances are your guides. Heed them when they surround you at your crossroads. They are the precursors to life-altering changes in your life. You will never know if it is for the good or bad, but it will greatly impact your life." Her voice was disturbingly grim.

Mercedes' best friend, Sydney, shook her head and leaned over to whisper in her ear, "I don't like the sound of it." She pushed the fallen lock of auburn hair behind her ear; her dark chocolate eyes matched her sleeveless dress.

"Shh!" Sydney's younger sister, Cassie, who sat on her right, silenced her. Her loosely gathered brown ponytail almost whipped Sydney's face as she turned her attention back to the psychic. Her demeanor was like a juror in one of her courtrooms, her attention wrapped up in the testimony of an expert witness. After biting her thumbnail, Cassie asked about taking a job in another law firm, while Sydney wondered about her future with her attorney husband, Patrick Trahison.

As they were leaving, the psychic stopped Mercedes and said in a low voice, "For he is your half of the puzzle as you are to his. One will always find the other." Before she could protest, Madame Claire continued ominously, "There are *other* souls in the labyrinth of life, great care must be heeded. Do not be deceived. *Rien n'est pendant qu'il semble."*

Before she could say anything, the psychic pressed her hand and abruptly walked away. She opened her hand, surprised to find her payment for the reading was returned.

"Wait!" she called out, but the lady in black had disappeared in the back room. The candles blew out as she passed.

"What did she say to you? Was that French?"

"I'm not sure, Syd. I really wasn't paying attention," Mercedes lied. She had both heard and understood Madame Claire's last words perfectly. French was a language Mercedes knew well.

"Do you believe this crap, Merc?" she asked incredulously.

"Do you?"

"Let's get out of here," Sydney announced.

"Yeah, it was fun until it got spooky."

The three close friends emerged from Madame Claire's subterranean sanctum, climbing the few steps up to join the masses along South Street, one of Philadelphia's famous streets in its equally famous Society Hill neighborhood.

It was a typical Saturday night turnout; South Street was jammed with people from all walks of life and representing every lifestyle, strolling or cruising in their convertibles and dodging the taxis that hovered like buzzards for fares. Colorful people with uninhibited fashions provided eye candy for the people watchers dining out in the open air along the many sidewalk cafés. Taxi cabs vied for fares and the sidewalk traffic mimicked the rhythm of the street.

"Oh look, another genuine psychic," Sydney said cynically as she pointed with her well-manicured finger to another huge neon sign that read, "Accurate readings. Find out your future. Reasonable prices."

As they passed by a small art gallery, Mercedes stopped dead on her tracks, wincing from the pelvic pain she suddenly felt. She clenched her pelvic area instinctively.

"You all right?" Sydney asked with concern.

"I'm fine. It's nothing." She smiled convincingly. The pain disappeared as quickly as it appeared.

Her gaze fell on a print of Edmund Blair Leighton's *God Speed*, displayed in the glass storefront window behind Sydney. The way the mounted Medieval knight, clad in red, was looking at the elegant lady with cascading long hair reminded her of a familiar past. The lady was tying her "favor," or symbol of love—an embroidered red scarf—on his left arm. Losing a lady's favor in battle was considered to be more of a loss than losing armor.

Sydney followed Mercedes' mesmerized gaze and asked, "Want us to go inside?" There was no answer.

Cassie echoed, "Hey, *Slayer*—want us to go inside?"

"Huh? What?" Mercedes responded, bewildered.

"Want to go inside?" Sydney repeated.

She immediately looked at her watch and replied, "No, that's all right. We'll be late for our dinner reservations at the Rock Lobster. And—" Sydney's cell phone rang, interrupting her.

"You're there already? Okay, give us ten minutes. *Ciao!*"

Without prompting, she said, "It was Donna. She's just arrived at the restaurant with Mallory and Renée."

Mercedes nodded, "Well, that settles it. Let's go."

She stole a quick glance back at the print as they turned the corner to hail a taxi. She immediately thought of Madame Claire. She was not certain of how to feel about what those bittersweet words predicted for her. She had freewill and could forge her own life with her own choices, provided she made the right choices. Suddenly, she felt a sharper thrust of pain in the same place that took her breath away—it was almost unbearable. The unwelcome pain made her nervous, but the French words echoing in her mind made her shudder even more: *Rien n'est pendant qu'il semble.* Nothing is as it seems.

Chapter 1

March 17th, St. Patrick's Day

"How am I going to convince Mercedes to go?" Myles pensively debated his strategy to maneuver the only female engineer on his staff into taking an impromptu business trip.

"Frankly, I don't care." Wade Meyers, his boss, looked at the company's youngest vice president of engineering. "Wallace Water Industries has the chance to close a deal for a multi-million dollar buyout of that medium-sized, water utility outside of Las Vegas, and it's too promising a deal to pass up. They want her out there. And you know the opportunity surfaced only because of Mercedes' participation in the Annual Water Industries Convention in Anaheim last summer."

Oh boy! This is going to be more difficult than I first imagined, he thought. Myles stared at his monitor, scanning the page with her travel schedule and shook his head, muttering, "Her schedule shows she's completely booked. She's heading out from here to St. Louis and then to Phoenix for a monthly project site meeting." Scrolling back to the previous page, he added, "Philly to St. Louis to Phoenix. No wonder she's even logged in as a road warrior since she returned from sick leave."

"Problems?"

Myles looked at his boss. Her exhaustion was becoming apparent, but there was no evidence of it in her work. "No. No problems. I admire her ambition and drive to get things done. Her work is top notch. She's very organized."

Actually, the word *anal* came to mind, and he knew that an unexpected addition to her busy itinerary would prove difficult.

"She told me last week that she has plans to relax next weekend."

"Make it happen. You manage a staff of twenty-two highly educated engineers spread out among the planning, design and construction departments. You're used to contending with a fully loaded schedule and handling projects in thirty-four U.S. states and three countries in Europe. You can handle her, can't you?"

Myles looked over at his phone and started to pick it up to call her in to his office. Quickly, he replaced the phone on the receiver and thought, *If only this was a European trip. I wouldn't have to sweat this out right now. I wouldn't have to walk down to her office and practically beg her to go. Damn!*

"Like I said, make it happen."

As his boss stood up and left the office, Myles made a decision. Noting Mercedes was scheduled to leave in less than five hours, he picked up the phone again.

"Barb?"

"Yes, sir."

"I need a favor." He knew his charming fifty-something secretary was smiling.

"Yes sir, what?"

"I need to rearrange Mercedes' travel itinerary."

"I take it this will be a surprise to her?"

"Yes." He outlined what he needed done, and with a sigh he added, "I need to include all the perks you and I can think of too." He knew he needed to ease the burden of his last-minute request.

"Okay, I'll get back to you as soon as possible. It shouldn't take me long."

Myles leaned back in his chair as he hung up the phone. He knew Mercedes' type-A personality in the work arena all too well. *Yet she's a completely different person outside of the workplace—a sweetheart*, he thought. He had been unsuccessful in a couple of his attempts to get her to compromise in the past. When she managed to state her case with conviction, she could even persuade him to forgo adding a particular project to her list of tasks. He walked away not knowing how skillfully she had played him to her advantage. She was merciless.

It's that damned smile! he smirked, thinking with consternation about that incident.

He sighed deeply. *She enjoys verbal sparring. Might explain why she has so many lawyer friends. I know not to get her started. Oh no—especially not with her pet peeves: assignments, advancements, and even conduct. Ugh—I'll never hear the end of it.* He shook his head in frustration and returned back to his work.

After what seemed like just a few minutes, his secretary was knocking at his open door, interrupting his thoughts. "Excuse me, Myles, but here's what you asked for earlier. And don't worry—everything is all set. Let me know if you need anything else." She placed the flight package to Las Vegas in his in-box.

"Thanks, Barb! I really appreciate your efforts in getting this to me on such short notice."

"Surely." She smiled and left quickly for her desk.

While he continued his private negotiations with himself about what perks to offer Mercedes, he swiftly gathered all the necessary paperwork for her trip, along with copies of the project files, and placed them neatly in a brown accordion file organizer, simply labeled as *Las Vegas*. He glanced at his watch, noting that he had three hours left before her flight took off.

The walk from his office to hers was a long one, which gave him more time to prepare his case. There were four buildings in the corporate complex and the engineering department was located in the building adjacent to the executive offices where he was.

He crossed a skyway above Vine Street and then went down a flight of stairs to her corner office. Standing in front of her door, he looked at her name placard: *Mercedes P. Sinclair, Director of Engineering.*

Through her closed door, he could hear Mozart's *Clarinet Concerto KV 622.* It was through her love of classical music that they had found common ground for a friendship. He viewed her as the sister he never had. Though he was biased in his protective nature toward her, he remained impartial otherwise. After a deep sigh, he knocked with confidence on her door and turned the doorknob to enter her office as the music began its hypnotic adagio tempo.

He had always noted that her office was an atypical engineer's office. It was more like a cozy study with her paintings and wall art, healthy greenery and eclectic accessories from her travels. Only her desktop and the phone lines gave a hint of chaos.

Mercedes was using the hands-free phone headset while she worked at her desk—he noticed that five of her six phone lines were lit. She signaled for him to wait for a moment, giving him a wide, friendly smile before becoming very distracted with her phone conversation. Putting aside a small metal puzzle, she turned the music down and jotted a hurried note to herself in her planner: *Blazer/long-term parking*, while listening to a loud, irate electrical contractor on the phone. After a few moments, she ended the call, saying, "Right, that's all I'm agreeing to. No, no exceptions. Send it over immediately. Thanks."

"Hi Myles. Be right with you." She clicked on her intercom. "Donna, can you take my incoming calls? Thanks. Yes, yes, I'll be sure to visit the St. Louis Museum of Art when I'm there. I promise."

"Myles, it's good to see you!" Mercedes smiled, "Always a pleasure." She had noticed the obvious concern on his face, which had remained in place as he had impatiently taken a seat across from her desk.

As always, Myles was impeccably dressed, and his appearance normally matched his sanguine presence. He was less than six feet tall with light brown, neatly cropped hair. The greenish designer suit he was wearing matched his light green eyes, which were often hidden by the bookish pair of designer glasses he always wore. She wasn't surprised that he also wore a green shamrock tie in honor of the holiday. He was after all celebrating his Irish heritage.

At that moment he wasn't smiling, but whenever he smiled, it could light up the room for a few seconds before he shifted to a serious look and began discussing the intricacies of hydraulic flow calculations or started a staff meeting.

In meetings his serious look made him appear imperious, especially because of the deep timbre of his voice when he spoke. Nevertheless, he enjoyed cubicle humor, had a hearty laugh and instinctively said, "I've got hand!" whenever something worked in his favor, especially in a battle of wits.

Judging from his body language, he needed something urgent from her. She noted the file that he was carrying. Mentally she prepared herself for a negotiation or a fun witty debate with him as she undocked her laptop from the docking unit that linked it to the mainframe.

"Happy St. Patrick's Day, Myles! How are you? What brings you to our side of the tracks?"

"Mercedes, I need a huge favor from you." He didn't mince any words, and when he didn't even acknowledge one of his favorite holidays, her curiosity was piqued. *It must be really important*, she concluded.

"A favor?" About to give him a quick protest, she stopped when he held up his hand with his palm facing her, interrupting her thoughts.

"Before you say anything, please hear me out."

"Ok." Reluctantly, she conceded and sank back into her chair, her fingers joined in a classic steeple against her lips as she waited for the facts. "Go on."

She prepared to end the conversation quickly. She had to make a quick personal stop en route to catching her flight.

He cleared his throat, "Mercedes, I got a visit from Mr. Meyers today and I need you to go to Las Vegas. The people from Nevada insisted that you personally attend the final negotiations on the water deal. They want you to close the deal. Would you do me a personal favor and add this trip onto your St. Louis trek? I'll make it worth your while."

"And?" There was a pause.

"Actually, I need you to be there all week for another matter."

"What other matter?"

"Your paper on hydraulics. Nevada Utility wants you to present it at a conference they're hosting. It's also in Las Vegas."

"I may be able to swing the negotiations—but a conference too? I highly doubt it."

"Mercedes, we need a presence out there, especially when we are about to close the deal with them. You can do it efficiently and kill two birds with one stone. What do you say?" He punctuated his question with a smile.

She grabbed the small metal puzzle on her desktop. In her hands, she began to unravel the puzzle while she kept still, looking through him, beginning a mental checklist of her itinerary.

Myles had seen the small metal puzzle on numerous occasions. He knew it was her thinking tool. He waited impatiently.

"You know I'm also scheduled to go to Phoenix for three days after St. Louis."

"Yes. I'm taking you off the Phoenix flight. Victor Lamond has been working with you on the project from the start, so he'll be a natural fit to take your place. Anything else?"

She unconsciously put the puzzle back together. She flashed a disarming smile at him, and lowered her voice an octave, which she knew would unsettle him.

"Let's see. You *need* me. But, I *don't* need to accept. This is entirely a *huge* personal favor. Have I heard these facts correctly?"

"Precisely," he nodded quickly.

Putting the puzzle aside again, she rose from her chair, walked around her desk, and then carefully leaned against her desk with her arms folded. He watched her graceful movements, noticing how she looked like a prowling lioness with her chestnut brown hair gathered up with a mane comb. She was very fashionable—but professional—in a deep olive-colored suit with a short skirt.

The look on her face and her poised posture, a posture he knew too well, alerted him that she was not done with her careful tactics.

Smiling charmingly, she asked, "And what exactly is in this for me, Myles?"

"I'll have a limousine for you anywhere."

"A black stretched limousine."

"Yes, of course."

"You know how irritating it is to travel and rush. What else do you have for me?"

"The use of the corporate jet so you won't have to rush and you'll be comfortable traveling."

"Very nice," she sounded pleased. Taking the seat right next to him, she slowly crossed her legs and leaned over. With her chin resting on her palm, she continued, "Las Vegas. I heard there are interesting places I could go and visit in and around Las Vegas. Perhaps unwind from my non-stop lecture circuit. Some entertainment, too?"

"Go ahead and pamper yourself while you're there. I've heard it's nice and expensive too. I could certainly arrange for a one hundred percent increase on your expense account."

"You know what this means, don't you, Mr. Ward?"

Now what? He shook his head and shrugged slightly at the same time.

Feeling as giddy as a kid left alone in a candy store where everything in it was free, she leaned closer and said assuredly, still grinning, "You *owe* me big."

He barely refrained from shaking his head in defeat as his immediate thought was, *But, of course, she's not going to make this easy on me.*

Not trying to mask his anxious expression, he said, "Yes, I know."

The friendly little smirk she gave him showed that she felt triumphant, and he could see her thoughts had spontaneously turned to something else.

"Organizing your new schedule?"

"Yes. I had a feeling that the Nevada assignment might be coming my way."

"You were essential."

"Probably." She knew she had been, as she had prepared the Preliminary Feasibility Study Report for the project. Facts and figures, including the graphical charts, appeared swiftly in her mind like pages in a book. She could even read them in her mind and mentally note everything she required within them. Mentally, she also created to-do lists to add to her planner. For her, the process was instantaneous and natural.

Myles noticed that as she was thinking, she was softly humming a popular opera libretto. What he didn't know was that, at the same time, she was mentally sketching a cartoon caricature that she would later add to a handwritten note she had composed earlier. His eyes caught a new addition to her wall.

"Where did you get the tapestry?"

"A gift from my parents. It's a replica of the original tapestry they saw at the Whitworth Art Gallery in Manchester. Each lady represents courage, caring, love, wisdom and fidelity. The original was woven in France."

"I like it —especially the two women dressed in armor: courage and fidelity. So, does the tapestry have a title?"

She nodded, smiling, "*Tribute to Women.*"

"Fitting."

"Myles, I hate to kick you out, but I've got to rush out of here!"

Quickly she got up from her seat beside him and returned to the chair behind her desk, picking up her hands-free headset, planning on making a call to the in-house travel department to make the necessary changes to her travel itinerary.

Before she could make the call, Myles immediately interrupted her with a cocky, yet playful tone in his voice, "Mercedes, knowing you couldn't resist my lucky Irish charms, I took the liberty of arranging all the necessary, fine details of your trip."

With that comment and a victorious smile, he withdrew a thick packet out of the file he held, adding audaciously, "Here's your itinerary, your flight package with the agreed perks, the project files, and—oh, here's a bar of Godiva milk chocolates, and Irish green M&M's for that sweet tooth of yours."

"*Oh, mon Dieu!* Myles Frederick Ward! You're impetuous!"

With a wink and making a firing gun motion with his right-hand, he grinned even wider, "I've got hand!"

She chuckled and promptly popped a green M&M into her mouth.

Chapter 2

March 19th, Aladdin

It was a short ride from the McCarran International Airport to the Aladdin Hotel and Casino on South Las Vegas Boulevard. In the privacy of the black-stretch limousine, she watched the decadent display of neon-lit casino hotels and resorts whistling by, one after the other. It was her first visit to *Sin City*.

Her flight from St. Louis had been long and tiring, but was made comfortable due to the corporate jet's first class amenities.

Arriving at the Aladdin hotel, she was a little disappointed to see that it was a typical hotel and not a ridiculously ornate theme-hotel like others along the Vegas strip. Though she preferred to stay at the imaginative Medieval "castle" Excalibur, she felt the Aladdin was appropriate for a business venue.

She was pleasantly surprised to be checked in to an executive suite on the thirteenth floor for her weeklong stay. It was almost 10:00 p.m. as an eager young bellhop took care of her luggage. His nametag caught her eye, since his was the same name as the pilot on the jet, the limo driver, and the guy at the front desk. A cold chill ran down her spine and she quickly dismissed the odd feeling which accompanied it. She was amused with the bellhop's obvious attempt at flirting as he escorted her to her room. It reminded her of the similar flirtatious reception she had received from another brazen hotel employee, who had eagerly fraternized with her just yesterday in St. Louis.

Yet the name of the young man in St. Louis escaped her. He had said that he was an aspiring pilot and only working temporarily as the head concierge at the former train station turned luxury hotel until he landed a job with a major airline.

He had been quite the Latin Casanova, a very attractive young man of twenty-nine from the Dominican Republic. He was a few inches taller than she with a smile that lit up his brown eyes and fashionably styled brown hair that complemented his manner of dress.

She let him accompany her on her planned visit to the St. Louis Art Museum and she had enjoyed his company; although she was a bit miffed when he tried to show off his driving abilities in his white sports car, recklessly speeding by the beautiful historic mansions along the Lafayette Square Historic District.

She was greatly amused with his painstaking efforts to impress her when he surprisingly took her to three separate restaurants, each dedicated to one course of the meal. His choice of desserts hadn't been appetizing.

"I'm sure you'll enjoy licking honey off me—or would you prefer whipped cream?" She remembered him asking.

From his well-rehearsed actions, she knew he had performed this exact ritual with the same precision with other unsuspecting female hotel guests. His well thought-out words dripped with sensual seduction. He protested incessantly as she expertly rebuffed him while intentionally beguiling him by speaking fluent Spanish in an equally seductive tone, convincing him to take her out dancing instead.

She even punctuated her offer with a conciliatory kiss, and he simply hadn't been able to resist her feminine wiles. After a sweaty night of dancing, he took her on a unique tour of the city aboard a small private plane he piloted.

Such encounters were the typical results of her boredom in strange cities. She always attracted unexpected, adventurous encounters, welcomed or not. These encounters magnetically drew to her like *red on a rose*. The welcomed ones were opportune chance encounters like the one that brought her to Las Vegas, but unlike the one in St. Louis.

At least he had been a gentleman when she once again rebuffed his advances, frankly this time, and he had graciously backed away with the greatest of restraint. It was clear that the effort on his part to restrain himself had been physically painful, but thankfully, she had remained unscathed.

Thinking of it now, she felt somewhat guilty because she had been merely testing him the entire time, hoping he would be something other than the calculating, charming womanizer which he apparently was.

As the new bellhop left her room, she thought, *Oh well, I lost his phone number and I can't remember his name. He would've made an interesting distraction, regardless, on my next visit to St. Louis.*

Looking out the window of her suite, she realized she often played the role of a man, remaining devoid of emotion. It suited her well considering how she controlled her personal emotions with ease. Her closest friends dubbed her *Slayer*, which was short for manslayer. It greatly amused her, but she really didn't see herself that way. Yes, she had more male friends than her female counterparts, but that was quite natural for her, having grown up in a household of men and working in a male-dominated profession. She even kept close ties with her former lovers, considering them her dearest friends.

Lately, her personal life had been a whirlwind of change. She had dreamt of having a loving relationship like her parents, who just celebrated their forty-first wedding anniversary. And, for a few precious years, she had been living her dream; but sadly, in a few short months her divorce from her husband, Mason, would be final.

She was very comfortable with her new "single" status. She had reveled in her independence, finding solace in being alone. Yet she also enjoyed meeting new people in her travels, mostly men. She hadn't quite understood why many of her women friends protested her behavior, until her best friend, Sydney, had explained it to her. She remembered Sydney saying, "Merc, all this talk about your promiscuous ways is because it always seems as though you have a date with a new lover in every state that you're assigned in. Come on—you even label them with their respective states. Let's see, last month it was Mr. Oklahoma and Mr. California! Now can you blame them for thinking this way?"

She had said, "Sydney, you know it's only half true! None of them were my lovers! I can barely remember their names! I know it's demeaning to label them that way, but it makes talking about them easier—don't you think? You know that I would never break my personal rule of being a 'one-man woman'. Don't get me wrong—the temptations are sometimes irresistible—but succumbing would betray everything that I am!"

"I know you're a devoted egg. Like me with my Patrick, faithful to the end! But you've got to admit, it's not as interesting for us to talk about your strictly platonic dates as it is to talk about our versions of your escapades during our get-togethers, especially over tea. Oh, come on, Merc, the ladies need to spice things up a bit!"

"Well, since you put it that way, I guess there's no harm for them to live vicariously through me!" She smiled at how they both had shared a hearty laugh at their wrong conclusions.

It was easy to misconstrue her vagabond behavior but those were strictly platonic friendships. She would certainly dine with them, spend time with them, and often engaged in intellectual conversations; yet, it would never go beyond that unless she allowed it.

As with everyone, she preferred the company of a friend over a night alone in an executive hotel room. Admittedly, most of the friends were men, but she also had many female friends, worldwide. When she was in a new place, she could be bored beyond belief—something she was famous for.

When a male friend wanted more from her, she would simply rebuff him. At first, she would be tactful and sweet. She wasn't a malevolent spirit who would knowingly lead a man on or be unkind to him. However, she did put men through a rigorous test, knowing it would successfully reveal the face of their true character. And if he persisted when she wasn't interested, she would be very blunt and brutally honest with him. Sexually driven emotions, especially romantic feelings, could not be forced out of her. Never without her consent.

Another rerun of St. Louis was not in the cards tonight. She was far too exhausted and she was definitely not interested. She just wanted to get this whole week done and over with, so she could enjoy a much-needed rest. As she settled in the suite, she unpacked her things, wrestling with how she had even decided to accept this unscheduled business trip. Smiling, she said aloud, "Myles! You and your sweet chocolates!"

Regardless, she was still quite jet-lagged and too tired to even eat a meal from room service. But a nice, long, luxurious soak in the tub would be refreshing. Perhaps she'd curl up later and read a couple of chapters of the newest Anne Rice novel that she brought along on her trip.

She placed her laptop computer next to her briefcase and her portable CD player on the bedside table along with her black CD case. She went back to her briefcase, took out the book and her planner. Glancing at the clock beside her bed, she debated on whether it was too late to call her mother. With the time difference it was almost midnight in Florida. *Too late.* Quickly, she got up and sat at the desk. She opened her laptop and logged on to the Internet to check her e-mail.

As she scrolled through the dozen or so new messages, she ignored the Instant Messages or IMs popping up on the screen with only brief glances. People who knew her realized that she wouldn't interrupt her work to respond to IMs. Instead, she would contact them later.

It took less than an hour to handle the urgent messages. As she was finishing the last one, she noticed an IM pop up on-screen which she gladly answered since it was from one of her big brothers.

"Yo, Merc. Got time to chit-chat?"

"Yo back, Raiden," she smiled as she typed his call sign. "Always. Are your legs tired?"

"Huh?"

"They should be. You've been running around in my head all day! <haha> Seriously, what are you doing?"

"Very cute. I got it :) Anyway, same old, same old. I've got only a few minutes to chat, though. Where are you?"

"Sin City."

"Las Vegas? Playing?"

"Right." They both knew that she didn't spend enough time playing, nor did he.

"You know you should do like Mom did, join some beauty pageants, meet guys, and have fun."

"Lucas Mateo Donato! She did those pageants for the scholarships—not to meet guys!" Indignant on her mother's behalf, she blasted him, but she was laughing as she typed it.

"Now, now, don't be using my name in vain. Easy, Merc, I'm just teasing."

"Lucky that you are <grin>."

"I heard your art show was a success."

"Wish you were there."

"Me too. I really tried, but you know how it is."

"It's all right. Understandably you couldn't come." She had hoped he wasn't feeling too badly about not making her show, so she typed, "I'll zip up some photos from the show so you can check it out."

"Excellent. What's up with Luccio? He mentioned his firm entering a harbor design competition in his last email. Have you heard anything? I also heard he's taking Kiley and Leandro snowboarding." She smiled, knowing how close he was to his fraternal twin.

"But Leandro just turned two!"

"Two is the best age—no fear yet!"

"A true Donato! He even looks more like his father."

"I think he'd look more exotic with Kiley's green eyes."

"Uh-huh. Oh, Luccio's firm won and he's the lead architect on the team. Send him an e-card."

"Excellent news and I will. Now how's everyone else?"

"Luis decided to start his own dental practice. Lázaro is trying to decide whether to work for the FBI or teach at Florida State."

"Tough call. He's better out in the field with his instincts profiling these criminals."

"True, but he's a mirror image of Mom, excellent as a teacher and doctor."

"I bet he wishes he can do both like Mom. I'll email him my two cents."

"Leo is still clueless."

"That seminary stint really screwed him up."

"Royally. He's sculpting right now."

"What about his writing?"

"And his painting, the ceramics, the computers... the women! Right now he's going through models left and right. Alana is the current one."

"The Hawaiian?"

"That's the one."

"Don't worry about Leo. He'll figure it out. So, what are you really doing in Las Vegas?"

"Working :("

"Really? You working?" Her work took her all over the country and to parts of Europe, which was one of the reasons why she took the job. She was a confessed workaholic, though she didn't need to work at all because she had been financially independent since she was twenty-two years old.

"Are you getting your life under control? Are you okay with where things are with Mason? I'm worried about ya, little sister." She smiled at her brother's question. Both of their lives were in a constant state of flux.

"As okay as I can be. Besides, I'm a tough nut to crack." She changed the subject by typing in a short question, hoping he would get the message. "Are you on exercises?"

"Tomorrow."

"Any new scars?"

"Not yet. I heard about yours though."

"It's barely a flesh wound."

"Hey Merc, I can't help thinking of the fact that Nellis Air Force Base is right near you. If you see any pilots from Nellis while you are there, and if any of them were over in the Gulf, tell them 'thanks' from me. Those fighter pilots saved my life more than once!"

She murmured, *Les chevaliers du ciel* (the knights of the skies) as she typed, "Yes, I remember. I'll even kiss them for you."

"I said thank them, not swap spit!"

"My, my, aren't you the overprotective brother?"

"I may be grateful to those flyboys, but I don't trust those viper jocks anywhere near my little sister, especially the lonely married ones. Horny sons-of-bitches! They're the worst kind. They'll say anything to score."

"That holds true for any married guys who wander. Vipers!"

"Thankfully I won't have that problem."

"Yes, I know. Forever the bachelor."

"Amen!"

"Where are you exactly?"

"That's classified. If I tell you, I've got to shoot you <just kidding>."

"Seriously, where are you?"

"Seriously, I can't tell you except that it's in a different continent."

"I understand."

"Before I sign off, I've got a new riddle for you. You ready?" Challenging each other with brainteasers was part of her family's tradition—a battle of wits that their mother passed on to them.

"Excellent because I've got one for you, too. Go ahead—I can take it."

"What is the beginning of eternity, the end of time and space, the beginning of every end and the end of every place?"

"Come on, you've got to give me a more difficult riddle than that."

"Sounds like you're stalling ;)"

"Really? How about if I tell you that the answer is the letter 'e'." She didn't tell him that she had heard of it before. She giggled.

"Not bad."

"Oh no, you're not going to get away that easy. It's my turn. Ready?"

"Shoot."

"That which hath been is now; and that which is to be hath already been; and God requireth that which is past." There was a pause and Mercedes stared at the screen trying to visualize Lucas' thought processes.

"You're taking too long. Now look who's stalling."

"Why are you so fond of biblical riddles?"

"Gotta put those twelve years of Catholic school to good use :) Seriously, I like being biblical, makes me feel omnipotent. Besides, I like to keep you on your toes. And you might learn a thing or two about the universe. So, do you give up?"

"No, no, I never give up. I'll just have to think about it some more. I do have to run. I promise I'll answer your riddle. Be good and don't forget about the pictures. Love ya!"

"Love you, too. Be careful wherever you are!"

"I promise. Bye."

Smiling as she turned off the computer, she stood up to start a recently released U2 CD, hoping it would help her relax.

Loosening the bonds of her ponytail, she felt the soft waves of her hair.

She habitually changed the style of her hair, but she never wore it short above her shoulders. For the spring and summer, she would highlight her hair with blonde streaks to accentuate the bronze tan that she so easily acquired.

Running her hand through her hair, she knew that in the autumn and winter it would return to its natural umber and sienna colors while she remained active with snow sports and other outdoor-related fun.

She went into the scrumptious bath area, deciding it was time to soak for a few minutes before going to bed.

I need this so badly, she thought as she started the tub filling with water. After she took off her fashionable attire, she rubbed her aching neck muscles. *I can't believe I'm thirty.*

Then she sighed, wishing she wasn't as short as her mother. She stood exactly sixty inches tall, barefoot; she could easily pass for nineteen or twenty if she wished. She constantly got carded whenever she ordered wine or accompanied her friends to the clubs. College guys never believed her when she turned down their advances, citing her age. She always took it as a compliment, especially when she was with friends who were younger.

Looking down at her breasts, she sighed again. *Wish I had C-cups*. Her breasts were small, firm, perky, and well suited to her petite frame. But she was every bit of a woman.

She naturally preferred the company of older men; men who possessed mature child-like qualities, not childish and immature. There was a vast difference between the two. Though a handsome face and a fine chiseled body certainly didn't hurt, she was drawn to men with intellect, passion, insight, and power, but who were also gentle and romantic. She was also a sentimental soul, and a gentleman with impeccable manners could touch her heart. They were definitely more interesting to be around.

Not long ago, Howard Wallace, a dashing, debonair, powerful man who was twenty-three years her senior and CEO of Wallace Water Industries, had taken her hand and kissed it, saying, "You are certainly the loveliest engineer I have ever met. You are a breath of fresh air in the midst of us men. You grace us with your beauty, dear lady."

Of course, her knees buckled at his very nice compliment. It had been at the corporate Christmas formal dinner and later he had sought her out, bringing her a glass of Merlot, giving them a chance to talk about worldly things.

They were so spontaneous with each other that the difference in their ages had been irrelevant as they shared engineering-related jokes, quite comfortable with each other. He had asked her to address him by his nickname, *Bud*, which no one except his own close-knit circle knew.

She had been completely smitten, feeling almost like a college freshman with a giddy crush on her math professor. Their conversation had continued until it was unexpectedly interrupted when his wife missed his company.

Mercedes smiled, thinking of him, his beguiling smile and their conversations. He was certainly the kind of mature, child-like gentleman she adored.

The tub was filling and she slowly sank into the hot water, surrounded by thick aromatic bubbles. Gently leaning back, she thought of how often she downplayed her looks because of her profession. But she did know how to use them. *If my looks open the doors, then God help you when I'm through those doors!*

Sitting there, she was very amused with that thought, knowing that she possessed a powerful asset but that it could also prove to hinder her personally.

She frowned as she lightly touched the one-inch surgical incision healing on her bellybutton. She felt the tiny twin punctures, right above her pubic line. They were from an invasive laparoscopic procedure performed twelve days earlier. She could still feel a twinge of pain from each side. The lyrics of U2 were appropriate at this moment: *with or without you, with or without you.*

She breathed deeply, inhaling the fragrant scent; she closed her eyes, reflecting on what led her to this moment and remembering when it all began.

* * *

She was attending a charity ball for the Children's Hospital of Pennsylvania at the Philadelphia Museum of Art. In the Impressionist Wing of the museum, she was engrossed with Van Gogh's *Still Life: Vase with Twelve Sunflowers*. Whenever she looked at it, she would feel herself weep, for it so moved her. She felt lonely without Mason. He was supposed to accompany her to the function, but he was resistant as usual. Lately, he frowned on anything which did not procure him the almighty bottom line. He constantly debased her artistic interests, as a mere luxuriant frivolity that he could not understand. Yet, when it came time to entertain his business partners, he would insist on throwing lavish dinner parties, endowing her with what he often referred to as her wifely duties. She thought with repulsion, *Wifely duties.* How those words sickened her. She was expected to be the perfect hostess and conversationalist. She could feel the resentment steadily growing for him, realizing that she had become the perfect perfunctory wife. She sighed, thinking how he wasn't always like that.

Her thoughts turned to what she had been longing for: a child. Perhaps now would be the right time to start a family. It seemed like the naturally perfect progression of things in their life. He might stop focusing his mind so much on work and spend more time with her when she became pregnant. She heard how pregnant women would glow in their happiness due to the miracle of life growing within them. She wondered how wonderful that would feel: to finally see the baby at the moment of birth. It was a moment she had often thought of. And she found herself silently humming a French lullaby that suddenly crept in her unconscious musings.

We could go on a second honeymoon for our fifth wedding anniversary; perhaps it would soften him back to his former self. We could really use a very long vacation. It has been so long since we have just simply kicked back and relaxed. Wouldn't it be so romantic to conceive our child on the yacht where it all started? She amused herself with the possibility.

And so that evening while in bed, she talked to Mason about her wish to start a family.

"Babe, are you sure that's what you want?"

Smiling widely, she quickly answered, "Absolutely! Besides, this huge house could use the sound of little happy children. And you'd make a wonderful father!"

"I'm not sure."

After giving him a loving soft kiss, she said, "You'll be great at it. You've had lots of practice raising your little brother. And look how good Max turned out! You're a natural. Now imagine what our son is going to be like. He'll have your thick, wavy brown hair, your gorgeous hazel eyes and your good looks. He'll be a perfect gentleman, a romantic who loves his mother with a passion!"

Teasingly, she continued, "I can imagine our son sounding just like you with your strong Philly accent. And hopefully he won't have your notorious temper."

Mason looked rather pensive and distracted with thoughts that she couldn't decipher. Ignoring her cajoling, he asked seriously, "But are we ready for this?"

She embraced him tightly, reassuring him, "We're more than ready."

In her arms, he whispered lovingly in her ear, "Okay then, let's have a baby."

A few months had gone by and each time Mercedes took a pregnancy test, she felt her heart break because it would always read the same: negative. Mason tried to console her.

"Babe, if it is meant to be, then it'll happen. C'mon, stop being so desperate. It's no big deal! I don't mind if there's no kid. I'm too selfish to share you, anyway." Then in an attempt to make her feel better, he handed her a thick wad of one hundred dollar bills, teasingly saying, "Here. Why don't you go shopping? It always makes you feel better."

His gesture angered her and she replied, disgusted, "Mason, stop making light of this! You know how much this means to me. I want us to have a child. No matter what!"

He angrily shouted, "Whatever! I'm tired of this shit!" as he threw the cash on the floor, rushing out of the room toward the garage, where he hastily got into the car he bought himself when he turned thirty. He revved the engine loud and hard.

From the window she saw Mason peeling out of the garage in his vintage black convertible Camaro, recklessly speeding down their long driveway.

Tearfully she thought, *Why is he being so callous? Why doesn't he share my feelings?*

The following week, after a visit with her doctor, she came home with uncontained excitement. Mason was in his study, sitting at his desk, busily going over his schedule for the week. His back was turned toward her when she came in.

"Mason?"

Without looking at her direction, he replied, "Yeah, babe."

"It's about my doctor's visit this morning."

Still distracted, he was shuffling his paperwork, huffing in frustration before he answered, "Everything go okay?"

She moved closer to him, standing behind his chair and draping her hands onto his shoulders. She leaned down and gave him a playful nibble on his ear and whispered, "It will be."

He stopped what he was doing then turned to face her, "What do you mean?"

"Instead of telling you, let me show you," as Mercedes handed him a pill bottle.

He read the label aloud, "Clomiphene citrate." Looking puzzled, he asked, "What the hell is this?"

Smiling, Mercedes said, "It's a fertility drug."

"A FUCKIN' WHAT?"

Startled by his loud reaction, she repeated with a stammer, "A, a fertility drug."

"Youse got to be kiddin' me!"

"No, I'm not joking. Face it, everything seems to be normal with you and the problem is clearly with me. So my doctor prescribed something to help me along. Mason, the best part is that we could be pregnant in a couple of months! Isn't it great? We can start right away. Actually, right now!" She began kissing him but Mason pulled away from her.

"Babe, we need to talk about this."

"Mason, we've been trying for several months! We've gone to these doctors and finally there's something that will insure us a pregnancy—what's there to talk about? Aren't you as excited as I am?"

"Are you sure it'll work?"

"The doctor told me that the chances for success are higher than before. There might even be a greater chance of having twins since it runs in both our families. And I say, the more, the better! Mason, I can feel in my heart that it'll work. I'm so excited." She began kissing him again as she implored sweetly, "So let's start. Please, babe?" But this time, he unexpectedly pulled away from her.

Flabbergasted at his actions, she asked "What's wrong now?"

Frowning and pensive, he replied, "I can't."

Alarmed, she questioned him again, "'I can't' what?"

Shaking his head, he answered "I can't do this."

"You're scaring me. What do you mean?"

He looked at her gravely and said seriously, "Babe, I don't want to have kids."

Puzzled with his words, she nervously looked into his eyes. "You mean no kids right now?"

"No, I meant no kids—EVER."

"You can't mean that. You're joking right?"

"I'm serious as a fuckin' heart attack."

She searched for a change in his demeanor, but he remained as serious as ever. Her disbelief turned to sorrow, her eyes misted and she nodded her head. She could do no more, for she couldn't speak past the tightness in her throat.

She paused for a few moments, feeling her sorrow turning into rage. Finally, she offhandedly shouted, "If I can't have this baby with you then I'll have it with somebody else!" Without waiting for a response, she stormed out of the study. Fighting the wave of tears welling up in her eyes, she screamed in several different languages, *"This is not happening to me!"*

* * *

She breathed deeply as she slowly came out of her reverie, shook her head at the memories, and sighed deeply in frustration before berating herself, *Okay, Mercedes, stop this torture. Just relax.*

Then she let out a deep sigh. Her muscles, tired and aching from traveling, were easing under the soothing magic of the heat and the water.

Her stress peeled away in layers as she savored the quiet pleasures of her bath. Her body relaxed and her mind grew silent as she closed her eyes and listened to the sweet serenade of the music playing in the next room, relaxing totally.

In what seemed like only moments later, she was startled awake by the ringing of the phone. Luckily, the voicemail picked it up. She didn't want to get up, but the water had turned tepid and the bubbles had almost disappeared. Reluctantly, she unplugged the bath and sat in wait until all the water drained.

Standing, she turned on the shower to rinse and wash her hair and then got out of the tub, dried off, and went about her evening ritual.

Exhausted, she knew she was not going to attempt to read, so she slipped on her favorite soft, deep burgundy silk pajamas which felt deliciously luxurious next to her skin.

She walked tiredly to the windows, wanting to look at the stars. She strained to see the stars because the glaring lights of the city blocked the beauty of the night.

The room felt too closed, so she unlatched the lock on the windows to let the delicious cool night air into her suite. She loved the feel of the cold temperature against her bare skin. Still wishing she could see the stars, she continued to stand there until sleep beckoned her, forcing her to crawl into bed. As always, she found it difficult to sleep on her first evening in a strange bed.

To help induce the deep relaxing sleep she needed, she got up and placed a dab of lavender oils on the light bulbs of the lamps, infusing the air with the sweet fragrance and then changed the CD to the relaxing sounds of the modern

Gregorian chants of the musical group *Enigma*. She got in bed and pulled the covers up, centering all the pillows as she covered herself with only the sheet.

Drifting off to sleep, she heard the words "*dit moi*" from the song, which sent a wave of overwhelming sadness through her. *I know it means 'tell me,' but tell me what?* The words were like a strange premonition and she was one who never took those feelings for granted.

* * *

Suddenly, she could smell a distinct scent flooding the room, a scent she couldn't quite place. Her eyelids were heavy and she kept them closed as she breathed deeply, recognizing the scent. *Candles? Here?* The scent was unmistakably from candles and it permeated the air.

She could hear low, muffled whispers. Many voices surrounded her, as if in prayer, standing vigil as she slumbered. The sounds were like the vespers she heard in church. She shifted her body, deeply breathing in the misplaced aroma. The whispers grew louder and louder, becoming more and more audible, in an orchestrated prayer.

She heard the chanting in unison, "*Ave Maria, gracia plena, dominus tecum, benedicta tu, in mulieribus et benedictus fructus ventris tui ihesu. Amen.*" Though it was in Latin, she knew the prayer well—it was the *Hail Mary*.

She struggled to open her eyes so she could discover the source of these voices. She felt uncomfortable when the air became dense and thick with sadness and melancholy.

Fear and apprehension never entered her mind, only curiosity. As she fought for awareness, a clear voice, familiar in its deep and tender tones, interrupted the multitude of voices in prayer.

She felt the presence of a man who said, "*My sweet lady, prithee awake.*" His voice pleaded with her, the sound of which she had heard all her life.

Desperately, she fought the strong hold of sleep. Her lids fluttered, and then, finally, opened to find her vision blurry. She tried to adjust her eyes to the darkness of the room. There he was kneeling beside her, in silhouette. A strange glow of light filtered through the shadows behind him, framing only the most basic of his features. She felt quite at ease, comfortable, as though she intimately knew this man. None of his features were distinct. She figured that this must be a delirium of some sort. Again, she heard him saying, "*My love, how fare'st thou?*" His deep, sensual voice now filled with obvious joy in her wakefulness.

The voices she heard earlier were quickly silenced, replaced with normal speech, but she was alarmed. The words she heard were in French and the prayers, in Latin. All of the words, including those of the familiar stranger, were in French—but what greatly distressed her was her recognition of the thirteenth century French colloquialisms he was using! She found it quite strange yet delightful; she was thinking in modern English, but speaking in thirteenth century French as well.

Where the hell am I? she wondered, with only a slight trepidation. She then turned her head from side to side and strained to focus her eyes. Her heart began to beat nervously when she heard the distinct cries of a baby. She was bewildered. *A baby? In my hotel suite?*

She looked at him; the darkness still blanketed the details of his face, yet she smiled at him in recognition, nonetheless, very uncertain. She whispered, "Who are you?"

His voice reflected her angst when he replied, "*Ma chérie, thou knowst me not.*" She wasn't sure if she heard him correctly, but her attention turned to the people, mostly women, who were kneeling at the foot of her bed.

When she heard the cries of the baby again, she observed one of the women, dressed in a bodice and dress with a square-cut neck and bloused sleeves, quickly stand up and run to the baby's cradle on the right side of her bed. In her haste the flare of her skirt at the hem rustled against the bed. The baby stopped crying when the woman started to sing a familiar lullaby, "*'Tis the day of our lady, a most beauteous babe to behold. Blessed with a child of God, born on this our Lady's Day.*"

Again, bewildered, she thought, *Strange, I know that song. Lady's Day? That sounds familiar. Where have I heard it before?* She began to think hard about it, as the singing continued. Then, it finally came to her. It was from a class on Renaissance Art. Much of the art was religious and devoted the lady, the Blessed Virgin Mary. The Medieval calendar had placed *Lady's Day* on March 24th in celebration of the Annunciation, when the Archangel Gabriel visited the Virgin Mary. In the modern Catholic Julian calendar, that would fall on March 25th but the holy day of obligation for Mary was January 1st. Since she was brought up as a Roman Catholic, she knew she was right.

She strained to look at him again and implored with a voice filled with desperate confusion, "Please tell me what is going on. Please tell me who you are." She tried hard not to panic, but she could sense her control breaking.

The room felt very cold and damp. The strong scent of a newly lit candle flooded her senses. She then felt him take her hand, which was lying outside of the sheet, pressed it to his lips, and gently whispered, "*My sweeting, 'tis I.*"

Okay, that didn't help me at all, she thought with annoyance. Then she felt something trickling down her hand, which he held. Suddenly, she realized that they were his warm tears. He was weeping and it tugged at her heart. "Why are you crying?" she asked him, with genuine concern.

As quickly as those words left her lips, a sharp radiating pain shot up from within her belly, took hold of her and wracked her entire body in absolute torment. She took her free hand, held her stomach and braced for the pain; she then arched her back against the bed when the surge of pain hit her with tremendous force.

"OH GOD!!" she screamed, feeling like she couldn't breath and gasping desperately for air. Immediately her thoughts turned to her recent surgery. An infection must have set in, which was why she was feeling these incomprehensible pains.

"A DOCTOR, I NEED A DOCTOR!" she cried aloud, instinctively reaching over for the phone to call 9-1-1 so she could get to the hospital, because this was a definite medical emergency. But when she couldn't find the phone, she then thought that perhaps she was already in the hospital. It would explain why they were trying to help her. As another wave of pain hit, she tightened her grip on this familiar stranger's hand, whose strength she could feel as he helped her brace for it.

"HELP ME!" she shouted, her body now drenched in sweat, "OH GOD, THIS HURTS! Please, I need MORPHINE! NOW!"

The steady flow of her own tears was streaming down the sides of her face from the agony of this unknown pain. Alarmed, her womb felt incredibly raw and sensitive. Then, she heard an elderly man's voice speaking to him, "*My lord, by your leave. Prithee, mayhap thou away this hour. We shall attend to milady.*"

"Thou? Milady? What the—" she was going to utter an obscenity, but before she could say another word, she grasped for him again to help her brace for another painful surge.

He fumed, "*FIE UPON THAT! NAY! I stay! Jamais! I will ne'er leave my wife, 'tis her hour of most dire need! Wherefore? Thy bewitched magic canst undo her pain.*"

Immediately, he commanded in a strong and angry voice, barking with a rage to everyone present in the room, "*Enow with all thy dismal-dreaming prayers. Away, now! Go to!*" He then called out, "*Nurse! Bring thou hither our child! Quickly!*"

"Our child? What? My wife! Me? Someone tell me what is happening! And, why the hell am I speaking in FRENCH!" she shrieked, but her concern then shifted to how sick she felt and how weak her muscles were, and her spirit seemed to fade.

Many left the room in silent protest. The room was still too dark for her to make any detailed features out, but she knew that she was no longer in her hotel suite. This place felt quite ancient, yet she knew this place very well, which disturbed her greatly. As she was thinking this, she felt him loosen his hold on her hand, but only for a few moments. Then, a baby was placed on her chest.

When she looked down at the baby, she noticed she was no longer wearing her silk burgundy pajamas; but instead, she was clothed in an off-white cotton ruffled chemise with full long sleeves, which to her horror, was stained with blood.

"OKAY, I'M FREAKING OUT!" she screamed in panic, still trying to understand what the hell was happening.

She calmed down when she felt his strong hand on hers again. He bent and covered her mouth with his. The kiss was long and luxurious, mingled with love and worry. His lips were moist and soft on hers. She responded to his kisses—his familiar, tender, loving kisses.

The tiny baby on her chest took hold of a tendril of her long hair and tugged it gently. She immediately felt a deep bond and an incredible rush of pure joy, and happiness filled her heart as she held the baby closer to her and kissed its tiny little cheeks. She saw that the baby girl had just been born, as the blood and birth fluids still covered her and clung on to her thin silken hair, and stained her swaddling bands.

At that moment she stopped the barrage of questions and silenced her mind. She finally stopped crying and mustered all her strength to fight the sharp pains, incessant with their torturous attacks. Her heart began to beat in its normal rhythm when she looked down at the beautiful infant she held with her right arm.

The baby was looking up at her. Her sweet little mouth made suckling noises while her eyes remained closed. Mercedes watched her closely, noting how beautiful she was in her struggle against her tiny heavy lids, but the infant did open her eyes and looked right at her. In that instant Mercedes felt all pain leave her body. All she felt was love for this new life and for this man who was kneeling next to her, holding her, giving her words of comfort and reassurance.

This is impossible. This is not real. Yet she felt it deep in her heart that this was very real. The warmth of the love she felt was undeniably true. She held in her arms two of the most important people in her life. *My own family.* This was her husband. This was their child. There were no explanations, nor did she want any at this moment. She drew in a deep breath so she could hold on to the memory. Her tears became uncontrollable.

Finally, she asked him, "Let me see you." She wanted to see him in the light—his face and his eyes. Before he got up, he leaned over to kiss her passionately. He walked beyond her view, where she could only guess that he was getting one of the candles. She kissed her child again as she waited in eager anticipation for his return. Her eyes began to clear as the candles illuminated his path toward her.

From a distance she could finally see the light color of his hair; he was tall with broad shoulders with well-defined arms and legs. He was wearing a knight's surcoat without armor; a coat of arms was emblazoned on it, but she couldn't quite see it clearly, except that it was red. His young handsome face was battle hardened and unshaven, his eyes filled with concern as well as love and devotion. He smiled lovingly at her as he approached the foot of her bed. As he was getting closer, her heart beat faster and faster. He set the candle down at a table right next to her bed, and his back was slightly turned. She was smiling slightly, but suddenly began to wince and then screamed as an unexpected swell of pain bore down on her. It was a pain of sheer intensity, more powerful than the previous waves of pain. The pain possessed her and swallowed her up completely. It caused her to shut her eyes as she screamed, "MAKE IT STOP!"

As the pain began to ebb, she felt her spirit waning. She struggled to open her eyes again because she wanted desperately to see his face up close, but her vision blurred, a darkness was approaching—a deep sleep.

As she gasped for a breath, she heard him faintly, *"Do not away! Prithee stay! I love thee! And, by God's wounds, I shall find thee again! I swear it by our love! I shall find thee again! Je t'aime! NO!"*

She could hear him sobbing in agony as he cradled her in his arms, and held her in a tight embrace. She sighed deeply and took what seemed to be her last breath. Suddenly a great force, like a vacuum, pulled her into a bright void, floating on a current of absolute solitude. The pain was gone. There was simply peace in her solace. She turned to look at him again, but the visions of him faded, her arms were outstretched toward him. She screamed, "NO!"

* * *

Springing upright, she awoke instantly. Her breathing was erratic and her heart was pounding wildly. Her silk pajamas were drenched in sweat and she could feel her eyes were swollen with tears. *What's happening to me?*

She was back in her hotel room. The air was no longer filled with the scent of candles, but with the sweet fragrance of lavender. A chill went up and down her spine when the cool breeze from the open windows lifted the sheer curtain from its place. In the background she heard the Gregorian chants from the last track of the CD. The music sounded almost ominous.

Involuntarily, she felt her belly where the small incisions were, feeling a slight tingling of pain. Making an intense effort, she slowed her breathing and meditated to calm her spirit.

After a few moments she got up from the bed and moved to the window, looked up at the dark night sky, and offered silent prayers, barely aware that her prayers were said in Medieval Latin.

Chapter 3

March 20th, The Conference

Mercedes was unaware of what time it was; she hadn't had a restful night's sleep. Actually, she hadn't had a good night's sleep in quite some time and was becoming concerned that the lack of sleep might affect her focus, which was something she couldn't allow.

Her memory of last night made her tremble, and her heart felt heavy with sadness. The visions had been even more vivid than others in the past; and each time she felt like she was experiencing the dreams for the very first time. After it was over she sketched and wrote about the dream in detail in her journal, as she always did.

If it was a dream, a phantasm, how could all of my senses have been so acutely aware? I even understood the old French dialect! Each time she would literally awaken fluent in another ancient tongue. Whatever the explanation, she knew it was more like a long forgotten memory than a dream, and it had haunted her since college.

Because of her dream she began to research and paint obsessively about Medieval themes. Her vacations would often end up in Europe, hoping that she might one day discover if the places and the people she saw in her dreams really existed. If they were real, how would it affect her?

Where are you now? Are you near? she wondered, knowing her question was futile.

Standing in front of the mirror, she quickly gathered her hair into an updo and secured it with a pretty, jeweled comb. She was wearing a gray houndstooth pantsuit with a double-breasted jacket. After adding a coat of burgundy lipstick, she slipped on her sling-back shoes and noticed the message light on the phone. There had been a call she hadn't answered last night while she was in the bathtub. Glancing quickly at the digital clock, she picked up the phone and checked her messages.

A warm tingle ran through her as she heard the voice of Grant Larcher, the aristocratic physician she was seeing. "Hello, my angel. I wanted to make certain you arrived okay. I'll call you later."

The second call was from Myles talking about the logistics of the Nevada negotiations, and the third call was from her secretary, Donna Burke, with information she needed about her presentation materials.

Donna, 27 on Thursday—send flowers. She jotted the note in her planner.

To Mercedes, Donna looked like she was Cleopatra or Queen Nefertiti with her natural Nubian beauty, though she was originally from Trinidad-Tobago.

Mercedes admired her sense of style, especially the way she dressed fashionably in extremely bright colors and youthful attire, but it was definitely her hair and her face which made her extremely beautiful.

She admired how Donna styled her hair in varied artistic weaves or curls or waves with jeweled combs and accessories that adorned her head like a crown.

Donna carried herself with a regal air of confidence, and Mercedes felt she was a walking contradiction, much like her. She was highly educated, had completed graduate studies in marketing, and was clever, witty and creativity, yet she didn't seem to aspire to anything more than her position as a secretary.

Mercedes shook her head, wondering how she could help, how she could point Donna toward a path where she would truly shine. Smiling, she knew she would do so. She was lucky to have such an efficient and smart woman whom she considered to be a friend assisting her with tedious, mundane tasks.

She added another note in her planner, *Donna = Nubian Queen, next painting*. She could see the painting clearly in her mind, and she knew immediately it would be a perfect belated birthday gift for her.

Pausing for a moment to think about whose call she should return first, she looked at the clock again.

I should phone Grant first. But based on her internal clock, she knew she was running late. She couldn't afford to be late, especially at the beginning of her hectic week. She decided to call Myles and Donna first. *Grant might be in the middle of surgery anyway, so he'll have to wait until after my day is over.*

Switching into her business mode, she dialed Myles' number.

"Hello, this is Myles."

"Myles. Mercedes here. Just checking in."

In his usual deep tone, he said, "Good morning, Mercedes. I've emailed you the directions to the Nevada Utility office along with the meeting agenda. They want to feed you first before the meeting at 2:00 p.m. A business luncheon is scheduled for 12:30 p.m. Also, I received a faxed copy of the conference roster, and it doesn't look like there will be any conflicts with your presentation. You're scheduled as the first presenter everyday, except for today. That should give you a chance to catch up with the details. Now, on Thursday afternoon, there's a second meeting, also at two, to wrap up the rest of the formalities. Any questions, so far?"

She thought through her quick mental checklist. "No. I've got it covered." With a teasing tone to her voice, she said, "It was my light reading on the plane. And, Myles—thanks for stocking the plane with my favorite snacks. I really appreciate the personal touches."

"Hey, I just wanted to show you that I really appreciate you being there. Besides, Mr. Meyers made it explicitly clear that we weren't to spare any expense for you because of the Nevada deal, so I can't take all the credit." She could hear his sincerity.

"Well, in that case, I have other conditions I'll need to discuss with you later." She grinned, almost able to see his smile. "And, keep the attention to detail coming. I can use a little more continuous pampering."

"I will. Do you want to tell me more about those conditions?"

"Would love to, but I'm really running later than I'd like. Myles, can you be a lifesaver and transfer me to Donna?"

"Not a problem. I'm sure you'll let me know if you need anything else. And,

Mercedes, I'm going to have to send you over to Barbara. I'm inept with the phone system, as you know. Hang on a sec."

In the background, she was amused to hear Myles' muffled voice asking Barbara to give him instructions on how to even transfer the call to her desk. She and her other coworkers were really comical in many ways. The irony of engineering minds was that nothing was ever simple. Simplicity was not part of an engineer's vocabulary. To explain the simplest of tasks to an engineer, a full schematic was needed, along with detailed specifications. Simplicity was another lesson she needed to master.

After a couple of attempts, she was successfully transferred to Donna.

"Hi Donna. How are you doing and how are the extra copies of my presentation materials?"

"I'm fine, and the copies are being delivered overnight. We have got to get Myles to give you more notice. Normally, I'd have all of your materials already waiting for you, but these one day turnarounds are tougher."

"Do you think I'll have enough for all three days?"

"Yes," Donna's regal voice floated over the phone line, "and if you need more, I'll make sure you'll get them immediately."

"Thanks, Ms. Burke. I owe you."

"Yes, I know. Bye now."

Finally, hanging up the phone, she grabbed her laptop and briefcase and headed for the elevators that would take her right down to the conference area, which was conveniently located in her hotel.

When she entered the conference room, which was large enough to hold over a hundred people, there were only a few other people there. She nodded hello to several, and as the room filled, people began to mingle and the ritual of exchanging business cards for future collaborations began. She recognized a few familiar faces among the growing nametag wearing crowd. Her excitement burgeoned, as it normally did whenever she had the chance to participate in a conference where she could share her theories.

Conference packets with the roster of presenters and schedule of the sessions for the week were on the table. Just as Myles had mentioned, except for today, she was listed as the first presenter for the next three days.

As she perused the schedule she grimaced, surprised to see a familiar name, Calvin Garvey, was listed as the host on Wednesday. *I can't believe this asshole is here! Merde!* She cursed in French as she quickly scanned the room, but she didn't find him in the crowd. He was not one of her favorite people. Immediately, she put him out of her mind, as someone insignificant at the moment. She turned her attention to the people filling the seats, nodding to familiar faces and acknowledging other people as she made eye contact with them.

After briefly scanning the room, she took out her planner and quickly evaluated her schedule for the week. She didn't have the luxury of wasting time, though she sometimes wished she could digress from the technicalities of her role. Regardless, she was accustomed to her hectic pace and contented with it because she drew much of her motivation from the things that diverted her from her work.

Doing her work and receiving feedback from her peers this week was going to be thoroughly enjoyable.

As the seats around her filled up, she wrote a couple of memory joggers about the calls in her phone logs. She flipped to the notes she had made over the weekend before leaving for St. Louis. In one entry she had jotted *Sydney's suspicions* next to a call from her best friend. Flipping to the page for the following day, she jotted down, *Check on Syd—AM*. The host then took the podium, interrupting her thoughts.

"Welcome fellow engineers! I hope you are all enjoying your stay here in Las Vegas. If you've never been here, the Hoover Dam is a must-see. After all, it is one of the marvels of our profession," the portly host began to chuckle. "You know that you're an engineer when you're at Hoover Dam, you know the Q of the falling water!" The audience understood his attempt at humor and offered polite laughter.

After a brief outline of respective topics, the host reminded everyone that if they wanted continuing education credits for their attendance, they needed to complete the necessary paperwork. He continued with housekeeping chores, reminding everyone to fill out an evaluation for each presentation and presenter.

Mercedes always delighted in receiving peer reviews because she was in her element doing presentations. She consistently received accolades for her sagacious observations and effervescent approach.

Since the morning sessions were mostly filled with formalities, logistics, and presentations outside of her interest, she had chosen to sit in the back and begin to work silently on her laptop on design calculations and specifications for the upgrade of a century-old water treatment plant in Phoenix, choosing to multi-task during the pockets of time when the conference did not warrant her full attention.

As the morning continued, she updated her progress reports and completed preliminary budgetary estimates for three new projects in the West Coast region. During breaks, she refilled her tea, preferring the taste of it to coffee.

At the luncheon, she joined the multitudes and shared in brief conversations with the people sitting at her table before saying her goodbyes. She went out to the lobby to make several business calls. She had several minutes left before the conference convened. She decided to phone her mother.

"Hello, who's this?" The deep, familiar accented voice of her father came over the line to her.

"Hi Daddy."

"Hello my little red rose. Is everything okay?"

"Yes, everything is fine. I'm just calling to let you and Mom know that my travel plans changed. I'm in Las Vegas for the company and I'll be here for a week."

He sounded distracted when he replied, "That's nice, *mi pequeña*. All I need is to hear your voice to know that you are fine. Hold the line and let me find your mother."

She could hear him calling out loudly for her mother in Castilian followed with a loud musical whistle. She smiled when she heard her mother returning his whistle with her own distinct musical response. She thought how original it was for them to have a personal way of calling each other when they were not in each other's line of sight. Unfortunately, she never learned how to whistle though she tried.

The other line picked up and, almost immediately, she heard her mother's voice. "Sweetheart?"

"Hello Mom."

Before her mother could answer, her father spoke briskly in Castilian, "*Okay, I'll leave the two of you to catch up. Little one, are you coming to visit us next month? And, mi amor, when you're done on the phone—would you help me find my screwdriver? I just had it in my hand and now I can't find it!*" Her father hung the phone up without waiting for a response from either one of them.

They both burst out laughing.

"*Dios Mio!* I don't know what to do with your father!" She sounded exasperated but her giggles continued.

"I'm glad to hear nothing has changed. Dad is lost without you!"

"I don't think it'll ever change! So tell me, what's new with you, *iha?*"

"I'm in Vegas!"

"Las Vegas? How exciting! What brings you to Vegas?"

"Work. Myles talked me into taking on a Vegas project at the last minute. I got here last night and I'll be here for a week."

"You sound exhausted. Are you okay? Did the trip wear you out?"

"I actually feel pretty good despite all the running around. Myles sweetened the deal and offered me lots of perks. I was flown in one of the company jets. I feel quite pampered." She thought of how skillfully Myles had handled her and excitement gripped her when she began to think of all the possibilities of the favors he was to return.

"Perhaps you could ask Myles to give you an extended vacation after all this traveling. I'm worried that you're not getting enough rest, especially now. I don't think you have given your body enough time to fully recover yet."

"Sounds tempting and I do have my eye on France. We just got a sizable contract in the Loire Valley. It would be ideal to have a working vacation there. You've been there, haven't you? What was it like?"

"I'm not sure, sweetheart. Your dad was more fascinated with the Eiffel Tower and the Louvre so we passed on a tour in that region. You know how stubborn he can be when it comes to anything related to architecture or art. Anyway, I'm sure it's beautiful there with all the vineyards, chateaus and castles."

Her mother was still talking about the Loire Valley when she abruptly interrupted her and blurted out, "I'm reluctant to deepen my relationship with Grant and I'm not sure why. We've been together almost a year!"

"Sweetheart, Grant is a nice man, but perhaps you're having second thoughts. The long separation period is supposed to give you and Mason the chance to work things out. I'm sure Grant understands that."

"Mom, Mason and I both want the same thing right now. We're better off divorced than married. We really don't want to end up hating each other, which is what would happen if we kept up the 'we're happily married' charade. You understand."

"Yes, of course. I hope you don't mind if I call Mason. I need him to talk to him about a builder."

"Please do. Nothing has changed just because we're divorcing." Almost immediately, she heard her mother sigh.

"Sweetheart, I'm afraid some things will most definitely change."

"I don't want to imagine any unexpected changes."

"Unfortunately, there's nothing to prevent it." She knew her mother was right.

"Dearest, I sense there is something else troubling you. It doesn't feel like it's about Mason. Care to tell me about it?"

"I'm also worried about Sydney. She suspects Patrick is cheating on her. I don't think he's capable of being unfaithful."

"Have you spoken to her about it?"

"Not yet with the non-stop traveling I've done. I haven't had the chance really. I need to catch up with her soon."

"What you need is to recharge your batteries from all this gallivanting around," she sounded very motherly, "but that's not what's really troubling you, is it?"

Why do I even try to hide my feelings from my mom? She conceded reluctantly, "You're right. It is something else. I had that same nightmare again and I've been seeing my signs—you know which ones I mean. The most obvious is that there are entirely too many people associated with this trip who share either the *same* first or last name. For instance, the pilot on the company jet, the limo driver, the guy in the front desk and the bellhop were all named Travis!"

"Well, you know not to take those types of feelings for granted. Just be aware of your surroundings while you are there. Just keep your wits about you. Remember what I told you."

"I know, I know, *Haz el bien sin mirar a quién.*" It was an old Spanish Proverb meaning "Do what is right, come what may."

"As far as your nightmare, try not to think too hard on it, my dearest. Simply trust your intuition when logic fails to present an answer. Praying helps, too, so don't forget to say a prayer for guidance. It never fails with me. Now tell me, have you recuperated from the art show and everything else?"

Mercedes decided to momentarily ignore the "everything else" question and just focused on the art.

"Having a solo art show at the Nouveau Gallery was just too good an opportunity to pass up."

"I really liked the name you picked out for the show, *Enchantment.* That name was a perfect fit."

"I was glad to see a lot of people there. I was equally nervous with many of my nerdy colleagues there too. They haven't seen that part of me."

"I must have heard them tell you a dozen times, 'Mercedes, I can't believe you're an engineer! You've really missed your calling!'"

Mercedes laughed softly, as she had that night at the compliment.

"What can I say, thanks to you and Dad, I have two equally powerful hemispheres in my brain. It gets me in trouble sometimes, but it's been well worth it."

"Your father and I enjoyed your art show. Your art defies singular categorization. The opening was so rich, it was almost like a theatrical drama—and the way you unveiled *Under a Spell* was just beautiful. Exceptional." Hearing her mother's praise meant the world to her.

It had become a tradition for her to spotlight one exceptional piece among the series of paintings in her show. A silk cloth was usually draped over it and she would customarily unveil the painting, signaling the official opening of the exhibit. Following the unveiling, she would give either a short, moving speech, or a poem she had penned specifically about the unveiled piece. For her most recent show, she had chosen a moving soliloquy from Shakespeare's *A Midsummer Night's Dream*.

"I honestly wasn't sure if you and Dad would like that painting since it's a self-portrait in the nude."

"*Au contraire*, it's a beautiful self-portrait and your pose is tasteful. I love the way you cleverly used your long hair, cascading down to cover the most intimate areas of your body."

"I received many offers for that piece, surprisingly from females."

"I can understand why. It conveys a powerful statement when you look at it. Rather, sad, though. Did you sell that painting?"

"Couldn't sell it. I'm not ready to part with it, not just yet."

"Do you think you will ever be ready to part with it?"

"I don't know. I don't think so."

"What about your writing?"

"My muse has left me. I couldn't capture the depth of emotion that I had wanted. Each time I ended up staring at a blank page, and it was frustratingly difficult to try and force the effort." With a melodramatic voice she expressed her frustrations after a deep sigh, "Nothing beautiful could ever be created without being struck with the fiery passion of true inspiration. I've lost my words."

Just as she finished her sentence, she could hear a loud bang in the background, which was followed with constant hammering. Then she heard her mother laugh, followed with a loud yell, "Lindor Donato! What are you doing now?" There was no response because her dad evidently couldn't hear her mother over the hammering.

"Sounds like Daddy found the hammer, not the screwdriver," she giggled. "So what project is he working on now?" The hammering got louder and she heard her mother telling him to stop. Suddenly, there was silence. She could only hear a muffled conversation, which was followed with her parents laughing.

"*Oh, mon Dieu!* I don't know what he's into now, but he's constantly doing something around the house. And he has no concept of time either! Why did I marry a big kid?" She was laughing as she said it.

Mercedes could hear kissing sounds and then her mother giggling.

"Dad, Mom, I can hear you, you know!" She smiled knowing her father was smoothing things over with her mother. They were very affectionate with each other.

"Your dad is quite romantic." Mercedes sensed her mother's smile.

"Women are still shamelessly flirting with him. Just the other day, your dad and I were at the mall. I had to pick up another bottle of perfume when those ladies at the counter were busily flirting with him. They were paying more attention to him than to me!"

"Dad must've loved all the attention!"

"Of course and he never smelled so good." They both shared another laugh.

"Has Dad been painting lately?"

"He's been working on a very vibrant oil painting but when he ran out of paint a week ago, he suddenly stopped working on it."

"I'm surprised that he didn't immediately run out and get more paint."

"Oh he did, sweetheart, but when he got back, he claimed to have lost his artistic momentum. Like I said before, you and your father are so much alike. He claims his muse left him too. Meantime, he's gravitating toward the tools."

"Which explains all that hammering!"

"I can only guess what he's up to!"

"I heard from Lucas last night."

"I'm glad. He called a couple of days ago, telling us he got re-assigned again to some place that he couldn't tell us about. He's very hush-hush about his whereabouts. You know how he is."

"I know, he told me." Mercedes missed her five brothers but she was closest to Lucas.

"They're all fine—busy with their own lives. Luis just called yesterday, saying he wanted to hear from his little miracle sister."

Her birth had truly been a miracle because she had been in terrible distress in her mother's womb with her umbilical cord wrapped around her neck. The doctors had hurriedly performed an emergency C-section delivery. Her mother almost hadn't survived the birth and whenever she saw her mother's long vertical surgical scar, she'd cringe.

"Anything new with any of them?"

"Leo, he's in the Bahamas with Alana. He, he might be proposing to her—"

"The model? But they've just met!"

"They're in love."

"They're in lust! Mom, I can't believe you approve of this."

"Let's be happy for him, dearest."

She sighed and was silent for a few moments.

"I can't believe I didn't remember this earlier. Sweetheart, your godmother, Veronica, is in Las Vegas now. I just got a letter from her not too long ago, telling me that she is in Las Vegas to be with Angel. Of all places, she was in Zimbabwe. I'm sure she would love to see you. Perhaps you can squeeze in a visit with her—in between your meetings?"

"I would love to see her. What's her number and address, Mom?"

Quickly she grabbed her planner and jotted down the information from her mother. As they were about to continue talking, the other line picked up and once again Mercedes heard her father's strong accented voice.

"*I'm sorry to interrupt my two favorite ladies, but, mi amor, I could really use your help now.*"

Her mother replied in Castilian, "*All right, but first let me say goodbye to our daughter and I'll be right over to help you.*"

"I need to get going anyway, Mom. The conference is getting started again."

"All right then." Mindful of her husband listening in, she continued in French, "*But please don't forget that when logic fails, trust your instincts. Okay, sweetheart?*"

"*I will, Mom,*" then she shifted to Castilian, "*Love you, too, Dad. And, Daddy—I will be over next month. Mom, I'll talk to you when I get back, okay?*"

"*Love you, mi pequeña.*"

"*Hugs and kisses through the line, little one.*"

Besides her name, Mercedes also shared her mother's uncanny ability for languages. After only a few hours of listening to a conversation, both she and her mother could speak the language like natives. The many things they shared in common made them the best of friends, and often she easily shared her deepest secrets with her mother.

She felt her mother was, in many ways, a woman ahead of her time in her thinking. She remembered how she would ask her father about how he had proposed to her. "It was with a serenade and a poem I wrote," he had said. She often wondered if she would ever be as lucky as they were.

One of her cherished childhood memories was watching her parents while they danced the waltz. Her father had taught it to her when she was ten; she had literally danced on his feet while they swayed to Johann Strauss' *Blue Danube*, and they had danced the waltz for their father-daughter dance at her wedding.

She instinctively looked at her watch. *Damn, I'm late!* She quietly snuck back to her seat and while she sat in meeting after meeting, she found herself wondering what Grant was doing.

Chapter 4

March 20th, Grant

When Grant's pager went off, he immediately picked up the closest phone. "Is everything all right?"

"Yes, just checking in on my big brother, that's all." The voice was sweet and southern.

"Abigail! I hate it when you page me like that. Y'all know it's only for emergencies," he said. Though he no longer spoke with a deep drawl, now and again he would occasionally let out a "y'all," or some other colorful descriptive.

"Quit being ornery and tell me, how's my favorite pediatric surgeon?"

"Just fine. What about you? Which country are you invading next?"

"I'm fixin' to jet off to Paris for another fashion week and maybe to New York City. Just as well, I'm tired of fighting off well-bred southern boys. I'm feeling adventurous. I want to try something new. You busy?"

He sighed. "I have a non-ending stream of paperwork and patient records, or so it seems."

"So, is Temple all you expected it to be?"

"Absolutely." He had accepted the job not only because of Temple's reputation, but also because of his fondness for Philadelphia. After graduating from the University of Pennsylvania's School of Medicine, he had been on the lookout for opportunities to return to the *City of Brotherly Love*, even though he was from an affluent Memphis family, rich in southern traditions. "How are Mom and Dad? What about you?"

"If things get any better, I may have to hire someone to help me enjoy it!" she said, her drawl was stronger. "Momma's busy with her M.F.A. students. She's also hosting the book club this weekend. And Daddy, he's at another brain convention."

Grant had grown up wanting to be just like his father and follow in his footsteps. His father was a surgeon, as his grandfather had been before him and so on. Medicine was a Larcher family tradition, as were the arts.

He leaned back in his chair, thinking of his mother, whom he adored.

"Hey, are you coming home for their fortieth wedding anniversary party? Everyone else is."

"Really? Is Hugh going?" he asked about his elusive younger brother who was in the secret service.

"Yes. Leo, Caleb, and Daniel, too."

"How are my little brothers?" he grinned thinking about them.

"Well, Hugh is in some undercover thing again. Momma is beside herself with worry. Leo is nursing some science experiment, hoping to get another research grant. I never could understand why he likes fungus. Gross!" she said, sounding like a prima donna. "And Caleb just got the nod for the Atlanta Young Architect Award."

"What about Daniel? I heard something about him going into private practice."

"Humph! I'm not speaking to him."

"What is it now?"

"What good is it to have plastic surgeon as a brother when he won't give me breasts!?"

"He's a reconstructive plastic surgeon, Abby—the operative word is *reconstructive*. Besides you've got more than your share in that department," he chuckled and went on, "Vanity, thy name is Woman."

"Oh hush with that vanity stuff!" she said, clearly flabbergasted; then, expertly shifting her tone, trying her best to appeal to his sentimentality, she drawled, "Come on, you'd complete the set if you went to the party. We could all sing to Momma and Daddy at the party like old times."

"I really want to be there, but I won't know my schedule until a few days before the party. There might be—"

"A gig?" she quickly asked.

"No."

"Still dreaming about becoming a musician? Just quit medicine and go where the wind blows to play your music," she said, remembering one of their conversations. "You certainly don't fit the profile of a doctor with your long hair and everything else. Shoot—you've got longer hair than I do."

"Hey, I keep it neatly tied back so I don't threaten my older patients or the parents of my younger ones."

"Sure you do, and you keep it long because you know it makes you look like a rock star and that women find it very sexy."

"It's not my hair they love," he said, shifting to a drawl, "it's my smile and southern charm they can't get enough of."

"I'm not sure that it's fair that someone could be so good-looking and so unpretentious too." She paused before saying, "Did I say that out loud about me?"

He grinned at her teasing and chose not to add that the real reason he was popular with women was because he was very attuned to a woman's need for sensitivity and romance.

"Are you still wearing glasses? You don't need them, you know."

"I need them!" he said. Though, it was just for reading.

"Sure you do. Would you please stop hiding your eyes? You can still look like an intellectual without those wire rims. Do these women know that you rival Einstein?" She continued, "Besides, you look younger without them, too. I can never understand why anyone would want to look older."

At thirty-five, Grant could pass for twenty-five, although he never tried to do so. He kept himself very fit, working out as often as his time would allow. His workouts complemented his average height, making him appear larger than he was. He was also tough as nails and never backed down in a confrontation.

"Okay, *Jet*—what are you up to?" he asked, using his personal nickname for her.

Sighing, she said, "Oh, nothing. I just called to rile you up a bit."

"Good luck." He always retained his unruffled composure until he was seriously provoked.

"You're just like Daddy!"

"Why, thank you, I'll take that as a compliment." He credited his composure to his father's stoic refinement and class.

"Have you heard from Mercedes?"

"She's out West in Las Vegas. At a conference."

"That's too bad. Bet you miss her."

"Yeah, I do."

"Y'all make a nice—"

A beeping noise broke through; it was Grant's pager again. He was needed on the pediatric floor. "Sorry, but it's my cue. I've got to jet. No pun intended."

"Real funny, smart-ass!" Quickly shifting her tone, sounding a bit motherly, she said, "Make sure to be nice to your patients and remember to sing for them too. Those little guys need a touch of your humor when they're in the hospital. Physician—heal thyself, get those silly patches and quit already. By the way, you owe me a chess rematch!"

"Yes, I'll sing. Yes, I'm on the patch. And, yes, I'll *whup* your spoiled behind. Love you, bye." He chuckled when he hung up the phone, having enjoyed the brief phone call with his only sister. They just loved to tease each other.

Needing to win was at least in part due to the timeless hours of chess with his father, and in part due to the fierce competition in every possible sport that he had participated in with his four brothers and Abigail. Those activities had trained his mind's acuity and patience.

He smiled, thinking about the *Larcher Riders*, as his brothers and closest friends were collectively known within their circle. They were always known as a terror to contend with when they were hanging out together in town.

Whenever he returned to Memphis, they would gather up for a ride through the trails in the nearby woods, followed by an intense game of paintball, and, finally, a rowdy game of poker or 9-ball.

Ten hours later, after he was deep into his 36-hour shift, he found a couple of hours to get started on the rest of his dictation.

He was heading to the Medical Records Department in the basement of the hospital, when he passed the cafeteria. It was almost 1:30 a.m. and he knew he needed to at least get a sandwich and a strong cup of coffee to deal with a couple of hours' worth of paperwork.

He had been on his feet for eight straight hours in the operating room and he couldn't remember the last time he sat down for a meal. Thinking about food, he could feel hunger pains gnawing at him and the urge to have a smoke was strong. He had promised Mercedes that he would quit and times like this made it difficult to resist.

Although the hour was late, the cafeteria was crowded as usual. For him it had been one of the quieter nights at work. He had four and a half hours to go, and then he would get at least an hour of sleep in the doctor's lounge before beginning morning rounds with a fresh batch of fourth-year medical students.

Looking at his pager to check the time again, he wondered why he hadn't received word from Mercedes.

Abruptly, his attention was turned to the subject of his meal, as the man behind the deli counter prompted him for his order.

"An Italian hoagie, extra tomatoes, no onions, a bag of chips and a large black coffee, please. Wait—scratch the large coffee! Make it an *extra* large cup of strong black coffee. Thanks."

He scanned the room for a quiet table where he could jot down a few notes before he forgot them. Getting settled, he took a legal pad out of the folder he was carrying and then took out the neatly folded note he had placed in his lab coat pocket before starting his shift. Mercedes had left it for him in his sock drawer a few days earlier. He grinned thinking about how she managed to leave notes in the most unexpected places. He unfolded the note and began to re-read it again, hearing her voice in his mind.

"Hi Grant,

I'm so sorry I missed you. I should've called, but as usual, I'm multi-tasking, so while I was en route to the airport, I decided to drop in instead.

Woe is me! Jeff told me I had just missed you by minutes! Well, I couldn't resist sneaking into your room and leaving this in your sock drawer. You're going to need a fresh pair of socks sooner or later!

My schedule is quite hectic for the next ten days since Myles insisted this morning that I squeeze in a lecture in Las Vegas after my seminar in St. Louis. I couldn't get out of it, though I tried, yada-yada-yada....

Here's my itinerary:

- Weekend seminar in St. Louis on Friday and Saturday.

- Leave for Las Vegas on Sunday for workshops/lectures/meetings from Monday to Thursday.

- Home on Friday for much needed rest.

No, I didn't forget about Shakespeare's Much Ado About Nothing at the Mann Center Saturday night. It is just my all-time favorite—next to Hamlet, of course.

I'd love it if you could pick me up at the airport next Friday. Perhaps we can grab a bite to eat at Bookbinders. Intrigued? I'll call as often as time will permit me.

Not to worry, I promise to take my antibiotics for these dreaded wounds!

Don't miss me too much!

Mercedes"

He mumbled, "Wrong, I already miss you very much." Sipping his coffee, he noticed the difference between her beautiful penmanship and his scrawling on the notepad, chuckling at the fact that he was doomed, as doctors often were, to have illegible handwriting because he was constantly rushing from patient to patient.

Almost a year ago they had started going out, but their relationship wasn't as serious as he wished. Thinking about the year they spent together, he jotted a note to send a card for her. Hopefully, she'd be surprised.

Lately, she had been more distracted than usual—even hard to reach at times. He wasn't sure what he was doing wrong. He was consistent, always kept his promises, and tried to make her laugh whenever he could.

At times, she was aloof, convincing him that it was largely due to his damned impossible 36-hour on-call schedules over the past two months. She also warned him that she would get melancholy around this time of the year and inundate herself with art-related activities, accept additional assignments and dive into research work until she was exhausted.

It didn't seem like it was a mood disorder, such as Seasonal Affective Disorder; it was inconsistent with what he expected because her despondency only happened after one of her nightmares which occurred during any given month.

The episodes had become more frequent since her outpatient surgery, resulting in her becoming an insomniac. When he tried to prescribe sleeping pills, she resisted, which frustrated him more because she would never talk about it, but purposefully seemed to push him away when he wanted to help her.

After one of her night terrors, she would just cry with murmurs, in French or Latin and cling to him for comfort. He wasn't even surprised when she spoke, unaware of doing so, in French or Latin, since she had an inherent talent for languages, much like his ear for music. He could pick up a tune after hearing it once. But the way she screamed and sobbed uncontrollably after she woke up distressed him.

After she woke, she would assure him it was nothing—expertly feigning normalcy. But he knew she was having reoccurring nightmares, and it usually took her a day to recover.

He suspected she was actually dissociating, reliving a certain event partially or in its entirety. Flashbacks often happened with his patients who suffered Post-Traumatic Stress Disorder. During his psychiatric residency, he had cared for war veterans and victims of traumatic events, but Mercedes didn't fit any of those categories.

He had explained it to her, but she would dismiss it, mercilessly teasing him about being a silly worrywart. Well, she was right. He was worried and concerned about it.

He beamed, thinking of his plans to pamper her when she returned from her business trip. He had planned a weekend filled with theater, wine, dinner, dance, and personal attention that would lift her spirits and hopefully help him get over missing her so much.

It was hard to believe there had been a time when he hadn't known her. The first time he saw her had been only just before she separated from Mason.

While at a medical conference in Philadelphia, his mother had convinced him to attend a small black-tie affair at the Philadelphia Museum of Art as the representative for the Larcher family. His family name was quite celebrated in the museum endowment circle.

He hadn't wanted to go, but afterwards he had actually thanked his mother for bamboozling him into going. That was the night he had first met Mercedes.

He had gone to the Saint-Genis-des-Fontaines Cloister of the museum, a French Medieval cloister from the heart of a monastery featuring architectural elements from the late thirteenth century Abbey of Saint-Genis-des-Fontaines.

The twelfth century fountain in the center of the open courtyard had originated from the Abbey of Saint-Michel-de-Cuxa, and the rooms made him feel oddly at home.

Yet his boredom was palpable. For years he had been hobnobbing with other prominent guests with whom he had little or nothing in common.

He eventually worked his way from the Saint-Genis-des-Fontaines Cloister to the Impressionist Era wing of the museum, needing to escape the loud chatter, which had sadly been drowning out the moving andante of Tchaikovsky's *Violin Concerto*. He followed the trickling soft sounds of water to the center hall where there was a small circular water pool, surrounded with marble benches, complementing the ambiance of the gallery filled with the works of Van Gogh, Renoir, Degas, Cassatt and Monet. It was an area he loved and one that let serenity seep into him.

Admiring Monet's *Marine View, Sunset*, he perceived an exquisite perfume and instinctively turned to find out who was wearing it.

The woman was delicate, a petite brunette. Her back was facing him, and he noted how her gracefully coifed hair was crowned with delicate gems that were shimmering under the museum spotlights.

He let his eyes follow the contours of her shoulders and the plunging V-back of her crimson silk satin gown that accentuated her carefully sculpted frame, wondering if her face would match the rest of her quiet elegance.

She was studying Mary Cassatt's *On a Balcony During a Carnival* and then fixed her attention on what was obviously one of her favorite masterpieces, Van Gogh's *Arles Sunflowers*.

The museum had Van Gogh's *Still Life: Vase with Twelve Sunflowers* in their permanent collection and he had wondered if it made her as emotional as it did him.

She was oblivious to the gaiety around her, seemingly wanting only to immerse herself with the brilliant colors of each masterpiece. She hadn't looked lonely, even though she was there without an escort.

He knew the exact second she felt him staring at her from behind and he noticed how she brought her left hand up, tucking back a loose tendril of hair behind her ear, deliberately flashing a diamond studded wedding ensemble that looked rather grand on her dainty hands.

As he stood there smiling to himself, a voice behind him asked, "Dr. Larcher? Dr. Grant Larcher?"

Enraptured, he was a little startled as he had turned to find out who was addressing him.

A sophisticated-looking, silver-haired man thirty years his senior continued, "Hello, Dr. Larcher. Let me introduce myself. I'm Ned Hayward, curator of the museum. How are you this fine evening?" He promptly extended his hand to Grant.

"Ah, yes, Mr. Hayward. I am enjoying the beauty—the beauty of the art, of course. Thank you for asking." He remembered their handshake and recalled politely saying, "My mother has spoken a great deal about you. How nice to finally meet you, sir."

The beautiful woman turned her head slightly toward them. He remembered wanting to see her face closer—in full light.

When she finally looked toward them, she smiled in recognition at the older man. Grant was delighted to see her turn toward them and was powerfully smitten by her smile. She looked magnificently regal with Johann Pachelbel's *Canon in D* serenading her slow, sensual strides toward them.

The older man also noticed her approach; his eyes lit up and a smile formed on his lips, showing his delight.

"Mrs. Sinclair, you look enchanting as always," he said clasping her extended hand with both of his. She answered sweetly, "Why, thank you, Mr. Hayward. You're compliments are much too kind."

It was then that her eyes had locked with Grant's as she smiled shyly.

Ned turned to Grant and asked, "Dr. Larcher, have you met Mrs. Sinclair?"

"No," he remembered almost blushing as he smiled at her, saying, "I haven't had the pleasure."

Mr. Hayward promptly and formally introduced them. "Dr. Grant Larcher, let me present the lovely Mercedes Sinclair. Mrs. Sinclair and her husband, Mason, are some of our most generous benefactors—as are the members of the Larcher family, of course."

Knowingly, she extended her left hand. Taking her hand in his, he slowly brought it to his lips and gently placed a warm kiss on the back of it, fully aware of the marital signals she was sending; signals that did not matter to him at that moment.

She gracefully excused herself from the company of the two men and returned to the colors of the Impressionists.

* * *

"Doctor Larcher—please dial 14625. Doctor Larcher, 14625." The intercom jarred him out of his daydream and returned him to the cafeteria of the hospital and his cold black coffee. Sighing, he got up and went to a phone near his table.

Chapter 5

March 20th, Mason

"Mr. Sinclair?"
"Yes, Jen. What is it now?" Mason was annoyed with the interruption.
"Mrs. Donato is on line one."
"I'll take the call," he replied, sounding delighted. "That reminds me, would you call my realtor and find out when the closing date is on my house?"

Quickly, he pressed the flashing button, "Mom, how are you?"
"Hello, Mason. I'm fine, dear. Do you have a moment?"
"For you? Always. What can I do for you?"
"I was wondering if you could help me locate a reputable builder in Florida. Dad and I just closed on a property in Crystal River just last week. He has the architectural plans ready and we just need a builder to get started. We're hoping to get the house finished before June. Could you point us to the right person?"

As he was listening to her talk, he went through his Rolodex and pulled out a business card. "As a matter of fact, I have just the builder you need. He's a good buddy of mine and he won't steer you wrong. Better yet, why don't you leave this to me? All I'll need is a copy of the house plans and your budget. I'll take it from there."

"Mason, that's so generous of you. You must be very busy. Are you sure we're not intruding on your time?"
"Not at all! Don't be silly. I can't believe you would even think that."
"Well, with everything that's going on, it's really hard to say."
"Mom, just because Merc and I are divorcing doesn't mean anything should change between us."
"She said the same thing to me today."
"She did? How is she doing after the surgery?"
"She's well and out West on a business trip."
"It's just like her to get right back into the mix."
"How about you? How are you, dear?"
"Good. I'm good. I've got a full plate with work, so there's never a dull moment."
"And your mom—how's Bridget? How are your sisters and Max?"

He automatically looked at the family photo on his desk and said, "Max is joining the Marines in a couple of months. I'm hoping that'll shape him up. Mom is fine. She's trying her hand at opening a restaurant downtown. Bree and Briana are helping her get it started. They seem to have everything under control except they can't agree on the theme and name of the restaurant. I tried to help, but I got a prompt thrashing and it's just as well, since I really couldn't get a word in edgewise anyways. I bowed out knowing if I insisted, my mom would rip my head off. You know how she is."

"Sounds like an exclusive ladies project, Mason. And yes, I do understand."

"How's Dad doing?"

"He's still quite distraught over the two of you, dear. He tries to hide his worry, but he can't fool me."

"I hope he'll understand that it'll work out for the best in the long run. I'd hate to have him think differently of me. He's the only father figure I've known."

"He loves you and understands. He—actually, we just wished that things could be different."

"Yes, I know—me too. But there's not much to do when you've got two very stubborn people with their minds made up and—"

The intercom interrupted him. "Mr. Sinclair?"

"Hang on, Jen."

"Mason, let me get going, you sound really busy right now."

"Okay, Mom. I'll talk to you soon. Hello to Dad."

"Take care. We love you."

"Me, too."

Immediately, he acknowledged Jen sternly, "Yes, what is it?"

"Max is on line two. He said it was urgent."

He looked at his phone but found none of the lines blinking. "He must've hung up. Would you get him back on the line?"

"Yes, sir."

He looked at the family photo again. He remembered Mercedes had taken the picture and his thoughts wandered to their early beginnings.

***

It was at the opening of Club Bertucci where Mason met Mercedes. He had built the club for his best friend, Dominic. He was grateful that Dominic believed in him enough to let him build it. It was his first major project. He had just started his own business enterprise as a contractor with one motley crew, and some borrowed capital from the bank. The club gave him enough capital to increase his crew size and he was able to pay off the bank. He hated to be in debt. He would rather starve than owe anyone. And he was starving since he was still dependent on each contract thrown his way. They were hard to come by since the competition was fierce.

Mason knew he looked good. A couple of things he never compromised on were his looks and his clothes. He made sure he was dressed like a million dollars. His buddy, Dominic, talked him into becoming a bodybuilder to earn some extra cash in the local competitions. He could have any woman he wanted and after spotting Mercedes from across the room, he wanted her the moment he saw her. So he approached her with the same cockiness and charm, but, to his surprise, she turned him down!

Shit! That was a first! Shaking his head in disbelief, he headed back to his friends.

"*Porca l'oca!* Youse got fuckin' shot down, crashed and burned!" Dominic ribbed him loudly after witnessing the entire scene.

I'm never gonna fuckin' hear the end of this! he thought, a little annoyed about what just happened. This was going to be a challenge, and he never refused a challenge, especially in front of his best friend. He stopped, turned so he could look at her again, but she had disappeared. Frankly, Mason was a bit relieved because he felt she was way out of his league, anyway. She was too cultured for him. He usually liked his women with teased big hair and huge breasts—the ones from South Philly who dressed slutty.

No, he thought, *too high maintenance.* He didn't want that in his life. He simply couldn't afford it. As he was thinking this, he saw her appear again in his line of sight. She was just coming out of the ladies' room and he thoroughly checked her out. She was a breath of sophisticated elegance; she wore a slim-fitting sleeveless cream sheath halter dress which accentuated her perfectly tanned body. Her hair was layered and long with light brown highlights. She literally knocked him out with her smile.

She looks like one of those sexy hula girls who just got back from spring break, he thought. He had never seen anyone so amazing to look at. If he played his cards right, he could have sex with her right there on the dance floor. But he could sense that she was not the type that would do that. *Too much class. She's not here alone. No, not her,* he thought. *She's here with someone.*

He had to turn his attention to his friends, who had just shoved a beer in his hand while they mercilessly jibed him about her and then congratulated him on the club.

"There she is again," Dominic said, grinning at him. "If youse don't got the *coglioni* to try again, I do."

"Yeah, *cacchio*, watch this," he said, taking his chances on the dare. Following her up the stairs, her perfume was intoxicating. *She's mine*, Mason thought, *I've got to have her.*

* * *

Sighing at the memory, he sat back and stretched as he cast his eyes on the red dragon painting on his office wall. It was one of Mercedes' early acrylic paintings.

He unconsciously felt his right bicep where a dragon tattoo was hiding under his sleeve. He tried to convince her to get a matching tattoo, but she surprised him when she refused, being the artist that she was. Instead, she designed the tattoo on his right bicep, which he showed off as often as he could.

When she had sketched it, he remembered wondering what the hell Mercedes saw in him. He saw himself as this cocky, good-looking, well-dressed, yet crude-talking, jealous, half-Irish, angry Neanderthal with only a high-school education.

Boldly, he asked, "Why do you love me, babe?"

"What? You don't know?" she teased.

"C'mon, just tell me," he pressed, feeling a little insecure.

"I love you because of your raw passion for everything in life!" She raised her eyebrow, asking, "Should I go on?"

"Hell yeah!"

"You've got natural instincts to make things happen. You know exactly what you want and you get it. You got me, didn't you?"

"You're right. Okay, keep going—what else?" He was genuinely curious.

"Okay, it's also because you see right through people, but you have the compassion to let other people believe in themselves. You give confidence where there is none. You truly bring out the best in everyone. And I especially love the fact that nothing scares you. You stare fear right in the eyes and have it scurry away with its tail between its legs."

"Look who's talkin' about being fearless! You try everything at least once," he grinned. Then, with a serious tone in his voice, he recounted, "You weren't scared when you fell off my bike the last time we rode the trails. That was a twenty-foot fall, babe! That was scary shit!" He remembered how a branch got caught in his front wheel and the bike flipped over, throwing them off the embankment. He cleared the bike and was safely thrown off, but her leg got stuck, causing her to fall like a rag doll with the bike. As she went airborne, Mason saw the bike fall on top of her. He closed his eyes thinking that the bike landed on her, crushing her skull. The impact knocked the wind out of her and she passed out. Thankfully she was wearing her helmet, so in place of getting her skull crushed she received a severe concussion, a broken right wrist and ankle, a fractured collarbone, and a dislocated right shoulder with scratches and bruises all over her body.

"I can still feel the pain," she winced at the memory, putting her pencil down and presenting the sketch to him. "You like it? You can make it a red tattoo."

Looking at it, he shook his head.

"No good? Or no red?" she asked, frowning.

"No," he said, but his head was nodding. "I fuckin' love it! And yeah, I'd like it in red." Looking at it again, he said, "And, babe…"

"Uh-huh."

"I promise you—I'll never let anyone or anything hurt you," he said, not sharing how she had scared him more than she would ever know. When he found her unconscious down on that embankment and wedged in on her right side, he thought he had lost her.

A life without her was unimaginable. She was there with him every step of the way. Without her, he would still be piss poor and struggling to get his business off the ground.

He was living with his fiery Italian mother and siblings to make ends meet. He had been the man of the house since he was ten years old, when his father, whose name he bore, decided to just walk out on the family. He had not seen or heard from him since. His father simply vanished into thin air, and Mason couldn't care less if he showed up in his life now, especially now that he was an adult. It would be for best if the bastard stayed gone anyway. He didn't care what his reason was for leaving.

Mason never forgave his father. He hated how he had become an adult and, more importantly, a surrogate father to his siblings overnight. He took care of everyone. Everyone relied on him. He never asked for all the responsibilities dumped on his young shoulders. This ultimately left Mason with a nasty taste in his mouth about marriage and children, especially. He was not going to put himself in a position where his kids could be abandoned for whatever reason, even death. He had a well-known reputation as the consummate bachelor, but all that changed when he met Mercedes.

She breathed new life into my sorry ass existence, he thought. She showed him another life, one he never thought he would be part of. He was still a street punk at heart. He thought, *I just can't get into all that artsy-fartsy shit she loves so much. Art, books, philosophy, poetry, plays, the orchestra, the opera, the ballet and all that fancy shit! She loves to travel and I can't even get in a plane without a fuckin' sedative!*

A man should be so lucky to have a gorgeous woman who was every bit a lady, smart as a whip and talented beyond belief. *Damn! I felt smarter just being with her.*

"What are you reading?"

"Shakespeare."

"It's barely in English! Why do you read it?"

"For the gore and sarcasm," she teased. "But seriously, I read it because it inspires me. I enjoy the wisdom in his writings too. He talks about destiny and love. Listen— 'One half of me is yours, the other half yours. Mine own, I would say; but if mine, then yours, and so all yours,'" she said, quoting *The Merchant of Venice.*

"It does sound pretty cool when you say it."

"All it really means is I love you," she explained as she smiled and kissed him.

There was never a day he could remember that they didn't say *I love you* or hugged and kissed. It took a lot of getting used to. He never saw that type of affection in his own family. He saw a lot of bickering, resentment, bitterness and sharp words, but not a whole lot of affection.

She was very slow to anger too. But when she was pissed, she would blast him in so many different languages that it made his head spin. He would hightail it out of her sight as fast as he could. He would provoke her in the way he was use to. He was quick-tempered and had grown up with all that shouting and fights that would last for days. No, it was different with Mercedes. He had not known so much peace in his life. Whenever he flew off the handle about something, she would just listen to him rant and rave like a madman.

"Are you done?" she would ask, then there was that smile again. She would talk to him in her sweet voice, but in a low, relaxed tone which would calm him right down.

She also didn't mind getting her hands dirty. She had worked as a construction inspector in college, and she could hang with best of them. Even the crudest of men treated her with respect. It was the way she carried herself. *She's...* he paused, trying to remember the big word, he had just learned from her. *She's never ostentatious,* he completed his thought as the word finally came to him. She wasn't arrogant like he tended to be. He barked orders right to their faces and swore up and down at the men. With Mercedes, all she had to do was smile and remain silent. And when she spoke, people paid attention. He paid attention. He learned how to really listen. He was as stubborn as a mule, so it took some practice. He was still working on it.

"You're so devoted to your mom," she observed.

"Anything wrong with that?"

"Nope," she grinned, "A woman can always tell how a man will treat her by simply watching the way he treats his mother. And you treat your mom—"

"Like a fuckin' queen!" he exclaimed proudly. She giggled at his crudeness. And he loved his mother. He would do anything for her, too. He was doing something so natural, he didn't even know she had been watching him. Good thing she wasn't looking at the way he treated his father. He would have never been able to step up to the plate.

"The true nature of a man lies in the unconscious," she said. He wasn't sure exactly what she meant, but he liked the sound of it.

He especially delighted in her fiery side. Her heat. Laughing softly to himself, he thought, *Shit! If my homeys heard I couldn't keep up, they'd fuckin' crucify me!*

She was everything to him. He struggled to find a flaw in her, but she'd quickly tell him, "Babe, you see me as beautiful because you love me. But I have my flaws—I'm just as stubborn and hardheaded as you. My passion also blinds me if I'm not careful. Though my heart is always in the right place, my good intentions often get misplaced. And I'd trade my IQ for your common sense! Often the answer is right in front of my face, but when it's too obvious, I either dismiss or misinterpret it. I have a sneaking suspicion that I'll be working on that flaw for the rest of my life."

She was laughing as she talked about flaws that he didn't even think she had. She loved to laugh. She said to him once that she would rather die laughing than die of a broken heart.

"What keeps you smiling?"

"Love."

"That's it?" he grinned.

"My turn," she said, "What is it that you want out of life?"

"That's easy. I want to be rich. Not for nuthin', babe but I want expensive things that say 'Hey, look at me, I'm fuckin' rich!' What about you? Want to be rich, too?"

"Being rich is nice, but all I really want is to be happy."

"So you would not mind being poor?" He was truly puzzled.

"Not as long as I'm happy! Don't get me wrong. Money has its purpose. I just don't see it as the ultimate end. Money just helps along the way, makes life easier, more comfortable as I work for the goals I really want to achieve. Mason, I can live without money, but I wouldn't want to live without happiness, or for that matter, without love. And I'd give it all up in a heartbeat if given these choices."

"Well, babe, you're the richest and happiest person I know, because I'm poor and all I've got is all the love in my heart I can give."

"Then you hold within your heart everything I have ever desired," she said lovingly.

How ironic! Because now, he not only had all the love in his heart, but he was also rich.

Though she never asked for things, he vowed to shower her with gifts. He would give her anything she ever wanted or needed. Anything. Except he couldn't give her the one thing she had her heart set on: a child.

He tried to open his heart to having children. Each time Mercedes took a pregnancy test, it broke his heart to see how disappointed she was whenever it turned out to be negative, but he couldn't deny the relief he felt each time that it happened. And when she finally presented him with a sure thing, it scared him. Only two things scared him the most: the first was that she would stop loving him, and the other was having kids. He knew he couldn't deny it any longer.

* * *

"Mr. Sinclair? Max is back on line two."
"Yeah—thanks, Jen."

Chapter 6

March 20th, Club Utopia

In her room in Las Vegas, Mercedes was preparing for a quiet evening of room service, intending to read a couple of chapters from a new book. As she started to take her jacket off, she slipped out of her shoes and loosened her hair, wanting to get into her comfortable silks.

Suddenly, the little voice in her head urged her to go out tonight and whispered, *Check out the lay of the land. After all, this is Las Vegas. It should be fun.*

Restless, she picked up the hotel traveler's guide and flipped through the pages. Her colleagues were always telling her how great the entertainment and floorshows were there.

The Hard Rock Café and the Vegas strip looked somewhat interesting. She picked up a brochure for the Excalibur and flipped to the last page, which was her normal habit. She saw striking photos of the Tournaments of Kings, a dinner show complete with jousting knights, invading armies, dragons, fire-wizards and dinner at 8:30 p.m.

It piqued her interest, but she put the brochure on the table along with the others. *I'll go to the Hard Rock Café tonight,* she decided. She had made it a habit to collect their polo shirts and pins. *I'll grab a bite to eat there and afterwards I'll finally keep my date with my book.*

She also made a mental note to phone Grant when she got back before cozying up to read and trying for a restful night of sleep.

She looked at her wardrobe: business suits, travel attire and a little black dress. She always brought along one of her little black mini-dresses in case of unexpected business dinners. Otherwise, she would venture out to the nearest mall and buy a fashionable dress off the rack. But the black minis were small, light, and easy to pack, so she always had one in her suitcase. She had worn her suit jacket over it during her dinner date with the concierge/pilot in St. Louis. But she knew the probability of an impromptu business dinner in Las Vegas was high.

Debating on whether to wear it, she realized the dress was far too dressy for dining alone. She berated herself aloud, "I'm not here to impress anyone!"

After tousling her hair with hairspray and placing a dab of perfume on her wrists, chest and neck, she put on her black mid-calf stiletto boots, freshened up her face, and headed out the door.

Downstairs the doorman hailed a cab for her.

In the cab, she said hello to the driver, smiling as she always did.

"Where to, Miss?" The balding driver, probably in his late forties, met her friendly smile with one of his own.

"The Hard Rock Café, please."

He grinned, "I love that place. I still remember the first time I went there after I moved here from New Jersey."

"Really?"

"I'm from Cherry Hill. Do you know it?"

Her smile widened and she said with open delight, "Know it—I grew up there!"

"Hey, is Olga's Diner still at the Marlton Circle?" Not waiting for her answer, he remarked, "Those damned circles. I sure don't miss the nightmares those things used to give me!"

"You know Olga's?" She was surprised he was asking about it. It was her favorite diner.

She leaned forward toward the cab driver, talking to him through the small glass opening which separated them. "Yes, Olga's is still there! My friends and I go there all the time right after the movies. Do you remember their bakery?"

"Remember it? How about their banana cream pie! Wow, I can actually taste it right now," he said, smacking his lips. "I read somewhere that they baked the presidential inaugural cake one year."

She smiled back, "Your sources are correct! And the circles are gone, including the Marlton Circle." After glancing at the little sign showing his name, she said, "By the way, Owen Shoemaker, I'm Mercedes."

"Nice to meet you, Mercedes," he said, smiling at her through the rear view mirror, saying quickly, "It's a small world indeed."

As the cab continued along the road, he kept talking about other places they both knew and he also suggested different places along the Vegas strip where she might want to go.

Pulling up at the Hard Rock Café, she handed him her business card. "If you get back East, give me a call."

He gave her his card, too. "I've enjoyed talking with you, Mercedes. You call me if you need anything while you're here, and if I get back East, I'll surely give you a call."

She glanced at the meter, took a few bills from her purse and paid him, adding a generous tip.

"That's too much. I can't take that from a fellow lover of Olga's!"

"Sure you can." She smiled, insisting he do so. "Call if you get back East. We can share a slice of banana cream pie at Olga's."

Her words weren't idle ones. She often made new friends as she traveled, and she meant what she said when she said that she would enjoy keeping in contact with him.

"Thanks."

"You're welcome, Mercedes."

Inside the café, she purchased her collectibles and sat at the bar area until she could get a table for dinner. She often dined alone on trips, but frequently she ended up meeting someone interesting before her meal was done.

Sitting at the bar, she wondered, *Will tonight be any different?*

Automatically, she scanned the room. As the bartender came over to her, she ordered one of her favorites, "Tonic and lime, please."

The bartender nodded, smiling before he moved away to make it.

She looked down on the bar counter, stared at a video poker screen and murmured, "It's amazing where they put these things." She had even been greeted by slot machines at the airport gate.

"I manufacture them." The man seated on her right said softly, almost to himself.

She turned toward him. His intoxicated grin greeted her, and he introduced himself. "I'm Walt Calabrese. I'm vice president of a gaming company."

He was a very attractive man with short blond hair and light blue eyes, but nothing annoyed Mercedes more than a verbose, arrogant, wealthy man, who would try to engage her in pseudo-intellectual conversations. She was not impressed easily, especially by material wealth and rhetoric.

She decided it would be easiest to humor him to pass the time and avoid the boredom that suddenly descended upon her. She decided to amuse herself with the playboy executive, laughing politely and nodding at the right places. In between ramblings he kept giving her coins to play the machine *for him*, between flowery propositions to fly her to Paris.

The bartender noticed her predicament and gave her a sympathetic smile whenever she looked at his direction. She decided it was time for a respite and called the bartender, "Hi, can you tell me where the ladies' room is?"

"Sure. Over there, just down that hallway."

Minutes later, Walt was still at the bar waiting for her when she got back, but she decided to pass on dinner and get back to the hotel.

"Oh, come on," he pleaded with her. "Come with me over to a club that's right near here."

"No, thank you."

"Let me drop you off at your hotel. My limo is right outside. Consider it my way of apologizing if I've been too forward."

It was only 10:30 p.m., and she couldn't help thinking, *The night is still young. It's really early, and I am desperately bored!*

His desperation was obvious, and even though he was boring her, she felt like having fun. Suddenly gripped with a strange excitement, she decided to accept the offer.

"Okay, let's go—to the club."

* * *

Within moments he was leading her to a VIP lounge softly illuminated by neon and strobe lights where they sat on large, comfortable sofas.

It was an intimate atmosphere; she saw a number of couples being more intimate than she liked to be in public, and many people were staring at her.

She was used to the staring whenever she entered a room, especially a nightclub, and she knew both male and female eyes were on her.

She enjoyed having men looking at her with a hunger. She fully understood and even enjoyed their gazes, but the women who looked at her were often judgmental, which irritated her, even though she accepted it as just womanly posturing.

The club was actually fun. Before long Walt was attracting more women as he lavishly threw his charm and wealth around. He also made it clear she was going to be his main conquest for the evening, treating her as his prized trophy.

It was a sentiment that brought her some distress. She detested being regarded as the ultimate accessory in a man's wardrobe.

As he became more and more intoxicated, he also became more insistent on kissing and fondling her, finally suggesting, "Hey, let's go back to the limo for a private party," and he grinned drunkenly, "I'll fulfill your every fantasy."

"You're very flattering, but I'm going to have to pass."

Moments later, Mercedes noticed another man approaching them.

"Dance?" His question to her was more in his eyes than his words. Before she could reply, a drunken voice coming from beside her interrupted the man. "Get lost, asshole!"

Walt had drunkenly stood up from the couch where they were sitting and rudely, deliberately shoved the guy and then took a swing at him. Thankfully, he missed in his stupor.

"Walt! Please, stop it!" Mercedes sprang to her feet.

He caught her arm and quickly pulled her back down with him to the couch. Without apologizing, he sneered, "I've got to let them know you're with me!" Shifting his tone, he said, "I just can't help myself, Mercedes. You've bewitched me."

Stretching his arm around her, he pushed her lightly back against the couch, whispering lustfully, "I must have you. And, I won't take no for an answer. C'mon sexy, I know you want me, too. Stop resisting me, babe." He forcefully kissed her, and the taste of his kiss was pure Scotch. He disgusted her with his actions. Almost immediately, he excused himself to go to the men's room, at which point she took the opportunity to leave his exasperating company.

She hadn't even had a chance to dance; she decided to at least accomplish that before leaving, so she casually walked toward the dance floor. She stood right at the edge, looked around and she was reminded of the time when she and Mason first met.

* * *

From the second floor overlook, Mercedes and her boyfriend, Joey Pitman, watched the frenzied crowd dancing on the dance floor below; her body was unconsciously moving to the rhythm of the club music as she stood in front of him. He was leaning against one of the couches along the railing.

Turning around, she said smiling, "Hon, let's dance."

"What?" Joey said, gesturing to his ear and leaning down closer, as he was a foot taller than she was.

Reaching up and putting her arms around his neck, she tiptoed with her stiletto heels as she pulled him closer. Looking into his pale blue eyes, she pleaded with a kiss, "Let's dance, please?"

"Hon, let's wait for a slow song," he said in her ear, shaking his head. "How about I get you something cold to drink?"

Frowning with a deliberate pout, she said, "Okay, tonic and lime please."

"Sure," he said and quickly turned to his dark-haired friend standing next to him. "Drew, I'm getting drinks, want something?"

"I'll come with you," his friend said then turned to his date, asking with a gesture, "Terri, want a drink?"

"I'll have a Margarita!" said the pretty brunette.

After Joey and Drew left for the bar, the two ladies danced where they stood.

"I like this club, but it's too crowded!"

"You're right!" Mercedes nodded.

"Hey, it's the new song by Madonna!"

"Right again!" she said matching her smile and started singing along, "*Como puede ser verdad...* it all seems like yesterday, not far away..."

Sighing, she wished for a slow song so she could be dancing instead of watching. Glancing around in search for Joey, she saw him still waiting at the bar. As he waved at her, she blew him a kiss and he playfully pretended to catch her kiss in the air, placing it in his pocket. She giggled.

Joey was her sweet gentle giant, a tall heavyweight and the senior captain of the collegiate varsity wrestling team. He was soft-spoken, handsome, and possessed an intellect that matched hers. She felt that he had one of the purest souls she had ever met. It didn't surprise her that he had captured her heart. They had talked about getting married after graduate school.

Looking around again, she smiled at a few guys who were obviously staring in her direction and she was enjoying it. She turned down offers to dance, including a well-dressed guy who approached her with a cockiness that secretly excited her. She wanted to say "Yes" very badly, because Joey didn't really dance. *What's the harm? It's only for a dance.*

"Terri, I'm going to check what's taking them so long. Wait right here!"

"Okay!"

She fought her way through the crowd and when she finally reached Joey, she wrapped her arms around his waist.

"We're next. The bartender is getting our order right now."

"Okay," she said as the music changed to a slow song. As she looked up at him, he gave her a soft kiss and said, "Next song, I promise."

"All right. I'm going to the ladies' room and I'll meet you back upstairs. Terri is waiting there too."

On her way back from the bathroom, she passed a group of dark-suited men; one of them was that cocky guy who had asked her to dance earlier. He was shorter than the rest of his Guido friends, who were obvious in nudging him toward her. She quickly noted the bulging arm muscles through his designer suit.

He looks like movie star, she thought and smiled at him before quickly turning to climb the stairs to the overlook.

As she searched the crowded, darkened room for Joey, she felt a gentle tap on her shoulder.

* * *

"Hey sexy, wanna dance?"

The question shook her out of her daydream. She smiled at a young clean-cut man, who was slightly intoxicated, but shook her head, "No, thank you."

A few young men, using the usual lines, asked her to dance but she turned them down because her urge to dance had waned. *Okay, time to get out of here.* Yet something kept her standing there.

She instinctively looked around the dance floor as she began to feel a peculiar yet fascinating feeling. After a few minutes she dismissed the feeling until she saw a figure silhouetted against the backdrop of neon and strobe lights, standing at the edge of the dance floor.

He was wearing a black t-shirt that accentuated the breadth of his shoulders, and he stood there with a commanding presence, looking fit and hard. He was smiling at his male companions when she first noticed him—he had a dazzling smile. His neatly cropped, light brown hair signified he was in the military. She surveyed his physique, liking what she saw.

In a matter of seconds, she was wondering if he would have a warm, masculine scent that matched his body. Were his eyes blue or brown or...?

A shiver ran up and down her spine. She felt a strong sense of familiarity and couldn't help but notice that he was now looking at her very intently. She thought, *Do I know him? Is he really looking at me, or am I just imagining it?*

With a provocative little grin, she decided to find out. She intentionally locked eyes with him and deliberately flashed him her best come-hither smile. He smiled back.

Strangely, she found she couldn't tear herself away from his gaze or the delightful surge of excitement that was coursing through her body.

Chapter 7

March 20th, Phantom

Joe Tristram stood at the edge of the main dance floor. He was near the bar in front of the VIP lounges, along the south side of the club. It was his first time at this two-story dance club, which was fairly new with a large main floor which was open to the above floors. The bars were directly in front of the multi-level dance floor. A huge accrual of neon and strobe lights lit the entire place. The drumming beat of the music emanated from the strategically placed, high-tech, surround-sound system.

He unconsciously scanned the crowded room. He wasn't looking for anything specific, or rather, anyone. He was there in the company of his two fellow fighter pilots from Nellis Air Force Base. It had been a long week participating in flight combat maneuvers. Today was his first real chance to unwind. Since he had given up drinking for Lent, he was left with the taste of his non-alcoholic beer which did not satisfy his thirst.

He just happened to turn his gaze to the left across the dance floor, and there he spotted her standing in front of the north-side VIP lounge by the stairs. He marveled at her and took in every detail of her exotic beauty.

He noticed her white, fitted, long-sleeve seamless top, which clung tightly to her. Suddenly, his mind's voice whispered, *Yes, clinging to her like red on a rose.* He liked the way it sounded, so he smiled and repeated loudly, "Like red on a rose."

No one heard him between the deafeningly loud music and the blended noisy chatter surrounding him.

As he kept his eyes fixed on her, he sensed something very familiar about her, but he couldn't quite place it. Perhaps they had met before, but he knew he would never have forgotten meeting her. *No, not her.*

While he watched her furtively, she spurned the advances of several men. He tried to project his salient interest across the space between them. The moment came when they locked eyes and he knew she was smiling directly at him. Her beautiful smile struck him with the same inexplicable familiarity he felt when he first laid eyes on her. He had an incredible need to be near her. And when she looked at him again, his need had become primal. But it was beyond the physical attraction; it was something else, something more. *Why am I so drawn to her? I must've known her, but how?*

The next moment he found himself pushing his way toward her through the crush of bodies. When he came up close to her, he knew he was smiling, "Hello, dance?" and "Yes, thanks." He took her hand leading her out onto the dance floor. As they began to dance, he felt spellbound by her beautiful smile. Seeing her smile struck something deep inside of him, heightening the adrenaline that pulsed through his veins. He couldn't believe his luck, or how it had happened so naturally and quickly, like it was pre-ordained.

Within seconds he stopped thinking and began just enjoying the music. He also enjoyed the way she was rhythmically, lasciviously moving her hips in tune with the beat.

Mercedes loved dancing, enjoying the way she felt as she moved freely in free-form dance. And she knew she could learn a lot about a man by the way he danced.

It was also a great way to seduce a man. She could express her interest by merely dancing in a certain way. Closing her eyes, she smiled, reveling in the thunderous cadence of the music. She felt seductive.

The strobe and neon lights were bathing everything in a ghostlike glow, giving the dance floor a surreal, eerie appearance. The music added to the mystical semblance, and she danced with sensual indulgence, feeling the excitement tightening more than his breathing.

He reached out and pulled her closer for a slower song, letting their bodies meld together. He could feel the heat of her, her body pressed against him, and he responded with a twitching in his crotch betraying his growing excitement. Embarrassed, he tried to pull back, but she began to move her hips sensually against him, showing her consent. With the slow music guiding them, he reciprocated with selfless abandon.

Mercedes welcomed the pressure of him, enjoying his sensual touches against her body. The scent of him stimulated her, and she was losing herself in the moment. With a start, she realized where they were and quickly looked around, concerned that Walt would find her; but her worries vanished when she looked up into this stranger's blue eyes. She—they were lost in the crowd, in a dance with an unknown man who was managing to surprise and excite her, without great effort. *Was there more to him than just a dance?*

They had unconsciously moved to a part of the dance floor unlit by the stream of strobe lights. No one was taking any notice of the two of them.

God, she's beautiful! He didn't know what it was about her that moved him so.

He hadn't been this powerfully attracted to a woman for a long time. He was in heaven in this club with a similar name. Having this gorgeous goddess in front of him, so close to him, within his grasp—he wanted to touch her, to kiss her. Spontaneously, naturally, he slipped a finger gently under her chin, tilted her face upwards, and covered her lips with his.

Mercedes responded willingly to the touch of his lips on hers. Normally she would never act so fast, so soon, but with him, she felt an immediate closeness. It didn't make sense to her. In her mind she was screaming to herself to stop, to not succumb to the heat of her passion—not with a stranger. *But was he? Was he a stranger? It felt so right to be with him.*

Joe found it more and more difficult to stop touching her. *God, I haven't even asked for her name yet!* There was a soft lull in the music and he began to ask, "What is—"

Before he could finish asking, she said, "Mercedes, Mercedes Sinclair." At his look of pleased surprise, she added, "I just realized I hadn't told you my name yet!"

"Are you reading my mind?"

She simply smiled.

"Mercedes. I've always loved that name. And, here you are as beautiful as your name." He couldn't help smiling. "Hello Mercedes. I'm Joe. Joe Tristram."

"Joe Tristan?" She leaned into him letting herself brush lightly against his chest, feeling herself blushing in response to the sensation, as she repeated his name in his ear, making sure she heard it, correctly.

"Tristram."

"A pleasure to meet you, Joe Tristram." He felt a surge of excitement when he heard her say his name. With a sweet smile, she shook his hand playfully.

Indulging her, he returned the handshake, and said, "Nice to meet you, too." Spontaneously, they both laughed at the silliness of the moment.

As the music changed to a faster tempo, Joe took her hand, guiding her away from the dance floor to a nearby table where a couple of other guys were sitting with a small cluster of attractive young women.

"Mercedes. These are some buddies of mine. Mike Bernard—we call him, *Spyder*. Mike Ritter—he's known as *Hannibal*." The touch of his hand on her back was unassumingly protective, as they smiled a greeting to her.

It was easy to remember their names: Mike and Mike. But she was more intrigued with their call signs.

Spyder was an attractive man, and she could tell he knew it. Unlike Grant, he wasn't at all unassuming with his physical attractiveness. Instead, he was blatantly aware of it, and she could sense he had used it to amass the growing legion of women at the table. He oozed charisma. His smile was tantalizingly sweet, allowing him to expertly manage the ladies who sat near him. They were all smiling and wide-eyed from listening to his stories.

One of the more buxom girls, Vanessa, moved closer to him, saying, "Spyder, please tell us some more stories about being a fighter pilot. I just can't believe all three of you are fighter pilots."

Mercedes raised her eyebrow at Joe, questioning. He nodded, confirming what the young woman had just said, but clearly unimpressed by what they did. When she heard the words "fighter pilots," she immediately thought of Lucas and her heart skipped a beat at the coincidence. She glanced back at Joe and smiled wondering if he, too, was at the Gulf War.

Spyder, probably made bold by his drinking, granted Vanessa's wish. "It's the best job in the world. We get to fly these F-16's and travel everywhere while helping our country. It just doesn't get any better than that—except perhaps spending an evening with you."

With Joe sitting beside her, lightly touching her, she listened to Spyder as he spoke. Joe exuded a silent sense of command—his eyes were lit with excitement as the guys spoke of their flight experiences. She was distracted with her observations, oblivious to the conversation, except when she caught the tail end of Spyder's story. She just heard him say, "But nothing beats flying a Viper."

Curious, she asked, "A Viper?"

Spyder explained, "The Viper is what every self-respecting fighter pilot calls an F-16 aircraft."

Vanessa flirted, "So you're a Viper driver. I bet you look sexy in your uniform."

"Why, yes, I do," he said flirting back. "You like men in uniform?"

Vanessa nodded and smiled coyly as she sat closer to him.

Hannibal laughed and mumbled in Spanish, "*What a line! Horny bastard!*"

Mercedes giggled when he said it. He turned to her, "You understood me, didn't you?" Then, they began a conversation in Spanish.

"*How did you learn the language?*"

"*From wooing my beautiful Mexican girlfriend, Adriana, a few years back,*" he answered with an inebriated grin, as if thinking of a memory. "*I really wanted to impress her and it worked.*"

"*You miss her.*"

"*Yeah,*" he said, taking a gulp of his beer, "*but I've got my buddies to entertain me.*" He glanced over to Spyder and called out, "*Oye ese! Chupame la polla!*"

Mercedes matched his loud laughter; Spyder didn't understand that Hannibal had just said, "Suck my dick" to his smiling face.

Vanessa was clearly the most impressed and began to ask endless questions, starting with, "Spyder, how did you get such an interesting nickname?"

Hannibal and Joe snickered when they heard the question. Hannibal blurted out, "'Cus he got pegged with a *Spyder* paintball gun at point blank range during a game!"

Spyder shot him a "fuck you" look, and barked, "Lies! All lies! Don't listen to him!" After he stealthily flashed the middle finger at the two jocks, he leaned over and whispered in Vanessa's ear, telling her the details. She giggled and exclaimed loudly, "It swelled up! Oh poor baby, maybe I can take a look at it later." From Spyder's sly smile, he was looking forward to whatever it was that Vanessa wanted to do.

"How do you get a call sign anyway?"

Hannibal responded, "Embarrass yourself or do something stupid. It could also fit with your last name. Anyway, your buddies give it to you."

Spyder chimed in, "Yeah, but if you piss and moan about it, you'll get a new call sign that you'll like even less!"

"Actually the call sign doesn't have to be an embarrassing event," Joe clarified, "It could be something cool, but usually it's due to a screw-up. The call sign becomes official when the squadron has a naming ceremony."

"Naming ceremony? What happens during this ceremony?"

"Fun and games!" Spyder teased, "Actually, the naming ceremony is usually held on a Friday evening with lots of beer."

"Sounds like a frat party!"

"Close, but the beer is there to help with the decision-making process," he said, trying to sound serious. "The nominee is brought up in front of the squadron. Then he is ceremoniously thrown out of the room until the squadron decides on an appropriate name and the storytelling begins. One by one, each squadron member tells stories about the guy. The stories only have to abide by what we call the 10% truth rule."

"Truth rule?"

"10% truth and 90% story," he explained.

"Lots of bullshitting, I bet."

"You have no idea!" he roared, and then continued, "Anyway, the guy who tells a story gets to nominate a name when he's done. And then, the yelling begins."

"Yelling?"

"Yes, the rest of the squad yells out alternate names. The louder the yelling, the better!" he laughed, taking another gulp of his drink.

"In the front of the room is the Sergeant of Arms. He lists all the prospective names on a dry erase board for final voting. Finally, the nominee is brought back into the room where he sees all the possible names on the board, some good, some bad, and some are hilarious! Anyway, each story is briefly recounted and the process of elimination begins. Each name is voted on and judged, one by one."

"So basically, it's a popularity contest."

"Exactly!" he awarded Vanessa with an intoxicated kiss, becoming distracted.

"Please finish the story," Vanessa coaxed.

"Where was I?"

"The voting," she reminded him.

"Oh yeah, the voting," he repeated, "The voting is based on the volume of enthusiasm from the squadron. The name that attracts the loudest yells becomes the nominee's new name. Finally, to make it official, the Sergeant of Arms then proclaims, 'So it is said, so it is written, you are now known as', well, in my case, 'Spyder'."

"Well, I've got another name for you," she teased, and whispered it to his ear. He laughed and awarded her with another kiss. He looked over to the rest of the group and said, "Sorry, she won't let me tell you."

"You might just get a new name after tonight," Hannibal jibed.

"Oh yeah, fly boy, what?"

"*Romeo!*" Hannibal taunted.

"Fuck you, man!"

"Hey what's that about?" asked Vanessa.

"Don't you dare fuckin' tell her!"

Nevertheless, Hannibal began to share the story. "Earlier, Spyder—I mean *Romeo*—asked this babe to dance. She said her name was Juliet." He burst out laughing, and exclaimed, "Juliet was a man!"

"I couldn't fuckin' tell, and neither could you, asshole!" Spyder exclaimed but with inebriated laughter.

Mercedes laughed along with everyone. She was also amused with the call sign explanation; she wondered silently what Joe's moniker was. At that moment, he leaned to whisper in her ear, "I'm going up to the bar. Do you want a drink?"

"Thanks. Yes."

Before leaving, he nipped her ear gently. It tickled her and she laughed softly. He walked away before she could tell him what she was drinking. She hoped he wouldn't bring her a beer. She never particularly enjoyed the bitter aftertaste.

While he was gone, Spyder started looking at her lustfully. "If I told you that you had a tight body, would you hold it against me?"

Flattered, she replied, "Thank you. No." As she had anticipated, he went right on entertaining her without skipping a beat. He was in the middle of telling her a funny story when he unexpectedly yelled, "*Phantom!*" and looked over her shoulders. She wasn't sure what he meant until she turned around and saw Joe rejoin them. He offered her one of the drinks he was carrying.

"Thanks." Seeing it was one of her favorites, she smiled and wondered how he could have guessed what she wanted to drink.

Joe sat down next to her, feeling her smile melting him. He wanted to talk to her, to find out more about her, but Hannibal engaged him in a military-related discussion, attempting to impress the ladies.

Vanessa continued her questions. "Why are you called Hannibal?"

"I bit someone's finger off."

"Wow! Did you really?"

Laughing, he said, "Well, almost, but it was in self-defense. I had a guy in a headlock while another guy was trying to gouge my eye out and his hand slipped down so I instinctively bit down on his finger. My buddies started calling me Hannibal the Cannibal. Later on, the story began to evolve drastically. One version was that I bit the guy's finger completely off and swallowed it. Anyway, the name stuck."

A couple of the ladies were grimacing at the thought. Hannibal continued, "If you think that's disgusting, Phantom saw a Saudi getting his hand chopped off for stealing. How's that for punishment! What was that town called?"

"Al-Hufûf."

"You really saw it?" asked another buxom woman who was seated next to Spyder.

"Yes, Wanda—it's Wanda, right?" Joe said and took a sip of his drink, then looked at Mercedes who was listening intently as he spoke.

"Phantom, remember during the Gulf War when we flew through the oil fields in Kuwait?" Spyder prompted another story.

"When the Iraqis realized we were kicking their asses out of the country, they set all the oil wells on fire to wipe out Kuwait's bread and butter. The oil fires literally blacked out the sun."

"Ladies, it was something out of Dante's Inferno," Spyder interrupted, "It looked like hell on earth! It just shows how sick Saddam Hussein really was, to mastermind something like that."

"War *is* hell." It was Mercedes who spoke.

"Amen to that!" the pilots said in unison, raising their drinks.

Mercedes kept her attention on Joe, studying the way he carried himself with such quiet confidence. He winked and smiled at her in the midst of the conversation he was having with Hannibal. She noticed he wasn't drinking alcohol and neither was she. They were both completely sober.

Over the next few minutes, they ran through a myriad of small talk. They both tried to cram as much detail about themselves into what seemed to be merely a few short minutes.

"Captain Joseph P. Tristram," she read from his military identification; she didn't notice any other photos in his wallet. "You're three years older than I am and we're both Sagittarians," she observed, "Hey, my middle name also starts with a 'p'."

"What does it stand for?"

"Pilar."

"Pilar," Joe echoed the name, sounding surprised.

Wondering about his subtle reaction, she was delighted when he pronounced it perfectly. Without prompting, she explained, "It's my grandmother's name. And yours?"

"Peyton, for my dad."

"Is your call sign from something embarrassing or was it cool?"

"Neither, it's from a series of practical jokes that I orchestrated against a guy named Will Eamonn, who had pulled a stunt on me. In turn I slowly tortured him. I started out with small pranks that lead to bigger, more elaborate schemes. He never knew that it was me who did it to him, and neither did anyone else. I was completely anonymous," he said, grinning. "I can pull a straight face whenever I need to."

Her right brow rose. He continued, "My identity wasn't discovered until a practical joke I did while we were at Incirlik Air Base in Turkey. When we were flying A-10's, I poked a nail through the side of a shaving cream can and tossed it through his window. The shaving cream sprayed all over the room."

"That must've been a mess!"

"Slightly, but that wasn't all. When the screaming was really good, I discharged a chemical fire extinguisher through the vent in his door." He laughed at the memory, and then said, "Anyway, it was my final prank and I've been know as 'Phantom' ever since. And no one ever tried to pull a stunt on me again. As you can see, paybacks are hell in a fighter squadron."

"My brother Lucas was in the Gulf War too. He's known as *Raiden*, for the God of Vengeance," she said, a grin escaped at a memory. "Like you, he takes his practical jokes very seriously."

"He's in the Air Force?"

"No, he's a Navy Seal."

"Impressive."

"He does it mostly for the adrenaline," she shared. "As a matter of fact, my brother asked me to extend his heartfelt thanks to every fighter pilot that I might bump into. And since you're a fighter pilot, I must thank you." She then leaned over, and gave him a soft yet deep kiss. She said sweetly, "And that was a thank you from me."

"Please, thank me again," he said smiling.

Out of the corner of her eye, Mercedes saw Walt in a drunken stupor searching for her on the dance floor. A wave of discomfort and disgust took hold of her and she felt a great need to leave.

"Joe, I must go." She stood up and he stood up with her, taking her hand and holding her back. "No! Not yet Mercedes. Don't go. Not just yet."

Walt was coming closer to them, and she didn't want him to cause another unwanted scene. Worse yet, she knew she would let Walt whisk her away to prevent a senseless fight.

She could handle Walt if she could avoid an awkward situation and getting Joe involved in her problem. She apologized, "I'm sorry, Joe—but I must leave now."

Taking out a business card, she handed it to him. Smiling a little sadly over what she knew she had to do, she added, "If you are ever in Philadelphia—"

She wanted to say more, but Walt was too close for comfort. So she quickly turned and briskly walked away, carefully dodging her drunken predator. She was relieved to see Walt heading into the VIP lounge with another woman in tow. She hastily got her things from the coatroom and headed for the exit, wanting to return safely to her hotel.

Joe was in total disbelief. He watched her leave, not knowing exactly what to do next. What he did know was that he wasn't going to let her disappear from his life like this—no way!

As she turned and started to walk away again, he hurriedly followed her, calling out her name, but the music was too loud for him to even hear himself. He continued to press on through the crowd and in his mind, he called out to her, *Please stop! Turn around, Mercedes—right now!* And at that very moment, she uncannily did.

Reaching her, he said tenderly, "Please, Mercedes. Let me take you back to your hotel. I promise I'll be a complete gentleman. I just want to make sure you get back safely. Please trust me."

She surprised herself when she said, "I gladly accept your charming offer."

Their bodies folded together. She had heard people talking about melting into someone's arms, but until that second she had never known what they had meant. *Why is this so different? So good?*

They walked back to the table, and he reminded his friends that he was the designated driver. Although Spyder and Hannibal protested about leaving the club, especially the company of the ladies they had amassed for conquest, they agreed to leave.

* * *

When they arrived at the Aladdin, he hurried to open the passenger door for her and she slid gracefully from her seat into his arms. After a much too brief kiss, he asked his friends to wait in the car while he saw her safely to her room.

"I hope Spyder and Hannibal didn't mind leaving."

"They'll get over it." He added, "I'll bet you they'll be out like a light when I get back."

"And what are the stakes?"

"Name it."

"Hmmm," she said with a flicker of mischief in her smile.

At her door, she searched for her key card, thinking, *This could be the last time*

I see him. She wondered what would happen next. She turned, and uttered coyly, "Thank you."

He lowered his head, and kissed her.

Softly, gently, she allowed him to kiss her once, twice, before returning his advance. Before they knew it, they were inside her room responding to a hunger they couldn't contain. She fell backwards on the bed, and then he knelt before her. They kissed passionately. Their heat intensified, and they groped at each other, locked in the kisses they were sharing.

He slowly began to pull her white shirt up, gently kissing her stomach, and she wanted desperately to go further with him. "Mercedes," he whispered.

Fighting her needs, she pushed him back a little, choosing to wait, not rush, knowing even without touching him how perfect he would feel. Reluctantly, she had pulled herself up and tucked her shirt back in.

He sighed deeply at her actions, releasing his pent-up tension, unconsciously showing her how much he needed to be with her. She wasn't sure what to say. Something about the way he knelt before her at the bed sent a powerful sense of *déjà vu* coursing through her. She stared at him bewildered.

"How about dinner and a show at Excalibur tomorrow evening?" She asked awkwardly. It was the first thing that entered her mind.

"Name the time." He didn't hesitate in his response. Still kneeling before her, they smiled at each other. He looked so handsome in his angst and so very familiar.

"Until tomorrow at 7:00 p.m." She gave him one last gentle kiss.

Spontaneously his mouth opened a bit more, his tongue caressing her lips, as their mouths molded together. They once again were kissing deeply, locked in a tight embrace, their hands roaming and bringing mutual pleasure with each shared caress.

Within seconds, they were breathless.

Almost collapsing in each other's arms, a capricious laughter took hold of them, as they said in unison like a couple of teenagers, "This is agony!"

With great restraint, he took the initiative. "If I don't leave now, I won't be able to leave!"

He rose and picked her up in his strong arms. She circled his neck with her arms, letting her fingers test the texture of his short-cropped hair as they kissed and held each other, trying to find the strength to last through the night. He set her down, sighed deeply, quickly turned, and walked out the door, letting out another deep sigh as he looked back one more time at her beautiful smile.

She closed the door, touching her lips, feeling his lingering kisses. The phone began to ring, and while she debated about answering, it went into voice mail.

Her body was still warm from his torrid kisses.

Once again, the phone rang and she decided not to answer it. She needed to compose herself.

The phone rang once more and she ignored it, wanting to savor what she had just experienced.

* * *

Joe kept thinking of her incredible smile, the taste of her lips, and the warmth of her in his arms. Seconds ago, he had this wonderful creature in his arms and the rush was driving him insane!

For a few seconds he stood outside her door, hoping she might open it like a scene in a movie and pull him back inside. He knew she was so close to having him stay. He wondered if he should have tried harder. *No, she's worth waiting for.* He would continue being a gentleman.

He had been around the world and had encountered this situation before, but something was quite different this time. She wasn't a one-time conquest. He felt like he knew her and that they would be together.

As he walked away, reality kicked in when he remembered his two friends waiting outside the hotel in the car. He quickly ran through the hotel hallway, feeling as excited as a child and already thinking about tomorrow.

Her smile. Her smile made him feel that way.

Standing beside the car outside, he laughed at seeing Spyder and Hannibal passed out drunk in the backseat, propped up against each other. *She should've taken the bet.*

It was already 0245. Their morning brief was in less than six hours. The thought of the morning's sortie gave him another adrenaline rush. But, it was because of her that his adrenaline surged to his loins.

Getting into the car, he looked in the rear view mirror. The sight of the two sleeping jocks caused him to shake his head and laugh softly.

He hated thinking of the hangovers they were going to face. He was glad he hadn't been drinking. Regulations prohibited drinking before flying, and being the designated driver also had helped him to stay sober. And it was Lent.

She hadn't been drinking, either. Was it just another coincidence? How had he known when he ordered her drink what she wanted? *Tonic and lime.* How had he known that?

Driving in silence, except for the gentle snores coming from the back seat, he headed toward the hotel where his squadron was staying. In his mind he kept revisiting the events of the evening.

If he had not looked when he had, he might have missed her completely. She was so comfortable to be around. They had an almost instant rapport, and it had been clear they could have talked all night. They could have easily been mistaken for old friends, but friends didn't feel as good as she did in his arms.

Originally, Spyder, Hannibal and he weren't even going to be at that club. Hannibal had suggested going to a tropical themed club elsewhere down the strip featuring babes in bikinis, serving the tropical drinks. *Tropical. The way she moved. The way she looked.*

He was particular about getting involved with anyone. Sure, he was drawn initially to physical beauty as all men were. He liked a woman with an athletic body, sexy, and well-endowed with beautiful hair. It was the stereotypical male fantasy—a woman complete, of course, with a gorgeous face and matching killer smile.

He was equally drawn to inner beauty, tenderness, a huge heart, talent, and intelligence. More importantly, he was searching for an ambitious, passionately driven woman who would be a worthy match for him. He was searching for the other half of his puzzle. So far, he hadn't encountered a woman who embodied all or at least a majority of those qualities.

What is she really like behind those features that melted him? He just couldn't get the vision of her out of his brain.

Pulling up at their squadron hotel, he spent a few comical minutes trying to get the two sleeping beauties to wake up and get out of the car.

He laughed, seeing their waking reactions to their cozy, awkward positions in the backseat. He could hardly wait to tell Mercedes about it tomorrow, to make her laugh and to see her smile again.

* * *

An hour or so later, Mercedes quickly picked up the phone when it rang again. She knew who was calling at such a late hour.

"Did I wake you?"

"No, Grant, I'm still awake. I'm sorry, I should've called you, but you know how it is," she said softly, unconsciously touching her tongue to her tingling lips. "What time is it in Philly?"

"It's almost 5:30 a.m. here. I'm planning on catching an hour of shuteye before my rounds. After that, it looks like I'll be in surgery most of the time until my shift ends Wednesday morning."

In the midst of forming a sentence, his pager went off, and she heard it and him as he muttered, "Damn!"

He had to call in right away. Hurriedly, he said, "I've got to answer this page. Leave me a message when you can, all right?"

"Yes, yes, of course I will," she quickly replied. He didn't want to hang up, but he was needed urgently. "I've missed you, my angel."

"Ditto." Ditto was her predictable answer whenever he professed something to her.

"Good night, Grant. I promise I'll talk to you soon."

Chapter 8

March 21st, Red Flag

Hannibal drove Joe and Spyder to Nellis Air Force Base the next morning. At the front entrance, the prominent words, "The Home of the Fighter Pilot", were displayed in bold letters on the large, prominent brick façade situated conspicuously at the entrance. They passed through the checkpoint and parked at their designated area.

Inside, they quickly started getting ready for the day's sortie. As Joe pulled his flight suit on, he wished he was part of the standard Air Force coffee crowd; but he hated the taste of coffee, so this morning he found himself searching for a vending machine and a much needed Mountain Dew caffeine jolt to start him on his day.

He finally found one near the hangars. A chief master sergeant was already at the machine waiting for his soda to drop through.

Though Joe only had five hours of sleep, he felt excited thinking of this morning's maneuvers. He couldn't keep from smiling with thoughts of Mercedes, either. He felt exceptionally good, so as he got nearer, he cheerfully greeted, "Good morning, Chief!"

The chief retrieved his Coke, surprised to see anyone in the area so early. When the chief looked up, he quickly noted the captain's rank. "Good mornin', Captain. I'll be out of your way in just a sec."

"Not a problem. Take your time." The chief looked about his age but since he had an E-9 rank, he was definitely older than he seemed.

Joe recognized he was of Italian-American descent, as opposed to his own French and Irish roots. The chief was solid, stocky, with dark brown hair, olive skin, and light brown eyes. He could tell from his uniform that he was part of the aircraft maintenance crew.

"Hi, I'm Captain Joe Tristram. Call me Phantom. And you are?" Joe introduced himself because he wanted to know the people on the ground crews whom he depended on to get him off the ground. He also liked getting to know other people, especially at a new facility. The nametag on the breast of the chief's uniform was out of his view.

"Sir. Chief Master Sergeant Frank Lloyd Petrone." He maneuvered the Coke in his hand, quickly introducing himself formally with a salute. "Good to meet ya, Phantom. Everyone calls me, *Uncle Lloyd*."

Joe acknowledged his greeting, extended his hand in a friendly handshake, saying with a smile, "Hello, Uncle Lloyd."

After noticing the patch on the right shoulder of the flight suit of the friendly, young fighter pilot, Uncle Lloyd said, "Phantom. Here with the 555th Fighter Combat Training Squadron?"

"Yes, the Triple Nickel. I'm here for the Red Flag exercises. Hey, maybe we'll see each other on the flight line, or squadron ops."

Uncle Lloyd nodded. Phantom was a new face on the line. "First time here in Nellis?"

"As a matter of fact, it's my first time TDY—I mean temporary duty— here," Joe replied.

"It's my second." He wondered which squadron the pilot was flying with. "Are you flying with the Red or Blue forces?"

"Today, I'm part of Blue Air."

Uncle Lloyd grinned knowing how exciting it was to participate in the large force exercise, especially for a first time player. "Then we'll definitely see each other. I'm assigned to work with Blue Air, too. Like I said, it's my second time here. I was here as a young staff sergeant, working with the 422nd when Red Flag maneuvers were just implemented, I think about five years into it. I still remember how excited I was just being part of it, even though I was on the ground with the aircraft maintenance crew." He opened his soda can while Joe retrieved his drink from the vending machine.

After a gulp, Uncle Lloyd commented, "*Youse* must be excited to fly today."

Joe couldn't place the accent. "Youse? Hey, Uncle Lloyd, where are you from?"

With pride, he said grinning, "Born and raised in Philadelphia. South Philly to be exact. Philly cheese steaks and the Liberty Bell! Watching the Phillies with a cold beer and munchin' on soft Philly pretzels. Ever been?"

Hearing the chief say Philadelphia, Joe's thoughts immediately turned to Mercedes, and thought how interesting it was to meet someone else from that area.

He shook his head, "Never really had the pleasure, but I've been at the Philly airport, and I drove through the city. I've never had the opportunity to act like a tourist."

Thinking of Mercedes' smile, he said grinning, "I'm planning on taking a trip, once I get a chance. I'd like to visit some friends, check out the scenery, and maybe even watch a Phillies game!"

The chief nodded, "Where are youse from?"

"Well, originally Tallahassee, Florida. Fighting Seminole Country and the Mexican Gulf."

"Hey—my son, Pete, is a freshman at Florida State! Small world, huh?" He paused, and said, "I sure miss him. He's living with my ex-wife. Just couldn't hack the military life. You know how it is."

Joe nodded, "All too well."

As they sipped on their drinks, they continued their casual conversation, talking about themselves and past assignments. They got along well despite the differences in their age, rank, and background. It was unfortunate that they couldn't be in the same crowd; they had the same *esprit de corps* and pride in serving their country. But at the end of the day, Joe would head to the Officers Club, while Uncle Lloyd would go to the NCO Club.

"I've got to bolt, Phantom. It was good chattin' with youse. I'll see ya around, aight? Have a good flight today and check six!" Tossing his soda can into the trashcan, he scored a few imaginary points.

"Thanks, Uncle Lloyd." He checked the time; he needed to get to the morning brief. He hoped he was going to have a chance to shoot the shit with him again.

He finished his own drink, took a shot at the trashcan, and scored his two points as well. They laughed and walked down the corridor together.

Almost immediately Joe looked around, a little puzzled. "Somehow I've gotten turned around this morning. Which way do I go to get to the Red Flag main briefing room?"

"You're in luck. It's on my way to the tool bin."

* * *

Joe entered the briefing room and took his seat with the rest of the squadron, his excitement at an all-time high.

Ninety-five young fighter jocks of all ages, eager to do battle out over the desert, were sitting at attention: trim, fit and confident. Up front a tough-looking, equally confident leader, known as *Nitro* and wearing the rank of a lieutenant colonel, was standing there in a green flight suit. He was a tall, imposing man with a deep commanding voice, and he demanded rapt attention.

"Gentlemen, I don't care what you heard about Red Flag outside this room. I am here to educate you about the most realistic, combat-training exercise in the history of military war games. The objective is simple," he paused and scanned the determined expressions of his audience, pleased by what he saw.

Joe noticed the commander's voice increase in force, keeping everyone's attention and fueling his own adrenaline. He was here solely to participate in Red Flag.

Grinning, Nitro continued in an austere voice, "The objective, gentlemen," he paused, "the objective is to maximize combat readiness, capability and survivability of participating units. What that means to you is we want to turn you into mean fighting machines.

"How do we accomplish this? Well, I'm going to tell you. We accomplish this by providing realistic training in a combined air, ground and electronic threat environment.

"And another thing, gentlemen, this affords us a free exchange of ideas between players!" He cleared his throat and then began compellingly, "The USAF Red Flag Center provides Air Force graduate-level training on the following weapon systems: A-10, B-1, B-52, EC-130, F-15, F-15E, F-16, F-117, HH-60 and RC-135 platforms."

He smirked, making Joe feel like he was looking right at him, "Did you get all that?"

Joe nodded along with everyone. He listened to every word that Nitro had to say. It gave him a sense of pride to be part of it. Though it was serious, he was going to thoroughly enjoy it.

"That's it, gentlemen. Do any of you have any questions at this time?"

There weren't any questions, there never were. His severe demeanor kept everyone in check and they were eager to fly. They were ready to fill the desert sky with war.

Joe was fully aware that, as an inexperienced wingman in the F-16, everything he did today would be recorded and debriefed in a giant room with all the participants watching.

Today's flight was going to be exciting. He would be number four of about eight F-16's. They would fly out in the desert as part of a seventy-five aircraft package, which would include every type of jet in the Air Force inventory.

As part of the Blue Air Forces, they would strike targets as well as escort other bombers. They would use various tactics to attack Nellis' range targets: mock airfields, vehicle convoys, tanks, parked aircraft, bunkered defensive positions and missile sites. The targets would be defended by a variety of simulated ground and air threats, giving them the most realistic combat training possible.

Somewhere in the desert, they would surely be ambushed by scores of other Air Force assets, who would be playing the part of Red Air with a mission of attacking Blue Air and preventing their penetration of the target area.

Red Air threats would include electronically simulated surface-to-air missiles and antiaircraft artillery, communications jamming forces, and an opposing enemy air force of Red Flag Adversary Tactics Division pilots. Those pilots would be flying the F-16C and were specially trained to replicate the tactics and techniques of potential adversaries.

Even though it was just a training sortie, everyone prepared, briefed, and flew it just like it was a mass package going out into the middle of Iraq.

The rest of the day literally flew right by and the flight went well. He and his flight lead were even able to bag a simulated kill against one of the Red F-16's before continuing on to drop bombs on their assigned target.

Although the day had been tough, his mind kept wandering to other places, to her. He kept seeing Mercedes' smile and thinking, *Why do I feel like I have already known Mercedes for years?*

All day long he had kept telling himself, *Compartmentalize*. That was how flight surgeons described how Air Force fighter pilots could handle many tasks at the same time.

Anything that wasn't relevant to the next few seconds of flying at five hundred knots, five hundred feet off the desert floor had to be crushed and set aside for another time.

After the debrief, he decided to skip the typical gathering at the Officers Club, recounting the day's events, shooting at their watch with the opposite hand, signifying what a great job they had done controlling the skies. It was one of his favorite times, but today he had other plans for the evening and he couldn't get to her fast enough.

Chapter 9

March 21st, Serendipity

When Mercedes woke that morning, the first thing on her agenda was a call to Sydney. She frowned when the answering machine picked up.

"Hi Syd, it's Merc—your vagabond friend. I'm sorry I missed you. I'm in Vegas. I'm staying at the Aladdin Hotel and Casino. Just ask the hotel operator for me. Call me as soon as you get this. I hope we won't get stuck in a perpetual phone-tag. *Ciao!*"

On her list, she noted—*left message, call later PM.*

After a quick shower, she put on her power suit—red, of course.

At the conference room, she sat with her fellow presenters at a long table. A silver-haired gentleman began making the formal introductions of the panel. She was glad to be the first presenter.

"Thank you," she said, her confident voice carrying to every corner of the room. With her remote control at hand, she began to present her paper. Her presentation was well organized and she used her visuals to guide the audience through her key points systematically and confidently.

After what seemed to be just a few moments, she was taking questions from the audience. The question-and-answer portion of a presentation was always her favorite part. She loved the opportunity to teach and share her knowledge with her colleagues. She also welcomed constructive feedback that would allow her to delve further into her research.

"Looks like I have only enough time to answer one last question," she said, noting the signal from the host. She nodded at a young dark-haired engineer on the second row who had his hand up first.

"Ms. Sinclair, do you foresee the usability of these Computational Fluid Dynamics models relative to other applications?"

"Aside from air flow, heat dissipation and dispersion of air pollutants, I predict at least seven other applications will benefit from CFD modeling," she said, smiling.

After she elaborated on her predictions, she thanked the audience and got in the waiting limousine.

* * *

Seven authority figures from the Nevada Utility greeted her, including, Emery Homestead, CEO; Evan Sheridan, President; and Omar Yusuf, VP of Acquisitions, all of whom she had met in Anaheim. They were all well dressed in a palette of gray and indigo hues except for the ladies in their company.

Emery was a tall, soft-spoken (yet imposing), boyish and gentlemanly African-American in his fifties. He formally introduced the dignified Spaniard in his late sixties, standing next to him. "Mercedes, I'd like you to meet Nevada Utility's current owner, Señor José Enrique."

"A pleasure to meet you, Mercedes," said Señor Enrique, welcoming her warmly with his thickly accented voice.

"Hello, Señor Enrique. Nice to meet you."

"And these are our corporate counsels, Everett Patterson, Jude Pandorin and Laila Fursey." Finally, Emery turned to a brunette with a short blunt haircut, dressed in purplish-blue suit. "And this is our VP of Engineering, Edna Chadwick."

After the formal introductions, she was whisked away immediately to a nearby, quaint restaurant with a blues motif where the formalities melted to friendly discussions.

At the restaurant she managed to put everyone at ease with light humor and her efforts to be friendly. She despised defensive posturing.

Emery was the first to follow Mercedes' lead, entertaining them with his own brand of corny, delightful humor.

"Here's a joke I just heard. 'To the optimist, the glass is half full. To the pessimist, the glass is half empty. To the engineer, the glass is twice as big as it needs to be!'"

"That's a good one!" Joining in the laughter was Everett, a boisterous, balding, fatherly gentleman in his late forties; his face flushed in a lighter crimson than his tie. "Jude's got a good joke too," he added, turning to him smiling. "Come on, *Mr. Pandorin*, tell the joke."

"You tell the joke," Jude protested, sounding incredulous with his smiling light blue eyes.

"No, no, go ahead—you've got better delivery, Jude. I'll just butcher the joke if I try."

Jude was a little younger than Everett. He was physically fit with well-formed biceps bulging under his grey suit. He was short and he looked youthful, but his deep, croaky, commanding tone gave him an intimidating presence even as he shared quips and inside jokes with Everett.

"Okay, you've twisted my arm." Before he started telling the joke, he took off his jacket and rolled up his sleeves. Finally, he began to tell a joke about three engineering students who were gathered together discussing the possible designers of the human body.

"One said, 'It was a mechanical engineer. Just look at all the joints.' Another said, 'No, it was an electrical engineer. The nervous system has many thousands of electrical connections.' The last said, 'Actually, it was a civil engineer. Who else would run a toxic waste pipeline through a recreational area?'" The group roared at the punch line.

Mercedes noticed a tattoo peeking from Jude's rolled sleeves. She remarked, "I designed a tattoo once. It was of a dragon."

"Mine is a Harley tattoo."

"You've got a hog?"

"Oh, yes one," he grinned.

"Been to Daytona for bike week?"

"Haven't missed one in years!" he shared, and spoke fondly about his memorable Daytona bike week last summer.

The women were sitting near each other and their conversations shifted from friendly humor to career experiences in a male-dominated profession. The three of them took an instant liking to each other.

Laila was a lovely blonde from Kentucky in her mid-thirties with a fiery disposition that rivaled Mercedes. She was also wearing a red tailored suit, except with pants. She spoke loudly and with authority, and was passionate about workplace conduct.

"Ever thought about being a lawyer, Mercedes?" Laila asked curiously, in a soft drawl.

Mercedes shook her head, "Funny you should ask me that. My friends are mostly lawyers and are constantly trying to recruit me. But after hearing their war stories, I opted to pass on the idea."

"Best place to affect change," said Edna, an attractive Brit, who appeared to be in her mid-fifties. Of all of them, she was the diplomat who listened intently and observed her surroundings. She used words carefully, speaking with zeal when the topic was of interest to her.

Opposite them was the older generation, schooled in traditional engineering long before the dawn of sophisticated modern technological gadgets, like calculators, laptop computers, portable cell phones and palm pilots.

Omar was a tall, lean man in his sixties with silver hair and a soft voice. He had eyes the color of the earth. "Mercedes, are you enjoying your stay in Vegas?"

She thought of Joe when she answered, "Yes, I am. It's a city full of surprises—it's magical."

"Illusion, Mercedes. It's all just an illusion," Omar said, smiling.

Evan, who sat adjacent to Omar and looked as if he was about the same age as Omar, joined the conversation. He said, "There's an old Jewish saying that says, 'A half-truth is a whole lie.' That's what Vegas is famous for, its half-truths and illusions."

Mercedes smiled and said, "I heard of another Jewish proverb, 'What you don't see with your eyes, don't invent with your mouth.' I suspect it talks about lies but touches on faith."

"Ah, but you must never put your faith in illusions."

Mercedes noticed that his well-trimmed beard and full head of dark brown hair peppered with gray made him very charming and appealing, as did his dazzling white smile. Part of his charisma was due to his high intellect.

The oldest among them was the patriarch, Señor Enrique, who had an irresistible charisma. His silver hair glistened with pomade in a 1950s style. The volume of his accented voice escalated to a loud crescendo and his fawn eyes lit up with pride when he spoke of his humble beginnings as a Spanish immigrant and openly shared some details of his life.

"There is no denying that this is the land of opportunity. When I arrived in this country, I didn't even own a car. And now," he said, smiling at Mercedes, "now I drive a Mercedes. Two of them!"

Mercedes giggled and shared, "You remind me of my father, except he would say, 'I have *three* Mercedes: my wife, my daughter and my car.'"

"I like the way your father thinks," he said.

As dessert was being served, Laila asked Emery to explain the strange circumstances that had initiated the entire buy-out plan.

"Well, the story goes back to our arrival the day before the convention started. After checking into the hotel, I decided to join a couple of other facilitators for a fun-filled day at good old Disneyland.

"Well, mind you—I was the oldest in the group. I love roller coasters—yes, at my age I still love them, even though they could give me a coronary. But I kid you not, I really do love roller coasters. A coronary on a roller coaster might be a wonderful way to go!

"The first stop was Space Mountain. I was seated next to Mercedes and she was hysterical, screaming in the dark. I couldn't help but laugh because I was screaming even louder than she was!" He started chuckling. "At the time I had no idea that she was an attendee at the convention among other things. I thought she was just another tourist. So, I thought nothing of it until my group headed to another roller coaster called—well, the name escapes me."

"Big Thunder Mountain Railroad," Omar quickly interjected.

Nodding at Omar, he said, "I'm getting senile in my old age!" He laughed along with everyone else. "It was Big Thunder Mountain Railroad. And when I got on the ride, who was sitting next to me?"

"Mercedes!"

"Thanks, Evan," he smiled with a nod. "I still thought nothing of it until I stood in line for the water plume ride. And you would never guess who I randomly sat next to in the ride."

"Mercedes!" exclaimed both Omar and Evan in unison.

"Imagine that. Three times in a row! Well, we promptly introduced ourselves as we reached the plateau of the ride, and since we were sitting in the front, we were thoroughly soaked at the bottom!" His arms extended out as he said it.

"After the ride was over, we began to talk about the experience and I dropped a couple of buzz words relating to the design of the ride and its water delivery system. She told me, much to my surprise, that she had toured the facilities to study the water systems for the park. I asked her if it was for school. I must admit I thought she was a college freshman, maybe a senior." He looked at her direction, and said, "My apologies, Mercedes."

She smiled, and quickly replied, "I'm not going to be offended by that, Mr. Homestead!"

"Please, Mercedes—I'm feeling old again. Please call me Emery," he said, smiling at her. "Okay, where was I? Ah yes, when she told me she was helping with a feasibility study with the Disney Imagineers. Imagine my surprise! I mentioned I was attending the convention. Again, she surprised me when she told me she was not only attending it, but she was also a presenter. How ironic! I was hosting the session. I knew her professional background and read her paper. I even planned on discussing a few things I found interesting when I finally did meet the face belonging to the name, which was simply listed as *M. Sinclair* on the presenters' list and on her paper. Well, as you can imagine, I was astonished! And the rest, ladies and gentleman, is as they say—history."

"A truly amazing coincidence!" Laila remarked.

"I believe in coincidences," Omar added.

"Well, after hearing that story, I'm inclined to believe in it," Laila shared.

"Having lived through it, I am a believer," Emery said.

"It was serendipity!" Señor Enrique exclaimed, "A fated moment."

"You believe in fate, Señor Enrique?" Mercedes asked. Side conversations began with her question.

Proudly, Señor Enrique confided, "Call me a romantic, but I believe in fate. It was fate that led me to meet my beautiful wife Maria." The mere mention of his wife's name caused his cheeks to flush a deep red. "We've been married for forty-eight years!"

Mercedes matched his wide smile, noticing his demeanor shifted to that of a young man in love.

Their business meeting started promptly at 2:00 p.m. in a large corporate meeting room. Unlike other rooms in which she had conducted meetings, the area had an ambiance of opulent elegance. The colors had been carefully chosen: hunter green, deep burgundy, cobalt blue and gold. The wall-coverings, Berber floor carpets, period pine and mahogany furniture, and decorative pieces were all elegant, and the room was lit by neoclassical sconces on the walls and recessed lighting in the shaped ceiling, instead of the usual fluorescent bulbs humming overhead. Framed paintings of past company leaders adorned the walls, and large plants and floral arrangements on the tables along the side gave the room a welcoming warm feeling. Overall, it had a distinctively old Spanish flavor with a classic matador painting displayed prominently at the back of the room.

On the conference table, thick contracts and filled coffee mugs were waiting for them. She sat on one end of the table while the charming Señor Enrique sat on the other. She smiled pleasantly at everyone and realized she was the youngest in the coterie, which prompted her to quickly shift to her business mode.

Laila asked the first question. "What about the future cash infusions, Mercedes?"

"The proposed management buyout calls for Wallace Industries to make cash infusions into Nevada Utility of $49.5 million for an approximately 55% fully diluted ownership."

The negotiations continued and hours later, an initial agreement was reached.

Edna asked for a clarification. "What percentage is Wallace Industries going to retain at the signing of the term sheet?"

"We expect to retain a 63% fully diluted interest in the new company at the signing of the term sheet. Otherwise, there's significant risk that our transaction may not close." Noting the time, she asked, "Are there any other questions on the table at this time?" She was thankful that there were none.

After the negotiations, but before returning to the hotel, she was in for a treat. There was enough time for her to see the Hoover Dam. In the limousine she asked the driver to pull over at what looked like a good vantage point where she could view the historic engineering marvel.

When a jet flew overhead, she looked up and followed the white trail it left in the sky until the aircraft disappeared. Joe. She smiled with thoughts of the date they would be going on, of how she might feel, and of what he would really be like. How would they act toward each other?

She stood there for a long time, enjoying the unusually warm breeze which unraveled her classically styled business coiffure.

Inside she was filled with a peaceful calm. Simply enjoying the amber colors of the setting sun, she thought of Joe. Flashes of her restless night crept into her thoughts and something about her dreams made her shudder. In her mind one thought raced through: *He could be the one.*

Chapter 10

March 21st, Tournament of Kings

By 7:00 p.m. she was ready for their date. She was keeping her mind preoccupied by tapping away on her keyboard, making notes about the day's meeting and feedback on her presentation.

Then, the soft knock came on the door. A frisson of excitement flowed through her, but she carefully masked it.

Breathing deeply, she rose from her chair. Her heart was beating so hard it nearly stopped her breathing. Her hand trembled nervously as she gingerly opened the door.

As the door opened, Joe was standing there quietly, and for a moment he didn't look up at her, wanting to savor the first sight of her.

Mercedes was breathtaking standing there before him in a classic black designer mini-dress. Her hair was a lustrous, flowing mane, and the scent of her perfume was luscious and sweet.

He took in every detail of her delicate frame, unable to hold his smile of joy and pleasure inside. A night in her arms would be heaven.

She gazed at him, smiling, wanting to know him in every way, equally overwhelmed by her desires.

On their way downstairs, he almost never took his eyes from her face. Sometimes it made her feel self-conscious, but at the same time, she was drawn to his eyes. It was as if they were the only two people in the world. When he laughed, she involuntarily put her hand on her heart, trying to slow its rapid pounding. Constant pulsing, tingling sensations filled her. In the car he reached over and took her hand, held it to his lips, softly kissed it and rubbed her palm with his thumb.

She felt an overwhelming desire to lie naked, crushed against his strong body. *Is he feeling the same sensations?*

On their way to Excalibur, they eagerly exchanged stories of their days. It felt like they had done this—engaged in conversations about their jobs and their likes and dislikes for many years.

He guessed her favorite color was red. She surprised him, knowing his favorite color was blue. Both were primary colors, colors she regarded as very significant in her life.

"Did you know that Tristram was one of the Knights of the Round Table?"

"Yes, he was killed by his own uncle. A real sad story for a great knight."

"But even worse for King Arthur."

"Why do you say that?"

"Guinevere betrays him for his best friend, Lancelot."

"It just wasn't meant to be," he said, sounding a little pensive and then seamlessly shifting to an upbeat tone, "So what does an engineer as beautiful as you do in her spare time?"

"Boss men around more," she laughed. "Seriously, I paint and write poetry in my spare time. I also read a lot."

"A left and right brain thinker. Fantastic! What can't you do?"

"Stop time," she blushed when she said it.

"I've been working on that one too." He gave her hand a gentle squeeze. "Tell me about your paintings, your poetry."

"I paint about my thoughts and how I feel. Lately, I've been painting self-portraits. I'm also self-taught. And the poems I write are about my paintings."

"I'd love to see your paintings and read your poetry."

"Perhaps one day you will."

He mentioned a recent trip to New Orleans and her eyes lit up. It was the hometown of one of her favorite female writers, and since she hadn't been there, she was eager for him talk about it. He asked her to think of him when she visited the *Big Easy* and tasted her first *Béarnaise*. It was a promise she would keep four years later.

He said that he loved beautiful things, classic cars, and that there was one particular Porsche he had wanted since he was nineteen. He talked about the Air Force, his experiences during the Gulf War, the perils of flying, and how it felt to experience the high G-forces that could stun a pilot, causing him to plummet to the earth. The plane would be, in his words, "a lawn dart" that would ultimately crash to the ground. He witnessed it several times in his career. He was silent for a moment.

"What it is like to be alone in the clouds with nothing but solitude?"

He tried to articulate that feeling, but she could tell he felt he couldn't quite make it clear enough.

"It must be one of the places that Jules Renard spoke about when he said, 'there are places and moments in which one is so completely alone that one sees the world entire.'"

"You have a gift for words, Mercedes."

"Thank you. You have a way of bringing it out of me," she confessed.

"What else do I bring out of you?" he asked purposefully.

She blushed again, and changed the subject.

"Lucas was in northern Baghdad in Iraq, near a military complex. His position was compromised somehow and he told me an Air Force package of twenty aircraft flooded the sky. The Iraqis scrambled when they saw them."

"Really, that's interesting because on my first combat mission, I was part of a twenty aircraft package, dropping CBU against AAA sites north of Baghdad. I remember the AAA muzzle flashes looked like fireworks on the fourth of July. My RAW gear was screaming at me as I recovered the jet after bomb release. I remember seeing the white bursts above and behind me. It was amazing to watch the sub-munitions detonate on their targets all over the complex."

"I know that a CBU is a cluster bomb but I'm not familiar with the triple A or muzzle flashes. And what's a RAW gear?"

"AAA's are anti-aircraft artillery. They're the big guns that shoot planes down. The muzzle flashes are the lights you see when they shoot. RAW gear is not an acronym but it means radar awareness."

"Radar awareness?"

"Basically it's the device that lets us know that bad guy radars are looking at us."

"You are amazing. I'm honestly awestruck!"

"Thank you. You're just as amazing, you know."

A block or two from the Excalibur, she began a play of words on his name and rank, amusing him. "Hmmm.... Captain Joe. Captain Joe Cool." She became pensive and looked at him for a moment.

Finally, she said, "Joe, my Captain. JC. Yes, that's it. That'll be my personal call sign for you, *JC*."

"I like that. I like the sound of it on your lips." The call sign would be uniquely hers, and whenever she called him JC, it would acknowledge and celebrate the unforgettable times they would be having together there in Las Vegas.

He wanted to cherish every moment with her, thinking, *Now is what is important. Not the past, nor the future—but now!*

At Excalibur they walked leisurely through the lavish opulence of the casino with their hands entwined in a lover's knot. They were seated in the arena for the Tournament of Kings show.

The show was filled with pomp and circumstance that realistically presented jousting knights in chivalrous duels for the favor of the beautiful lady.

The setting seemed perfectly natural to both of them, and once again they were oblivious to everything but each other.

He was a great conversationalist, witty and charming. She often found herself drifting on the current of his deep, sensual voice, allowing his voice to embrace and caress her, sweeping her into a reverie. The cadence of his voice held her spellbound. It calmed her and in the end, exhilarated her.

And it distracted her. When he asked her a pertinent question or for her opinion, she was at a loss for an answer, having been oblivious to the words. She would smile and candidly tell him that she hadn't heard what he asked.

Luckily, he would say he understood, since the crowd had begun cheering for their designated knights, each of whom was dressed in bright colors. The arena was divided according to the colors, and their section was rooting for the red knight.

As Joe continued to talk to her, she remained oblivious to his words, thinking, *where have you been all my life?*

Her heart beat faster because he paused at that very instant and leaned over and gently kissed her lips, whispering and echoing her thoughts, "Where have you been all my life?"

She felt her hairs stand on end as electricity coursed through every cell in her body. There was something invisible at play, and she was not going against the current of fate. Did everyone around them sense how connected they were? Why did it feel like an invisible coil was holding and binding them together?

She didn't want the evening to end. *I haven't felt this way—this intensely, this quickly. Not even with Mason or Grant.* With great effort, she kept her composure and continued to enjoy the rest of the show with him.

After the show he drove along the Vegas strip so she could view the ornate landscape. As she had expected, the strip was littered with themed hotels displaying the excesses of the gambling town. She enjoyed his tour of words as she looked at the blazing vista of the thoroughfare. The allure of the Vegas strip was like a beautiful but deadly siren, beckoning the unsuspecting along its path. It was clear that many had gazed upon the temptress and undoubtedly been smashed straight into the depths of a sea of debt.

It was late so they didn't have enough time to roam around on foot, to visit all the usual tourist landmarks of the city. Reluctantly, he drove her back to the Aladdin. He was filled with angst. Every time he looked at her, all he could think about was making love to her. *Should I remain the consummate gentleman?* He sighed.

Mercedes also dreaded their inevitable parting at her door. Walking along the long hallway, she decided to surrender herself to whatever was going to happen next.

No plans, no thoughts. She simply wanted the spontaneity of the moment, whatever it might be. She hoped he would be as consistent in his desire for her as he had been all evening. She desired him equally.

At her door her heart began beating abnormally fast. She took her key card and, before opening the door, she turned and looked into his eyes. Whatever she saw there encouraged her to take his left hand and lead him inside. She felt compelled to do it. It felt quite natural, and when the door closed, she placed her hands upon his face.

He smiled at the touch, clearly happy to agree to her silent invitation. Her hands moved to the back of his neck and she drew him closer for a gentle kiss.

His mouth opened slightly. The tip of his tongue traced the shape of her mouth, caressing her own tongue, which responded by exploring his. His arms tightened around her, palms splayed against her back, creating warmth against her dress. Too soon, she broke the kiss. Her eyes opened, meeting his intense blue gaze reflecting the same passion she felt.

"Thank you for a lovely evening," she whispered, aching for him but still wanting to take things slow. She started to pull away, but he wouldn't let her go and she had no intention of resisting.

"The pleasure is all mine," he said softly, kissing her again, and then reluctantly drawing back slightly.

The smoldering storm in her eyes threatened to fog his impassioned mind, and his own breathing was as rapid and excited as hers.

"I can't stop myself—you feel so good," he confessed in a whisper.

"JC," she said his newly given name in a sultry whisper.

The whispered sound of her nickname for him made him shudder as a raw hunger gnawed at his control. Her feminine scent left him tortured, "Mercedes, if you don't tell me 'no' now, I...I won't be able to pull back."

Tenderly he let his hand touch the side of her face, stroking her soft skin with his fingertips. "Tell me, Mercedes," he whispered, "tell me you want me as much as I want you."

She was staring at him as her desires warred with her logic. The small voice inside her head that she expected to be saying she shouldn't be doing this, shouldn't let him continue, was surprisingly silent. In its place, a strong feeling of *déjà vu* took hold of her.

As he felt her fingers flexing restlessly behind his neck, he pleaded in his mind, *Please don't refuse me, Mercedes. Say yes. Say it.*

"Yes," she whispered, her lips softening tremulously. His relieved eyes smiled radiantly, and she repeated, "Yes, JC—yes, I want you."

Spontaneously, they melded together, letting the passion grow between them as those surges of energy began flowing back and forth. They surrendered to the intense throes of passion for one another.

She felt completely carefree, wanting nothing more than to give into the powerful emotions she was feeling. His hands slid down to grasp her buttocks firmly and pull her up against him.

She slid her hands behind his head, pulling him closer, trying to deepen their kiss even more. His lips were soft against hers. She closed her eyes and stood on tiptoe to better reach him.

She reached down between them to touch him. At her touch, he gasped involuntarily into her mouth and dueled with her tongue, lost in the sensuous feelings.

He began running his hand up inside of her thighs making her shiver at his touch. His hand moved higher under her dress, as he gently began squeezing and caressing the naked skin he found there.

As his expert hands and skillful fingers explored, she started going mad with desire. She wanted him between her thighs and she began willing him to touch her there, to quench that burning desire. In consent, she slowly parted her legs before his touch.

He felt her feminine arousal and the press of her body as she moved harder against him. His breathing became ragged, deep with excitement. He moved his hand lower, toward the core of her, still kissing her mouth, feeling her body quiver and tremble at his touch.

He hungrily kissed the nape of her neck, touching her through the soft material as she moaned deeply and arched against him, feeling his fingers deep within her tingling, silky walls.

She jerked involuntarily, breathing heavily, moaning as her mind was reeling. Each delicious wave of sensation exploded through her body and radiated out from within her. She was more aroused than ever before and she wanted more.

She felt the approach of a flood rushing to burst the wall containing it. The wall crumbled before the rush of pressure within her. A series of powerful constrictions shattered her, leaving her deliriously light-headed with every pulse. She wanted to touch him without any restrictions.

He felt her gently pull him free, and the feeling of him exposed sent his mind reeling. His body was ravenous at her touch. He couldn't believe this was happening. It was like a dream, but she was right here in his arms as he kissed every part of her that he could.

Mercedes was lost in a world of her own, again close to the edge, beyond coherent thought. She closed her eyes at its approach and she moaned when she felt the delicious wave surging within her.

Her hand was moving, and he groaned. He could feel the pressure building, becoming too difficult to hold back from its powerful force. She brought him to the edge, and he finally lost control as powerful sensations consumed his whole body.

Slowly, he became aware that he was holding her against the wall. He had been the entire time.

She opened her eyes, which were unfocused. Breathing heavily, she looked up at him. They both smiled gasping, both needing time to regain their senses. Both knew what they had shared was only the beginning.

She walked over and put a U2 CD on a low setting. He sat on the bed, still recuperating from the dizzying sensations. She came up behind him and placed her hands on his shoulders. He let out a sigh as she started to give him a delicious massage.

Intoxicating shivers ran along his spine as he enjoyed their building passion.

"Relax." He was on his stomach, and she straddled his back, placing her thumbs in the middle of his neck, her fingers working his muscles. She felt his head sink into the bed as he relaxed.

She pushed her thumbs hard against the muscles at the top of his shoulders, kneading, breaking the tension she felt. Then, holding her fingers still, she worked with just her thumbs, moving up from between the shoulder blades to separate the strands of muscle there.

A small shudder ran through him and, with her palms facing out, she began to stroke the length of his back, moving up toward his neck as his muscles rolling under her thumbs. She let her fingertips brush his sides. He sighed as she continued the movement of her hands up and back down his back. *What did his sighs mean?*

Moaning softly with content and sighing again, he said softly, "Yes, that feels so good. You've got magic hands, Mercedes."

"Thank you," she said as she traced the outside of his arms and then across his shoulders before moving down his back using just enough pressure to relax him totally. "There is more to a good massage."

He turned over greeting her smile with one of his, enjoying the sweetness of her foreplay.

"I could get lost forever in that smile," he whispered as she leaned in to cover his smile with a deep passionate kiss.

The more she touched him, the less it felt as a physical craving. It was becoming more intimate than she could ever imagine. Not lingering, she continued her kisses downward.

He stroked her long dark hair softly as her warm breath caressed his skin. His body was crying out for another release. He pulled her face up to meet his in a fierce kiss, letting their passion take control of their movements.

An unexpected pinprick of pain from her healing puncture made her tremble, and a burgeoning feeling of apprehension swept over her. There was not a doubt in her mind that she wanted him completely, but she couldn't move forward and welcome his penetration.

They haven't talked about protection. She had none.

Suddenly she pulled away. She needed to be cautious, even though she wanted him, ached for him. She was still healing and she couldn't risk it.

As if he was reading her mind once again, he simply stopped her and placed his finger softly on her lips, "Shh…" He pulled her gently toward him, kissing her gently. He slowly put his hand into his pocket, relieving her worries. "Please don't think I was being presumptuous."

She responded with a kiss as she took the packet from his hand and began removing his shirt. Her even white teeth clenched the edge of the plastic wrapper, leaving it dangling from her mouth.

Smiling, she scanned his beautiful torso and longed to feel his flesh pressed against hers. She placed her hand on his smooth chest and continued her sensual exploration. With a slow rousing urgency, they continued to explore each other's bodies, peeling away their coverings. He caressed her with his lips, tongue, and hands.

Her desires were so heightened that when his hands touched her, they seemed to linger after they had passed.

She positioned herself between his legs, continuing the rhythm of their foreplay. She carefully opened the packet and gently sheathed him with a seductive motion. She was above him, her knees astride him. He placed his strong hands on her hips and watched as she closed her eyes, tilted her head back, and allowed her silky dark hair to cascade down her back against his thighs.

He had never seen a woman who could match her exquisite island beauty. The vision of her would never fade in his mind. Her full, luxurious lips were curved up in a sweet smile. His eyes followed every sensuous curve of her body. He could feel her tightening around him as her hips undulated. She was moaning in her dance, heightening her pleasures.

"Yes!" Their bodies matched each other's rhythm with an exhilarating blend of force and passion.

Slowly, he pulled himself up to meet her mouth, kissing her harder and rougher. They were facing each other, with his hands behind her back, holding onto her shoulders. She unfolded her knees, wrapping her legs around his waist, her arms holding onto him in a tight embrace. His face buried in the sweet scent of her long flowing hair pulling him deeper into her.

He rocked her forward, opening his legs, as she fell back onto the pillows. She felt his gentle strength.

Never had a woman pleased him this greatly before. She pulled her knees and turned over onto her stomach, arching and inviting him, encouraging him to continue.

He welcomed her invitation, wanting to take her body and soul for his own. The short, soft moans escaped her lips and escalated to screams of sweet passion.

The flood broke deep inside her, and she started to convulse uncontrollably. She was aware of every inch of her body and its sensitivity to his every touch.

Feeling her pulsing, listening to her screaming his name, he couldn't hold back any longer against the heavy grip, the mounting pressure inside him. His breathing quickened, his heart was pounding in rhythm with their bodies. He closed his eyes and he too was lost in the sensations.

With one last determined movement, he gripped her hips, pulling her tight against him. His whole body was on fire. The fire consumed him until he collapsed on top of her lithe, shaking body.

He let all of his weight rest against his arms so as not too overwhelm her. Their breathing slowed, and they kissed caringly until their bodies returned to their normal states.

He carefully pulled himself up with his arms and rolled over next to her. She was glistening in sweat. Her breathing was erratic, but still she smiled playfully at him, asking to his amazement, "JC—again?"

It had been so long since he had felt such a high level of ecstasy. In fact, he wondered if he had ever had. This incredibly sexy, passionate woman had made love to him with an insatiable appetite.

At her request he let out a soft laugh and simply embraced her, but she was quite serious. She knew he needed time to recover, so she simply nuzzled at his neck and lingered in the moment, embraced by his scent.

Lingering in sensuous silence, he was resting his head on his right hand, caressing her lightly, tracing her profile and enjoying the sensual sight with her left breast only partially covered by the sheet. Her soft skin exuded a light bronze, sun-kissed glow without a single tan line. She had a flawless complexion. She didn't need to wear make-up, though her lips wore an alluring, deep shade of crimson with a complementary hue outlining her soft pouty lips.

The dark eyeliner on her lids gave her the elegance of a 1950s diva. On her left ear, a diamond stud earring sparkled next to a second golden, dainty earring. A delicate gold crucifix was unobtrusively positioned on her throat, hanging on a thin fragile gold chain that he touched fleetingly, feeling its slightly rough texture.

The scent of her was fragrant and tantalizing. His caresses continued downward from her throat to the middle of her breasts. He gently pinched her nipple, which hardened with his touch, pleasing him. He traveled downward to her navel, where he discovered her small healing incisions. He gently uncovered her, and just above her soft mound, he saw the triangular pattern of her delicate wounds.

His touch was so soothing; it induced her eyes to close, allowing her to enjoy each tender caress. She slowly became self-conscious as he approached her navel, yet she felt her wariness fading as he carefully began to glide his touch near the perimeter of her scars, consciously not touching them, as though he did not want to take any chances of inflicting even the slightest pain.

"Are you curious about them, JC?" she asked in the softest whisper, while her eyes slowly opened and she gazed at his profile. His eyes were still fixed on her wounds and he seemed to be lost in thought and in his delicate exploration.

"Do they hurt?" he asked in a voice filled with compassion, as he leaned over to kiss her belly, close to the periphery of her incision.

"Once in a while I feel a pinprick. Nothing more," she replied, reaching for his face, beckoning him to kiss her lips, "I would like to tell you about it." His gaze shifted to her eyes, and silently he listened to her with undivided attention.

"A year ago my marriage with Mason ended and in six months, the divorce will become final." Sorrow tinged in her voice, "I wanted children. He didn't."

"I'm so sorry," he said, gently stroking her hair and waiting patiently for her to continue.

"After months of soul searching, I returned to my doctor to get a clear understanding of my future options. I underwent a laparoscopic procedure twenty days ago. My doctor discovered and promptly removed rare genetic obstructions of my fallopian tubes with a laser." Looking at him, she shared, "My dearest wish is to have a child—with or without a partner."

"You would raise your child alone?"

"Yes. I've thought it through—all the problems of single parenthood—and I've made plans. I would have the baby and then go back to work accompanied with a traveling nanny, or an *au pair* on my business trips. I have everything planned out, my work schedule, even college trust funds, which I've already established."

"But is it fair for a child to grow up without two parents?"

His strong convictions and his need for a traditional family structure tugged at her heart. Her tone suddenly turned sullen as unpleasant memories of Mason emerged in her mind.

In a sharp, hurtful voice, Mason had yelled at her, "NO! I will NOT subject a child to being born into this UNFAIR WORLD!"

Struggling to speak, she finally said, "Life is never fair."

Joe noticed the change in her mood. He wanted to know what she was thinking, what had changed her mood. He wanted to share more about himself and his thoughts on the subject.

"When I was in the Gulf War, a journalist asked me what I was fighting for." Without sounding virtuous, he continued, "I told him that although I was fighting for my country, I was really fighting for the future—for my unborn children."

He looked at her in her eyes, "Mercedes, I strongly believe a child should be nurtured by two parents. I didn't have that same luxury. I grew up in a family torn by a bitter divorce, and I was shuffled between two parents, especially during the holidays. I made a vow to myself that I would never screw things up for my own kids. No matter what!"

She asked with great care, "Would you even stay in a loveless marriage for the sake of the children?"

"Yes."

His answer saddened her deeply and it sent a powerfully strange premonition that silently overwhelmed her heart. "I am so sorry, JC. I cannot even begin to imagine what it was like for you growing up." With as much compassion as she could, she added, "I wish I could say I know what that was like, but I've been blessed with a close, loving family and with parents who have been together forever."

She began asking questions she had long struggled to understand. "Would it be unfair to a child to later discover the truth about all the unhappiness he or she had been witnessing? Would a child be devastated to learn that his or her parents' marriage had all been perpetuated because of a sense of parental obligation?"

He didn't answer, seemingly pensive.

She noticed his silence and respected it; but she wanted him to know her thoughts. "What I don't understand is how two people who fall deeply in love could later hate each other so passionately! It's beyond my capacity to understand."

"I don't understand it, either," he said, remaining pensive.

Not wanting to spoil the earlier mood, she carefully chose her words, deciding to share something from her father. "My dad had once said that the most important thing that a father can do for his children is to love their mother."

Just saying it, she felt a sense of relief, but she noticed he still remained uncomfortably serious and contemplative. She touched his smooth face and gently kissed him on his cheek. With that, a smile emerged on his face.

Happier, she asked, "Are you hungry?"

"I'm famished!"

She felt a chill, so she wrapped herself in one of the satiny sheets before picking up the phone and ordering food from room service.

He put on his pants and something caught his eye on the desk. He walked toward the desk and stared at it. He waited until she was off the phone, "Mercedes, who are they?"

She turned to find him looking at the screensaver emblazoned on the screen of her laptop computer, which had been running all day long, even during their lovemaking. Walking over to join him, she wrapped her arms around his waist. He took the seat at the desk and pulled her onto his knee. He gently kissed her on her neck, unconsciously rubbing her back as they both looked at the screen.

"The lovely lady on my left is my best friend, Syd." She paused unconsciously feeling the velvet touch of his cropped hair.

"My best friend's name is Sid," he remarked, "And the guy on your right, is that Mason?" He was surprised to feel a slight tug of unexpected jealousy.

She was smiling when he asked the question. "No, that's not Mason. That's Grant."

He was puzzled. He hadn't heard that name before and they had spoken at length about everything. So with piqued curiosity, he asked, "Who's Grant?"

She wasn't quite sure how to answer him, so she jokingly said, "He's the lead singer of a local alternative rock band. I met him backstage and ever since then he has become my personal boy-toy."

He believed her. The guy looked like he could be in a band. He was about to say something when she said, "Actually, Grant's more a rock star hopeful who happens to hold down a day job as a surgeon." She added guiltily, "I'm, I'm seeing him right now."

"Mercedes, I would be a fool to think that a beautiful, intelligent woman like you wouldn't have a handful of men at your beck and call."

"Ah, that's just it. I'd rather not have a handful of men at the moment," she smiled at him sweetly. "Just you." The words slipped out quite naturally—and they surprised her.

* * *

Joe answered the door when room service arrived. Mercedes was in the bathroom putting on comfortable clothing.

Coming out of the bathroom a few moments later, feeling refresh, she was pleased with how the server had set the table and with the small arrangement of flowers in a simple, elegant vase.

"I love the flowers."

Joe brushed a hand across her shoulder as he held her chair, "So do I."

"Then you would enjoy my own private English garden at home."

"I'd love to see it some time," he winked and gave her a soft kiss.

While they dined, their conversations were very spontaneous. He shared more details of his turbulent life.

"I'm very close to my sister, Tammy. She's a good-looking, blue-eyed brunette."

"Just like you?" Mercedes teased him.

"Yes, good-looking just like me," he said, almost blushing.

"So what's she like?"

"Independent. A free spirit. Bubbly personality. She loves to have fun. Like me, she seeks out activities that give her an adrenaline rush, but she's also protective and more guarded in her interactions with other people. She was a masseuse once."

"Is that how you recognized the massage I gave you?" Mercedes had given him a deep tissue massage, *shiatsu.*

Nodding, he asked, "How'd you learn it?"

"Joey Pitman. My boyfriend in college." She smiled, remembering him. "He helped me survive a lot of stress. My engineering courses were pretty demanding."

Mercedes looked up at him, "Are you and your sister the only two?"

"No, there are actually six of us. Two are from my father's other marriage, Martin and Jillian. My other siblings are Colette and Ken.

"My parents went through a bitter divorce before I was ten years old. Divorce is too common and it hurts kids badly. That's why I'm against it. My parents went through nasty child custody battles and those battles scarred us, especially with our future relationships."

"Tell me about your parents."

Joe nodded, "My father, Rick, is a hardworking entrepreneur. He's driven, ambitious and pretty liberal, but he can be very demanding. After the divorce he married his shrink and it seems to be working out for him."

"What about your mother?"

"My mother, Margot, is a beautiful woman. For a while she was dating a doctor, but so far she's remained single."

"Maybe she's still searching of her own true soul mate." Mercedes said with empathy.

"Maybe. Unfortunately, my parents are both attracted to extreme addictive personalities. Holidays and visitation weekends were excruciatingly bad for all of us. It also kept me from being close to my half-brother and sister."

"You must be the oldest."

"Yes."

"Interesting. You and I are on the opposite sides of the same family structure. There are six of us in my family too."

"I'm sure your family reunions aren't few and far between. Not to mention the bickering. Once there was a huge fight between Tammy and my stepmother,

Jessie. When Jessie is sober, she's a kind, understanding person, but when she's in her dark moods and she's had a couple of martinis, she's like a Dr. Jekyll / Mr. Hyde. As a kid, it was very confusing."

Frowning, he said, "My father is more in love with her than she is with him, so it gives her a natural advantage. She comes off as a sweet motherly type, but she has an attitude like she's the matriarch. Being a shrink really didn't help her to be a good mother. She tries to keep a strong hold of the family reins. Anyway, her fight with my sister came about when she came across Tammy's diary and read about how my sister loathed her. She had written that Jessie was a fake and some other non-flattering adjectives about her feelings and my stepmother went ballistic."

"How bad was it?"

"My father and I had to hold them back from each other. That was probably my first lesson from my father about the art of diplomacy with an enraged woman. It's been useful from time to time."

"I don't know if I want to hear about when," Mercedes shot him a look then smiled.

"Probably not." He grinned. "Well, the fight between Jessie and Tammy lingered on for days. The atmosphere in our house was very tense. It was really uncomfortable to be there for long periods of time. Tammy still resents Jessie to this day. That relationship still causes Tammy problems in her personal relationships. She's reluctant to commit with any man. She chooses to live with them instead. She's had three children with different fathers."

"Is she unable to love anyone?"

"Actually, Tammy loved each of the guys deeply. She just didn't want to marry anyone of them. She was faithful and devoted to each one and she's really devoted to her children. She protects them fiercely, like my mother protected her."

"Is she happy?"

"Right now she is. She just got engaged with plans for a July wedding. I think he's also an engineer."

"Really? That's wonderful! What about Jessie, is she still tyrannical?"

"AA has tempered her. She's been sober for over fifteen years now. I have to credit her for her strength."

"I see, physician heal thyself!"

"Exactly. Things are much better now that we are older."

"And wiser?"

"Perhaps."

"Tell me more about your mother, Margot."

"My mother is soft-spoken, intelligent and outgoing."

"What was she like as a mother?"

"An absentee mother. She constantly travels. Growing up, I was left to my own resources and imagination. I learned really quickly about heartbreak, and I decided I wouldn't turn out like either of my parents. Hopefully, I haven't."

"What do you make sure you do differently?"

"I make sure I'm very truthful when I share my feelings with anyone. I'm very selective before I commit myself to a serious relationship."

"What does that mean?" Mercedes was pretty sure she knew.

"I'm careful. I'm not into superficial relationships, but some of my buddies say I flit from one woman to another, like a bee going from flower to flower in a large, beautiful garden. I enjoy my freedom, and in some ways I like to have a sense of control in a relationship."

Mercedes nodded, knowing he was actually saying that he held his guard up to protect his bruised heart, building an invisible wall around him. His sister had been doing the same thing in her relationships, and so was she.

Through the night, they shared secrets neither had felt free to share before. They joked and laughed like children.

She was inside his mind and he was inside hers. They felt an unknown force—an immense power—that caused them to feel very much alive.

They were attuned to each other in ways that were beyond physical.

He enjoyed making her giggle, and her giggling often escalated to hysterical laughter. Although he had no way of knowing where she was ticklish, his hands were automatically drawn to her secret spots. He truly enjoyed being with her.

He noticed how she easily brought out the side of him that was childlike and fun, as well as sensitive and gentle. For him, she was his fantasy made flesh. He knew many men had been swept away with a smile like hers. But it was her beautiful mind, inner strength and beauty that captivated him. Talented and successful in everything she put her mind to; she had depth and a very sentimental soul. It almost felt as if she was someone he had known and loved before.

Mercedes sat back and studied him as he was lost in his own thoughts. She knew how intelligent he was. It showed through in every conversation. Intelligence was a natural aphrodisiac for her and so was insight.

No man had ever shared such poignant thoughts with her. He couldn't know how much his insights meant to her; yet, she sensed he knew it. His passion kindled a fire in her soul that had lain dormant for a very long time.

The warmth of his touches and his gentleness engulfed her, and she willingly immersed herself in what he was willing to share with her. Since she and Mason separated, she had suppressed her feelings, unwilling to yield her control; but in his warm, tender embrace, she could relinquish her control without thought.

Within moments they were again making love with as much fervor as the first time they made love. The passion never ebbed, and they didn't stop until he had to leave at two o'clock in the morning.

Before he left, he tucked her in and caressed her hair lightly as she slumbered. He watched her sleep and then left quietly.

* * *

About an hour later, she woke instantly when the phone rang. With her eyes still shut, she fumbled to find the phone. Was it Grant?

Disoriented, she fell back against the pillow, but the ringing persisted.

Finally more awake and alarmed, she hurriedly attempted to pick it up, knocking the handset off the cradle. Once she retrieved it, she was greeted by the distinct sounds of inebriated crying on the other line.

"Sydney?" she whispered with concern, her voice raspy from sleep.

There was no answer, so Mercedes became insistent, "Syd, please talk to me. What's the matter, sweetie?"

"Merc, my life is over!" Sydney screamed through her sobs, repeating, "My fucking life is over!"

Fully awake, Mercedes noted it was shortly after four in the morning and she sat upright against the pillows. With a soothing voice, she said, "Sweetie, let's try to calm down, okay? Deep breaths, please." She heard Sydney trying to calm herself. "That's it, slow deep breaths."

Mercedes listened to Sydney's struggle to get calmer, very worried at the sadness and apparent rage that she had heard in Sydney's voice. "Tell me what's wrong?"

Sydney took several more deep breaths, and finally was calm enough to talk. "It's Patrick," she started to cry again. "I'm leaving him!"

That was not what she had expected, so with a start, Mercedes exclaimed, "What?" Trying to comprehend what was happening, she wanted to know more details. "Why are you leaving him?"

"I just got the surveillance photos and, I, I…" her voice trailed off and she started to cry harder with each breath.

Mercedes waited patiently, listening to her troubled, drunken friend as she thought of the Trahisons. They had just celebrated their fifth year wedding anniversary in December; they had started having marital problems a year ago after Sydney decided to shed her career as an architect to become a full-time mother to their two young children, Luke and Amanda.

Sydney began to be suspicious of her husband because his work had been taking him on impromptu business trips. For her peace of mind, she needed to know if she was just being paranoid because of the friction already thick in her marriage or whether there was another reason for her concerns. She had hired an out-of-state private investigator to get the information she needed and, in case she was wrong, to make certain Patrick's unstained reputation remained intact.

Patrick was a highly respected real estate attorney who was part of Mason's power circle. She knew Patrick before she met Sydney—she actually first met Sydney professionally and they had become fast friends when they worked on a project together in New Jersey. Sydney's firm had been hired to design the architectural façade and interior spaces of a project that Mercedes had also been working on.

Sydney was the sister Mercedes always wished she had. The parallels in their lives led them to believe they were kindred spirits, and each felt the other was more like a sister than a friend. The many things they found that they shared in common often took them completely by surprise.

Mercedes had hoped Sydney's suspicions were unfounded, but if she had pictures, pictures did not lie. Still waiting for Sydney to calm down, Mercedes was concerned that she had only three hours until she had to get ready for another day of presentations, but she was not about to abandon her friend in her desperate time of need.

"Do you know what really hurts most? Patrick didn't even have the decency to have an affair with a woman who is more beautiful or intelligent than me! I could understand if she was a fucking supermodel Einstein but no! He had to add insult to injury!" Regaining her composure, she said, "Remember that blonde with the terribly obvious fake breasts at Dante's St. Patrick's Day party?"

Dante was Patrick's law partner. Mercedes had gone on one date with him shortly after she had separated. Sydney had set them up! And she did remember the unnaturally voluptuous blonde with Dante.

"The Atlantic City showgirl?" She remembered how Dante was showing the blonde off to his fraternity of over-priced lawyer friends like she was a highly coveted classic car.

"Yes. Her."

"I remember. She was one of the reasons I never accepted another date from him. I had no urge to join his list of conquests." Mercedes continued to search her memory for the woman's name but she came up blank. The showgirl had been very attractive and quite uninhibited with her sexuality, but she paled in comparison to Sydney's classic European beauty. Their bodies were equally voluptuous, but Sydney's was natural.

Mercedes unexpectedly found herself saying, "Jill."

"Yes, that BITCH!" she fumed. "Oh God! I'm beautiful. I'm intelligent. I'm substantial. I gave birth to his children! Why is this happening? Please could someone tell me, why this is FUCKING happening?"

Mercedes didn't have an immediate answer. Sydney was a very strong and special woman whom she respected. She had admired her courage and strength for a very long time, especially during tumultuous moments of her life with Patrick.

Those moments were usually about his job or her preoccupation with their two kids. And it had been especially difficult for both of them when she was pregnant with her daughter. Their lack of physical and emotional intimacy coupled with the constant separation because of his work during those trying late months of pregnancy and the first few months of birth had been a tremendous challenge of their marriage and love.

Those problems had put a wedge between them, causing a void that strained their relationship. It didn't surprise Mercedes that ambivalence and resentment had developed between Sydney and Patrick. She had experienced the same feelings right before she and Mason separated.

She did find comfort in the fact that her dear friends loved each other deeply, despite their rocky marriage. She felt they would both withstand the test facing them, unless it wasn't truly meant to be.

She had a theory about soul mates, which she had not fully thought through. She hoped one day she would be able to share it with Sydney. And right now, she wished she could spend more time with her dear friend.

Sadly, her nomadic travels had not afforded them the time to really sit down and have a heart-to-heart. She kept penciling it in her hellish schedule, but something always came in the way, like this morning with her upcoming presentations.

She desperately wanted to comfort her friend, to ease her broken heart. "I'm so sorry, Syd. I really am. I don't know why this is happening either. I truly do not know why."

Frustrated and concerned, she kept trying to find the words to console her. Finally, she offered convincingly, "But I do know this. You are beautiful. You are intelligent. And you are a terrific mother! Not to mention so many other things that you are as well—you're witty, kind, compassionate and honest! I can go on and on!"

"Then why did I drive him into the arms of another woman?"

From Sydney's grim tone, Mercedes knew her friend was not looking for a response. She merely wanted to say those words out loud, perhaps to make some sense of her pain.

"Where are you now? What about Luke and Amanda?"

"I'm home. The kids are asleep and Cassie's on her way."

Mercedes was relieved to hear that she wasn't going to be alone. "Where is Patrick?"

"He's away. Very convenient, isn't it? He's away on a two-day business trip in New York." Sydney couldn't hold back her anger and shame, and for the next few minutes she went into a well-desired tirade until she was finally exhausted.

"Merc, promise me you'll call after your lectures."

"You know I will. And remember, Syd, every problem comes to us with a gift in its hands." Feeling unable to bear more of her friend's torment, she felt the need to turn on her usual charm and added in jest, "You could use a new, red-hot convertible, right? Then hire a Chippendale-type cutie with nothing more than a little bow tie and floss-like thong to drive you around. I think you deserve some mindless entertainment, a guilty pleasure if you will, while you decide what you want to do."

"I might take you up on that, Slayer," she said, starting to laugh giddily despite her horrid state. "I can always count on you—always there with the right words and the jokes. You're my rock, woman!"

Mercedes felt a little relieved. By the time they finally got off the phone, she could tell that Sydney felt much better, but Mercedes also wished her friend could see things clearly, without the accompanying hateful rage and searing pain.

Her mind racing, Mercedes couldn't fall back to sleep. She grabbed the pillow and simply buried her face in it before letting out a frustrated scream, exhausted. She finally drifted soundly to sleep with her arms wrapped around one of the pillows.

Chapter 11

March 22nd, Big Sky

Mercedes woke with a start when the phone rang again. She quickly sat upright, her heart beating nervously with concern, as she picked up the phone, "Syd?"

"Good morning, this is the hotel automated wake-up call. It is now 7:00 a.m."

The computer-generated voice brought her a sense of relief and she fell back to her pillow, not wanting to move her slightly aching muscles. Fifteen minutes later, the digital alarm clock went off, but instead of an annoying buzz, it was blaring Sarah McLachlan's *Hold On* at maximum volume. She always had a back-up wake-up call, knowing how she was easily lulled back to sleep. Her schedule had been hellish and sleep had become another one of her luxuries.

She turned down the music, got out from her bed and, still naked, walked toward the window to admire Vegas landscape. A deep cleansing breath made her feel suddenly invigorated. Her thoughts fluctuated from Sydney to Joe, Joe to Grant and her schedule for the day; but ultimately, her thoughts lingered on Joe. Smiling, she gave herself an embrace with him in mind.

Her thoughts shifted to Sydney and she picked up the phone and dialed her favorite florist in Philadelphia. "Good morning. I would like to order six long-stemmed, yellow roses with Stargazer lilies and Alstromeria. Would you also include a one-pound box of assorted Godiva chocolates? ...Yes, I'd like to have a note attached to it." Mercedes thought quickly of what she wanted to say, "Please have the note say:

"Syd,

Don't ever forget—not even for a day—how very special you are. Hold onto love for love never fails! I'm here for you, always listening with an open heart, or ready to kick you in the ass when you need it <smile>.

Love,

Merc"

After she gave the florist her payment information and Sydney's address, she added to her order, "Also, for tomorrow, would you send your Blooming Masterpiece arrangement to another person at another address? I want the roses to be red, yellow, pink, white, and peach, along with limonium and greens in a glass."

She had almost forgotten about Donna because of her pre-occupation with everything that had been happening. Mercedes knew she had to keep focused despite of the turmoil.. It was growing difficult, but it was manageable if she let part of herself function on autopilot.

After giving the florist the additional information, she got into the shower and, unable to get the tune from the radio out of her head, she started singing,

"Am I in heaven here or am I in hell...
At the crossroads I am standing...
Hold on, hold on to yourself for this is gonna hurt like hell..."

She was still humming the rest of it as she got dressed, went downstairs and grabbed a cup of tea on her way to the conference area.

The room was filling up as she took her seat at the presenter's table. She was first on the agenda.

She grimaced when she realized that today's host was Calvin Garvey. He worked for one of Wallace Industries' subsidiary companies outside of the Philadelphia area. He was a tall, lean man with thinning brown hair, showing the middle stages of male pattern baldness. Clearly, he was trying to salvage whatever he could by combing his hair over to cover what he obviously didn't have.

She had never noticed the exact color of his eyes; she always felt uneasy around him and had avoided looking into his eyes, knowing she would find his look distasteful. Nothing about him was too memorable. A year ago after a weeklong engineering roundtable and workshop, his conversations at the dinner party had been laced with innuendoes. She had rebuffed him as nicely as she could, citing nepotism, which left him embarrassed and rejected. He always left her feeling perplexed and disgusted, but because of his professional abilities, she had no choice but to continually give him the benefit of the doubt. He was supposedly a happily married man with a handful of children and she regarded most family men highly.

Whenever she was assigned to work with him on a project within his area, he would be a perfect gentleman at first. After a short while she would be faced with the same discomfort. She frowned, realizing Myles had just assigned her again to a three-month long project with Calvin. Perhaps he would rise to the occasion.

As he stood at the podium, he addressed the audience in a deep tone, "Let's welcome our first presenter, Mercedes Sinclair from Philadelphia. Ms. Sinclair's expertise is in environmental hydraulics. She will be presenting her recently published paper on *Urban Fluid Dynamics*."

On his way back from the podium, he winked at her, showing her a definite lack of professional respect. She gathered her notes and walked to the podium.

Needing the lights dimmed for her PowerPoint presentation, she ignored his wink and forced a smile at him, asking him softly to have the lights dimmed.

Immediately, he took advantage of the situation, leaning toward her and gesturing that she needed to come close and whisper her request in his ear. Keeping her disgust hidden, she used the microphone, "Mr. Garvey, thank you for your kind introduction. Would you please dim the lights so we can get started?" She offered him a forced smile.

At the conclusion of her presentation, she received warm applause for her technical discourse and her new work. She decided to stay and listen to the next set of presentations.

The speakers who followed her were equally interesting and at the end of the day, she gathered her things, eagerly thinking about the time she was going to have with Joe.

Before leaving the presenter's table, she took out her planner to add her daily entries. She was in the midst of her entry when she heard Calvin's voice, "Mercedes, would you be interested in joining us for dinner at Spago's?"

She looked up and checked to make certain that he really meant to include other people in the dinner invitation. A growing group of other presenters were standing a few feet behind him.

Before she had a chance to respond, he added with a knowing smile, "I understand there's a full-sized replica of Michelangelo's *David* just yards away from Spago."

"Why, Calvin, I am delighted that you remembered the details of my trip to Florence," she said, trying not to sound facetious.

At an in-house workshop several months ago, she and the others had been asked to share one outstanding personal experience with the group. She had gladly recounted her November pilgrimage to Italy; a trip she made solely because of her wish to be standing in front of Michelangelo's *David* on the day she turned thirty.

She remembered how he talked about his college's football team, and she asked, "And, how did the thundering herd of Marshall fare last season?"

"The *Big Green* was stronger than ever!"

She glanced at her watch. It was only 5:00 p.m. She was apprehensive, especially when he took a seat next to her, "Mercedes, it's just dinner among colleagues, really. Please come with us."

"May I have that in writing, Calvin?" Her deliberate smile was meant to give him a bit of discomfort, but he ignored it. As he talked, she evaluated her options, deciding she didn't want to eat alone while she was waiting for Joe. So, she allowed him to think he had persuaded her to join them.

Clearly pleased, he asked, "How about if I meet you at your room?"

"That's okay, Calvin, but I'll meet you and the others in the lobby in an hour. See you then." She checked in at the front desk for another business package from Donna. There was also a card waiting for her, which she immediately recognized as Grant's distinct scribble.

Upstairs in her room she opened his note as she listened to Mozart. She had taken it from Grant's collection when she dropped off her note in his sock drawer. She smiled, knowing Grant always played classical music in the background while he performed surgery, believing it would seep into the unconscious, soothing his patient's fears. She wished it would soothe her right now.

"My Angel,

You may think it childish of me, but I wanted to celebrate the day we met again in Big Sky. A few nights later, you showed off your prowess on the pool table, and I don't mean the wicked English you used to finally sink the 9-ball! I thank my lucky stars every day that our paths crossed again.

I miss you desperately!

Love,

Grant"

She never thought of him as childish, quite the contrary, she adored him. She found him a formidable challenge in debates. She didn't even have to feign losing. Yet somehow she suspected that he purposefully let her win some of those rebuttals. She also loved his surprises and his very touching sentiments. He was always considerate of her feelings and especially of her need for personal space.

She remembered when they met again in Montana after their first meeting at the art museum.

* * *

It had been an impromptu weeklong ski trip, which she almost hadn't made because of an unusual blizzard that hit the northwestern portion of the country. But her plane had landed safely before the snowstorm hit.

She was the fifth wheel at the ski resort and she hadn't minded. After a day on the slopes and fine dining at the Mountain Village, everyone wanted to unwind at the bar and grille in the Huntley Lodge, enjoying the acoustic music and games. Since the others had been paired up, she had strolled over to the pool tables, deciding to play a competitive game.

A couple of guys had been playing very well. One was built like an ox and the other was short with thick curly hair. The short one, whose name she heard was Jerry, was an arrogant son-of-a-bitch. He was constantly showing his crooked smile, laughing sarcastically, and speaking loudly.

"Yow, baby! I'm hot tonight. Oh yes, somebody wants a piece of this!" he said, looking over at her direction. His verbose and cocky attitude repulsed her.

The opportunity to teach him a lesson in humility was irresistible, as was the chance to give him a run for his money at pool.

She knew how to play pool very well, having learned while being competitive with her five brothers. Her parents had given them a pool table for a Christmas present when she was twelve.

But before she could challenge him, someone beat her to it. She remembered standing there patiently waiting, silently hoping the new opponent would trounce the overconfident jerk in the next game.

The new challenger was calm in his demeanor and was smiling. He never took his eyes off his opponent.

"Nine-ball okay?"

Jerry cockily replied, "Hey, dude, 9-ball. Sure, it'll be a quick game. You know what—I'll even do you a solid. You break."

Without complaints, the table was racked and ready for his break. The sound of the breaking balls was loud. Off the break, he sank three balls: the one, the three and the six.

"You've gotta be kidding me!" Jerry yowled in disbelief before starting to callously taunt him, "Lucky shot, dude, lucky shot. You won't get another ball after I get a shot."

The calm stranger expertly controlled the cue, sinking the 2-ball into the side pocket, with impressive inside English. Then, he executed a three-rail kick shot, successfully sinking the 4-ball to the far corner pocket, which left the cue in good position for the 5-ball sitting across from it. Suddenly, Jerry was left looking quite grave and angry, but still incessantly attempting to destroy his concentration. Yet it didn't seem to have any effect, and the other player shot smoothly, completely oblivious to Jerry's mental tactics.

With good cue ball direction and speed, he easily made the 5-ball in the opposite corner pocket with a soft stroke. The 7-ball was hiding behind the 9-ball leaving an awkward angle. The guy was engaging Jerry in deliberate stare-down contests between his silent pauses when he studied the position of his object ball. He seemed to triumph each time Jerry would look away from his intentional gaze.

Mercedes had only seen this good of a game on ESPN during a 9-ball tournament. Watching with a smile, she saw a move she only witnessed on the small screen as he skillfully performed a *massé*, gingerly swinging the cue ball around the 9-ball to sink the 7-ball with ease into the side pocket.

The player paused, studied the table, sighed and then took his position at the cue. She knew he was going to finish the game in the next shot. She was grinning openly as he did a trick shot to finally end the game. He hit the cue ball into the object ball, hitting the 9-ball, using the full effect of his stroke speed to sink the nine into the pocket. The cue smacked it so hard that the sound of his forceful attack echoed loudly in the room.

Impressive! Now that was certainly worth the wait. She couldn't have given Jerry a better trouncing than this man had. Yet she was so focused on the winner's game and demeanor that she didn't really pay close attention to how he looked or to his face.

She wanted to tell him how much she enjoyed watching him expertly play the game. He had his back toward her while he gave Jerry a firm handshake, as if to show what good sportsmanlike conduct was truly like.

She stood quietly behind him waiting until he would turn around and find her smiling. When he did, his eyes lit up and smiled widely, and before she could give him a compliment, he surprised her when he said charmingly, "Hello, Mercedes," stepping closer to her and moving within her personal space.

She was startled when he said her name, but having him standing so close to her didn't feel uncomfortable. She smiled, gazing into his eyes, immediately beginning a mental search to match his face with a moment. "We've met?"

He refreshed her memory when he took her left hand and pressed it to his lips.

At the touch of his lips, she was reminded, *Ah yes, the handsome well-bred gentleman at the Philadelphia Museum of Art who was admiring me from afar. How delightful!*

"Dr. Larcher—it is a pleasure to bump into you again. And I must tell you I truly enjoyed your pool game. You could be a professional pool player the way you handled that man! I was watching your game so intently. I, I didn't recognize you without your glasses, so please forgive me." She realized she was blushing and smiling coyly when they locked eyes. She could finally see his smiling light brown eyes behind the fallen blond hair. *Very nice,* she thought.

She saw by his glance that he had noticed she was no longer wearing her wedding ring. It made her blush even more.

"The pleasure is all mine. Please, call me Grant," he said, smiling, "Care to join me for a drink?" Her hand was still in his as he led her slowly to a table nearby and pulled her chair out for her. A server asked for their drink order.

"A glass of Merlot for the lady, and Cognac for me, please."

Mercedes was pleased with his choices since Merlot was her favorite wine.

"Are you here with your husband?"

"No, I'm here with my cousin Michael and his friends," she said warily. His quiet presence and his undemanding silence drew the words out of her. "I'm separated now."

"Oh, I'm very sorry to hear that."

She believed the sincerity in his voice. "Are you here on vacation with someone?"

"My parents rented a chalet nearby. They invited my friends, me, and Abigail for the weekend."

"Oh," she said, surprised to hear the disappointment in her own voice.

Grinning, he said, "Abigail is my sister."

Unable to hide her satisfaction, she was thankful when the server arrived with their drinks. They began talking about their families and discovered they had more in common than they had realized.

"Your mother sounds really amazing."

"She is," she said proudly. "She even had six children on top of that!"

"And so did my mother, five boys and a girl."

"Me too! I mean, I'm the only girl and I have five older brothers." The hairs along the back of her neck began to prickle. "Please, go ahead."

"Then there's Leo, short for Leonardo. He—"

"Unbelievable! I have a brother named Leonardo," she said, tickled with another coincidence. With unusual ease, she shared, "Leo left the seminary—breaking the vow of celibacy. Many would-be nuns left with him in shame."

"Now, you might not believe this either, but my brother Leo also left the seminary except he married the would-be nun."

"*Oh, mon Dieu!*" she exclaimed, feeling the tingle wave down her back. "What are the odds of that? I mean…" She caught herself in mid-sentence, beginning to feel self-conscious about the signs. "I'm sorry. I'm rambling, please continue."

Smiling at her, he said, "No, really I don't mind. I enjoy listening to you. When you talk, I like the way your eyes light up to match your incredible smile."

Blushing at the compliment, she insisted that he continue.

"My youngest brother, Daniel, was in the Navy. After he was discharged, he became a—"

"Hey, *Drake!*" Grant quickly turned around and waved at the group of men, approaching their table.

"Drake?" she said, a little puzzled.

"Yes, it's my middle name but the guys use it because—"

"He walks like a duck." A strong hand suddenly rested on his shoulder, belonging to a tall friendly man, too young to have graying hair. "Pardon the intrusion. Hi, I'm James."

"Hi James, I'm Mercedes. So he walks like a duck, huh?"

"Nah," he said, his head shaking with a grin. "I guess he hasn't told you about the Larcher Riders."

Before she could ask a question, the dark-haired man standing next to James extended his hand with a smile. "Hi, I'm Dave," he said, glancing over at Grant, "A good friend of the dragon."

"The dragon," she repeated, a little bewildered with his comment, as she shook Dave's hand.

Grant continued with the introductions, "Towering over Dave are Mark and his brothers, Andy and Brian. The guy with the silly grin is Gary, next to him is Chris, and the three guys standing behind them we call *Fat Man, Chino,* and *Troll.*"

After they took turns saying hello, Mark, the tallest of the group, called out, "Hey Gary, a round of drinks for everybody!"

"Yep," his youthful friend smirked, badly masking the lingering melancholy behind his light eyes. He quickly finished his beer before he darted to the bar.

"She's hot," his inebriated, short friend said to Grant, trying to whisper, while looking at her.

"Thanks, Troll," Mercedes said, smiling at his comment.

"Mercedes, I'll fight Drake right now," he said with an overconfident grin. His face was wind burned and cherry red.

"Troll, let's go," said the fair-haired friend, named Chris. "Gary needs help carrying the drinks. Besides, Drake only needs to hit you once and you're out!" His voice was firm and deep.

"Shut up, *Belly!*" he cried out, reluctantly getting up from his seat next to Drake.

"Come on, little man," said Andy, getting up with Troll. He had towered over him by a foot. "You're coming too, Brian?"

"Oh no, I've got something more challenging in mind," Brian said with his gaze at a smiling lovely voluptuous blonde talking to a cute brunette at the bar. At that moment he locked eyes with her, clearly relieved that the attraction was mutual. "Excuse me, I just got my cue."

"I'm with you on this one," said Fat Man, a curly-lashed friendly man of size; he was staring intently at the brunette. "I think I found my soul mate."

After the four friends politely excused themselves from the group, Mercedes asked Grant, "How long have you known your friends?"

"Mostly from high school, except for James, whom I've known since kindergarten."

"We actually met at his fifth birthday party," James said, smiling, "I gave him six Matchbox cars and we've been friends ever since."

"My friendship is easily bought," Grant joked.

"Now tell me about the Larcher Riders."

"We ride our cycles," James looked at Grant and added, "competitively."

"Snowmobiles and snowboarding in the winter," Dave offered, becoming distracted after an attractive Latina walked by, smiling at him.

"And the nicknames?"

"Those are our avatars when we ride to—"

"Have fun and raise hell!" Mark piped up with a grin, "That's why we're all here—for the rush!" His smiling dark eyes filled with the promise of innocuous mischief.

"The only cure for adrenaline junkies," the most reserved of the group finally said.

Mercedes quickly noticed his wedding band and asked, "Chino, is your wife here with you?"

"Yes, Krissy will be joining us later," he said, smiling and adjusted his glasses as if by habit.

Suddenly, a melodious southern voice was heard. "Y'all better come and play pool with us!"

Joining them was a striking twenty-something all-American beauty—cornsilk hair, glowing skin, white-toothed smile—fashionably dressed in indigo blue to match her eyes; her arm was around an attractive guy who wore sunglasses and had a beer in his hand.

"*Bubba*, what are you doing with my sister?"

"She's my date for tonight, Drake." After a brief handshake, he introduced himself, "Hello, I'm Joe. Joe Bellamy. Nice to meet you. And this beautiful lady is Abby."

Unlike the others she met earlier, Mercedes didn't hear a southern drawl from this man, and she tried to place the familiar accent.

"This is Mercedes. An engineer and fellow art lover from Philadelphia," Grant said smiling.

"From Buffalo?" she asked Joe.

"Close. Rochester, but I live in Memphis now. Southerners are much friendlier people," he said, looking at Abigail.

Grant said gesturing at them, "Now I don't know how comfortable I am with this—my best friend and my little sister."

"Oh hush, Grant! Stop spoiling our fun," his sister interjected. "C'mon, y'all can be partners." She squinted at Grant and challenged him. "Scared?"

Grant looked at Mercedes, "Shall we?"

"Yes, we must," she answered, matching his grin.

Together Grant and Mercedes made a powerful team, playing seamlessly as she racked and he shot the break. Later, as they kept playing against each other, she won but she couldn't imagine how she beat him.

After that night he convinced her to forsake her skis for a snowboard. He taught her to ride, and she loved watching him carve the powdery black diamond slopes like a sculptor. In contrast, she would crash again and again during her lessons and he would rescue her from steep falls. That first day they shared an intimate gondola ride when he melted her with his smile as the sun warmed the almost platinum color of his hair to match the fires she was feeling.

After a couple of days of his private snowboarding lessons, she managed to move along the slopes quite well, until she foolishly tried a trick move in the pipeline. She was feeling confident of her control, but overestimated her momentum and landed hard on her right shoulder, which she had dislocated before. She was crying in severe pain.

"Relax. I got you." He helped her to her feet.

"Okay, now bend forward at the waist. It might hurt a bit."

"I'm ready," she said, bracing herself for the imminent pain.

As he pulled her arm steadily down to stimulate the gravity effect, he applied a gentle side-to-side rotation at her wrist. At his professional steady pull, her shoulder fell into place. She slowly lifted herself up and smiled when he wiped away her tears.

"I'm so lucky you're here," she said and kissed him, but not purely out of gratitude. He welcomed her lips and began kissing her deeply.

"No, I'm the lucky one." He took his scarf off and created a makeshift sling and swathe to prevent a repeat dislocation. "Come on. I have to bring you to the hospital for x-rays. Doctor's orders."

She was grounded from the slopes, so they passed the time with their own fun at the lodge, waiting for everyone to come back from a day of fun. He would teasingly serenade her with his guitar while she nursed her healing shoulder.

That evening at the chalet, she sat down for a quiet drink by the fireplace with Grant and his family. She silently observed his mannerisms and his natural interactions with them.

"Instead of Jet, I should call you *hominy*."

"I'm not a grit!"

"No," he grinned at his sister.

"Then whatever do you mean?"

"Well," he said, still grinning, "*hominy* times do I have to tell you how pretty you are."

"Well butter my butt and call me a biscuit!" she exclaimed happily, but shot a glance over at Mercedes. "I do like that one, Grant, but I think it belongs to another pretty face."

Both Grant and Mercedes looked at each other and felt a slow rise of crimson on their faces.

"Momma, I think they're in love," she said mischievously.

"Abigail Savannah, now hush—where are your manners?" Her melodious voice was soft and motherly. Though petite and rubenesque, she exuded poise and an inner strength that becomes apparent simply through the cadence of her voice. When her voice lowered, it commanded attention with subtlety.

"Well, it's written all over their faces."

"Have you been to Memphis, Mercedes?"

"No, not really—not as a tourist," Mercedes said, thankful for the change in subject. "I'd love to visit soon, Mrs. Larcher—Dr. Larcher."

"Oh, sweet girl, please call me Anne," she said as her dark umber eyes lit up her lovely smiling face.

"Please call me Arthur," his father said, smiling. He was a tall aristocratic, confident gentleman with striking blue eyes. His strawberry blond hair, peppered with silver, was neatly combed, as was his well-trimmed mustache.

"Thank you, Arthur—Anne," she smiled, glancing at Grant. "I'm looking forward to visiting."

"You are welcome to stay at our home. We've got plenty of room. There's more to Memphis than Elvis' *Graceland*. It's the home of the blues and—oh, have you heard of the Peabody ducks?"

"Peabody ducks?"

"They're trained Mallard ducks at the Peabody Memphis Hotel. These ducks have become a Memphis icon. It's really the sweetest thing that you'll ever see. Everyday, these ducks march on the red carpet to the music of…" she paused, turning to her husband. "What song did they march to, dear?"

"I believe the song is John Philip Sousa's *King Cotton March*, honeybunch."

"Yes, that's the one," she smiled, continuing her story. "Anyway, these ducks waddle from the elevators to the marble fountain in the lobby." She giggled, "Now all this is done with the pomp and circumstance of royalty, just so they can enjoy their daily swim."

"I'd love to see that!"

"You've also got to see the Brooks Museum. Maybe Grant can show you around." Turning to Grant, she said, "I hope you'll be able to come home too. Such busy schedules my children have—I miss them all!"

"Of course he'll come home, Momma. He'd be excited showing off our fine city to his lady love."

"Abigail, would please pass the wine bottle?"

"Here you go, Daddy," she said, understanding his subtlety.

"Thanks, Abby." After freshening his wife's glass, he turned to Grant, "Have you tried this Cuban cigar, son?"

"No, sir, I haven't, but I'd love to try if you have another one."

"Yes, I do. Let's have one after our drinks. And Mercedes, you are welcome to join us for one as well."

"Yes, I'd like that—thank you."

Mercedes enjoyed the shift of Grant's voice when he spoke "shop" with his father. She also enjoyed his father's deep formal cadence, which shifted only when he spoke to his wife—the tenderness was apparent.

"Why neurosurgery, Arthur?"

"The functions of the *amygdala*—those almond-shaped structures within the basal ganglia of the brain—lured me. The *amygdala* participates in the regulation of emotion, attention, memory and decision-making." His voice resonated with intelligence and southern class.

"The seat of feeling in the brain," she offered.

"I see you know your *amygdala* as well," he said, sounding pleased. "Well, that's one interpretation."

"I'm familiar with how it enhances memory during stress—events are well remembered."

"That's the flashbulb effect," Grant said, joining the conversation. "Patients, who've experienced severe trauma, have both a flashbulb memory of some images of the traumatic as well as an unusually fragmented episodic memory of the entire event."

"Really?" Mercedes asked, genuinely impressed. "So it truly influences memory storage and consolidation, enhancing the memory of events that happen during a state of emotional arousal. Even a nightmare?"

"Yes, even a nightmare," Arthur said, setting his vodka martini down. "Its function remains an enigma. The debate has continued for almost two centuries."

"And it's not continuing here tonight, dear."

"No, not tonight, honeybunch."

"I'm glad y'all stopped talking about the *magdala*," Abigail said, without masking her boredom, purposefully mispronouncing the word. "It's just not complicated in the world of fashion. I'm glad all I have to have is a good eye for fashions and trends. And buy it." Turning to Mercedes, she said, "By the way, I just love what you're wearing tonight. It's Versace, isn't it? I just love that red color."

"Yes, it is."

"I thought I recognized it on the runway when I was in Milan. Have you been?"

Shaking her head, she replied, "Just to Rome, Florence and Venice."

"Aren't you going to Rome soon, Momma?"

"Yes, your father and I are going on a pilgrimage there," she said, gazing at her husband, "It'll give us a chance to catch up."

"Looking forward to it, honeybunch," he said smiling.

Grant's parents were so much like hers in how they were with each other. *Another pair of soul mates.* It gave her hope.

After enjoying an authentic Cuban cigar, Grant drove Mercedes back to her hotel at the ski resort. She began to feel nauseous.

"Ugh! I feel like I'm going to be sick," she said, grimacing. "I think I need to lie down."

Grant chuckled, "I warned you not to smoke the whole thing."

"But, but it tasted so good and sweet." Lying down, she said, "I'm never trying that again! How can you stand it?"

"Here, have some ice chips—you'll feel better. I promise."

After a few minutes, the nausea passed, but she began wincing with pain.

"What's wrong?"

Pouting, she said, "My shoulder. I feel like my body is falling apart."

"Let me check." After a professional examination, he said, "It looks fine to me. You just need time for it to heal."

"Are you sure? Could you look a little closer?"

"Sure, right here?" he asked, a little flushed, as he felt her bare skin.

"Yes, just a little closer," she said sweetly.

"Oh you mean, right here."

"Uh-huh." Their lips met and with careful maneuvering around her dislocated shoulder, they both peeled off the layers of their clothing without breaking the kiss they shared. His heart was beating hard, but no harder than her own.

As he lowered himself upon her, her skin quivered. She devoured his kisses that matched hers. She could feel the effort with which he kept himself in check.

Little by little, he let her go. She was delighted with his control; she had never experienced it with any other man.

Without blushing, he paid attention and listened to her suggestions and surprised her with a few of his own. He knew exactly the right places to touch her which would immediately have her seeing fireworks.

"Wow! Something they taught you at medical school?" she asked breathlessly.

"I did a lot of homework."

They laughed and made love again. They spent much of their time indoors that vacation.

"Stop, stop, I need to get something to drink. I'm parched!"

"Wait right here, I'll get you something to quench that thirst. Now don't you go anywhere, *purdy darlin*?" Smiling widely, he got up from the bed to put on his clothes.

"I'll be waiting right here," she said, matching his smile, and admiring his fine bare physique. She waited for him impatiently.

"Here you go. I got us tonic and lime. I find that it quenches my thirst quite nicely." Smiling, he began stroking her leg.

Suddenly, she started draining the drink down her throat.

"Whoa, slow down now or you'll choke."

With southern inflections, she said, "I've got another thirst that needs some other kind of quenching," pulling him down their newly rumpled sheets. She giggled under the sheets.

"I'm happy to oblige," he said with a very deep drawl. "You are why art exists and songs are written. You make mortal men want to weep."

She loved to listen to him turn on the southern charm, and equally charming was how he tried to shake his natural speech inflections. She still heard his drawl when he was very excited about a topic.

Even now, they tried to cram as much quality time together as possible while fighting both her travel schedule and his damnable on-call schedule. Yet their relationship suited her well because she too had a crazy schedule and she valued her personal time alone.

She cared deeply for him and she viewed him as the proverbial good doctor—the good guy. But it was his bad-boy edge that excited her, especially when he rode his motorcycle. She'd ride with him through the streets of Philadelphia, feeling free and reckless. She adored his musician persona with his dark shades, tousled long hair, leather jacket, and diamond stud on his left earlobe that matched hers.

She went to many of his band gigs in different bars in Philadelphia. She loved listening to him sing, especially right to her. He would often try his new compositions on stage, and the ladies around her would be swooning, but he paid zero attention to any of them. His eyes and his sexy smile were glued on her.

* * *

When the music of Mozart had stopped, Mercedes sighed deeply, placing the note in her purse after reading it again.

She fought to hold onto the warmth of her memories and Grant's image, but her thoughts continually turned to Joe, as if her mind knew exactly where her heart was heading.

Chapter 12

March 22nd, Sydney

"The chocolates were sinfully delicious, thank you. Why can't Patrick be as thoughtful as you? I can't remember the last time my husband gave me flowers just because."

Mercedes heard Sydney's deep sigh and the sound of her lighting a cigarette.

"God, Merc, I feel so angry! I wish I could do something to hurt him!"

"I don't know if I like the sounds of that. You've got to think things through with a clear head." Sydney's behavior was very uncharacteristic of her, which unsettled Mercedes.

"Oh, but I did," Sydney said nefariously, taking a long drag from her cigarette.

"When did you start smoking?"

"When my filthy, no good, rotten, son-of-a-bitch husband cheated on me!" The reply was loud and angry.

She hoped that Sydney wouldn't delve into one of her conspiracy theories, but she did. "Do you know Dante has lusted after me for some time now? I had hoped that when I set him up with you that he would forget about me. But, oh no, you turned around and rejected him! Now he's putting the moves on me." There was a menacing tone in her remark.

"Syd, I didn't know."

"Well, if you don't want him, I may just take him up on the offer and show Patrick that two can play this game. As you put it last night, it might be time for me to have some mindless entertainment while I'm making up my mind about what to do."

Oh no, you don't! Mercedes shrieked in her thoughts, realizing she had inadvertently played into Sydney's insidious plan. She wasn't going to allow herself to be Sydney's scapegoat. It was never going to happen.

It was also frustrating because she understood where Sydney was coming from. It was quite natural to strike back. Her wound was fresh and needed immediate relief.

Mercedes felt her mind racing as she wondered how she was going to convince her to forgo her plans. It was going to be difficult to dissuade Sydney, knowing her fierce determination.

Infidelity was not the answer; it was not the way to mend her heart or her broken trust. Trying infidelity as revenge against Patrick would inevitably hurt her, not Patrick. That was the nature of self-fulfilling prophecies. She needed to diffuse this quickly!

"Sydney," Mercedes pleaded, "I'm sorry but I must protest. I care too much for you to accompany you down that sort of a dark path. You know it's not the answer. You've got to stop and think—think really hard, before you give in to that lying little voice of despair that's tempting you, trying to convince you to do something when you're feeling vulnerable! Please, sweetie, you're not thinking clearly. Deep in your heart, in your soul—you have to know this isn't going to turn back the hands of time! Promise me. Promise me, right now, you won't do a thing, okay? When I get back in town, we'll talk, but for now don't do anything foolish to hurt yourself. Please, just promise me!"

And when she only heard a deep sigh, she asked again, sweetly but demandingly, "Promise?"

"How can I, Merc? If I do what you want, I won't get what I desperately want! I want your blessings and for you to agree to help me with my plans. I want you to agree with my decisions and to tell me I'm right! God, Merc! I want to feel better about my decision to be just like Patrick. I need to stop feeling this pain!"

Sydney was stammering, and Mercedes could tell from her tone that she was confused and very frustrated. Torment filled Sydney's voice, "I—I don't know. Damn it, Merc! I don't know!"

"Syd! Promise me. Please."

"Why are you always the voice of reason? I know I should listen to you, but I don't want to!"

"Promise me!" There was no answer except for a deep inhale.

She knew when Sydney's emotions overwhelmed her, she did things she regretted and used her stubborn pride to justify everything to make her feel that she was doing the right thing.

"Do you still love Patrick?" she asked bluntly.

"Oh God!" she gasped, "with all my fucking heart! Despite his callousness, his disrespect, I still love him. I desperately love him!" Agony filled her voice, and she started weeping and debasing him profusely once again. "I hate him! I hate him! I hate him!"

Mercedes was alarmed at her friend's tearful outburst, and she couldn't help but cry with her. She felt so much empathy for her friend. She knew the angst of love Sydney was feeling. She knew it all too well. Unintentionally, she said aloud, "With love, we must suffer. With love, we must forgive," and immediately regretting her spontaneous soliloquy.

Sydney immediately began to sob louder, crying, "Stop it, STOP IT! I CAN'T! I JUST CAN'T!"

In between sobs she kept explaining how she wanted to get revenge, and finally be vindicated without being so irrational. "I want to forgive him, I really do, but this pain is unbearable! I'd rather die and finally end this pain, but I can't! I can't leave my children, I can't—they need me. Merc, what am I going to do?"

"All right, Syd. It's all right. Please relax, sweetie. Just relax. Would you do that for me? All right, let's calm down—refocus. Get your control back. I'm here. I'm not going anywhere. Okay?"

Throughout their entire conversation, she could hear her continually smoking, and now she heard her swallowing a drink quickly and then pouring another glass. "You can't drown the pain away. It's not the answer."

"Right now, Mr. Bacardi Rum is the only answer I've got. I just want to get drunk, and be numb to everything."

"Is Cassie there with you?"

"No, she took the kids to a movie. She'll be dropping them off at Mom's to give me some space while I think of what I want to say to Patrick when he gets in on Friday." Sydney's voice seemed to gain a measure of control and she was even a bit cynical when she said with deep sarcasm in her tone, "If the bastard ever decides to come home."

Mercedes knew not to go another round in Sydney's roller coaster with her menacing phantom conversations. *I just despise phantom conversations!*

She just wanted to make sure she was calm and safe. She said lovingly, "Syd, sweetie. Know that I am here for you. No matter what! I just need some reassurance that you're going to be, all right tonight. I've got to know you're going to be fine. Would you do that for me, please?"

As if realizing that she had put her best friend in a precarious situation, Sydney quickly reverted to her old self, saying ruefully, "I'm so sorry, hon. I've been dumping all of this shit on you." She sighed and said sincerely, "Honestly, I'm actually feeling better now. Much, much better. Believe me. I'm planning on staying in and just sulking all night. I promise you I won't do anything I'd regret later. I promise."

Relieved to hear Sydney's promise, her *word*, Mercedes knew there was no question of its honor. Finally reassured, she said, "I'll check in on you later, okay?"

"Sure. Okay." Before hanging up, Sydney added, "Thanks for putting up with me, you're precious."

Sydney's voice was a bit slurred, but to Mercedes it sounded like Sydney had reverted to normal. She heard Sydney pour another drink, which was worrisome. "Bye, Syd. Remember, take care of yourself."

"You too, Merc. You too."

Mercedes glanced at the time as she hung up the phone. She was running late so she decided not to change for dinner, but she hurriedly made one more call to leave a clever numeric message on Grant's pager, thanking him for the anniversary card.

Then, she swiftly grabbed her pocketbook and headed out the door to the elevator.

Chapter 13

March 22nd, The Call

Joe was wearing his aviator shades when he entered the briefing room, but he took them off when he took the open seat next to Hannibal in front of Spyder. The three of them started recounting the flight as everyone else was filing into the briefing room.

Nitro stood in attention before a large white screen that was positioned against the wall. His appearance was a silent demand for attention and it was heeded.

He began talking about air combat excellence as he gestured for one of them to turn off the lights.

Joe began to feel the effects of sleep deprivation as he struggled to listen to Nitro. Nitro had started a computer-generated videotape of the day's sortie and expanded his discourse on air combat maneuvers, or ACM. Joe was thankful that this was the last de-brief of the day.

Joe knew he had done well again today during the sortie. He observed and paid attention to his lead, following him like an unshakeable shadow. Nitro was winding down on ACM, shifting to MiG tactics and technology, when Spyder leaned over and whispered, "Phantom, you look like shit! Long night?" Hannibal also gave him an inquisitive look, making it clear he also had noticed Joe's exhaustion.

Joe glanced at Hannibal and just smirked before turning to Spyder. But before he could say anything, Nitro walked by them, saying almost directly to them, "So we had best be sharp, gentlemen!" Nitro turned the lights back on and returned to the front of the room, barking out, "Dismissed."

Joe quickly gathered his notes and put his aviator shades back on, pre-occupied. He left the briefing room before his buddies and hurriedly headed toward the life support shop and his locker where his flight gear on a peg, was stored.

Hannibal and Spyder quickly caught up with him, curious about his apparent lack of sleep. "Hey, Phantom, out all night?" They knew he was secretive about his personal life, and each of them wanted to take the opportunity to find out more about current events.

"A certain gorgeous, tropical woman!" Spyder blurted out. "I want details."

"Sorry, that's classified," he said, almost laughing. Joe made it a policy never to mix his personal life with his career. It was a rule he kept fiercely and relentlessly. There was no way anyone was going to pry personal information from him, especially sensitive and compromising details.

"Come on, Phantom," Hannibal probed, "Why are you being so mysterious about your personal life, buddy?"

Joe saw the two of them look at each other and watched as they tried to double-team him, expecting their joint covert efforts would succeed in prying loose some details of his secret rendezvous.

"What are you hiding, Phantom?" Spyder shook his head, as if acknowledging he had tried hard before, but always managed to hit a brick wall.

Hannibal grinned, "It's clear who captivated her attention, and whoa! I believe Phantom's definitely smitten with her, too. Remember, we joked about it while we waited in the car?" He turned to Joe, "In fact, we made a wager that you were going to score with her that evening."

Joe ignored the jibe and grinned at them, knowing their imaginations were not as sweet as the real thing, the intimate details—all of it!

"C'mon, Phantom. Something must've happened, inquiring minds want to know," Spyder pressed.

For a moment, the temptation to share the incredible details of her was irresistible. Joe felt like he was bursting at the seams. He felt incredibly happy and he wanted to shout it out. Everything with her felt like it was part of a movie scene he never thought he would be in.

There were so many coincidences and feelings of *déjà vu* that had almost seemed too uncanny. He and Mercedes were so attuned to each other. They seemed perfectly matched. They even looked great together.

Joe began to smile, thinking of her and the previous night. Then, wallowing in the idea of torturing the two jocks, he said, "Spyder, give it up. Nothing to tell. No. Stand down, Hannibal! Don't you get started, either!"

Spyder said, grinning, "I don't believe you! Something definitely happened."

Joe laughed and said, "You know what, something did happen—you flyboys passed out two seconds after I left the car! You should've seen how sweet the two of you looked, clinging onto each other in the backseat. I laughed my ass off. But, hey, believe what you want. There's still nothing to tell." He laughed, trying to shake their confidence.

Hannibal shook his head, "Yeah, I do remember waking up and Spyder was up against me. His arm draped around my shoulder!"

"Shut up, Hannibal!"

After a fit of laughter, Hannibal said to Joe, "Damn! Where do you find the energy?"

"Energy?"

"Yeah, energy for Red Flag *and* a woman. What's your secret? How do you manage to function, let alone stay awake? I'm damned useless after a day of sleep deprivation," he confessed.

"Yeah, been there—done that—and damn! I won't hesitate to do it, again!" Spyder shared with a grin.

Inevitably after pressing him further, they gave up, understanding his silence and respecting his privacy while still hoping he would open up one drunken evening. Alcohol often loosened up even the most silent tongue. Since Joe gave up drinking for Lent, the opportunities never presented themselves. Regardless, he kept his drinking in moderation anyway, because he was taught one too many lessons about the serious ramifications of drinking to excess, so he never put himself in a precarious situation when he could control it.

Their suspicions and inquiries were hitting too close to home and it was getting uncomfortable. Yet, Joe never yielded but kept his impenetrable guard up. He simply continued to ignore both of them. They were still speaking together, a murmur of voices, distant and inconsequential.

Spyder and Hannibal's banter simply blurred into the background, mixing with the voices of the other pilots in the shop as all of them hurriedly changed and, sensing he wanted his space, they headed off with a friendly wave toward the Officers Club without waiting for him.

* * *

Joe remained stoic and began to peel out of his combat edge G-suit. He had other important things in his mind: a phone call he needed to make.

When he got back to the squadron's hotel, he picked up the telephone handset and dialed.

"Hello?" The voice was melodiously sweet and womanly.

"Hey, Eva—how are you?" He wasn't sure how he felt, hearing her voice when all he could think of was Mercedes, but he had the entire phone conversation ready in his mind. He knew exactly how he was going to handle himself and where the conversation needed to go.

"What have you been doing?"

"The usual. Working at the gym, still getting paid to keep in shape," she said trying to sound nonchalant, though he heard her sigh. She went on, "I went to the salon today."

"Got pampered, I hope."

"I had my hair layered and highlighted with this nice shade of auburn. I also couldn't resist a perm. I hope you'll like it." She sounded tentative.

"How short is it now?"

"I can still pull it into a ponytail." There was a pause.

"Eva?"

"Yes."

"Are you all right?"

"Not really. I was just at the *Hearts Apart* program over at the Family Support Center. I think I'm getting a little more patient, but I'm still hoping things will change. Everyone keeps reassuring me that I'll get use to your long temporary duties. I miss you every time you're gone. Damn it! I'm tired of having to attend this Family Readiness shit!" He had hoped that she wasn't resenting him for his long absences because a TDY was simply a fact with their lives in the military.

For the last couple of years, they had been having an extremely rough time, in part due to his constant TDY's that often lasted for three months. And right now he was realizing that Eva never quite lit the fire in him like Mercedes had in just an evening. In the beginning she had, but it fizzled out within the last year, and, like Mercedes, he had an insatiable appetite for a passionate, physical relationship. Worse, he felt he was pretty rough to live with anyway because of his strong type-A personality.

Flight surgeons assessed him as having the stereotypical fighter pilot's personality. He was independent, controlling, active and goal-directed. He was the ideal candidate for his type of flying assignments. He was cautious in close personal relationships. He hated uncertainty or failure, and sometimes he found himself intensely uncomfortable with strong personal emotions. There were many things in life he could not control, though he tried. He knew he wouldn't be able to deny the strong feelings he was having for Mercedes. He welcomed them.

Eva and Mercedes. Both occupied his mind. They were beautiful women with Spanish heritage, except Eva was a hot-blooded Latina, seven years older than Mercedes. Uncannily, they shared the same middle name.

He met Eva shortly before the Gulf War. He had been charming, and she had eagerly fulfilled his voracious appetite, but fulfilling it was more for his benefit than hers. He tried to be romantic, sensitive and gentle, but was not entirely consistent with her. At times he would slip into a mood of indifference; at other times, he was a genuine pain in the ass!

She had once said, "*Mi amor,* I love hearing your voice. You're such a sweet talker. You know just what to say. You just know how to melt my heart and you know it, don't you?" He knew she was desperately in love with him. It gave him the upper hand.

"You're really quiet. Is something troubling you? Is something wrong?"

Joe felt the tension growing between them, and he knew she couldn't understand why he just wouldn't open up to her.

"*Amor*, I miss how it used to be when we were dating. We had such a wonderful romance. I was like putty, but lately, lately it's been difficult. You're away on so many different assignments and I'm here alone continually. I don't want to be a complainer, but like right now, I don't have any close friends nearby, and I spend my time always pining for you to come home." Joe heard her trying to find ways to bridge the miles between them.

Their reunions were always intense. The last time he came home, after months of separation when he was in another desert location, they had been together practically every night, until she had to protest, unable to keep up with him. He then went again for months in yet another desert location. The realities of life caught up with them.

"Eva, I can't change that. It's part of being a fighter pilot." Joe knew her life became routine, even mundane and somewhat weary. He also knew that inevitably, the vicious cycle of separation would begin again and her emotions would return into a frenzied state. It was an endless roller coaster ride.

"The loneliness is tearing me up. It's unbearable at times, especially in the bed at night." She sighed.

"Maybe you need to get out more when I'm gone. You know I trust you."

"I know. You've had no reason not to." There was a hint of guilt in her voice. "I did run into a friend from college, Billy Tavish, a week or so ago. Remember Billy? I think I told you about him a while ago. Anyway, it was nice to see him, to rekindle our friendship. I'm really glad that you don't mind that I love to keep in close contact with my friends, even my old boyfriends."

"Yes, I do remember you telling me about Billy and no, I don't mind." He never minded when she kept in touch with her old flames. He trusted her, and it gave her trust and confidence in him.

"I love that about you. I just wish you would show some raw jealousy, some protective anger once in a while, just to make me feel passionately wanted. I miss the passion, the early passion of our relationship. But I still love you."

Joe knew that somehow the passion they shared wasn't as complete as either of them wanted or had imagined it would be.

"Does Billy still have his college crush on you?"

"Oh, I don't know, but he kept saying how lucky you were to have me. He said it was really great to see me again too. I was flattered when he said I looked more beautiful than he remembered. We were tennis buddies back then. He remembered a game of ours when I beat him with my backhand. I think he was distracted which is why I won."

"I assume he's still in good shape."

"Yes. He's a licensed physical therapist now. Do you remember I told you he was in the same classes as me?"

"You were in a relationship with Kevin then, right?"

"Yes. I was exclusively seeing Kevin at the time."

"Did you play tennis this week?"

"Yes, we played a few great sets of tennis. He still handles his racquet much the same as he did in college. You've never met Billy, have you? The two of you could actually pass as brothers, especially at first glance. Maybe that's why I'm comfortable around him. Just the other day, he called to check up on me, knowing I was home alone. We ended up going to dinner and a movie."

"Sounds like a date," he teased.

"Now, why can't you say that with a jealous tone?"

"You know I don't get jealous."

"Yes, I know."

Joe was listening to the silence on the line, wondering what she was thinking. When she had first answered the phone and heard his voice, she had seemed excited to hear from him. But over the last few minutes her voice had changed, it was almost as if she had been waiting to speak to him and that what she was going to say depended entirely on him.

"Eva. Are you okay?"

"I'm fine."

He felt her answer was disturbingly cold. After thinking about it for a moment, he became a little annoyed with her curt answer. "That's it—fine? I haven't talked to you in a couple days."

"I know. I had expected you'd call sooner. I just wish you would check in everyday," she sounded irritated. "Where were you?"

He was slighted with the way her tone sounded. She wasn't the welcoming person he had known. It was a leading question, and he was annoyed, "What do you mean? I'm flying all day."

"All night, too? I've tried to get a hold of you, but no answer. I'm tired of leaving you messages. Good thing I have Billy to talk to now."

They had many similar conversations in the past year. Military life often made it difficult on a relationship, especially with the rigors of being a fighter pilot. The constant separation wore through the strongest of relationships. He had known many other men in his squadron who had to contend with troubled relationships and marital strife. He just didn't want to rehash any old conversations, especially with Mercedes on his mind. "Look. You know I don't need this right now. Why are you giving me such a hard time?"

"I don't like the way our relationship has been going, especially in past few months. You're avoiding things. Are you happy with me, Joe?"

He was caught off guard with her question, his mind jumped to Mercedes when she mentioned being happy. He responded, "Of course I am"

"Then, why don't you show it?"

"I didn't realize I wasn't."

"It just goes to show you that you aren't paying attention to the obvious. And do me a favor, please drop the charm, I'm not in the mood." The disdain was clear in her voice.

Her caustic remark destroyed his patience. He didn't want to get into verbal blows with her, especially today. Wanting a shift in the conversation he said, "The obvious? Eva, why don't you just stop beating around the bush and tell me, what is so obvious?"

Infuriated by his attempt to turn the tables, she simply blurted out, "We need to end this! End us!"

Hearing her words, he was genuinely surprised and secretly happy. It would make everything so much easier in the long run because he would have the opportunity to pursue Mercedes with a clear conscience. *Is there something going on with her, too?*

"End us? Did I hear you correctly?"

In a muffled voice, he thought he heard her say angry words in Spanish.

"Eva, I really can't hear you. Speak closer to the phone." The silence dragged on, yet he could hear her crying.

"You heard me, Joe. I'm fulfilling your unspoken dream. Your actions speak louder than your words."

This was not how he had imagined the conversation to turn out. She was trying to lead him somewhere, but he was not going to allow it. He despised head games and he would never let her win. Besides, he had other things he wanted to say to her. He wanted to get right to her point so he could be forthright about Mercedes. He said, "You know, Eva. This has been going on long enough. Why don't we just stop this right now and you can tell me exactly what's going on?"

There was another uncomfortable silence. A moment of uncertainty and foreboding invaded his thoughts but he quickly dismissed it. He was about to say something when she said, "I'm pregnant." Her sobs became uncontrollable.

He pushed the phone closer to his ear, wondering if he had heard her right. "Pregnant?"

"Yes. Pregnant."

The phone went dead, and the silence became a void surrounding him. He sat thinking about the phone call, the words still ringing in his ear. *Shit! I can't believe this is happening! Especially now!*

His feelings were threatening to overwhelm him. He had not anticipated such untimely news. He wasn't certain how to respond, especially since he was seeing Mercedes in just a few hours.

Joe had to consider more that just Eva's pregnancy. His entire military career was at stake. The military frowned greatly upon misconduct and love affairs were not exempted. He and everyone else in the military lived by the Uniform Code of Military Justice. Everyone in the armed forces had to have impeccable conduct. What he was doing with Mercedes was not a precarious sexual affair. It was not even close, but he knew it would be viewed as such, given the facts, especially by an outsider with zero insight about the strong emotions associated with the triangle he was in. Fate was playing a hand in his life and he knew it. His thoughts raced.

A beautiful love affair could be easily misconstrued and turned into something ugly. It would become a fiasco. There was no way he could defend himself properly. How could he possibly defend himself when he reached the same conclusion an outsider would reach? What he was doing was even grounds for dishonorable discharge.

He was not going to be dragged into the public eye to be dissected and scrutinized unmercifully. A spectacle. He could withstand it, but Eva wouldn't be able to. Nor could Mercedes.

He had to make an important decision. A detached decision. It had to be swift and final. There was no other solution. He called on his military training to help him handle the situation. He had to remain in control.

With his thoughts racing between Eva and Mercedes, he put on his headphones, and listened to music of *Enigma*. As always, the soothing chants of the

Gregorian monks put him in a relaxed mode, letting the music to lull him into a much-needed catnap.

By the time he woke, he had made his decision. It might not be the best decision for him, but when he thought of Mercedes, he couldn't help smiling.

Chapter 14

March 22nd, Fate

As it came closer to 9:00 p.m., Mercedes felt a need to listen to modern Gregorian chants to calm her spirit as she anxiously waited for his knock on her door.

The city lights were casting a magnificent blaze of color against the desert sky when she heard a soft rap at the door. Once again she could feel her heart beating as loudly as the chants of the monks.

She quickly opened her door and was greeted with an enticing smile from a devastatingly handsome man who was bearing two wineglasses and a bottle of finely aged Merlot.

"Hello, JC," she smiled shyly.

"Hi, how are you?" he said, kissing her softly as he entered the room.

"Much better now that you are here, my Captain," she teased. She shut the door behind her as he put the wineglasses on her bedside table. Opening the bottle, he took a moment to gaze at her.

She was wearing her red business suit with the short tight skirt, and the sight of her white camisole peeking through her jacket stirred him. He poured the wine and offered a glass to her, the most exquisite woman he had ever had the pleasure to be with.

"I enjoyed our evening at Excalibur last night," she said, taking the glass from his hand. "I've always been fond of the Renaissance period—the romance of Camelot, chivalry, magic."

He kissed her hand, enjoying the sweet perfume on her skin.

"To my lady." He raised his glass to her.

"To my knight in a shining F-16." Her soft response and laugh completed the toast. After their wineglasses touched, he took a sip of his wine and beckoned her to come closer. She gladly did what he wanted, smiling, closing her eyes as their lips touched. The taste of the wine and the moisture of his lips left her breathless.

When they set their glasses on the table, the moment turned unusually somber. She felt the distinct shift and looked at him for silent signs that would help her understand the instant chill that had run down her spine.

"We need to talk." His voice was almost as soft as a whisper as he gently brushed the tendrils of her hair off her shoulder. She sensed something was not right. Her thoughts began to race, but quickly she quieted her mind before kissing him gently on the lips. That kiss instantly turned into a series of passionate kisses that showed how hot the fire between them was still burning. She wanted to be with him, but she also wanted to know what he needed to tell her.

"Tell me whatever you wish, JC," she responded with a sweet shy smile. He gazed at her, wanting to let his hands caress her, loving the intimate feelings he felt.

Sighing deeply, he stroked his hands over her cheeks, once more kissing her with burning passion. For a fleeting moment he forgot what he needed to say. He just wanted to be with her, to make love to her. Should he wait until later? He didn't want to lose her. Not yet. She might end this evening and fly out of his life forever as soon as he revealed what he needed to share. His truth.

She was holding his gaze with such care. Her caring gave him the courage to take the risk. He had to be completely honest with her. He wouldn't attempt to lie to her now. It simply wasn't their way, and he knew it.

"Mercedes, I need to tell you more about myself. I need to be completely honest with you about myself," he hesitated for a moment before taking her hand in his and saying, "I'm married."

She instinctively looked at his left hand for a wedding band, though she knew he wasn't wearing one. She looked up and stared intently into his blue eyes, trying to comprehend his words. His eyes professed a tenderness and desire that caught her completely off-guard, as his words had.

In her thoughts she told herself, *It must be a mistake. Yes, of course, he must mean he's separated!* Was she grasping for straws? She had to be sure.

She stumbled awkwardly for the right words, "JC, I—I think, I understand. I mean, I do understand. I'm separated, but I'm still legally married." She still kept looking for an invisible sign to affirm her thoughts, "That is what you mean, right? JC?"

For the first time in her life, she was at a loss for words, unable to even come up with a silent prayer for the impossible. She even wanted him to lie to her. Then she realized how incredibly stupid she felt. She was loosing her mind to her heart—she needed to regain her composure, her confidence and her self-respect. She braced herself for the truth.

"No, Mercedes. I'm not separated. And—and there's something else I need to tell you." He braced himself for their final moment together and in a melancholy voice, he confessed, "A few hours ago, I found out my wife is pregnant."

Nothing could have prepared her for his words. They shattered her, sending a sharp invisible arrow firmly into her. She felt as though he had fatally wounded her. She had not expected the incredible burning pain in her heart that took her breath away and made her resolve crumble.

The silence between them was as still as a midnight solstice. Suddenly, the soft music in the background became deafening as the words, *dit moi*, invaded the silence. *This sounds all too familiar.*

She embraced the music and the words tell me, *dit moi*, over and over again in her mind. *Oh, mon Dieu! My premonition! Oh God—I knew, I knew this was coming!*

Inside she argued with herself viciously, not noticing that she had begun the doomed phantom conversation that would haunt her. Were his lips moving? She could only hear his words, "my wife." The words resonated brutally in her mind while on the outside she was strangely calm. She couldn't help but think—or was she remembering? She began thinking in different languages as she often did at times of crisis. *Pitié sur moi, mon Dieu! Why can't I think?*

She was flooded with emotions as Sydney immediately entered her mind. Her thoughts screamed, *How can I be true to Sydney, now? To what I was telling her to do? What about his wife? What is she like? I don't even know her name! Does she know? Does she know about me? About us? Of course not! If she did, she'd be devastated, just like Sydney!*
A shudder ran through her, *Good God! Now I'm the other woman! This is not who I am! His wife is pregnant! My dearest wish is now his reality, but he is having his child with her, not with me! He would never leave his wife, his child. His convictions were as strong as mine.* Shock flowed over her, holding her in an icy grip. *How could I be everything that I've always vowed never to become! No, NO! This isn't happening to me!*
It was a nightmare and she kept praying for a miracle. She kept hoping she would wake up any minute now! The phantom conversation, the dreams she felt so often were at their full height. She forced herself to think, knowing she couldn't. *Why don't I know what I'm feeling? Do I feel humiliated? Used? Disgusted? Am I angry? What am I? This is crazy! Frustrating! How can I let this affect me this way?*
She stood rooted, remaining as silent and calm as she could. The conflicts were tearing her logical mind apart. She hated it! She had never felt comfortable with anyone until him. She had always had to control her emotions and her heart. She built a formidable fortress around it, and in one swoop he had taken down her walls and left her vulnerable, and now she was almost bleeding. *Why does he possess such power over me? Why do I still trust him? WHY!*
She had always been able to detach herself easily from any relationship. Even Grant knew that about her. In her mind an argument was raging, *Be an ice queen! Don't waste any energy on a surreal relationship! Move on. This is fantasy! You have to move on. Life has to move on. It always does! Damn it, damn you!*
She coached herself, still not having spoken a word out loud to him. *Okay, be calm. Just do it—let go. Let go, right now! Shit! What is wrong with me? Why can't I do this! I feel completely powerless! What is the matter with me?*
She felt completely exposed. And numb. She felt the wave of numbness swiftly consuming her. She simply wanted to disappear.
Like the proverbial ton of bricks falling on her, she realized she was trying to resist fate! She believed in fate with all her heart. Something incredibly powerful, something beyond chance was guiding them, causing their paths to cross.
Her dreams, her life circumstances and her premonitions had led her to him. She was tempted, very tempted, to throw away all logic, to let destiny lead her to the right decision. All she needed was a sign, even a silent sign, to point the way. *Fate.* The little voice in her head said. *All he has to do is say one word. If he's truly the one, he will say the word fate!*
Her heart and mind were battling. She needed one word to nudge her off the precipice she was standing in front of. For him she would take that leap without any regrets. But without the right word from him, she remained motionless, standing in stunned silence.
She wasn't reacting as Joe had anticipated. He sensed her conflicted thoughts, and he knew he had to speak the absolute truth with the emotion he felt in his heart or he would lose her completely.
"Before you say anything, I want you to know that you make me feel like I'm totally alive again. I haven't felt this happy in a very long time." He paused and looked deeply into her eyes, wondering what the right words were to say. Finally, he said, "Fate...call it fate, call it destiny—I somehow know that this was

meant to be! Perhaps in a different lifetime we were together. I feel our souls are connected. I can be completely myself with you—good, bad or indifferent. I've never felt like this with anyone!"

Her mind was spinning, her heart was elated, and a voice inside her said, *He said it! He said fate.*

Hearing his voice and his words, she felt as if the memories of a thousand lifetimes were being released in her mind and at this crossroad, fate was guiding them to meet. She knew now was not the time to falter. She was not one to indulge in gambling, yet she knew for the first time that she was taking the biggest gamble of her life. She had to take the risk, now.

She made up her mind. There was no turning back. All the important things, everything in its collective whole, were not more important than this one moment. They were together at this very moment, facing each other after so very long. Knowing it, she surrendered herself to fate. Their fate.

God forgive me, she confessed in her mind. Without needing to utter a word, she simply leaned over and kissed him with all the passion that was inside her. She wanted him to feel her heart. She wanted her passion to give voice to the words she lacked the courage to say.

Feeling his lips on hers, she knew she would sacrifice anything even if she only had but a moment with him. For in that moment, she would have a lifetime with him and she was going to take it. Now.

From her kisses, Joe was overwhelmed with a sensation he couldn't describe, an instant crushing passion, shattering his senses and all rational thought. It was intoxicating. Spontaneously, he pulled her toward him and began to slowly kiss her neck and nibble gently on her ear.

She took his hand and guided it to her breasts, letting out a quiet moan when he touched her through her camisole. She lifted his shirt off over his shoulders.

He slipped her jacket off her shoulders, letting it drop unheeded as he lifted her camisole. Gently, he lowered her onto the bed.

She reached for the snap on his pants and unzipped them. She watched as he undressed in front of her as if in slow motion.

Without speaking he unzipped her skirt, knelt, lowered his head and started kissing and exploring her sensual body. His breathing grew deeper as he savored her perfumed skin.

She ran her fingers through his soft cropped hair and down his neck. He slowly ran his tongue up, over her stomach, kissing the soft skin between her breasts. He took the hot erect tip of one breast into his mouth while his hand felt the wet silkiness between her legs.

His touch melted with her soft whimper. Stiff with passion, he wanted her. And she wanted him. Her eyes now locked with his, she pulled herself up and rolled on top of him. Her stunning beauty was overwhelming in the soft light. Her long dark hair and slender petite body were shining in its soft glow. He felt her delicate hands exploring and touching him.

She could taste his growing anticipation as she lowered her head. His body responded in delight, and she took him to the point where he had to have her. He needed to have her.

As he guided her up, she felt her hot breath brush against him, along with her soft shimmering hair. With a natural ease, she slipped her knees around his hips, sitting astride him and flashing him a seductive smile as she lowered herself onto him.

He could feel heat flash over his body as every inch of him slowly, lovingly entered her. He reached out and touched her breasts, feeling them growing fuller in his hands. She took his index finger and placed it in her mouth, caressing it with her tongue.

She leaned forward and pressed both his hands against the bed unwilling to yield total control to him. He devoured her kisses as he moved rhythmically within her, beneath her. His matched her moans of delight as he kept burying himself deep inside her. He closed his eyes and listened to her short gasps of pleasure as she moved on top of him.

"Joe, JC." His name on her lips hurled him higher.

With one fluid motion, he was on top, their rhythm unbroken. She felt his gentle strength and the fire in his soul. Even with her eyes closed, she felt the intensity of each delicious wave rocking them.

He could feel her muscles contracting, causing him to gasp as his breathing became more labored. He could feel her nails digging into his back. His appetite for her grew instantaneously. They rolled over and he grabbed onto her from behind. Rapidly, he took her to new heights, over and over again.

She arched her back, melting her body with his, deepening their reunion.

Momentarily, a vivid vision flashed in her mind, triggering an ancient memory of their coupling in another life, in another time. At that very moment she knew they had just conceived their child. The vision was so clear; she could feel herself growing light-headed and her heart pounded erratically. She cried aloud and trembled beneath him, causing him to lose control. In a sinuous frenzy, she joined him as he reached his final moment. Their souls were completely intertwined and the seeds of bittersweet love were securely planted and renewed.

With the sounds of their breathing slowing between them, with their bodies locked together as firmly as two pieces of a puzzle, they felt something in their hearts that was beyond just their physical closeness. It was as though they had returned to themselves.

Silent whispers surrounded them, encouraging them to reach out regardless of any risks. They had tried to struggle against their feelings with logic and reason, but fate prevailed, mingling two flames, binding them together. The other finally filled the void each had always felt.

They made love again and again. They hungered for each other equally, and wrapped in each other's embrace, they fulfilled each desire until it was time for him to leave for the base.

Standing beside her as she lay there sleeping, he kissed her forehead and said softly "Goodnight, my lady."

Chapter 15

March 23rd, The Coin

It was 1320 as Joe, Hannibal and Spyder were returning from their afternoon briefing. They were engaged in a heated discussion about the maneuvers they would be executing in forty minutes. Quickly, they hurried their pace toward the life support shop to change into flight suits.

Joe checked to make sure he had his squadron coin in his flight suit pocket. As he felt it, he thought about giving it to Mercedes. He didn't want her to leave without a tangible reminder of their time together. Memories of her were now deeply embedded in him and he knew he would revisit them often.

His personal life was going to be changing, especially with a baby on the way. He remembered the vow he made to himself during the Gulf War and he was going to keep his word, whatever the costs. *Whatever it takes.*

Inside, he expected to feel terrible about his feelings for Mercedes, and he kept waiting for a slap of reality to send horrible, guilty feelings through him about their nights together. Normally, that would happen to anyone. Some of his flying buddies even neatly justified and explained their actions away as a momentary loss of judgment, but with Mercedes, it was completely different. With her he felt at home in every sense of the word.

He could freely express his gentle, sensitive side. A side few ever witnessed and a side that not even Eva fully brought out in him. The answer was simple—what they were doing was meant to be. He needed no explanations for it; he simply knew it was right just as he knew he had fallen in love with her.

"Phantom!" His thoughts were instantly interrupted by his squadron leader's roar, "Time to step to the jet!"

Tucking his helmet under his arm, he headed toward the flight line. Uncle Lloyd met him at the jet, and after exchanging formal acknowledgements of rank and a handshake, Uncle Lloyd walked him around the jet, performing a standard preflight and briefing him for a couple of minutes on the maintenance status of his aircraft.

In his typical Philly accent, Uncle Lloyd asked, "Yo, Phantom—not for nuthin', but you're lookin' pretty beat. How youse doin'? Fine to fly, man?"

"Actually, Uncle Lloyd—I'm pumped. I'm fired up to fly." Joe was surprised by the surge of energy he was feeling despite his exhaustion.

"Aight, Phantom. Know that it'll be a smooth flight 'cus I've got ya covered."

As they continued around the jet, they exchanged quips and military humor, laughing. They then checked the emergency systems and made sure the ejection seat was safe and armed, that the engine was good, and that there was no foreign object damage to the intake. Uncle Lloyd joined his crew as Joe climbed into the aircraft, feeling his excitement growing. He felt like a million dollars.

He strapped in and then checked his harnesses to ensure all of them were secured before he put on his helmet. While the ground crew finished prepping the aircraft for flight, he glanced at the cockpit controls, mentally checking switch positions. Starting from the left rear of the cockpit, he did a thorough preflight check of the myriad switch settings.

Confident everything was where it should be, he asked the crew chief to confirm that the jet was clear—fore, aft, underneath—and that the chocks were set and the fire bottle was ready. Getting a positive response from the crew chief below, he activated the jet fuel starter and when the RPM gauge showed 20% rotation, he advanced the throttle to the idle position and listened as the engine began to roar to life.

Next, they ran tests of the engine's emergency power unit and the standby backup modes, followed by a built-in test of the electronic flight controls. After checking the braking systems, he cleared off the crew chief, acknowledging he was going out as number two in the four ship and that it would be about a one hour flight.

He checked the inertial navigation system in NAV, turned on the radar and then the targeting pod and countermeasures suite. An intense feeling, one of personal seclusion and control, descended upon him. It was a feeling he truly enjoyed, knowing it meant he felt as one with his aircraft. It was as satisfying as melding into one with Mercedes had been the previous night.

The voice of his flight lead interrupted his thoughts, calling for taxi clearance on the ground. "Nellis Ground Tower, request Nickel 01 taxi with Charlie on the ATIS, highway two departure, clearance on request."

Nellis Ground Tower responded, "Roger, Nickel 01. You are clear to taxi runway two-niner."

Joe gave his ground crew the hand signal to pull chocks and then acknowledged Uncle Lloyd with a salute before taxiing out to the end of the runway.

As he waited for take-off clearance from the tower, Joe could feel his excitement peaking. Then he heard Nellis Tower, "Nickel 01, you are cleared take off runway two niner left. Contact Nellis departure on button 4."

The flight lead gave the "run it up" signal and they checked their engines at 90% RPM. With a head nod indicating everything was ready, the lead then checked them in on button 4 and roared down the runway. Fifteen seconds later, Phantom's turn came and he selected max afterburner on the throttle.

The single General Electric 110 engine's full afterburner kicked in one-by-one and with 30,000 pounds of thrust at his disposal, he was firmly pushed back into the seat as his aircraft rocketed into the sky. Airborne, he immediately raised the gear so it would be fully retracted before the jet reached the gears' 300-knot limit. At their initial level off point of 16,000 feet, they got clearance from Nellis Departure to climb to flight level 210 to 230, the block of space 21,000 to 23,000 feet above sea level. In less than four minutes, he was four miles high and twenty-five miles from the base.

He leveled off in the block and set his navigational data in the up front controls to steer point two, which would take him to the northwest range complex. He started to prepare mentally to fly their ingress route, but he found his thoughts were of Mercedes and the coin in his pocket. He looked right through his head's up display to gaze at the clouds as a vivid vision of her beautiful smile emerged in his mind. *I can't wait to hold you tonight.*

Chapter 16

March 23rd, The Stars

In every part of her, Mercedes could feel Joe's presence and suddenly everything felt right with the world. She was sitting in the Nevada Utility conference room with Señor Enrique and the rest of his team, negotiating the final stages of the multi-million dollar deal to purchase the utility. What she was doing was probably mundane compared to Joe's flight training at Nellis Air Force Base.

As she delicately hammered out the fine details that would close the contract, Joe's words, "I'm married," echoed in her thoughts. She shrugged them off and focused on the details of the buy-out.

An hour or so later, she turned to Señor Enrique and the rest of his team. "Let me call Myles and tell him we've reached an agreement. Is there a phone I can use?"

"Certainly." Señor Enrique nodded toward the door behind him. "Please, use the one in my office next door."

When Myles picked up the phone, she announced triumphantly, "Mission accomplished!"

"Fantastic! Mercedes, that's fantastic. Howard—Mr. Wallace—asked me to personally thank you. He said he wants to wine and dine you when you return, too. Put in a good word for me—will you? He is a hell of a person to have on your side."

Flattered, she laughed and she felt it was the appropriate time to present him with a few of her demands for the favor he owed. "Myles, if you want it, I'll get you 60% of the shares in the company, but first, about that favor you owe me..."

"Cashing in so soon?"

"A little. I'm going to keep my original table stakes, but I want you to know I want to be part of the French Connection."

His silence told her that she had caught him off guard.

"France. You're multi-lingual, too, right? There are three on-going projects there."

"Yes." she responded noncommittally, leveraging her advantage and waiting to see what he would offer.

"Which one? The Loire Valley?"

"Exactly." She wondered if he could hear her smile over the phone. His sigh was deep, as she had known it would be.

"I just got the team finalized and they are already scheduled to leave within the month." Before he continued, he remembered he had given her his word, so he reluctantly said, "Not a problem. I'll take care of the reassignments. Consider yourself—"

"Head of the team." There was no yield in her voice.

There was nothing he could say that would change her mind and they both knew it. She could handle the project and having her do so would add value. He

Under a Spell

surrendered to her demands with one word. "Precisely."

"Thank you, boss. You have been a dear. And you must be rewarded." She smiled thinking of the arrangements she had already made for him. "There are four VIP tickets for the Philadelphia Orchestra waiting just for you at the box office for this weekend's *Classical Music under the Stars* series. Oh, by the way, our favorite cellist, Yo-yo Ma will be performing. They're yours if you wish to have them."

"Lady, you've got style." He couldn't help but laugh softly, "You are a woman after my own heart. Thanks. I'll see you after you get back."

Going back into the conference room, she said to Señor Enrique and everyone else, "Myles and our senior staff asked me to thank you. They are very pleased. I will send them the contract by express mail, so they will have it in a few hours. As soon as the legal department gives their okay, the final signed copies will be returned to you."

Everyone in the room was happy with the outcome of the negotiations and handshakes were exchanged. Señor Enrique personally walked her back to her waiting limousine, opening the door before the driver could. She was pleased with his old world courtesy.

"We certainly enjoyed the pleasure of your company. It made the decisions less painful at times, though difficult to accept at first when such a lovely lady gave the terms. We would love to have you back in our fair city."

She smiled and surprised him by speaking in his native tongue, a Castilian dialect. *"It was my pleasure, Señor Enrique. I have learned a great deal from your experiences. Thank you so much for taking me under your wing, and sharing your wisdom of this profession. I am looking forward to returning and learning more from you, sir."*

"My dear lady, how did you learn to speak so beautifully? You must tell me. And please, call me *José*," he said, smiling, and quickly shifted to English, "I am thrilled to hear you speak so fluently in my native tongue. Aside from my own family and circle of friends, I have not heard the words of my language flow so smoothly for too many years."

"*José*," she smiled when she said his name, "I am fluent in many Neapolitan and Romance-based languages, including other Spanish dialects, Catalan, Galician and Basque. But it is so because of my father's grandparents. They were born in Spain and it is due to them and my father that I speak Castilian."

"You speak flawlessly. Your family must be very proud of you, *Mercédès*. They have raised you well." He pronounced her name perfectly, clearly knowing its origin was Spanish and that it meant "the Virgin Mary."

"*Your compliment is truly important to me. I thank you and am looking forward to working with you again, José.*"

They lightly embraced, then touched cheeks while lightly kissing the air, as was the acceptable Spanish tradition for farewells between particularly close colleagues.

As she slid in the back of the limousine, a sense of confidence and personal satisfaction filled her. Though the deal had been complicated, she had not only completed it, but had also made a new friend.

Back at the conference she went to the last lecture, which was on Global Positioning Systems (GPS) and their applications to engineering. It finished in time for her to return to the hotel to meet Joe before the night was very late.

As she left the meeting room, Calvin asked her to dinner again, but she declined, having already made arrangements to have dinner with her godmother Veronica.

Walking through the casino floor, she meandered through the slot area and blackjack tables toward the elevator, enjoying the overwhelming sights and sounds, but not in the least tempted by them. People were completely oblivious to time. There were no clocks, the food and drinks were cheap and the entertainment was designed to pull people out of their rooms and into the casinos. Las Vegas, not New York City, should have been bestowed with the nickname "The City That Never Sleeps."

Taking the elevator up to her room, she casually placed her laptop and briefcase on her desk and took her planner out, tossing it on the bed. She needed to relax for a moment. She needed music. Vivaldi.

She took off her suit jacket, kicked off her heels, propped the pillows and sank back into them. With her planner opened, she began her routine of checking and returning messages. She decided not to call Sydney nor even bother with Grant. She needed to distance herself for at least today. It was best, especially with Sydney. Especially now.

She called and confirmed her 11:00 a.m. flight back to Philadelphia, discarding the idea of extending her stay through the weekend. She didn't have any qualms about canceling her theatre date with Grant and, in fact, the temptation to do so was overwhelming. Perhaps, she could talk to Joe about it tonight.

Tonight. Her heart was still aching from the stinging pain of his truth and the knowledge that tonight would be their last night together.

It was 5:30 p.m., which meant that she had at least an hour to unwind. She flipped through her planner, checking the next few days. The weekend was filled. Tomorrow she had tentative plans for dinner at Bookbinders with Grant. She added *sleep alone* to the entry. Saturday morning she had the chance to sleep in. She was having dinner with Grant again at the Chart House, and then going to watch Shakespeare at the Mann and for dessert at the Painted Parrot. Sunday was a workout with Sydney, afternoon tea with the ladies and a poetry reading. For the workweek, she had her usual staff meetings and phone conferences, as well as luncheons, a training session, dinner parties and more meetings. It just went on and on.

The following weekend was Killington and snowboarding with the Godwin's. That would be a lot of fun, especially with ten of her adrenaline junkie friends there.

Tim and Rikki Godwin, her dentist friends, just built a new mountain chalet in the Pico area. Rikki had mentioned they would have the lift tickets, snowmobiles, and a mahogany pool table for entertainment.

Mercedes remembered that she needed to replace her badly beaten Burton Board and the tip for the cue stick Grant had given her for her birthday. A weekend of frolicking in the snow was never complete without numerous games of 9-ball. She had yet to break the table against Grant, who consistently took the break. Losing, not to mention having to keep racking the table, never settled well with her. Losing would gnaw at her, just like the tightening she was feeling in her neck muscles.

She rubbed the back of her neck to loosen the tight muscles. The calm sounds of Vivaldi were relaxing and she just wanted to lose herself in it. She penciled in a reminder to schedule a full body treatment at her favorite spa. *I could really use a few hours of pampering right now,* she sighed.

She set her planner aside and closed her eyes, needing a few minutes of peace before motivating herself to get dressed. But the solitude was all too brutal. Thoughts of Joe kept racing through her brain, forcing her to abandon the idea of relaxing. She wanted to take a bath, but she simply didn't have enough time.

She turned the music louder and then undressed, leaving a trail of clothes on her way to the shower. In the mirror she noticed a small somewhat circular bruise on her left breast where Joe's mouth had been. There was another on her right breast, but it was lighter. There were also bruises on her inner thighs. She smiled and shook her head. Her skin was so sensitive that she was surprised she didn't have more bruises. Stepping into the shower, she let the warm water run over her until it cooled compared to the rising heat of her body as she began to ache for him.

Standing there, feeling the water running over her and leaving her frustrated, she heard the phone ringing. Even before the voice mail kicked on, she knew it was Grant. When she got out of the shower, she reluctantly listened to the message.

"Hi, it's me. I hate these damned machines! Anyway, I wanted to hear your voice. After my shift yesterday I just crashed and, believe it or not, I just got out of bed a few hours ago. Sleep is my mistress—hope you're not jealous. I'll pick you up at the airport. In fact, I'll be waiting with my arms wide open.

"Okay—um, I made the dinner reservations at Bookbinders. You talked me into it. And I'll have the warm massage oils ready to work Vegas out of your body after dinner. Ah, Mercedes. You're so beautiful. I can't wait to touch you. I miss you. I miss you too much!"

She sighed deeply as she hung up the phone and quickly noted the time. Even though she was running late for her dinner appointment with Veronica, she picked up her clothes from where they were strewn on the floor. She hated clutter.

The new ebony chiffon body dress she had picked up while she was at the Forum Shops yesterday fit as perfectly as she had known it would. Adjusting the dress, she remembered the gallery that she had visited after Calvin showed her the replica of David.

In it she had found a reproduction of a stunning 1895 Gustav Klimt painting in an elegant gold-tone frame. The sight of the painting had immediately frozen her on her feet. Calvin tried to impress her with his knowledge of the arts, but his voice simply faded as she stared at the expression on the woman's face. Her eyes were closed. Klimt had shown her abandoning herself to the moment as her beloved was gently lifting her chin, about to kiss her. Mercedes thought of Joe and how the woman's face so beautifully captured how she herself felt when Joe had first kissed her.

The whole painting seemed to be meant for them. He had kissed her the same way on the dance floor. She simply stood there, wondering how she could possibly feel so strongly for Joe. Her heart skipped a beat when she finally noticed the title of the painting was *Love*, and that a man she hardly knew had taken her heart in almost an instant.

Shaking the image from her mind, she stepped into the main lobby of the Aladdin Casino where everything seemed to be in constant motion. There was no sign of Veronica, so she sat down on a comfortable overstuffed chair to wait. Dozens of people were checking in or out, and a steady flow of bellhop traffic streamed through the lobby as guests followed the bellhops and their luggage to the elevators.

Everywhere she looked there were groups of people with conference nametags. It was evening, time to relax and have a little fun, but they were still loudly discussing the lectures they had attended hours before. Other people were milling around while a few, like her, were sitting and waiting for their respective parties to arrive. She glanced at her watch again. Only ten minutes had passed, yet somehow she felt impatient.

Several couples caught her eye. They had obviously just gotten married, probably at one of the little white chapels that were famous in Las Vegas. Hearts were united and broken in droves. Sin City. *What happens in Vegas stays in Vegas.* The clichés disgusted her.

A woman passed by in a red dress with a white tulle veil on her head. The sparkle of her wedding ring ensemble caught Mercedes' eye and seeing it brought memories of Mason, of the time he had proposed to her eight years ago.

* * *

Mason had driven her to the Philadelphia Marine Center to attend Dominic's yacht party to celebrate his first multi-million dollar contract—a contract that Mercedes had a hand in landing and that had just made Mason one of the youngest self-made millionaires in the tri-state area. He was only twenty-two.

She was wearing the dress Mason had purchased especially for this occasion; it was in a sexy deep shade of red. The neckline was off her shoulders. She knew he enjoyed the sight of her soft bare skin.

Her long hair was pulled back into an elegant ponytail, adorned with gemstone clips. She was also wearing his gifts: a new diamond choker necklace, matching earrings with an inlay of her birthstone, golden topaz, and a diamond stud earring for her new piercing on her left earlobe. She had gotten the second piercing to match his. He was wearing the other diamond stud on his left earlobe.

"Mason? Where did you say his yacht was docked?" she asked loudly.

"Babe, it's the one in slip 6564."

She suddenly stopped on her tracks and started feeling faint when she saw that the fifty-four foot cruiser yacht sitting in slip 6564 was named *Mercedes*. Mason swiftly scooped her into his arms before she fell to the ground. He lifted her into the yacht, maneuvered his way through the deck, down into the salon by the forward stateroom, and finally laid her down gently on the large island berth in the master stateroom. He was giving her soft kisses on her lips, her cheeks and her eyelids, hoping she would awaken from her spell.

"I had the strangest dream," she whispered, with her eyes still closed, "I dreamt we had a yacht and it was named after me." He nibbled gently on her ear, whispering, "It is named after you, babe."

She shot upright and strained to focus her eyes. She was looking at her reflection in the full-length Cheval mirror across the room. She was sitting on the bed in the middle of an elegant master stateroom. Two dragonfly Tiffany table lamps she had wanted were on each side of the bed where framed pictures of them, in different sizes, were beautifully arranged. Her eyes rested a wall of gilded, bound books on the recessed bookshelves. The scent of roses filled the air. Everywhere she looked, there were orange-red & red-orange blended blooms. Not just any ordinary roses, they were the *Kordes Floribunda Mercedes* roses from Germany. They were just admiring them at Longwood Gardens not too long ago. She had commented on their beauty and name. He remembered.

He pushed a button on a remote and the sliding doors to the entertainment center automatically opened. The sounds of Gordon Dexter's soft jazz flooded the room. Mercedes was still in disbelief as she looked beyond the stateroom to the salon, where a table was formally set and the candles on the crystal candleholders were already lit. She was bewildered, and then a frown appeared on her face, "You do know what this means, don't you?"

He hated it when he had to guess at her questions, so sarcastically he said, "Okay, what's it mean?"

She shrieked, "We're yuppies!"

"FUCK NO!" he quickly shouted, as was his crude way.

"Then promise me we'll never change because of this," she implored. "We'll forever be in love, spontaneous and true to loving Philly cheese steaks over caviar and stuffed lobsters! Promise me!"

"Well, caviar tastes nasty but, about the stuffed lobsters—"

She stopped his wisecrack with a kiss. They were laughing as he took hold of her arms to help her off the bed, then he gave her a tight loving embrace. "I promise," he whispered and they kissed passionately.

As she walked, the glitter on her red dress seemed to dance under the soft glow of the recessed lights that lined her path to an impressive salon. He seated her at the table and walked over to the full service galley where he brought out a chilled bottle of champagne. The room was aglow with the warmth of cherry wood around them. He had coordinated the room décor according to her taste.

Easily startled, she jumped when the cork popped from the champagne, which he quickly poured into two crystal champagne glasses, spilling over the sides. Slowly, Mason lowered himself, got on one knee and took out a dainty black velvet box from his jacket pocket. He opened the box. It held a 5-carat diamond marquise, with two rows of three-tiered, emerald cut, Brazilian imperial topaz on a gold Elizabethan prong setting. It was a unique design which he had specially created for her. When he took her left hand in his, his hands were trembling. He took the ring and placed it on her ring finger.

Clearing his throat and saying in a well-rehearsed tone, "'Doubt thou the stars are fire; Doubt that the sun doth move; Doubt truth to be a liar; But never doubt I love.' Mercedes—marry me." Mason was quoting Shakespeare's *Hamlet* and tears were streaming down her cheeks.

* * *

That was an eternity ago, she sighed as the tears streamed down her cheeks, just as they did back then. She truly missed Mason. Most of all, she missed who they use to be together. It was during a time when she felt the joys of love at its height, but all that was in the past. Now, all she felt was deep angst and sorrow, for here she was, about to be divorced from him. Worse yet, she had found her untimely soul mate and Joe was not hers to have. He was only hers for just a few days, but she held onto hope. Her mind kept turning over their conversations, re-evaluating each phrase, searching for meaning. And each time she was left without resolve.

"This whole situation mimics a Shakespearean tragedy," she muttered quietly to herself, then decided to dismiss these thoughts for the moment. *To thine own self be true, Mercedes!*

Mercedes dried her tears and checked her watch as a black Jaguar XJ6 Vanden Plas pulled up. Veronica's familiar smiling face was beaming at her. Mercedes quickly got in and as they were pulling away, she saw a plane flying overhead. *Our souls are connected*, echoed in her mind.

"How are you, heart?" Veronica asked, noting the sadness in her godchild's eyes.

Mercedes quickly put on her happy face. "I'm fine, just a little tired from a hectic week. But look at you! You look wonderful!"

"Thank you. It's this car—do you like it on me?"

She loved Veronica like a second mother. She had introduced her parents to each other over forty years ago. Her mother and Veronica had remained the best of friends ever since. This woman changed her diapers, for goodness' sake! She married a diplomat from Italy and traveled the world more than ten times over. Her daughter, Angel, lived in Las Vegas, so during her annual three-month hiatus, Veronica would rent a house nearby to enjoy her family as well as the Vegas entertainment. Then she would be off to some remote part of the world with her husband, Mario. She loved talking to Veronica about her latest escapades. Veronica was gifted in her charms.

"Your mom told me about your out-of-country birthday tradition. How did you come up with such a nice ritual?"

"Since I wasn't born in this country, I felt that I should be out-of-country to celebrate it. It also gives me a great excuse to see the world."

"What a clever idea! This year, why don't you go to Paris on your birthday? Let's go together."

"I'd love that! Let's make plans soon."

"Heart, I hope you don't mind me asking, but how are you holding up with Mason?" she asked with concern.

"I'm fine. Really I am. Actually, it sounds really odd, but Mason and I are more concerned about everyone else around us. Like Mom and Dad, for instance. A couple of weeks ago we took them out to dinner to tell them together that we were moving forward with the final divorce papers. Mom cried and Dad was in disbelief because we talked about it as casually as we're talking now."

"Are there any chances of reconciliation?"

"Unless someone has come up with a miracle, then reconciling would be out of the question." She wasn't sure if she meant it.

"Right, your mom told me briefly about it. I am so sorry, heart."

"Don't be. Just like Nietzsche said, 'That which does not kill us,'" then in unison, they said, "'makes us stronger!'"

"I was just revisiting the past while I was waiting for you."

"Good memories, I hope."

Smiling with a bit of melancholy, "Yes, beautiful memories."

"I love memories, heart, especially beautiful ones. I am completely devoted and faithful to memories, but not to the people in them."

"Interesting statement. Why's that?"

"Because the memories will *never* change, but people do, which is why I enjoy looking back at them."

"I love the way you think."

Later, they were headed to the MGM Grand after dining on seafood at a New Orleans style restaurant. She didn't have any appetite for dessert, but opted for a hot cup of green tea with honey and a slice of lemon. The minutes seemed to pass so slowly. She anxiously checked the time when Veronica wasn't watching. Finally, when the check came, she swiftly took it out of Veronica's hand and before she could raise a voice of protest, the bill was paid. The dinner was lovely and relaxed.

Veronica sighed and said, "Heart, it was such a short visit. I had hoped we could have gone to an exhibit or maybe on an indulgent shopping spree."

The valet opened the car door for her, but before she slid out of her seat, she gave her godmother a tight squeeze. She missed her already and wished they could have spent more time together.

If it were any other time, she would have gone to an exhibit with her. Except today was very different, she simply couldn't spare a moment even if she wanted to.

"Very tempting. Perhaps when we see each other again in Paris—yes?"

"But, of course, heart. We'll have a lovely time in Paris. You enjoy the rest of your stay here. My love to your parents!" They hugged for a long time and touched cheeks, kissing lightly in the air, already looking forward to their French adventures.

Chapter 17

March 23rd, Her Gift

Though she had a lovely time with Veronica, she couldn't stop the frenzied butterflies in her stomach. For distraction she checked her email and found a message that made her smile. It was from Lucas and his email simply read,

"*Merc,*

The answer is today, the present or NOW. Take your pick :)~

It's Ecclesiastics, too, right?

Love ya!

Raiden

PS—here's another ancient puzzle for you:

'If I have a faith that can move mountains, but do not have this, I am nothing. If I give all I possess to the poor and surrender my body to the flames, but have not this, I gain nothing.'

C ya!"

She stared at his riddle for a while. She was having difficulty focusing, but finally the answer came to her. It was the very thing that she was struggling with. She replied,

"Hey big brother,

You are correct on both counts! I see your Catholic school education has not gone to waste :)

Now for your puzzle, the answer is LOVE.

Hugs!

Merc"

After she clicked the "send" button, she tried to mentally prepare herself for Joe, but it was no use. She felt like she was falling apart. She had no simple answers about what she should feel or say. Whenever she felt unraveled this way, she usually took out the small metal puzzle that her beautiful Mother had given her in college. It seemed silly, but it always worked on grounding her whenever she was faced with making an important decision. It may have looked insignificant to others, but it was an important part of her.

It was given to her on a significant crossroad of her young life. It was during her second semester as a pre-med student. She was so hell-bent on becoming the best pediatric surgeon in the country that she immediately jumped on the chance to be one of the five people to accompany her professor to a permitted tour of the neonatal intensive care units at the Children's Hospital of Pennsylvania (CHOP). In the midst of his lecture, a premature baby was distressed, then immediately went into cardio-pulmonary arrest. It was a madhouse with the rush of doctors, nurses and the crash cart. In a matter of seconds, the baby had completely flat-lined and time of death was called. This happened only yards away from her as she was quickly ushered away with her group. The event left her spirits shattered because she knew that she would never be the doctor she had hoped to be. The death of that child left her helpless and lost. At the dorms she called her mother, crying her eyes out, not knowing what she was going to do with the rest of her life. That was the time when she began having her phantasms of thirteenth century France.

A couple of days had passed after her nightmare at CHOP. While she was working on some assignments, she received a beautiful arrangement of flowers with a small gift-wrapped box from her mother. When she opened the box, she found a peculiar gift of a small metal puzzle. The interlocking puzzle consisted of two strong bent silver nails. The solution was to separate them from each other. It looked simple, but she learned that looks could be deceiving, or perhaps she was just thinking too hard again. She found a written note underneath it. It simply read,

"Dearest little one,

This little treasure has great, great powers. It is quite simple. First, clear your

mind and keep it silent. Second, open your heart. Finally, begin with the end in mind.

For it is not the answer that is important, it is the question.

Love,

Mom"

She took the puzzle from the box and stared at it. *Could it be that simple?* she wondered and began to free her mind of distractions. Suddenly, one of her first childhood memories flooded her mind. It was of sand being sifted through a sieve while cement was poured on a framed foundation, followed with visions of hollow masonry units stacked at her father's warehouse where she would play. She saw her father's office where she would sneak in to play with his lettering boards. She also saw the excitement in her face when she received her very first calculator. Then, she looked down at her papers on her desk at her advanced analytic calculus and physics homework, subjects in which she excelled.

Her eyes looked toward the framed picture of her boyfriend, Joey, who convinced her to take one of his engineering classes, so they could be together. She found that it held her interest; as a matter of fact, she had just finished his homework before she received her mother's gift. *Of course! It's been in front of my face the entire time. Everything in my life has always pointed to engineering!* Then, she looked down at the puzzle in her hand and smiled. She had separated the two nails from each other without realizing it.

With that small metal puzzle she had learned how to approach everything in her life. All it took was a completely different perspective. She also learned never to ignore the silent signs that surrounded her in her life. It was a lesson she never forgot.

As she searched for the metal puzzle in her briefcase and smiled when she realized how, among numerous other coincidences, the name *Joe* was very significant in her life. *How should I interpret these signs?*

She turned on her CD player to quiet her mind, and finally took the small metal puzzle out of her briefcase. She started to untangle it, but she stopped in the midst of her motion, when the image of her and Joe, locked in each other's arms, appeared in her mind. She looked at the puzzle again and saw the outline of their bodies conforming to the shape of it. Then she heard the familiar knock at her door.

"Hello, beautiful," Joe said sweetly, greeting her with a gentle, longing kiss. He gave her a tight bear hug without hurting her. She felt so many things being in his arms, one of which was complete joy. Time seemed to have stopped at that moment.

He noticed she was holding onto a puzzle in her hand. "Hey, I like puzzles."

She offered it to him as they walked over toward the chairs at the desk. He had unraveled it by the time he sat down.

"JC, I'm really impressed!" she happily exclaimed. She hesitated for a second before saying, "Please don't think it strange of me, but I would like you to have it. Think of me when you see it."

Smiling, he took her by the waist and guided her to sit astride his waist on the chair. He thanked her with a passionate kiss and while in their embrace, he said tenderly, "I will treasure it always."

She was almost in tears, causing her to hold him tighter. She regained her composure before she pulled away to look at him. She smiled knowing that he had no idea how significant that moment or the puzzle was for her. She never did tell him about it.

After he placed the puzzle on the table, he said excitedly, "I have something for you too."

She didn't expect anything at all, but she was curious to find out what it was. He took a silver coin from his pocket, but it was not a currency coin. It was something much different. He placed it in her hand.

He stared intently into her eyes and said lovingly, "I couldn't think of anything I could give you, but this coin holds a lot of meaning for me. I wanted to give you something so you would always remember our time together—a solid memory that this wasn't just a dream and that we really met and all of this happened.

"It is customary for a pilot to receive a coin after completing training on an aircraft. It is considered as a symbol of achievement. Each coin bears the mark of the respective fighting squadron a pilot served with." He went on to say, "This coin has already traveled over three continents with me. One of its uses is called a coin check. Any squadron member can call a coin check. Anywhere, anytime. So I must produce my coin; otherwise, the next bar tab from the group is on me and it could get very expensive, especially if there are many of us in a restaurant. So, I'm never caught without my coin."

"Now that you've given it to me, won't you be at risk?"

"Don't worry about it. There's usually a reserve coin in the safe at the base. Though, I hope there won't be a coin check tomorrow."

"Were you ever caught without your coin?"

"Yes, it was during a deployment from Aviano to Eglin Air Force Base and I forgot to take my coin with me. When we got there, a coin check was made and it cost me over a hundred dollars for a single round of drinks at the Officers Club! It just got worse from there until one of the guys felt sorry for me and gave me a spare he always had for emergencies. A spare coin was rare because they only give you one coin; luckily, he bought one from the squadron supply guy to keep as an extra."

"I'm glad Lady Luck was on your side," she said softly, "and I'll keep your coin with me always."

Their lips met and they kissed deeply. Breathless, she asked, "Did you fly today?"

"Yes, yes I did," he said, smiling. "And, I managed to have a great flight despite being so exhausted. You've worn me out!"

They laughed, which eased the tension she was feeling from the day. They talked like an old married couple, oblivious to the time constraints they were under. From time to time, there would be silence between them, but never awkward. It was a comfortable silence when both were simply enjoying each other's company.

When the second track of U2's *Joshua Tree* began to fill the room, she asked him to a slow dance. It was a moment she wanted to embed in her memory where she would always be able to retrieve it whenever she wished. She remembered he called it "compartmentalizing."

They danced as though they were standing still, just holding each other as if there was never going to be a tomorrow. She had wondered when they would dance like this again.

He sighed deeply, enjoying the moment of having her in his arms. He didn't want any of this to end. He didn't want to imagine her not being in his life forever. If there was a chance for them to be in each other's lives, however small it might be, he was going to take it. He didn't want to keep wondering about how life had treated her in the years to come. He didn't want to think of a life without her in it. So he said softly, "Mercedes, I want you to be in my life no matter how small a part of it I can have. I want you to always be there. Even if it means having only your words through a letter or maybe phone calls so I can let you know where I'll be deployed next. Promise me you'll keep in touch?"

"I promise," she whispered. Her heart was flooded with bittersweet joy at his request. She felt wanted with his need to have her in his life. She ached to be a part of it, even if it meant indirectly.

He thought back to all the events that led them to this moment in a dance. He couldn't begin to explain how he felt. He wanted to tell her everything he felt for her, but knew he couldn't because of the circumstances. So he shared with her the feelings he could tell her. "I can't believe how incredibly lucky I am to have met you that night. This doesn't happen to me. I feel like we were once very close like this. I think in a different life we could have been together."

With the coin still in her hand, she sighed deeply and wondered how he truly felt for her. It didn't matter at the moment. She felt his heart beating fast and strong when he spoke. She held him closer. It was enough for her to know he cared deeply for her, for it showed in his tenderness, in his words. Loosing herself in his arms, she just didn't want this dance to end.

But the dance was going to end. She wanted him to know many things. She began to say, "JC, more than anything else, I want you to be happy and do whatever it is you've dreamed of. And—" he didn't let her continue. He simply kissed her so tenderly and lovingly. She thought, *It all started with a dance, so shall it end.*

If her words weren't going to be voiced tonight, she decided her actions would have to speak for her. She placed the coin next to the puzzle on the table and began to pull her soft chiffon dress up and over her head, dropping it in a wrinkled heap on the floor. She stood before him in black lace. Her eyes pleaded with him to take her and her heart. She was about to unhook her bra when he stepped closer to her.

He looked deep into her eyes, as if he could see right through her soul. Their eyes were filled with passion and care, speaking all the words they needed to say. He kissed her deeply. His right hand was on the back of her head. He grasped her hair as he pulled her to him. She felt his arousal against her. He picked her up in his arms and laid her on the bed.

He began kissing and gently nipping her neck. Each kiss created a delightful shiver throughout her body.

"Mercedes" he whispered. The warmth of his voice caused her to let out a soft moan. She knew she belonged to him. Her whole body ached for him.

She watched him undress, carefully freeing himself of his shirt. His chest was bare and his breathing, already heavy. He smiled playfully at her as he took his cowboy boots off and slipped out of his clothes. He pressed his strong body against hers, with his kisses deep and tender. His hands traveled down the sides of her body. His hands grasped her buttocks, forcing their hips together. Their bodies ignited the fuel for their passions where they touched. His hands caressed her gently and tenderly, and then his touch became more urgent. He was magnificently engorged against her.

He slowly pulled her head back, brushing away her hair and exposing her neck. His other hand covered hers. His warm mouth tenderly kissed and nuzzled her throat; her flesh tingled and felt the pulsing inside of her. He swiftly unhooked her bra. His hand slid to her breast, driving her senses wild. She felt as though she was floating.

He pushed her legs apart wide at the knees. She was glistening, exposed to him, aching to be touched. She felt his tongue explore the tingling areas and, suddenly, she felt his fingers pushing away the silk and plunging deep within her. She moaned with pleasure as she felt the rhythm of his fingers quickening. He slowly withdrew and eased down her thighs as she lifted her knees.

Then, they were facing each other with their eyes locked. He took hold of her wrists and held them back against the bed; he had taken complete control of her. He parted her legs with his knees and she welcomed him as he lowered his hips. He entered her, slowly aware of every sensation intensified. They were now one sharing in the pleasure of their union. They lingered in that moment.

After a time he shifted her gently onto her stomach. Their breathing went from fast and ragged to free and deep. It seemed as if their bodies were made for no other purpose than this union. Their rhythm was slow, steady and full of meaning as their bodies spoke only of tenderness. They were lost in each other, locked within a timeless moment. Never had it been like this for them. On and on it went, each of them feeling the intensity of emotions as they fell deeper into each other.

Suddenly, she felt the tears in her eyes. She couldn't hold them back any longer. She bit her lip so a cry wouldn't escape from her lips as her back arched up to meet him. She was swept away on a tide of emotions. How she had longed to be with this man. Now he was hers. At that moment she thought, *I am yours completely!*

He looked down, not knowing she was weeping, and continued his slow rhythm within her. She had buried her head in the pillow to soak the warm salty tears from her face. She closed her eyes, immersed in the gentleness of his touch.

His breathing started to become ragged. Supporting himself on her hips, his muscles started to quiver with the strain she had built up in him. She began to move under him in a slow circular motion. He desperately fought for control. Now she had possessed him, body and soul. She had him completely and totally to herself.

He skillfully dropped down to support himself above her on his forearms and elbows. Still, she continued her maddening movements beneath him. He wanted this to never end. He wanted the sensations to go on forever, but everything she did drove him closer to the edge.

Suddenly, she lifted herself against him and turned over to her back. She wanted to see his face. She whispered his name and his mind nearly exploded at the sound of her voice. She concentrated fully on heightening his pleasure. She never took her eyes off of his. She wanted to remember every detail of him: his face, his scent and his passionate sounds. A delicious tremor quaked within her which seemed to go on forever.

Nothing would ever come close to how he felt at this moment. His heart was filled with more than desire for her; it was beyond the bounds of emotions that he thought he would feel until she entered his life. He knew he would never forget this moment for as long as he lived. When he looked at her beautiful face, he thought, *I will only feel this way with you, Mercedes*. Nothing else existed for him.

Finally, time froze for them. Words remained unspoken, though they knew they had loved each other completely at the exact moment when their souls finally became one in their joining.

They were bathed with the warmth of their closeness in each other's arms; she was lying on his chest, listening to his heart beating and feeling the sounds of his breathing. They knew they belonged together.

Still tangled in intimacy, he raised himself over her and said softly, almost inaudibly, "I will miss you."

"I will miss you more," she said in a pensive melancholy and then looked up. In response he kissed her forehead, pressing his hands deeply into her back. In silence they remained locked in each other's embrace, until the dreaded moment of scission came.

Chapter 18

March 24th, Lady's Day

"Mercedes," he said tenderly, "We're not going to say goodbye tonight."

He never wanted her to utter the word "goodbye," not even in jest! They would have to find a substitute for the word. Anything but goodbye.

"No goodbyes, JC, ever."

How she dreaded this moment. She wanted to bend the laws of physics and freeze time, suspending it just for them. She had no choice. It was time.

"Think of me even if you're with someone else?" he asked. Though in his heart he didn't want to imagine her so intimate with anyone but him, he had to be realistic. And for his own selfish reasons, he wanted to know she would still think of him during those private moments. He wished he could always be with her every moment, locked in her embrace, just loving her.

She lowered her eyes, fighting back mutinous tears that were threatening to break free. She couldn't speak, able only to give him a sweet smile.

In his mind he took snapshots of each moment they had spent together for the past four nights. Carefully, he tucked them away in his heart. "I will never forget." He would find whenever he made love, with whatever degree of passion, that he was impossibly and inescapably merged with the ephemeral body of Mercedes.

"I'll always be here," she placed her hand on his heart. "I promise." She knew nothing could ever make her forget him.

Putting his left hand on top of hers, he pressed her hand to his lips. They kissed passionately and held each other in a tight embrace.

Unbidden, a phantom conversation started in her mind. *I can change his mind. I can get him to stay a little longer. I'll surprise him and tell him that I can stay through the weekend. We can talk about being together again. We can be together. I can be anywhere, anytime. We can arrange everything so easily. As soon as my divorce is final, I'll maintain multiple residences. One will be wherever he'll be, so he doesn't have to worry about missing the milestones of his child's life. Oh God, what am I thinking!*

Suddenly, she was felt a penetrating cold running through her, frightening her. She was horrified with her thoughts. She had unwittingly started to succumb to that lying voice of despair. Inside she remembered his vows to himself, to his family, God and country! *Acting on these thoughts is tantamount to spitting on those vows. How could I disrespect those vows, ones I myself hold sacred!*

She and Mason had their own painful decision to make together. Nothing could come between them but themselves. They had decided that the best way to remain true to their love was to let each other go. Doing so was where they would find peace and happiness, but she still craved the life they could have if they stayed together. *What life?* Resentment would grow and their friendship, trust and love would inevitably die.

She would rather live alone than risk all that was precious to her. She had to do the same with Joe as she had decided to do with Mason. *I must do this! I must do this!* She kept repeating it in her mind. She had to let him go, even if it meant a life without him directly in it. He would become her sacrifice.

She vowed never to interfere in his life or his commitments. She had already beyond her own boundaries in the name of fate and she knew she couldn't go any farther. She had to remain true to herself. To be otherwise would not be who she was! She couldn't allow herself to become the source of his unhappiness. Not even for fate.

Sydney. Images of Sydney emerged in her thoughts. She felt the pain that had been in Sydney's voice. The anguish and sorrow that filled Sydney was filling her.

She made another vow to herself. *I must remain silent about my love for him until the time comes when he will be free to be with me in clear conscience. I must remain strong.*

With that last thought she let herself slip out of his embrace, as if to say, "Please go, and quickly, before I am lost to my desires." He quietly stood up, gathered his clothes and began to dress in silence.

She pulled the covers back, moved her hair away from her face and sat up against the pillows. Her heart was breaking as she watched him. Her breathing became shallow; the flood of tears and her need to be with him were loosening the grip of her control. *No, please no!* she screamed in her head, pleading for the tears not to come. Struggling to clear her head and control her breathing, she bore a searing lance of pain in her beating heart. She could feel her body trembling as she fought to remain as still as she could.

He picked up the small metal puzzle from her table, lightly touching the coin that sat next to it, and slowly walked over to the door. He turned the doorknob slowly and, as the door opened, he turned to look at her. Her smile was sweet and beautiful. He found himself looking at her mouth and wanting one more kiss. He wanted to lose himself forever in her smile.

Her smile is so beautiful! God, she's so beautiful. There's got to be another way! I don't want to go! He felt his heart tug at him. He wanted to remember her this way. He had to remember her this way. It was his only choice.

Burning the moment in his mind, he looked at her one more time, thinking, *I love you, Mercedes. We will be together again. I know it!*

He wanted to say the words, but he didn't have the right to do so.

No goodbyes. That was their agreement. Before he closed the door, he smiled and wanted to say something with depth, but the only words he could find were, "I'll see ya."

His heart was heavy as he walked down the hallway. Suddenly, he wanted to turn around and run as fast as he could back into her arms so they would never have to be apart.

They could fly away together somewhere. He smiled as he looked up at the lighted numbers on the elevators. *It would be heaven on earth!*

As quickly as he thought of heaven, he thought of the vow he had made to himself and his unborn child. As he stood impatiently waiting for an elevator, he thought, *It would eventually rip us to pieces. It will hurt us. My God, it will destroy us along with everyone else! I can't let that happen. I would never hurt you, Mercedes. Not even for a second!*

He looked toward her closed door at the end of the hall. He had sensed exactly what she was feeling and thinking at that very moment. It hit him so hard that his heart pounded harder, making him struggle for control against the emotions he felt. The pain became so overwhelming that he couldn't wait for the elevator. Thirteen flights of stairs would be a welcome release.

Inside her room Mercedes felt her agony growing. It had torn her apart to see him standing at the door, looking at her. She had wanted to run to him, to kiss him, to hold onto him one more time. She hadn't. She stayed where she had to stay, reaching out to him with her smile instead, holding her breath and her tears—just barely holding them off.

Her mind didn't register what he had said before he closed the door. At that moment, her tears broke free and she looked away. *I've got to tell him how I really feel. He needs to know!*

But the door had already closed. She immediately leapt out of bed, her heart as exposed as she was, and ran to the door.

She heard his footsteps fading.

He was gone.

Her legs weakened from the excruciating pain she felt in her heart. Her tears fell as she slid slowly to the floor, her back pressed against the door. She cried out loud, "NO!" Sobbing, gasping to breathe, she kept saying, "Please feel me, JC. Please." Her mind's voice saying, *I've fallen in love with you.*

As the tears came in waves, so did visions of a time long ago, of being cradled in the arms of a loving man who was desperate to ease her pain. She embraced her naked body, sobbing and rocking herself as a child would.

"No goodbyes, ever," she whispered, resigned. She sat there for what seemed to be an eternity.

With only the locks of her hair to cover her, she sat there nude just as she depicted herself in her self-portrait. Had she known all along?

At last, the words came to her for the poem she had struggled to complete for so long. It poured out of her heart through the little voice in her mind:

Most profound sadness takes unavowed

possession of her soul
Weeping, angry, consumed with pain
Suffering infinitely under a spell
alone in a shadowy place
Moldering, shivering in her mind's labyrinth
but not completely without strength
Quiet anguish trembling in her nakedness
exposed surpassing seductiveness
All else must wait in sacrifice
until the willful commission of scalding misery
runs through its deliberate confrontation
inflicting cruel and bruising pain
Feel the inner struggle and overpowering sorrow
in perfect torment
Mourning the tragic loss of self
Nothing gives comfort from the impaling agony
Retreats into the stillness as in the womb
void of sin and depravity
Continues on her passage numbed and infused with anger
Yearning for the transformation to begin.

Her words finally returned to her on this same day in her phantasm, on *Lady's Day*.

Chapter 19

Journeys of the Soul

"Professor, is it possible to have more than one soul mate? I mean, I've been in love more than once, so does it mean that there are many soul mates out there destined just for me?"

Mercedes welcomed the question from one of her far site students, speaking through one of ten large, interactive satellite videoconferencing flat screen monitors. Cameras were mounted on each monitor, labeled one through ten, located to the right front of her teaching station. A flashing green light would appear whenever a student wished to ask questions.

She quickly glanced at the roster on her slim computerized writing tablet with the first names and the initials of the last names of her class. Though it was only the first week of spring semester, she knew almost all the names of her thirty students. She habitually kept an electronic chart of names where she jotted down observations of their personalities and physical appearance.

She answered, addressing her entire class, "You may love *more* than one person, but there can only be *one* true soul mate for you."

The answer caused an obvious stir among her senior philosophy majors in her *Journeys of the Soul* honors class at Cornell University. She walked from the lectern toward the front of the class with her electronic tablet and sat on the edge of the desk by her glass of tonic water, crossing her legs.

Though she had just turned fifty-three, she looked like a woman in her early forties. Her raven-colored hair with rich henna highlights flowed in long straight layers to four inches below her shoulders. Her stylish pair of glasses looked rather dainty and academic. Her grey, ankle-length silk and cashmere sweater dress was accentuated with a burgundy pashmina cashmere stole and a pair of four-inch heeled, black leather boots. She never relented on her appearance or sense of fashion, maintaining her athletic, yet womanly-soft body with the help of her personal trainers. She worked out at least three times a week, practiced *Kundalini* yoga during her rest periods and participated in charity walks and five-mile runs whenever her time would permit.

Her stadium-style classroom at Goldwin Smith Hall was filled with gifted students. Ardent eyes were glued on her as they listened to her every word. The class was almost evenly proportioned gender-wise, and she was equally pleased to see a whole host of different heritages represented in their young faces. Some were familiar faces from previous semesters or her other philosophy classes.

In her classes her students were always on the lookout for a lively discussion about past lives, soul mates and kindred spirits beyond the conventional, scientific definitions of time and space.

She relished those discussions and the chance to impart her ideas whenever she could. She encouraged her students to think and figure out issues for themselves. She was merely a guide in their personal journeys of self-discovery.

She had an excellent reputation with students and, because of her standing in the department, she only taught select groups of seniors who were open to her New Age teachings. Her classes filled up quickly.

She paused, "Before I elaborate, how many of you believe there are soul mates?"

Most raised their hands, which pleased her, "How many soul mates were you destined to have?"

There were many zealous hands, but she called on one eager student whose hand had been the first in the air. He had an expression of impatient zeal bursting on his russet face. A quick glance at her chart gave her his name, William S. "Please, do us the honors, William."

His boisterous voice reverberated in the classroom, "The answer is many soul mates! I've encountered at least two in my life and I'm sure many in my past lives!" He chuckled with his last remark, as did a few others who shared his sentiments.

"Why do you believe so passionately that you've had multiple soul mates in this life time?"

He cleared his throat and gathered his thoughts while the room became silent in anticipation of his answer. "Well, I met my first soul mate, believe it or not, in grade school." His voice was serious. "She was my first love. We shared our first kiss and we were really close for years, but at the start of our sophomore year, she moved away. During my senior year in high school, I met another girl I was madly in love with and we were seeing each other exclusively. I even intended to marry her. One day, recently actually, I took her to Toronto to see the *Phantom of the Opera* for an anniversary celebration of when we met. During intermission, I was getting drinks for us and as I began to order from the bartender, the woman next to me spoke at the same time I did. We both said, 'Tom Collins with a twist of lime, please.' We turned to each other and locked eyes. She was gorgeous, but there was something about her, something in her eyes—it was so familiar.

"We smiled at each other, got our drinks and then parted, going back to our respective dates. I thought nothing of it until I was in a bookstore here in town. I was reaching for a book; I happened to turn my head to the tables nearby and who should be sitting there? The same woman! But what was uncanny was that she was reading the same book I was reaching for. I simply stared at her. Then she looked up and smiled at me in recognition. I wanted to approach her to say hello, but my girlfriend was at another table, and so I walked away feeling really strange about how our paths crossed that way.

"Anyway, I dismissed the encounter as a simple coincidence. Three weeks later, I took my girlfriend on a date to the foreign film festival to watch the French version of the *Count of Monte Cristo*. After we were seated, I got up to get the customary popcorn and sodas. I chose a random line and as I got up to the counter to order, I was stunned to see who was standing there taking my order. The same gorgeous woman! That was it. I knew we were fated to meet. It hurt really badly, but I broke up with my girlfriend. I truly loved her, but who was I to fight destiny?

"I'm happy to say that just recently I asked that gorgeous woman to be my wife and she said YES!" His body seemed to glow, exuding happiness and pride, when he finished sharing his story.

Mercedes initiated a round of applause. The rest of the class joined her and she cried aloud, "William, you have been truly blessed! We thank you!"

Accolades filled the room and a few of his friends and classmates were giving him high fives, even playfully punching him lightly on the arm to show their approval. He was also receiving text messages from his far site classmates.

Wanting the full attention of the entire class, she simply waited until the gaiety subsided before starting again, "Listen closely everyone. Before I talk more about soul mates, I would like to ask each of you to take a moment to meditate." She pushed a button on her handheld, which also served as a remote to the audio system. A slow rise of soft music filled the room. It was on a low volume setting, and she had selected one of her favorites, Mozart's *Clarinet Concerto KV 622*. She continued to tell her class, "I need for you to silence your minds, empty all the noise, distractions and racing thoughts."

She scanned the room and was pleased to see her students had closed their eyes in meditation. "Now, once your mind is still, please open your hearts to my words. Fill your hearts with as much positive energy as you can muster. If you are having difficulty, focus on someone you love deeply."

Many students were smiling widely at her request. She, too, was smiling, thinking of her own love for a man from long ago. When she felt everyone was in a state of heightened awareness, she slowly turned down the music and began her lecture, "Let me begin by reiterating the statement I made at the beginning of class. There is no law on earth proclaiming that you may not love more than one person, but there is an unspoken and unwritten law that there can only be one true soul mate for each of us. One pair of souls are married to each other, connected and eternally bounded in the sacred bonds of love.

"Before there was a universe, there were these beautiful, immortal, asexual, omnipotent and sentient beings, eternally connected with one another, created completely out of pure love, whose life forces were inherently predisposed to both positive and negative external influences.

"Let me take a biblical metaphor from Genesis: Adam and Eve. They are the epitome of soul mates. They represent many like themselves, like us. The Almighty Creator, who bears many names and many faces, created them with pure love. In this class we view God, not in the traditional sense of the great religions that have existed, but in the same manner we view ourselves. Your individuality is the epitome of God. Let me take Eve as an example for this metaphor of God. What makes Eve, Eve? Uma?"

"Her body?"

"Yes, but Uma, there's more. Eve is more than her body. Eve was created from the same source in the universe. Her body is composed of her DNA, cells, blood and organs. She also possesses a powerful yet mysterious brain, of which we only use a small portion. Our brains show that we are highly evolved."

She scanned the room and asked again, "Now, what else?"

"Eve also has a soul."

Mercedes smiled widely, "You are on the right path, Uma. Eve possesses a soul. It is our life force. It is the very same force that fuels the universe. No one has yet begun to understand what a soul really is, except we know it is immortal. It is pure energy."

She continued with another question. "Without a soul, do you believe Eve would be alive?"

As murmuring began, she answered her own question, "Of course not. Let's take artificial intelligence, for instance. No soul. Just an organized collection of circuits, hardware components, programming software, and so on—but it's not alive. There is no soul or awareness. Thus, in our metaphor, Eve is God. Just as all things in the universe as a collective are God. Each life force, which does not necessarily mean a living, breathing, biological entity, encompasses God. We all depend on each other, as our bodies depend on oxygen. We are part of each other and the universe, as we understand it. Without each of these parts, there could be no whole."

The murmurs grew louder, which always happened whenever she talked about soul mates in her advanced classes. "Now that we know the concept of God, let us return to the concept of soul mates and Adam and Eve in the Garden of Eden. The Garden of Eden is paradise. It bears many names: heaven, nirvana, utopia and so on. Adam and Eve are married and in love, soul mates for eternity. They are running around oblivious to their nakedness, unashamed.

"There is only one rule in paradise. 'But of the tree of knowledge of good and evil, thou shalt not eat of it; for in the day that thou eatest thereof, thou shalt truly die.' Contrary to popular belief, the fruit of knowledge is not an apple, which grows prolifically in our wonderful Empire State of New York."

There were chuckles in the class at her remark and then silence as students waited for her to continue. "Can anyone guess what the tree of knowledge could possibly be?"

Many hands were in the air, but she called upon Elle, an athletic brunette with a radiant smile who said with certitude, "Professor, it is a grape."

"Well done, Elle. Yes, the fruit of knowledge is a grape."

The far site student who had asked the first question at the top of her lecture blurted, "But it says in Genesis that it is a tree, not a vine."

She looked at the student from Heidelberg on monitor six and nodded, "Correct, Emmett, it is described as a tree. And older grape plants have canes that become trunks after a second season. All trees have trunks, do they not? Let's put aside the anatomy of a grape plant, shall we, and continue with the fruit, the grape. What is so significant about a grape? Creative brainstorms are welcome."

With that invitation, she received bursts of fervent answers, noting everyone who answered and following each voice with her eyes.

Duncan, another African-American student, immediately offered, "Wine, alcohol, intoxication." A handful of others followed his lead and offered their responses.

"Great buzz. Uninhibited thinking."

"Blithering idiot. Hangovers."

"Getting laid. Alcoholism."

"Warped delusions. False sense of reality."

Finally, "Forgetfulness."

Feeling her throat becoming parched, she sipped her tonic water as she listened. Finally, she signaled for a time-out and the outbursts and chatter quieted down.

"A false sense of reality and forgetfulness are right on target. Your other answers are also correct. The fermented juice of the grape in moderation is fine. It produces a sense of euphoria. Who wouldn't want to feel that? Consumed in avarice or excess, it becomes lethal. We see too many examples of that on campuses." She paused and continued, "Now, Genesis tells us Eve was tempted by a serpent, which is a metaphor for what?"

"Our curiosity," said Erin on monitor seven, receiving Mercedes' nod of approval.

"Exactly. There was no serpent per se. It was simply our curiosity. Eve, with her inquiring mind, wanted to discover why it was prohibited. Forbidden. What could be so bad? And what was death? Anybody?"

She acknowledged the student from Bombay on monitor two. "Unless you have a near death experience, you don't know—right, Professor?" he inquired with British inflections.

"Thank you, Ranjit. I agree." Turning back to the entire class, she said, "We'll devote another lecture about the subject of death a little later. For today we'll focus on soul mates. Let's return to Adam and Eve. We've said that Eve was tempted by her curiosity and subsequently ate of the fruit of knowledge. She discovers it tastes wonderful. Some bites are sweet and others are a bit tart. She keeps eating until she feels a blissful euphoria. She's delighted. She didn't die, but like all of us, she didn't know what death really was, so she harvested the grapes and innovatively crushed them into wine and work it into a cup. She takes this cup—filled to the rim with this delicious tasting wine and bunches of grapes—to her husband, Adam. She wiles him to take a sip and taste a grape. To please her, Adam agrees, but he takes it farther."

A loud collective male groan blended with female giggles; a serious young lady remarked, "Adam gets trashed, completely drunk."

"Yes, Kuan-yin, he does. Even worse, he passes out. Care to add to the answer?"

Kuan-yin quickly retorted, "Leave it to a guy to drink to excess and get completely out of control. Worse yet, they think they're in control. What a lethal combination—drunks with delusions!"

As a cluster of side discussions began, Mercedes clapped her hands loudly, only once. "Now wait! Please focus. I haven't gotten to the good part yet."

When the class fell silent, she continued, "The sight of Adam, then unconscious, sent Eve into hysteria as the last part of the law in paradise, 'thou shalt truly die,' echoes in her mind. It is a silent yet deafening edict in its finality. But, nothing is ever final. For Adams and Eves of all ages, death is merely a transformation. A transition into forgetfulness. Just as we remember nothing from birth, we remember nothing when we come to die. Thus, death should never be feared. The process of dying might appear painful, even frightful, but let me remind everyone of a very wise sage who once wrote, 'In the sight of the unwise they seem to die; and their departure is taken for misery. And their going from us to be utter destruction: but they are in peace.'"

The insistent blinking green light on monitor three distracted her. She acknowledged the young Italian, "Professor, the wise sage is you, of course—*si?*"

Looking directly at him, she shook her head and replied in Italian, "*Grazie, Salvador. What a marvelous compliment! I wish it were true; but I must confess it was not I.*" She translated quickly in English.

With a smile she added, "The wise sage was no other than wise King Solomon. And Salvador, it is written in the Wisdom of Solomon in the pages of the *Apocrypha*, the missing books of the Bible."

Addressing everyone, she said, "Remember, *nothing is as it seems*. Do not be afraid of death. Instead, respect and understand the enigma of it. Accept death as part of the terms of living a life in forgetfulness. Eve, never knowing what death was to begin with, was understandably confused and very frightened. Yet, she finds that Adam is still breathing in his repose, and so she is assured he is still alive. Remember, they are immortal beings not subject to the limitations of time or space as we know it.

"Eve holds onto hope and, more importantly, to love with all her might and tries desperately to revive him, to console him, lying down with him on the grass in the midst of this Garden of Eden. And she waits patiently for him to awaken.

"As time passes, mind you in paradise, 'a thousand years is as a day and a day is as a thousand years,' Adam awakes, but because of the forgetfulness from the fruit of knowledge, he doesn't remember to open his eyes. Therefore, Eve is happy and excited about his wakefulness, but what happened?"

The young man from Columbia, on monitor five chimed in, "He's not aware that he is awake, because his eyes are closed. He's frightened!"

Mercedes gave him a wide smile. "Yes, Umberto, it is definitely frightening for him because he thinks he is somewhere else, when in reality he is safely lying on the grass with his wife beside him, in the midst of paradise. And what about Eve?"

A strong female voice responded from the side of the class, "She is frightened as well, I should think. If I were Eve, I would be incredibly frustrated in trying to convince him to open his eyes! I would shake him, beg him, scream at him, pour water on him, and if needed, pry his eyes open to make him realize he only has to lift his eyelids or simply *will* them to open! What is the matter with Adam?"

The young lady was a new student. Mercedes didn't know her name, which was on a revised list, hidden somewhere on the desk behind her. "A very good question indeed. What is the matter with Adam? Any thoughts?"

She immediately heard a young man's voice. "Adam has forgotten. Like you said, he thinks he is somewhere else, so with his mind on autopilot, he must think he is in the dark or something. When Eve does all of those things to make him open his eyes, it must affect his false sense of reality because he's drunk with the grape, with the fruit of knowledge. Being drunk with knowledge, he won't listen; he thinks he's hearing voices or whispers, not the sound of his own voice in his head. He thinks he is responding to a universe he does not know, so he reacts instinctively. This altered state is tantamount to insanity! And he's unable to decipher his reality because his eyes are closed. For example, when a breeze touches lightly on his skin, his imagination manifests it as weather in his dream world. It's like being in a totally different dimension where the possibilities are endless because, as you said, he is an omnipotent, powerful sentient being. He's God!"

"I am impressed, William. It appears that finding your soul mate agrees with you. You're on the right track. Now let's turn our attention back to Eve. What does Eve do now? Before you answer, let your mind wander freely. Explore every possibility."

Mercedes called on the young woman with the strong voice whose hand rose as she finished her sentence.

"Professor, I believe Eve can do one of two things. She waits or she joins him with a mission to convince him to open his eyes. But how can she convince him? If she does the same thing, she would feel the same effects of forgetfulness. If she waits, it would be like a self-imposed punishment, a penalty or penance for eating the fruit of knowledge, and that would definitely be hell! I feel terrible for her because, as you had said, they are immortal, and so if she waits, it might be for a very long time. If she joins him in this Never Land, she may never find him, let alone tell him what to do!"

Sitting on her desk, Mercedes lowered her eyes. After taking another sip of her tonic, she sighed deeply and leaned back, her legs still crossed, her arms stretched wide to balance her as she looked up to see that the class period was over. "Yes, what can Eve do? We'll have to address that during our next class."

Hearing the groans of disappointment, she said, "You'll have to come to our next class for the answer. Now please check the syllabus for your reading assignment and think about what Eve could do. A good piece to read might be the soliloquy by Shakespeare in *As You Like It*."

In an oratory fashion, she quoted from memory "'All the world's a stage, and all the men and women merely players. They have their exits and their entrances, and one man in his time plays many parts, his being seven ages.'"

She turned off her tablet and added, "Think about that quote. I'll see you next class."

A number of students gathered around her, wanting to continue with the discussion. Mercedes entertained a few questions, but hurried off to her next class which was scheduled within the hour. First, she stopped at her office to check her messages. She uploaded her notes to the laptop, and scrolled through numerous emails that she downloaded to her handheld for later reading.

Finally, she retrieved her voice mail and listened to her first message.

"Hi beautiful, I hope your day went well." She instinctively touched her wedding band, smiling as she continued to listen. "It's been really hectic here. Unfortunately, I won't make it for dinner but I'll be home in time to tuck you in. Talk to you soon. I love you, bye."

A knock on her office door startled her. "Professor?"

"Yes, Kuan-yin. What can I do for you?"

"I missed the last Ancient and Medieval Philosophy class and I was wondering if I could get a copy of your lecture notes?" Her student's eyes fell on the credentials that hung on the wall behind her desk. "Wow! Your doctorate was from Harvard. What was Harvard like?"

"Much like Cornell," she smiled.

"Rumor has it that you were an engineer before you became a professor here at Cornell University."

"You've heard correctly."

"That seems like a really drastic change from engineering to philosophy."

Mercedes simply nodded and smiled at her, "Your tablet or handheld?"

"Oh yes, one sec." She hurriedly rummaged through her backpack and handed her a red computerized writing tablet.

Mercedes enabled the synch mode for the wireless transfer and within a few seconds, Kuan-yin had the lecture notes.

"I hope someday I can teach college too."

"It's a lot of work to get your degrees, but from what I've seen in class, you have the ability. Go for it."

She noticed her student was also examining her tapestry and struggled to translate the words on it. "You know German?"

"A little. I took it as an elective last semester. I thought I could translate it, but all I got is something the women—they, they something and into something life." She sounded a little flustered.

Smiling at Kuan-yin's efforts, she got up from behind her desk and stood next to her. Looking at the words on the tapestry, she translated with ease, "*Honour the women—they braid and weave heavenly roses into earthly life.*" She also offered a little history, "Marianne Stokes designed the tapestry and the text was inspired by Schiller's poem *Women's Worth* from 1796." Remembering an old friend's comment, Mercedes shared, "My favorites are the two women dressed in armor: courage and fidelity."

"They look powerful."

"Yes, they do."

Noting the time, Mercedes said politely to her young student, "Would you excuse me? I have to check the rest of my phone messages before I go into my

next class."
"Sure, no problem. Thanks for the notes."
"Anytime."
"See you in class, Professor Larcher."

Chapter 20

Epiphanies

Standing in front of the class, Mercedes picked up on Wednesday's lecture. "As you recall during the last class, we broke off with Eve trying to figure out how to awaken Adam and to get him to open his eyes. I quoted to you the soliloquy of Shakespeare's *As You Like It*: 'All the world's a stage, and all the men and women merely players. They have their exits and their entrances, and one man in his time plays many parts, his being seven ages.'"

The deliberate drama in her introduction set a serious tone for her lecture, exactly the effect she sought.

"Each of us is either an Adam or an Eve. Therefore, the stage has been set for the journey of those two soul mates. They are immortal. Their love is enduring. After Adam drinks and eats of the grape, Eve is left in paradise with Adam, who is in a state of forgetfulness because of the fruit of knowledge. Does any anyone want to tell me why it is called the fruit of knowledge?"

She was a little surprised at the lack of hands, yet she understood their hesitation, so she continued, "The reason is unassumingly profound in its simplicity. You need knowledge, you need wisdom to completely unlock the truth; therefore, once you discover the truth, you will know everything and everything will make sense. You will inevitably possess the gift of knowing.

"In Eastern philosophy, this is known as the state of *true enlightenment*. Once we reach this state, we will have been restored to our true selves—our former selves. We will be beautiful, immortal, asexual, omnipotent and sentient beings, eternally connected with one another, created completely out of pure love. Our life forces are inherently predisposed to both positive and negative external influences and, more importantly, to freewill! Thus, we are naturally flawed, imperfect. But, as you know, God is perfect. God is infallible. If we all encompass God, then how as *flawed* beings are we to achieve perfection?" She paused, not really looking for an answer.

"Freewill. Our freewill is another powerful gift. A gift, and more appropriately, a power that must never be taken for granted. With freewill we must bear enormous responsibilities. Since our life forces are predisposed to either good or bad and the battle of good versus evil, it is important to note that what drives us to be either is solely based on our freewill! Our freewill dictates and leads us to whichever path we shall take.

"We will attract one of these external influences, like *red on a rose*. If you willingly embrace negative thoughts, or *evil*, then negative/evil forces will be attracted to you. They will shadow you, keep you in the darkness and consume you wholly with rage and hatred.

"Your luck will always be bad and disappointments, heartaches, and medical maladies will suddenly occur in your life, one after the other, until you freely choose, using your own freewill, to embrace the good external forces of the universe.

"When you embrace those good intentions and good thoughts—and more importantly, welcome *love* into your soul—then positive/good forces will be attracted to you. They will shine and guide your path out of the shadows. When you emerge, they will bathe you in the brilliance of truth and love. Only good things will always happen in your life, and you will discover your health will improve, as will your luck and life circumstances. You will find you are loved tremendously and you will love equally in return. Inevitably, you will live out a long happy life.

"Should you choose the middle path that follows the teachings of Tao, you will have balance, harmony in the universe, a life of both positive and negative forces, of *Yin Yang*. Feminine and masculine. In simpler terms, life will taste *bitter* with the negative, life will taste *sweet* with the positive, and life will be *bittersweet* in between.

"When you are at a crossroad in your journey, facing significant life-altering choices, and you become fully aware of the positive and negative external influences of the universe that surrounds you, I urge you—do not be afraid! Have faith, take courage and strength from love and be wise. Once you do so, you will make the correct decisions! Remember, 'Behold I send you forth in the midst of wolves: be ye therefore as wise as serpents, but harmless as doves.' To put it simply, the path of good does not have red lights! But, as we travel that path, we must make wise choices because, whether for good or bad, positive or negative, it only takes one decision—one act of freewill to affect your life, your path, your journey and the lives of everyone within your circle of life.

"Now let us return to soul mates, to Eve and her life-altering choices about Adam. Last time we posed the question, what does Eve do now? What does she ultimately decide to do?"

She waited for comments but found none, so she continued, "Eve decides not to wait. She takes all the risks and responsibilities to find Adam, knowing their souls are eternally connected and that they will find each other, no matter what the circumstances may be.

"But, how will Eve maneuver in the world of forgetfulness, which she knows not, to find Adam? What will guide her through this labyrinth?"

There were several students whispering and she paused, hoping for a round-table discussion, but none of her students volunteered their ideas. All around her, she saw only eager expressions on faces waiting for her explanations.

"Ladies and gentlemen, in this world of forgetfulness, in this reality we call life, the powerful life force of God—the universe—will guide Eve as well as Adam. How is this manifested?"

She heard a male voice saying, "Coincidences! Like invisible forces guiding our actions and making us believe we are making conscious choices consciously, but our choices are really made at a subconscious level."

Looking at his direction, she nodded, "Yes. That's very good, but that is only part of it, William. Let's investigate those invisible forces. Those forces are manifested through an oxymoron that I refer to as *silent screaming signs*. And those silent screaming signs surround you every day. Importantly, they are completely unique to you and are always right there in front of you, perpetually dropping clues like coincidences, *déjà vu*, premonitions and the unexplained. They are also those whispers from that little voice in your head that you listen to in varying degrees and that can guide you along your journey.

"Whenever you get close to each other, more of those life signs appear, and you will either notice them or not until you are completely inundated with a deluge of signs—prompting your immediate attention! Those signs will become more and more apparent, even ridiculous at times, until they reach a point when you can no longer deny or ignore them. At that point they will become so painfully obvious that it will seem that the thunderous voice of God is startling you into wakefulness with a proclamation: 'Behold—open your eyes! Standing there before you is your Adam or your Eve, your true soul mate!' In the case of Eve, before she embarks in her journey, she seeks those personal signs unique to her, which will ultimately lead her to Adam. She is hoping against all hope that when she is in the state of forgetfulness, she will be reminded to remember and to recognize these signs and follow a path within this world of forgetfulness and make the necessary choices.

"This brings us back to the subject of *freewill*. Eve must contend with the power of freewill, because freewill dictates the choices both of them will make in their forgetfulness. Their journey will be difficult, harrowing, and often sorrowful. Often times, there will be missed opportunities in their search, but as William has personally discovered—the paths of soul mates will cross time and time again, like coincidences, until Eureka! They both figure out this was meant to be! It was destined, fated. They will end up together, for they truly do belong to each other.

"Now, why would Eve want to take the risks at all, knowing how freewill complicates her search for Adam?"

Her voice was raspy, as it normally became at times during class. Sometimes she would even lose her voice by the end of the day. She caught herself before she coughed and quickly sipped her glass of water.

She scanned the room, seeing the students still didn't want to interrupt her, eager to hear her ideas. After clearing her throat, she continued, "Eve takes those enormous risks because she embodies and possesses love, the most powerful force we know. With a strong arsenal powered by love, she knows she will never fail! For nothing is impossible with love! Trusting in the power of love, she has the courage and strength to eat and drink of the fruit of knowledge. As she begins to feel the effects of forgetfulness, she lies down on the ground in a loving and tender embrace with Adam. It is her desperate effort to protect him and be close to him while they journey together in this vast universe of forgetfulness. Like a powerful magnetic force, their love will cause their souls to gravitate to one another because the sacred bonds of marriage between soul mates are made in heaven *first*; therefore, these vows can *never* be broken.

"It is also a one way street! Heaven to earth, then earth to heaven. This reminds me of a Bible text, 'Whatsoever ye shall bind on earth shall be bound in heaven; and whatsoever ye shall loose on earth shall be loosed in heaven.' God married Adam and Eve, just like God marries every true pair of soul mates! Remember, 'What therefore God hath joined together, let no man put asunder.'

Recall that God is infallible; therefore no power can undo what God has done. *None*. Absolutely nothing will stand in the way of love.

"All right—when soul mates do find each other, how will they recognize each other? What measures has God, the universe, taken to ensure that they do not ignore each other or miss each other completely when they are standing inches from one another, just within reach, if only they knew? Okay. Time for some discussion."

At her behest, her students began to share their free-flowing thoughts. She encouraged them to talk and share, knowing that the process mimicked automatic writing, and allowed uninhibited thoughts to surface with a heightened awareness that led to self-realized truths.

After a few minutes, the green light on monitor nine flashed. Nathan, a boyish gentleman, said, "Professor, I read your book on kindred spirits, and I believe that it definitely applies here. The idea about a strong sense of familiarity. It would be like they have met each other before. Like, when you try to remember something that is on the tip of your tongue and later you blurt it out. Except with Adam, he won't know how he knows Eve because the memory of her will be dormant in his psyche. But he will feel very drawn to her, like a bee to a flower."

Larry, seated near Nathan, said, "Professor, I believe that Adam will be at the right place, at the right time. Not only that, there would be that sense of *déjà vu* all the time. Like they've met before, when the truth is that they really did meet, but in some forgotten time and place or dimension. It would feel funny, weird and strange at the same time. I know I would feel really uncomfortable, maybe even freak out about it."

Larry's pretty girlfriend Ginny, a young platinum blonde, added, "That reminds me of William's story. They'll somehow be able to read each other's thoughts, finish sentences and just know what the other is thinking. It'll be romantic when they do finally meet. We're all adults here, so I think I can safely say that their sex would be incredibly passionate and fulfilling. Their bodies would fit perfectly. There is nothing more satisfying than making love to the person you love! Talk about intense!"

Ginny was smiling at Larry and she gave him a quick peck on his lips. In turn, he took her hand and kissed it. They were staring into each other's eyes, smiling, before quickly returning their attention to Mercedes. Their public display of affection sent a warm feeling through her, and she noted there were many agreeing whispers on the subject of physical attraction.

The student from Tokyo on monitor eight, Izanagi, joined the discussion, "Which is why Eve will appear even more beautiful to Adam when he sees her. Adam would want to approach Eve. Even as Eve ages and her physical beauty withers, she will remain just as beautiful, or even more beautiful, in his eyes. When you look at someone through eyes filled with love, your soul mate is angelic, beautiful and even perfect. Love sees the inner beauty of the soul."

A fashionable psychology student, Nancy, said smiling, "All flaws, physical or otherwise, would be overlooked or simply accepted. It's like make-up or no make-up. Eve would still be very sexy to Adam. And as far as their lovemaking, their bodies would be attuned to each other's needs. Eve could just give Adam a look and Adam would jump on her without hesitation and vice versa. Or just thinking about each other would send them to heights of ecstasy. Their imaginations would become vivid. The sensations of their touches would be greatly enhanced, though comfortable. Their moments together would be a combination of physical and spiritual joining. When they'd be together, it would be like electricity with sparks flying everywhere. It'd be like all those stories about seeing stars or fireworks."

Without missing a beat, Rose, Cornell's current homecoming queen, a petite Italian beauty with a lovely smile, added, "I think it even goes to an unconscious level where scent comes into play. Eve would release more pheromones for Adam, basically marking him. So, Adam would naturally be attracted to her when she is close to him because she is emitting these special pheromones that are only meant for Adam. And their conversations would seem endless. Adam wouldn't be able to get enough of Eve. Their words would flow smoothly because they would truly be in synch with each other. They would just love to listen to each other's voices. Their voices would psychically massage and soothe their souls."

Ryan, a thin blond student who always sat in the back row, took the initiative, "Yeah, it would be like there was no one else in the room, even though you're both in the middle of a frat party or a football game or wherever. With me, I know I could tune out everything in the room and just focus totally on her. I would be mesmerized with her eyes, her face, with everything about her! And I wouldn't be able to stop touching her. I'd want to be near her and we wouldn't necessarily have to be making love either. I would be just as content holding her close and kissing her. Definitely a lot of kissing. It would be enough to just be quiet together, to listen to music, check out the stars, or just listen to her breathe. Just being with her would be a natural high! Wow! If you guys see my Eve around, send her to me—would ya!"

An infectious laughter took hold and a sense of warmth descended upon her class. The students were joyous with good-hearted humor.

Steve, a stoic young man with strawberry-blond hair and glasses, said seriously, "I think the best part is that you trust each other completely! No head games or stupid lies. No masquerades. Just plain honesty and total trust. I know I would definitely feel like a kid again. We would be silly but child-like, calling each other cute names, using some secret code that lets us know how much we love each other deeply. Others would think we're silly or sickeningly cute or even immature. But I'll be laughing when those same people encounter their own soul mates. They'll act the same way! I'd also be protective, not out of control like some intensely jealous maniac, but protective. There's no doubt in my mind that I'd trust my soul mate implicitly. There'd be no question about her word, either. Her integrity, her honor.

"I'd want her to be happy. I wouldn't have to put up any walls either. No guarded thoughts or feelings. I'd feel completely free to be me! It'd be like I could run around naked and show off all my flaws without worry or embarrassment. And disagreements? We would simply agree to disagree, and," he grinned, "then we'd have the most incredible sex afterwards!"

Though there was snickering at his last sentence, Mercedes also heard others commenting, "Yep, that's right!"

"Exactly! I feel you, dude!"

"It's happened to me!"

"Copy that!"

The camaraderie was interrupted when a longhaired Brazilian beauty on monitor ten named Estrella remarked, "Don't forget the tenderness. They would be sensitive to each other's needs, considerate and respectful for each other's feelings—never taking their own feelings into consideration, but always considering the other one. I know I would bear the discomfort if it would make him comfortable, much like my boyfriend draping me with his jacket because I forgot to bring one. He's willing to freeze for me without a second thought, knowing I'll be warm. I'd do the same for him, and so everything comes out naturally. It doesn't take effort to show gentleness. We don't need false intentions or forced feelings of caring. Whenever we're together, it feels like we're on our first date." She hesitated and then added a little self-consciously, "We're constantly fawning over each other, ceaseless in wooing one another. I definitely love the wooing part and just living to make each other feel good. And the laughter! We have so much fun just making each other laugh. I just love listening to my boyfriend's laughter! *Oh, meu Deus!* It feels fantastic to hear him laugh!"

Upon hearing her expression, which Mercedes often used, without any thought, Mercedes blurted, "*¡Eu sei exatamente como você sente!*" She didn't realize she wasn't speaking English until she heard Estrella, who was taken completely by surprise, exclaimed in her native tongue, "*Wow! Professor, I didn't know you spoke Portuguese.*"

Upon hearing her, Mercedes realized she was and she let out a soft laugh. Quickly, she acknowledged her and said, "Why, yes, Miss Ruiz. I picked up the language on a weeklong holiday to Rio De Janeiro during the Carnival." She turned her attentions to her class, saying with sincerity, "My apologies, class. What I said to Estrella was simply, 'I know exactly how you feel!'"

As the class started a number of small conversations, she was pleased with the personal insights from her students. Their discussions had generated good feelings, smiling faces, and warmth in the room, but she had to continue with the class, so with subtle grace, she joined the on-going discussions and steered them to the next lesson about wisdom.

"I am amazed with all of you. Joyful, as a matter of fact! Thank you everyone for sharing your personal thoughts and experiences. It sounds like many of you are feeling and describing the joys of love at their height. Love at the dawn of love…when all you feel is that wonderful giddy, butterflies-in-the-stomach, light-headed type feeling that releases all those wonderful endorphins that engulf your entire body. Now, imagine having all those feelings and having them last for the rest of your natural life!"

The excitement in the class was apparent as students shared their own experiences.

"It would be heaven on earth, Professor!" Larry offered.

"Yes, it would be heaven on earth," she echoed, smiling. "And—going back to Adam and Eve—it will be that way once Eve finally finds Adam. But, before they have that strong, loving commitment, they are faced with an obstacle. They are strangers to each other in this world of forgetfulness—remember?"

As heads were nodding, she said, "Listen closely, because this is where the power of love reveals its wisdom. Soul mates will *always* recognize each other because that recognition is on the subconscious level. It is with the windows of their souls that they will first recognize each other. Adam will look into Eve's eyes and he will recognize her life force, which will lead to an unconscious dance back into the depths of their buried memories. As I had said, Adam and Eve will recognize each other once their eyes lock. That recognition will be slow at first; and it will be quickly replaced with comfortable reminiscence, as familiar strangers inevitably become reunited soul mates.

"When they first meet, they are simply re-acquainting themselves. Mind you, in paradise, they know each other completely, for Adam and Eve are one! But in this reality of life, they must literally *rediscover* one another. Soul mates do not need a long time to reveal themselves to each other. To an outsider it would seem to be a whirlwind romance, because their emotions are already very strong after just a few hours together. The urge to be together constantly is inexplicable. It's as if each moment is very precious. Imagine how long they've spent looking for each other."

She paused for a moment before continuing, "There is another important reality to this recognition. Sometimes, an Adam will take more than a few hours, even years, to recognize his Eve. This happens when this Adam, with his freewill, chooses to refuse to see believe the true identity of his Eve often due to his external circumstances! Outside forces stimulate his freewill and encourage him to doubt or question the obvious! Again, it is important that you understand that freewill is all about choices.

"Wisdom is also part of the arsenal of love. Wisdom plays an integral role in the journey of soul mates at this crossroad. It is through the power of wisdom that Adam will come to know and make the right choices about Eve. Love will ultimately bestow the gift of wisdom on Adam and, at that moment of knowing, love will reveal the true identity of Eve to Adam. When will both Adam and Eve be more susceptible to finding each other?"

Among the eager hands filling the landscape was Minna's, a lovely blonde who was with child. In a girlish voice, she offered, "I think it would be when both Adam and Eve are not looking. I know when I'm not looking, I manage to meet someone at the most unexpected places. Then, when I'm out in a club with friends, all I manage to attract are the wrong guys, drunken guys to be exact, arrogant and full of themselves. My friends and I just laugh at them and don't think twice about rejecting them because when you meet them, it just doesn't feel right. But when I'm oblivious and not even checking anyone out, just simply out to have a great time with my girlfriends and dance up a storm, it never fails. There's a gorgeous hunk of a guy who boldly dances right alongside of me. We look at each other, smile and then keep dancing. The next thing I know, we exchange phone numbers, and maybe even meet elsewhere." She smiled warmly, "Honestly, that's how I met my husband, Austin."

Mercedes knew the warmth in that smile and it reminded her of her own nice memories many years ago. *Las Vegas.*

Quickly shaking off the memory, Mercedes underscored the young woman's comments, "Minna is exactly right. Their highest susceptibility would occur when Adam and Eve are not actively searching. That is when they can find each other a lot quicker. Why is this? If we link this point back to what Rose mentioned earlier about the pheromones and the unconscious level, Adam and Eve without active participation allow the universe to guide them. When they do this, their personal invisible signs are automatically recognized at an unconscious level. Therefore, Adam and Eve's respective invisible search parties embark on their mission, unbeknownst to the conscious awareness of their minds. Much like the pheromones, which were mentioned earlier, Adam follows Eve's pheromones and he recognizes her this way. On a larger scale it is the universe and the positive life forces and the magnetic pull of their love that now come into play. Those forces manipulate events and guide the course of their paths toward that inevitable crossing. To quote the famous phrase of the venerable R. H. Delaney, 'Love builds bridges where none exist!'

"But soul mates do not always end up as they should. Now, why is that?" Without waiting for an answer, she said, "It is because of freewill. Unfortunately, freewill does get in the way of soul mates. As you know, Eve anticipated this, even in the midst of forgetfulness. Class, what ramifications will the gift of freewill have on their reunion?"

Once again, she signaled the class for a little more free-flowing thinking. Frankly, she needed a few moments to become more detached from her own feelings, to compartmentalize her feelings from her lecture, because her next points would be dealing with the most painful part of the journey that faced soul mates who were separated. Silently she said a prayer for everyone, hoping they would never feel the bittersweet pangs of unrequited love.

William excitedly took the lead and said, "The word, Professor, is *pain*. I mean in my case, breaking up with my former girlfriend hurt very badly and even though I broke it off, I felt her pain because as I said, I truly loved her. But I knew in my heart that she wasn't my soul mate. However, that didn't make the decision to break away any easier. It was extremely painful."

Steve projected an interesting sentiment. "There's another thing, too. I think it's even worse when you are faced with your soul mate, but you are already committed to another person, someone whom you do love but now recognize is really not your destiny, your soul mate. It can be very frustrating. In William's case, he was lucky in the sense that he wasn't married. Breaking up with a girlfriend would be easier than divorcing a wife, and then if there were children in the picture, it'd make the choice to be with your soul mate appear impossible. You'd have to make a really difficult choice. If the right choice would be to leave a marriage, then by all means do it; but if the circumstances are such that you can't—then tough, right? I think it would be a classic Catch-22. I suppose you'd have to make the best of whatever decision you'd make. After all, someone still loves you and you still have love in your heart for that someone. So, all is not lost. It's just not complete. Like something is always missing in your life."

A female student on monitor one added in heavily accented English, "*Bon jour*. I believe freewill makes things difficult for soul mates. Sometimes impossible, I think, because the choices are already made. You feel like, ah, like you cannot get out of it. So you accept the responsibilities with your decisions. Sadly, you end up living your life with someone else! It will never feel the same as spending your life with your soul mate. Although I'm sure that a life with someone else, though sadly not your soul mate, could certainly still be a happy and content one because love does exist. For me, I know the love is definitely not as passionate or complete as it would be with my own Adam."

Mercedes enjoyed listening to the rhythm of Evelyn's voice. When she looked at monitor one, her speech transitioned in French as if without her notice, "*Thank you for sharing your extraordinary insights. It sounds like you are on the right path of your journey. I truly wish that you will find your Adam in this life. And once you do, hold on tightly to each other. Make wise decisions. Do not take anything for granted—however* small it may seem to be. And live in unconditional love for the rest of your lives without any regrets. I must say, Evelyn, you have a beautiful name, for like Eve, it means life!"

"Thank you very much, Professor! It's so nice to hear you speak to me in my language. Thank you for your wish for me. I hope that when I do find my Adam, I will make the correct choices with my freewill. And, yes, I promise to live in love for the rest of my days with him. And, of course, the rest of my future lives as well. But, if I would be so unlucky to miss my Adam in this lifetime because of my choices or his, I will certainly love whomever I am with, loving him with all that I am and will ever hope to become. I'd hope to live a happy life until I would be blessed with wisdom in the next life and to finally be with my true soul mate. For as you said, that is also the true nature of love."

Mercedes smiled and then promptly translated their words for the whole class.

After a second's pause, she prompted her students, "Does anyone else wish to share their thoughts on the ramifications of freewill?"

"Well, taking your lead on Shakespeare, Professor, as all of us are aware, Shakespeare's literature is filled with unrequited love and tragedies about star-crossed lovers. It's very sad! All that longing is excruciating! It's like that painting by Michelangelo on the Sistine Chapel where Adam is reaching out to God and their fingers almost touch but they don't. It's exactly like that. Adam and Eve are at each other's grasp, but never touching. Always together, forever apart. How awful!" said Tracy, a lovely brunette student, sitting directly in front of William.

The male student sitting two seats behind Tracy blurted out, "Pardon my French, but that sucks!" Many others voiced their agreement.

Not taking offense, Mercedes said grinning, "You're right, Seth, and I could share the actual French alternative to your sentiment, but not in class." Then, she took the opportunity to solidify her point and drove her lessons home, "I must admit that I find Tracy's metaphor of Michelangelo's *The Creation of Adam* captures my feelings on the subject succinctly. Let me cite my favorite bard, Shakespeare, in his *A Midsummer Night's Dream*: 'the course of true love never did run smooth.' With that, I must emphasize that soul mates may part sorrowful, but the torturous pain of parting will lessen. How can they survive it? Wisdom, once again. For with wisdom comes the understanding and acceptance that they will find each other. It is the nature of the journey of soul mates. Though Adam and Eve do not have the foresight or the conscious knowledge of when their paths will cross, it is with certainty they will meet again.

"Of course, as humans, we must naturally grieve the loss of our soul mate who was ripped away from us *again*! Therefore, the process of grieving could be a slow and painful one. Some may take a lot longer than others; some will simply bounce back within days. But when comfort is taken from the wisdom that their paths will cross regardless of circumstances, then they—you—will eventually continue with the business of life in a state of forgetfulness. Life moves on. One could even say that life is cruel and unfair because it waits for no one as we move on. One can view regret as an acceptable risk, but only when you know you did the right thing for each other, for love.

"This brings us back to the comment that Estrella made earlier about enduring discomfort for the sake of your soul mate and about making difficult promises or choices to ensure the happiness of your soul mate."

She had to pause again for a moment, because her thoughts suddenly flew back to personal moments when she had to make her own life-altering decisions. "At this juncture, I want, I need and I *must* stress to you, Adams and Eves of today, about another relevant fact regarding freewill. Love never allows freewill to hurt soul mates intentionally. *Never.* Therefore, love will not effect malevolent, life-altering changes onto the lives external to one another. That is not the true nature of love. Therefore, the tremendous pain of loss is also very temporary relative to the grand scheme of the universe. As William Wordsworth said, 'We will grieve not, rather find, strength in what remains behind.' After the grief of loss vanishes, you will revel in the love that remains intact. You will revisit those joys of love and celebrate, even in the absence of your soul mate. You will have been given the wisdom to view those moments with your soul mate—though brief—as a gift. A gift of reunited love. With soul mates, timing is everything!"

Suddenly, after finishing her last remark, a feeling of vertigo swirled over her, embracing her as though she was standing on a high precipice. Her senses began to numb and, lost in the moment and in her thoughts, she felt as though she was no longer in the midst of her classroom. An image of a past love, of Joe, emerged in front of her, filling her heart with intense emotions compelling her to quote something in Latin, "*'Ama me fideliter! Fidem meam noto: de corde totaliter et ex mente tota, sum presentialiter absens in remota.'*"

"That sounds so beautiful! What does it mean?" She heard the question in Joe's distinctly strong, sensual, deep voice, but the voice quickly transitioned into a younger voice with a Japanese accent. One of her far site students was smiling at her, patiently waiting for a translation, along with everyone.

Shaking herself out of her reverie, she translated with a smile, "'Love me faithfully! See how I am faithful: with all my heart and all my soul. I am with you though I am far away.'"

A little embarrassed, Mercedes noticed that some of her students appeared to have been fascinated with her impromptu soliloquy in Latin. She was known as a gifted linguist, but it was obvious they had never heard her, or anyone, speak in Latin with such emotion and passion.

"When the paths of soul mates finally cross, they are faced with each other. And, an inexplicable phenomenon happens. They recognize one another for who they truly are. I cannot stress this enough! But with freewill added to the complexities of the search, soul mates are most often under the mercy of unrequited love! Again, I wish to underscore this: soul mates decide with their freewill and are going to base their anguished decisions on what is truly best for each other, given the circumstances of life." She repeated the last line as though to remind her, "Given the circumstances of life. It really isn't as tragic as it seems, once you look at it from a different perspective. It is out of their immense love for each other that they—that you—both choose to let each other go. Freewill can easily be viewed as an enemy of soul mates, but when the truth is known and realized, it allows you to choose love. Remember, love never fails! Love always prevails, regardless of how terrible things may appear.

"Going back to my statement about how looks may be deceiving, when you choose love, you have been true to your love and your vows with each other. With love, we may suffer, but love is never unkind. *Never.*" She looked at Steve's direction, saying, "Therefore, there is no Catch-22! Love is always, always, a win-win situation! Just like in the moment when soul mates' paths do cross at that most opportune time, when freewill leads them to choose each other again,

Adam and Eve will live their lives, journeying together hand-in-hand, living in love, experiencing pure joy and unadulterated happiness in their reunited love, just as they would have in paradise. Thus they will witness, as I hope you will all witness in life, a monogamous, strong and loving relationship that is filled with mutual respect." She thought of her parents after she said it.

"It is *trust* bound by blissful peace and, more importantly, by unconditional love. This is when there is daily closeness, the unconditionally loving of one another that carries into the twilight of people's years of their love, in their forgetfulness. Inevitably, they will both open their eyes and be fully aware, returning to themselves as they were before their curiosity led them to partake of the grape."

She was pleased to see an insistent show of hands elevated in an almost orchestrated unison.

The young transfer student with the strong voice spoke, "Professor, once Eve finds Adam and they are reunited on earth as you alluded, they essentially remarry, thereby reaffirming their sacred vows that were originally made in heaven under the very eyes of God. Would this break the proverbial spell of forgetfulness? So when they literally die as humans, they would finally awake together in paradise?"

Mercedes appreciated her astute question. Usually it took several lectures before a student would make that observation. She quickly glanced down at her tablet for the revised student list, smiling as she saw the young woman's name, Mercedes T., and writing on the screen, *strong voice— insightful*, next to her name. *Of course, she shares my name. And, what a lovely coincidence!*

She looked at her with a warm smile. "Before I answer the question, which young Mercedes has just posed, would someone care to take an educated guess?"

As she expected, there were no takers, so she redirected her point, "Let me pose this question instead. When you have attended a fraternity party and gotten drunk—I mean a worshipping-the-porcelain-god type of inebriation—"

The comment put many of her student's into a laughing fit, and she laughed along with them. "I know what happens. I was young like you once. Now seriously folks, how do you feel the next morning? How long do the effects last?"

Without hesitation, a new voice belonging to a student called Theo, seated in the back row, said grimacing, "Hung-over beyond belief! You end up making impossible promises to never drink ever again!" Others, who seemed to have spoken from experience, followed his comment.

"Puking my guts out!"
"Getting stupid!"
"Wasting the rest of the weekend!"
"Wishing the headaches to magically disappear!"

Touching his newly shaved head, Theo added, "Depending on the severity of the drinking binge, I'm spinning on my bed with trashcans within puking distance for at least a couple of days."

The veiled woman sitting next to him, Aisha, said with all seriousness, "But if we were talking about an alcoholic, Professor, the withdrawal symptoms are wicked and painful. It could last for months until the alcoholic gets clean and sober, maybe goes to AA, and is strong enough to not yield to the temptations. Just one taste could put an alcoholic back on his or her same old path, having to go through that painful, cyclical process of recovery. That would be hell! Or at least one version of it! So, to tie into what the Professor said about Eve's angst in making her decision to find Adam, Eve would also know that it might take many, many attempts, even in their wakefulness, for the effects of the fruit of knowledge, just like alcohol, to be expelled. It would have to be purged completely out of their systems. Imagine if Adam was an alcoholic, or Eve becomes one, addicted to the fruit of knowledge during her attempts! Then their hell—her hell—becomes a reality!"

Theo interjected, "And as I understand it from the Professor's earlier comments about death, that would explain why we have the 'past lives' phenomena. Because Adam and Eve need to completely rid themselves of the effects of forgetfulness before they can truly and permanently return to their former state of grace!"

Another student added to the point seamlessly, "Ah! Now I get it! I read the Professor's last book about near death experiences or NDE. I believe I have deciphered it as well. The idea is that when either one of them has figured it out he or she will 'will' his or her eyes to open. Let me take Adam as an example, since my name is Adam. When Adam goes through the journey in numerous time periods or past lives, he dies each time. He goes through all the experiences that I've read about which occur in an NDE. You know: the tunnel, the vacuum feeling, sensations of hovering above your body, the blinding bright light, the warmth of peace, the love and other times, greeted by loved ones who have passed on. It makes perfect sense! Because in Adam's struggle for wakefulness, he'll feel like he was coming out of a tunnel or was being pulled by a vacuum force as he rejoins the universe! Of course, the light would be blinding because Adam has had his eyes closed to the truth for a very long time! The reason he feels the floating sensations is because he is in his true state—he is light and energy! He does not have the constraints of a physical form! And, of course, the love, warmth and peace would be there, because that's the state of mind or being he had before he got drunk from the fruit of knowledge. And, more importantly, the presence of loved ones is simply Eve greeting Adam in his wakefulness because Eve has returned or awakened before him! And—"

"Sorry to interrupt you, Adam, but just now I finally have another explanation for being gay. Of course, just as the Professor said, soul mates are asexual to begin with. God is asexual because God is all of us, the universe and whatever else we have not yet begun to comprehend!" said Ellen, a lovely shorthaired brunette with black glasses, who was open about her alternative lifestyle.

"Hey, you've got a great point there!" Adam complimented his classmate sitting next to him.

Suddenly, Henry from London on monitor four excitedly shared, "Yes—that's it! When both of them wake up separately, like in an NDE, a past life flashback or during REM sleep when we all dream, there would be a knowing! Of course! I mean, it would also explain about why people, especially me, feel a strong sense of longing, of knowing that there is someone out in the world for me. My soul mate, in my case, is *my Adam*!"

"As I was about to say earlier," Adam interjected. "I've read that many people who have returned from an NDE possess inexplicable gifts that they did not possess before their NDE experience. Gifts like clairvoyance, psychic abilities, healing hands, etcetera! This could only mean that each time Adam dies and gets reborn, his brain—as the Professor said earlier—becomes more highly evolved and accesses new areas in his powerful mind automatically, maybe like idiot savants or MENSA geniuses like the Professor. Maybe they've tapped into their powers, ones they had possessed all along, but ironically, just like Adam not remembering to open his eyes, they, or rather *we*, have forgotten how to access our inherent abilities!"

When he finished his sentence, Kwatee, an American-Indian student, added to his point, "To use the Professor's metaphor, it would be because in Adam's deep slumber, he briefly woke up on occasion bewildered, but still under the influence, so he only had glimpses of Eve, his true love, his one true soul mate! With just glimpses of the truth during his short bursts of wakefulness, he longs for love, just like all of us on earth always long for a love and search for it for all our lives! Romantic love, the stuff we see in romantic movies and books, it all makes sense to me now!" He laughed dryly, "I must be using more than 10% of my brain capacity."

Adam continued seamlessly, "To go one step even further, I believe that as I apply what the Professor was saying—that once the effects of the fruit of knowledge are completely cleansed and they have finally opened their eyes for that last time, it would be Judgment Day. I get it now! The end of the world as we know it! There is no destruction per se. It's merely the reality of life in utter eradication, in the drama of a physical Armageddon! There may be physical destruction with our bodies turning to ashes, but not our immortal souls. Adam and Eve will then have the wisdom of God, the wisdom of the law of paradise. Basically, the law set in paradise about not eating from the tree of knowledge of good and evil is there as the ultimate challenge—the end-all, be-all of puzzles rather than sin, because God loves us. It was simply misinterpreted as being a sin because they didn't know any different. And God, in his or her infinite wisdom, knows that. There are penalties for wanting to know all as well as incredible rewards for finally knowing everything."

Mercedes was pleased with all the answers and insights she had heard during their entire roundtable discourse.

Time and time again she wrote and presented her ideas, using many forms of storytelling in many languages and this time, had finally understood it almost on their own.

Suddenly, the class became very quiet, almost contemplative. It felt like a blanket of silence descended upon them. Mercedes recognized it as the first step of their journey to self-discovery. These were the moments when her students began to receive the answers from themselves, not her. It made her work even more meaningful. *Gifts of epiphanies*. Epiphanies of truth, she had learned and continued to learn in her own arduous journey of self-discovery. Epiphanies were the whole point of her teachings.

She stood up to address her class; some students were still in deep contemplation, while others were clearly disturbed with their own revelations. "Ladies and gentlemen, *señoras y caballeros, signore e signori, meinen Damen und Herren, donas e cavalheiros, mesdames et messieurs*, you must face the truth of your epiphanies, your revelations... your truths. Ask yourselves right now—with your freewill, are you ready to open your eyes? Are you willing to take the tremendous risks that you need to take? Are you ready to accept responsibilities? Do you have the faith, courage and strength to live in love and finally accept the truth of your very existence? Can you speak the truth with love?"

She paused, scanning the room, "You are the Adams and Eves of today. When you hunger for knowledge, when you thirst for the truth, your hunger needs to be filled by wisdom and your thirst quenched by truth! You see, it's really quite simple. The truth is the Word. The Word is God. God is love and love is *you*! The answers *and* the questions you seek are simple: you seek LOVE! For most of us, our backs have been turned toward the mirror of truth all this time.

"Now, I humbly ask you to please turn around and face your true self in all your splendid glory. Your true self is beautiful, omnipotent and immortal. You can see it in your face if you look. It possesses your soul. It is the very essence of life and the embodiment of pure love. It is YOU! At last, *nunc scio quit sit amor*; for now, I know what love is!"

Her passionate words were received with unexpected applause from her class; and with that, she bowed to them, smiling widely, "Thank you so much everyone! Know that we have only scratched the surface today. I will continue this lecture with an illustration about the true paths of soul mates in our next class. Let me leave every Adam and Eve in this class with two simple questions to ponder for the weekend. Remember the answers are obvious, simple, so try not to be distracted—it's truly not that complicated. What you need to do is first accept the fact that nothing is impossible! Okay, here are the questions. First, are the paths of soul mates parallel? Second, what roles do time and space play in the journey of soul mates?

"Excellent work, everyone! Enjoy your weekend and I'll see you all on Monday."

As students left, she saw varying expressions on their faces; many stopped to express how much they enjoyed the lecture, some asking questions relevant to it. Others, mostly the far site students, wanted to share more of their insights. Some students simply left in silence, perhaps thinking about what they had heard, while others talked about a frat party at Delta Lambda.

* * *

Once she reached the inner sanctum of her office, she closed the door, sat behind her desk and clicked on the online classical music station. The music of Vivaldi and Mozart was her companion while she unwound from a long day of classes. She smiled thinking of her students' reactions. They left her feeling rewarded, almost as rewarded as she was physically, mentally and emotionally exhausted from the lecture.

Before leaving to start the weekend, Mercedes wrote her class observations and answered emails, mostly from her family. Her thoughts turned to the new recipe that she had created. Taking out her handheld from her purse, she entered a checklist of the ingredients. As she was about to finish, there was a soft knock at her door. She noted the time. Her office hours had ended five minutes ago.

"Come in," she said, changing the volume of the music to the lowest setting.

"Professor Larcher?"

"Hello, Mercedes." Instinctively, she felt herself smiling back at the attractive young woman with highlighted, shoulder length brown hair that was neatly pulled back with a dark headband.

The girl was wearing faded, straight-leg blue jeans, low-heeled boots, an ivory mock-turtle sweater and a fashionable black, cropped leather jacket. She wore only a hint of makeup, and she had a backpack dangling on one shoulder. She was also holding a blue computerized tablet and a small paperback book.

Mercedes jotted down "saffron" and then put her stylus pen down, "Is there something I can help you with? A class-related question, perhaps?"

"No, Professor. I mean—I don't have a question about class at the moment. Although I have thousands in my head about soul mates and past lives. I'm, I'm just drawing a blank right now," she said haltingly. "I just want you to know, I mean, I just stopped back to tell you—that I truly enjoyed your class today. I have read every book you've written, and I have learned so much from you and from your books." Her excitement was apparent.

Mercedes smiled at the compliment, "I am greatly flattered. Thank you very much." As she spoke, she turned off her handheld organizer and placed it into her briefcase. She also turned off her computer and stood up. As she reached for her mid-length, black leather car coat which hung on a cherry coat tree, she said, "I'm sorry, but you will have to excuse me; I have to be going unless there is something else? You're more than welcome to walk with me." But the young lady simply kept smiling as though she was star-struck. After a few moments of awkward silence, Mercedes finally said to her student, "Okay then, I'll see you next class. Be safe this weekend."

Chapter 21

Her Book

Walking briskly out of the classroom and down the hallway toward the front of Goldwin Smith Hall, Mercedes opened the white double doors leading to East Avenue. Near the statue of Andrew Dickson White, she heard running footsteps from behind her and the young woman's voice calling out, "Professor Larcher! Professor—please wait!"

Mercedes stopped and turned as the young woman came up to her; her face was red from her effort to catch up.

Catching her breath, she said, "Actually, Professor, there is something, something I've been dying to ask you since the start of the semester. I'm so sorry to bother you again. It's just that I couldn't find the right words earlier. You see, I've waited for so long to meet you, to approach you, and finally, here I am standing face-to-face with you. I just wanted say—I mean I just wanted to ask... Oh my goodness! I'm rambling like a little child, please excuse my behavior."

Mercedes found herself intrigued by this young lady. She could empathize with her excitement; when she had met her own favorite author in New Orleans, she hadn't been able to find the words either. She waited patiently, with a smile, until the young lady calmed down.

Finally, the young woman asked, "Professor, would you please sign your book for me? Could you inscribe it personally to me?" With that the girl took the small book she was holding and presented it to her for signing.

Mercedes was thrilled and amazed with the book's pristine condition. She had not seen such a fine first edition copy of her first book for many years, especially not in the original paperback. The out-of-print and the first editions were now highly prized book collector's items, especially in the condition that one was in. Once she had signed it, its value would easily double.

Touching the book carefully, Mercedes noticed that it rivaled the copies in her personal library, and she was very delighted to see it and the care it had been given. She was eager to sign it for this young lady.

As she took out her black fine-tip pen from her briefcase, she asked, "Mercedes, is there anything special you'd like me to write in the inscription? And what is your full given name."

In a voice at an octave higher than her normal speech, the young lady nervously said, "Professor, please make the inscription: *To my greatest fan, Mercedes D. Tristram—*"

"Tristram?" Her heart skipped. She dared to ask, "Any relation to Joe Tristram?" She had not uttered his name aloud for many years and when she did, she felt a warm blush covering her cheeks.

Wide-eyed with excitement, the young woman cried, "Oh my goodness, my dad really does know you!"

Mercedes needed to be sure. With her heart pounding, she said, "Well, if he was known as 'Phantom' in the US Air Force, then he's the same Joe Tristram that I knew a long time ago."

"Yes, that's my dad! Phantom!" she said excitedly. "He's still in the Air Force."

Mercedes heard her briefcase drop to the ground, but she kept hold of the book.

A dozen thoughts rushed through her mind. She looked at the girl again, still unable to believe it. *She must look like her mother. Joe never described his wife to me.*

Unable to speak, Mercedes felt herself standing there in the same stunned silence as she had over twenty years ago when Joe confessed to her that he was married and that he had just discovered his wife was pregnant.

Standing before me is that baby. JC's daughter! Mon Dieu, she bears my name! Frantic with disbelief she felt her knees weaken, so she lowered herself to one knee in the guise of picking up her briefcase and the things that had scattered from it.

The young girl quickly bent down to help, asking, "Professor, are you feeling all right?"

Knowing her face turned from a deep blush to ashen, she tried to recover gracefully with a smile, "Yes, yes, I'm fine, Mercedes. Just a little clumsy, that's all." Then quickly, she asked, "Would you care to join me for a cup of tea in the Temple of Zeus? Perhaps you can tell me how you acquired your wonderful copy of my book."

"Yes, of course. I'd love to!"

Inside the Temple of Zeus, the dining facility in Goldwin Smith Hall, they sat down at a table near a window.

Needing to compose herself from her shock, she asked, "Would you excuse me a minute? I need to run to the ladies' room."

"Sure, Professor. Would you like me to get us something to drink?"

"Yes, a cup of jasmine green tea would be fine for me," she said, before walking away.

Inside the bathroom Mercedes stood in front of a mirror with tears streaming down her face. Memories of Las Vegas began to overwhelm her.

Joe's voice and his words echoed in her mind from that fateful night twenty-two years ago. *A few hours ago, I found out my wife is pregnant... fate... call it fate... but I somehow know that this was meant to be! Our souls are connected. We're not going to say goodbye tonight... I will never forget. Think of me, even if you're with someone else. Promise?*

* * *

Fifteen days after Mercedes got back from Las Vegas, she was surprised when she received a beautiful card from Joe. She had just gotten back from an overnight business trip. It was around 7:00 p.m. when she checked her mailbox and saw the card with *JC* in bold block letters and a South Carolina postmark. Her heart leapt and her crimson lips formed a happy smile. But she didn't open it immediately. Instead, she walked inside her townhouse and placed the envelope on her cherry side table along with her purse.

Quickly, she ran upstairs to her bedroom. She hurriedly changed out of her black suit into a red, cropped long sleeved tee and satin jacquard drawstring pants. She ran back downstairs, lit the logs in the fireplace and all the candles in her living room before walking to her surround sound stereo. Gregorian chants flooded the room. Taking out a crystal wineglass and a bottle of Merlot, she poured a glass and returned to the living room where she took his coin from her purse and smiled as she stared at the card.

Sipping her Merlot she sat down next to the fireplace on a plush area rug and sank back on multiple plush massive pillows. She took a deep cleansing breath, closed her eyes for a moment, and let every detail of his image appear in her mind. She just wanted to be surrounded with him entirely.

Opening her eyes, she swiftly opened the envelope with a silver, Medieval sword-shaped letter opener. Finally, she took the card out of its sheath.

Her heart was pounding fast, and she caught her breath before opening it, thinking how much his bold block lettering conveyed his strength.

As she read it, she could hear his deep, sultry voice in her mind. It felt like he was right there with her. Then, her thoughts raced as she read each line,

"*Mercedes,*

I can't believe we met then you flew so quickly right out of my dreams. Did it really happen? Or was it all a dream? This doesn't happen to me. You've made me feel like I'm seventeen again.

I am incredibly lucky to have met an intelligent, beautiful, caring and tender goddess. You are amazing! I marvel at your mind. I hold the puzzle in my hands, thinking of you, of your incredible smile. It's now permanently embedded in my brain.

I don't know if I truly believe in past lives, but we must've been very close in another place, another time. I know our souls are connected somehow.

You must from time to time drop me a note to let me know how you are doing. As I said, I want to be a part of your life, however small that part may be! I know there's no need to explain why it'll have to be a one-way communication. I do hope to hear from you soon.

As we promised each other that night, live your life fully and fill it with pure joy and happiness. I wish that for the both of us. Again, no goodbyes, <u>ever</u>.

I miss you so much,

JC"

She stared at the underlined word and smiled. Without realizing it, a phantom conversation began. She kept thinking the same thoughts from that last night at the Aladdin. *If you pick up that phone and tell me you want me with you now, I could be on the next plane out of Philly! We could be together in a few hours. Know that I never wanted to fly out of your dreams. I would've stayed. All you have to do is ask and I'll be in your arms right now.*

When she completed her last thought and realized what she was doing, she said aloud, "What is the matter with me! This is all too confusing."

She closed her eyes and revisited that last evening they had together, remembering every detail, every thought. *I miss you, JC.*

She stared at the crackling fire while sipping her Merlot, listening to the music, deep in thought, and reread the note over and over until it was well after midnight.

Finally, she got up from the fireplace, strolled to the French doors that led to her wild flower garden and looked up towards the dark night sky. *The stars are exceptionally bright tonight. I wonder if you're up there flying somewhere in the world, JC. And if you are, we're actually looking at the same stars no matter where you are. I hope you are safe.*

After she blew out all the candles, turned the music off, and made sure the embers were completely out, she finally got in bed where she wrote in her journal and composed a few poems based on her thoughts.

She couldn't sleep, so she stared up at the stars beyond the skylight above her until exhaustion took its toll. She fell asleep with his coin in her hand.

* * *

Unsure of how long she had been standing there, she was suddenly jarred back to reality after seeing a colleague of hers entering the bathroom.

Quickly, she turned on the faucet and washed away the evidence of the tears that had run down her cheeks after her sudden trip back in time. She powdered her face, freshened up her burgundy lipstick and waited a few moments to regain her composure.

When she approached the table, her young companion greeted her excitedly, "Professor, thank you for inviting me here. It's really an honor!"

"So tell me, how did you receive such a fine copy of my book?" she asked, bracing for all the stories her lovely young student was about to share.

"It was my father who gave me the book." Still in disbelief, she asked once again, "You really know my dad?"

Mercedes tried to read the signs of affectation on the girl's face, looking for a clue about how to answer. She saw one that she could easily interpret, so, taking the risk, she said, "We've lost touch over the years, but, yes, your dad and I are very old friends."

"From college?"

"No," she smiled warily. "When did your father give you the book?"

"The book was a birthday present from my dad," she replied smiling. Mercedes smiled with her.

With all the trust young people often showed in her, Joe's daughter said, "Well, it was my freshman year at the University of Florida when my heart was first broken. It was horrible. I walked in on my boyfriend with my roommate in his dorm room when I thought he was away at home.

"I was so hurt and betrayed by both of them that I stormed out and made my way toward the elevators. It was so embarrassing when he ran after me down the hallway, still naked! Before he caught up with me, I flew down the emergency stairs instead of taking the elevator. I was running down so fast I almost fell on my face. I felt completely lost. I couldn't understand what was happening to me."

"I'm so sorry you had to go through that."

"It's okay—I'm over it," she said, but the expression on her face told a different story. "I'm very close with my dad, so I called him. I cried telling him what had happened. I wanted to drop out of school because I felt like my life was over. What was the point? Here it was two days before my birthday and I was at my deepest, darkest moment.

"After listening to me *ramble*, my dad reminded me sternly that he hadn't raised me as some fragile flower. Well, the next thing I know—he appears at my dorm!"

"How sweet of him to surprise you like that," Mercedes smiled.

"Yes, it really was," her student beamed, "He had flown in just so we could celebrate our birthdays together!"

"You were born in December, too?"

"Yes, my dad and I share the same birthday"

"Really? What a lovely coincidence!" she said, but a tiny frown came to her. *Something's not right about that.*

"After dinner my dad gave me a beautifully wrapped gift—it was your book. He told me that the character in the book and the author were both named Mercedes, like me. Then he floored me when he said you were an old friend of his!

"After I read the book, I wanted to find you, but he also told me that he lost touch with you. I was disappointed but delighted to know he had a connection you. I couldn't believe it! I'm still in disbelief about the whole thing!"

Me too. Mercedes mirrored her statement in her mind.

"That night when he gave me your book, he also spoke of a small metal puzzle and the wisdom behind it. As a matter of fact, Professor—" Joe's daughter paused to reach into her backpack, where she carefully opened a zippered compartment to remove something silver.

The girl showed it to her eagerly, oblivious to Mercedes' shocked reaction. "Here's the puzzle he gave me. I accepted it, but only reluctantly because I knew it held a special personal meaning for him. I'd seen it before. In fact, I remember when I first saw it; he brought me along with him to his office at the base when I was eight. After he stepped out of the office, I was bored and I wanted to explore, so I started looking around to see what kind of mischief I could get into. After rooting through his desk, I noticed his bag sitting under the table and being curious, I began to look inside it. It had lots of zippered compartments and other stuff. In one pocket, I found the puzzle with a couple of good luck charms, but before I could play with it I heard his footsteps coming closer, so I quickly returned everything to its place. I sat on his chair and hoped he didn't see the guilt hidden behind my smile.

"After that, I knew he always carried it with him, but I never knew what it really meant until he gave me your book. He insisted that I needed it more than he did, so he gave it to me."

Mercedes was shaken to see the small metal puzzle and how this beautiful young lady was unconsciously untangling it as she spoke. *My mother's gift... my—our puzzle!* She almost reached for it.

"Professor?" Her thoughts were interrupted and she met the girl's eyes.

"I've read all your books and your writing made such a difference to me! When I discovered you were teaching here, it just made sense for me to come here. So, I transferred to Cornell to take your classes and had hoped to get the opportunity to meet and talk with you alone.

"Where are my manners! Here I am rambling on about my life. You must have other important things to attend to. Am I keeping you?"

"No, not at all, Mercedes. This is a delightful change in my routine," she said, touched with her thoughtfulness. "Every Friday, I have this habit of venturing over to the Johnson Museum of Art here on campus to sketch and write. Sometimes I listen to a chimes concert at McGraw Towers afterwards." She looked at her warmly with a smile on her face and added, "Your parents must be immensely proud of you. Tell me some more about you and your family. Do you have any brothers and sisters?" Her curiosity was getting the best of her.

"No, I'm an only child. I've always wanted a brother or a sister but my birth was a difficult one and—"

"You're a miracle, Mercedes."

"That's what my mom said."

"And she's right."

"I feel like I've known you all my life, Professor! This may explain why I feel so at ease in sharing all of this with you. To quote you, 'we are kindred spirits'—the kind you spoke about with your character, Sydney, in the book."

She wondered how this innocent young lady would react if she knew the character was based entirely on Eva, her own mother. She struggled to feign a smile in agreement, but the irony moved her. She was also touched by the way Joe's daughter was so effervescent, animated and passionate when she spoke, much like she was herself, especially when she was teaching. She hoped that her student was oblivious to the shifts in her moods.

"So, how's your mother?"

"Mom's doing well and happy to be back in Florida. She keeps herself busy with work. She's a physical therapist."

"Where in Florida?"

"Miami. She grew up there."

"That must've been hard for her—the constant moving."

"Not as hard as my decision to transfer here. She's completely against my being here."

"Cornell is an excellent school."

"Yes, but my mom doesn't agree with the real reason why I transferred here."

"I see." Mercedes wondered if Joe had confided in Eva about Vegas, which would explain the resistance to her daughter's decision. She wanted to know.

"It's nothing against you, Professor. It's just that my mom felt it was an impulsive—irresponsible decision, especially since it's my last semester."

Mercedes noticed the girl's voice was sounding hoarse so she freshened both of their teas, trying not to interrupt.

After taking a couple of sips, Joe's daughter continued, "She's also not excited with my decision to become a poet. She's afraid that poetry won't lead me to a 'real job'. She wants me to be practical, but I just want to do what I love to do.

"I want to write like Maya Angelou and Emily Dickinson. I want to be that next poet who will rival even the classics! You've spoken about it many times in your books—when you dream, dream BIG! I may have to struggle at first to make ends meet, but I will be living my dreams, just as I've fulfilled my dream of meeting you, Professor."

Mercedes was flattered and moved with her passion. Without giving any thought to what she was going to say, she asked the young woman, "Do you have plans for tomorrow evening? A date?"

"No, no plans, no date. My boyfriend, Kyle, is in Florida."

"Would you be interested in a private book signing at my home? I would love for you to meet my daughter, Carly. I think both of you will get along splendidly. She's a freshman here in Cornell, a pre-med major. Like you, she's an only child. As a matter of fact, she usually meets me at the museum around 5:30 p.m. on Fridays, but she unfortunately had an urgent errand to run today, otherwise, you could've met her today. Perhaps I can arrange for the three of us to have dinner tomorrow evening. Interested?"

Her student's eyes lit up. "Absolutely! Professor, name the time!"

She handed the book back to Joe's daughter and said, "See you tomorrow at 7:00 p.m."

Chapter 22

After Las Vegas

Mercedes was still overwhelmed with the irony, even after leaving the Temple of Zeus. *Where has life taken you, JC?*

She had continued to send him handwritten letters through the years, not knowing if he had ever received them. She had not heard from him since fifteen years earlier when he granted her an impossible wish.

As she drove out of the parking lot, she could scarcely concentrate. Instead, the uneasy feeling in her stomach overwhelmed her. She also found her mind revisiting those early years.

* * *

Three months after she returned from Las Vegas, she found herself on the phone in tears, sobbing, telling her mother about what had happened in Las Vegas and how her heart had been broken beyond repair.

In her despair her mother shared something that she never knew. Her mother said, "Dearest, I know how you feel, really I do."

Cynically, she answered, "How could that be possible! You have dad. Dad never did this."

Softly, she heard her say, "No, he hasn't. But, before your father, I was in love with another man. Later, while I was engaged to your dad, I almost broke it off to be with this man."

In disbelief, she gasped, "What? I don't believe you. I don't—I can't!"

The sincerity in her words was apparent. "But it's true sweetheart. I know how much you are hurting. Unrequited love is painful, dearest. I do know the pain very well. And I know this as well—you'll be fine. Everything will be fine. You are strong and you will get over him."

Curious to find out more details of this secret, she asked, "What was his name, Mom? Tell me about him."

After a sigh, her mother said, "His name was Joe—"

"I don't believe it!" The tears overwhelmed her and she became hysterical. She felt like a little girl wanting to be gathered close in her mother's arms.

Alarmed, her mother asked, "There's something else. What is it dearest?"

Mercedes blurted out the truth, "Oh God! I'm pregnant, Mom. Joe's the father!"

As the numbness in her body spread, she began to sob harder.

"*Oh, mon Dieu*! Sweetheart, you must come home now. You can't go through this alone, you can't. We're here for you. You know that."

"Mom, I can't, not right now."

"Sweetheart. You need to come home. I insist."

"No!" Tearfully, she pleaded, "Please understand and be happy for me. My baby was conceived out of love, and my baby is the only part of him I have. Please, don't tell anyone. Let me share the good news myself when the time comes. Please, Mom?"

"I won't, but remember if you need anything, I'm here. We'll all be here for you."

"I know you will be. I love you, Mom."

Hanging up the phone, Mercedes searched without success for a sense of uplift from having shared her feelings with her beautiful mother, yet, although she felt better, she didn't feel uplifted with her confession. And she didn't go home, either. Instead, she flew to France with her engineering team, absorbed herself in work and hoped to get her thoughts straight.

In France she enjoyed the pleasure of being pregnant, of having one of her dearest wishes come true, until a month later when she faced a pain greater than she had ever imagined.

***

Back in the states, Mercedes, Sydney and Cassie arrived at the Rock Lobster where the rest of the ladies, Donna, Mallory and Renée, were waiting for them at the bar. Mercedes was pleasantly surprised to find Mason there too. He was with his business associates as usual. They greeted each other with a friendly hug, and he instructed the Maître D' that he was picking up their dinner tab. He then joined his associates in the privacy of an enclosed table in the VIP section for his business dinner and conversation.

The Maître D' seated the ladies in the open-air section of the floating restaurant, where they had a great view of the Benjamin Franklin Bridge in the background. It was a nice warm summer night in July. Sydney was sitting adjacent to Mercedes.

"I heard the three of you went for a tarot card reading tonight. How was it?" Mallory asked, after carefully sipping her margarita without smudging her ruby lips. Her dark russet bangs and the chiffon skirt of her sapphire halter dress lightly stirred with the soft breeze.

"Well, I was told that I would get a new job soon," Cassie volunteered. "She couldn't tell me which law firm, but it was really uncanny since I just got a couple of strong offers this week."

"What about you, Syd?"

"She predicted that I'd be going on a trip for my own good. She couldn't tell me where or when exactly, except that it was somewhere warm. And I've been aching to go on a vacation!"

"Hope it'll be Tahiti!" Mallory exclaimed, her brown eyes flashed with nostalgia. "And you, Slayer? What prediction did you get?"

Mercedes replied cautiously, "It was too cryptic. I can't even tell you what it was really about."

"It had something to do with true love and signs," Cassie offered.

Renée interjected, "I could never go to a psychic! I'd rather not know anything about my future. It'd spoil the fun for me." Her head shook the golden layers of her hair.

"I'm with Renée on this, but I wouldn't mind knowing the million dollar lottery numbers!" Donna roared. The laughter and the side conversations began.

Turning to Renée, Mercedes asked, "How's the adoption going?"

Her crystalline baby blues told the story of her joy, and her usual soft voice increased an octave higher in her excitement. She said, "Two more months! We were told we're getting a boy—a rarity but we were lucky. He's only a few months old." Without prompting, she shared, "We've picked out his English name since he already has a Chinese name."

"What's the name?"

"He'll be known as Joseph *Fu-Hsing* Straubhaar," she said, barely able to pronounce the foreign name. "I looked up his name and it's actually for the Chinese god of happiness and symbolizes destiny, fate, love, happiness and success."

"What an incredible name!" Sydney exclaimed, overhearing the conversation. "It has a ring of success to it."

"It really does, doesn't it? Well, aside from what it means, Garrett and I wanted to keep his name because we wanted him to be aware of his heritage. We are so excited!" Her face flushed with a rosy color as deep as the floral sundress she was wearing.

"I agree," said Mercedes, aware of the coincidence; then, she boldly asked Sydney, "How's the marriage counseling going?"

"Ugh! It was awful at first, since I asked him to move out temporarily. But, he was vigilant about making things work for us. He really went all out and he swore, vowing to the heavens, that he would never do it again! He said he would make all efforts to make up for what had happened. Even if it took the rest of our lives, he said. He promised me he would do whatever it takes to save our marriage. And I believe him.

"I want to thank you for being there for me. You are such a friend—thank you for giving me the strength to go through this! If you hadn't, I would have cut off his precious jewels after saying, 'Patrick, I am doing this for your own good. This hurts me more than you!'" Her soft laughter almost hid the seriousness with which she had spoken.

"I am glad things are going better. I had no doubt that the two of you would work things out. Where there is love, there is no way it *wouldn't* work out! Now, quench my curiosity, what's up with Dante?"

She giggled, "Well, I have a funny story for you about him. After I told you about my lurid plans with him, I was literally knocked back to my senses. By the way I really meant to tell you about this immediately, but you know how it goes! Anyway, about a month after we spoke, Patrick didn't come home one night. I got so pissed off that I actually decided to try being with Dante. He picked me up and—get this!—I unexpectedly became violently ill. I couldn't do it! Just simply couldn't do it. I had gotten myself pretty buzzed so I'd lose all my inhibitions, but nothing. There was just nothing. So, after my foiled attempt at adultery, Dante developed a stalker mentality. He was like a puppy dog. He couldn't accept the rejection! I'm amazed at how this grown man reverted to childhood antics! Anyway, since he couldn't get anywhere with me, he hooked back up with that Jill—that wench. I heard he caught some STD. I think maybe gonorrhea or something itchy. Serves them both!"

Mercedes couldn't help but laugh and said, "Karma is funny like that. When you do something intentionally wrong, it bites you later in the ass really hard!"

"Whose ass are you talking about?" Donna interrupted. The laughter increased in volume as they began to share the details of it. The opinions were plentiful, and the laughter continued. Their server finally got all of their orders for their dinners, as they continued to chat about their latest escapades.

Donna said unexpectedly, "Hey, Slayer. Thank you for being an artist and for using me as a model for your painting." Her flawless mochachino skin seemed to glow against her coral off-the-shoulder dress. Sparkling jewels were intricately woven in her hair with rows of braids, artfully arranged like a crown.

"No, thank *you* for being such a beautiful model! I couldn't have found a more perfect *Nubian Queen*."

"If it wasn't for that painting, I wouldn't have met Avery at your art show. For that alone, I'm thankful. We're exclusively dating now."

"You and Avery? The magazine editor? He's not at all like any of the muscular, older men that you've told me about in the past."

"Yes, I know! He's everything that I never expected. Young. Portly. Moroccan. Nevertheless, he's incredible. There's something about him that I find so very lovable."

"It was meant to be, Donna. If it wasn't the art show, I'm sure that somewhere down the line, your path would've crossed with Avery's anyway. It was just a matter of time."

"Speaking of time, I hope you won't be angry, but I'm going to be giving you my two weeks notice at work. Avery offered me a job as a fashion director, and I've decided to accept."

Excitedly, Mercedes leaned over and embraced Donna. "That's the best resignation I have ever heard! I'm really happy for you." She took her fork, tapping it lightly against her glass, and said, "Ladies, ladies! I would like to make an announcement and a toast."

"Donna just told me she's quitting as my secretary. Yes, yes, I know—woe is me! But the perfect job—and it also sounds like the perfect man—have found her. If she wasn't going to quit to see if it would work, I probably would've had to fire her to show my support!" Mercedes raised her glass, prompting the ladies to raise theirs for the impromptu toast. "To Donna."

"Merc?" Sydney asked her quietly as the others turned to congratulating Donna, "I'm curious. Why aren't you having your usual Merlot with dinner, or even tonic? I don't think I've ever seen you drinking chocolate milk. Aren't you still lactose intolerant?"

As Mercedes was trying to figure out how to answer, the server came back with their appetizers, and the conversation turned to other things.

In the midst of dinner, Mercedes began to feel a tightening in her stomach along with a very severe cramp. She tried to ignore it, dismissing it as the second trimester's round ligament pains—a completely harmless pain which she had experienced before. In the last week alone, it had twice knocked her for a loop, stopping her dead in her tracks.

She continued with her dinner and conversation, mindful of the other episode, but not overly worried. It was probably nothing.

"You don't look well. Same pains like earlier?"

Shaking her head, she said, "I'm okay, Syd. It's the chocolate milk."

A few minutes later, she was doubled over by sharp, radiating, numbing pains from her belly unlike anything she had ever experienced. When the initial burst of pain passed, she excused herself and slowly walked to the bathroom, where she discovered she was bleeding badly. Inside her head, she could hear herself screaming, *Oh no, my baby!* She began to cry and as she walked out the bathroom, the pain took hold of her again. Unable to prevent it, she fell to her knees in tears holding her stomach.

Sydney, who had sensed that something wasn't quite right, found her there moments later, after having gotten up to go to the bathroom to check on her.

"Syd, hurry and please get Mason!" she pleaded in between her gasps.

"Okay, I'll get him and call 9-1-1," Sydney said before she sprinted to the VIP area and got him.

Sydney was searching for her cell phone in her pocketbook. Mason barked, "That's a waste of time! Temple Hospital is a heartbeat away. I can have her there before an ambulance can even get here."

"But it's Saturday night! The traffic—"

"Fuck the traffic!" He protested. "Frankie!" He yelled for his limo driver, "Get your fuckin' ass over here now!"

Mercedes could feel the fast beating of his heart against her as he tried to carefully place her into the back of the limo.

He screamed out the order, "Get to Temple Emergency Room now!"

Mercedes was in a fetal position with her head on Mason's lap. She felt as if her phantasm had manifested and tried to convince herself that this was a waking nightmare, not reality! But she felt Mason caressing her hair.

"We're almost there, babe. Hang in there." He felt her forehead, "Damn! You're burning up! Yo, Frankie—drive fuckin' faster!"

He was very angry, furious and cursing loudly. Both of them knew the driver couldn't go any faster, and she knew Mason's anger was because he felt helpless and couldn't help ease her suffering. She knew him well.

At the ER she was placed in a wheelchair and transported to a curtained area, then into a private examination room. Seemingly indifferent to her pain and screams of agony, a male nurse asked her to disrobe and put on a silly, blue-flowered gown—one of those that never failed to leave her backside exposed.

Hunched over in the wheelchair, screaming in extreme agony and facing his incessant requests, she felt her rage peak. With all of her remaining strength, she got up and ripped her burgundy mini-sundress off, sending the white buttons flying across the room. In just her burgundy high-cut bikini briefs, she fell back into the wheel chair, screaming, "Damn you! Get someone who can stop the pain, please! How about some fucking morphine!" She was in fetal position.

Mason yanked the gown out of the nurse's hand, scowled over at him as he helped her put it on. He then carried her to the examining table, and turned to the nurse who was holding his clipboard and a blood pressure cuff, patiently waiting to take her vital signs.

"Yo buddy, this ain't no strip club—aight!" he snapped and stepped closer, invading his personal space. "How 'bout youse do your piss-ant job, and get the FUCKIN' DOCTOR IN HERE!"

Though she was asked if she was pregnant, she couldn't tell them of her pregnancy because of Mason and kept hiding her belly. Standard blood tests were taken, and then a team of surgical doctors examined her and ordered other tests. As the blood was drawn repeatedly from her arms, her veins collapsed, which caused them to resort to drawing blood from the fine veins on her hands.

She had no idea how many hands were inside her pelvic area that night. She could barely speak due to the increasing pain. While waiting for the test results, the surgical and OB/GYN teams were taking turns, repeating painful pelvic exams and scheduling her for internal pelvic ultrasounds. Her sense of panic increased, knowing her pregnancy would be discovered during those tests, but then she realized that Mason wouldn't be wouldn't be in the room during the exam and she relaxed.

As she and Mason waited for an orderly to take her for the ultrasound, several members of the surgical team, residents and medical students were with her, but without an attending doctor. They were continuing their debate, but unable to come up with a clear assessment of what was wrong with her. There wouldn't be a medical consensus until the test results came back and were evaluated by the attending doctors.

Meanwhile, she begged for painkillers, but she knew very well that she would be unsuccessful. Until a diagnosis was made, the pain could not be masked or even dulled with pain medications.

Finally, she couldn't bear the pain any longer, and at the top of her lungs, she screamed, "I'M PREGNANT! PLEASE SAVE MY BABY!" Immediately, the OB/GYN team was called into the examination room and there was an urgent push to get test results.

Hearing her revelation, she saw the immediate change in Mason. All the color left his face and he simply stared at her as if she was a stranger. She began to sob.

Then, with controlled reserve and barely hidden rage, he asked, "Mercedes, is it Grant's baby?"

Her tears became uncontrollable when she looked up into his icy cold eyes. Sobbing, she couldn't answer him, and so she simply shook her head.

His voice still calm, he asked again, "If it's not Grant, then who's the father, Mercedes?"

Before she could answer him, the male nurse returned and asked Mason politely to leave, anticipating the arrival of the next medical team.

As Mason was leaving, he stopped at his tracks, turned and rushed back to her. Rage filled his voice and he asked again, "Who's the fuckin' father, Mercedes?"

She kept crying, not willing to tell him. Not while he was in this foul mood.

Enraged, he angrily yelled, "We're still married—damn you! I have a right to know! Tell me? Tell me, NOW! Who is he? Where is he? And does he even fuckin' know? Why the fuck ain't he here instead of me, huh? Why? I'M GONNA FUCKIN' KILL HIM!"

Upon hearing the strength of his rage-filled screaming voice, the nurse quickly left to get hospital security.

In the height of his rage, Mason startled her when he unexpectedly swiped his hand in anger along the row of medical instruments used for the pelvic exams on the table adjacent to her bed. The sterile instruments crashed to the floor, commingling with the white buttons from her dress.

The sight of his rage and the noise of the instruments crashing onto the floor frightened her, and she screamed incessantly, "Mason—stop it! PLEASE STOP IT! Please stop it. Please!"

Though his rage shattered her, she understood it and knew that there was nothing she could do or say to calm him down. She had to contend with such massive pains that she simply didn't have the extra energy to stop his tirade.

He tried to be oblivious to her pleas, but he couldn't stand the sight of her upset. "Mercedes! Can't you see—he's fuckin' KILLIN' YOU! I can't stand this shit! Don't you understand nuthin'? I still love you! I promised to protect you! I don't give a shit whether we're married or not! No one hurts you! NO ONE!"

Again, he startled her when he threw a chair against the wall. He was pacing back and forth with his fists clenched tightly. Luckily, no one had entered the room; otherwise, an innocent bystander would have been the unfortunate recipient of his displaced anger. An ugly scowl appeared on his face and it scared her, but as the pain surged from her abdomen, she forgot her fright. He was on his own and simply needed to restrain himself.

She could almost see him fighting to gain a sense of calm as the hospital's security officers finally arrived. At their arrival his anger escalated again and the arguments between him and the officers grew louder and louder. As the situation appeared to be out of control, Mason took control of the situation as usual. With a sense of high drama, he made his power known. With his rugged bad-ass self-assuredness, he straightened out his tie, saying without words, *If you're stupid enough to threaten me, I'll fuckin' sue you and this hospital, and I assure you—I will own your ass!* As the security officers watched hesitantly, he took his time, even beginning to brush the wrinkles out of his sleeves, slowly bringing himself back into his control mode.

He was an impressive sight. Impeccably dressed as always, his demeanor changed from that of a raging lunatic to a Mafioso-type persona. He handled everything with deliberate precision and within a few moments, he had gained complete reign over the hospital security staff. He was brutal in his negotiations with them.

Finally, he walked over to her bedside and sat beside her. He took his right hand and gently lifted her face, which was filled with physical pain and tears. He kissed her tenderly on her forehead, saying softly, "Mercedes, I'm so very sorry. I just hate to see you in so much pain! Please forgive me, babe. I didn't mean to scare you. I just wish to God that I could end this pain for you! With all that I got, I feel powerless, helpless to help you. Tell me what I can do for you, babe. Tell me."

She clung to him in an embrace that gave him silent absolution. There was no longer any need to usher him out of the area. Then, moments later, the test results confirmed the worst and she was immediately wheeled to the operating room for emergency surgery.

As she lay there, traveling down the hallway, she realized this was the very first time she had ever faced major surgery. She had always dreamed of being in the operating room, but as a surgeon, not as a patient. The whole process was intriguing. As people entered the room, she remembered the detailed discussions she often had with Grant, especially after watching an invasive surgical procedure performed on the Discovery Channel.

She was about to get first-hand knowledge, except from an undesirable vantage point. Nevertheless, she paid attention to everything happening around her. They had already taken off all of her jewelry and sedatives were introduced into her system. The severe pain would be subsiding in a few moments, and she watched another nurse setting up an intravenous infusion, adjusting the rates for the infusion of a saline solution. The orderly, whose nametag read Joe Solomon, arrived with a surgical gurney. Joe and two others carefully helped her slide onto the gurney where she was then strapped in snugly. The gurney was not equipped with an IV support hanger, so another nurse assisted by holding the IV bags and infusing pump gear high enough to ensure a steady flow.

She offered them her apologies for both her and Mason's behavior earlier. The nurse smiled and assured her that he had encountered worse scenarios. He also began to give her kind reassurances of her impending surgery.

Even as the sedatives started to take a hold, her constant need to learn manifested itself, and she urged him to explain what the surgical team was doing in preparation for her arrival.

The nurse gladly imparted his knowledge. He had been a surgical nurse before transferring to the ER. "As we speak, the operating room staff has completed sterilizing and wrapping the entire assortment of instrument trays. The operating table is also being readied according to your surgeon's plan. The correct anesthesia delivery equipment, including vaporizers and monitoring accessories are positioned near the operating table. Your surgeon is Dr. Paul Finley. He's a wonderful guy, very competent. You'll be in good hands, Mercedes. Trust me—okay? Dr. Finley and a surgical resident, I think it's Dr. Ashwin Wende, along with a nurse surgical assistant, a nurse-anesthetist, and the circulating nurses are scrubbing in for your operation. It's just like an orchestra fine-tuning their instruments before the curtain goes up. Oh well, Mercedes, looks like I must end my quick lesson for you." He had to stop his talk as they arrived at the operating room.

"What's your name?"

"Kurt Solomon."

"You two related?" she asked, referring to the orderly pushing the gurney.

"Joe's my brother."

"That's a good sign."

Before he left, he said with a warm smile, "Don't be afraid, Mercedes. Everything will be okay. You won't remember a thing about it. I promise."

"I'll hold you to that promise. Thanks, Kurt."

As the stainless steel doors closed behind her, and the cold air of the operating room quickly penetrated her, she felt at ease and unusually calm.

The masked and gowned surgical staff greeted her. They all had very soothing voices, but she only saw their eyes. They were in good spirits, and even tried to pry a smile from her troubled face. She was easily coaxed, especially after feeling the euphoric effects of sedation. To her delight, she heard classical music in the background. Dr. Finley was just like Grant, implementing music to calm the spirits of his patients. She felt her entire body relax. She felt only a small amount of discomfort, but no intense pain. In between brief introductions, the team was busy prepping her for surgery and transferring her to a bare, cold stainless steel operating table. She felt like she was on the cross, because of the way her arms were extended. Two people were busily inserting different needles into her IV lines on either side of her arms.

Finally, it was time to administer the anesthetic. The nurse-anesthetist, whose name was Dillon, asked her to inhale deeply through the mask, under the pretense of performing an oxygen intake test. She was not naïve. She surprised Dillon when she refused to follow instructions, making a very special request of him. "Can I see everyone's faces before you start?"

Happily, they granted her wish, and as she then drew in deep breaths of the anesthesia, she gladly welcomed the deep sleep and amnesiac effects. Counting slowly backwards from one hundred, she prepared her mind as she projected herself to a happy moment—in another place and time.

* * *

When a couple of months had passed after she broke it off with Grant, she realized she needed to take a long weekend vacation from her self-imposed, hellish work schedule, so she took a trip alone to Xcaret, Mexico, south of Cancun.

Legend had it that before important events, the Mayans cleansed their spirits there, and that was what she needed to do.

The next afternoon she was basking in the sunshine, lying on her stomach in the nude as usual, at her private little white sandy beach near the lagoon.

In the midst of her solitude, she felt a shadow being cast across her. She immediately became irritated. Someone was standing in her sun and, more importantly, invading her privacy.

She looked up to find a fine-looking hot-blooded Latino wearing a skimpy black spandex Speedo. He was smiling at her with a tropical drink in his hand. Not too many men could pull off that look, but this man certainly did. He had a well-chiseled form and a gorgeous bronze tan, along with light brown eyes, dark wavy hair and long eyelashes. He crouched down, offering her the drink, speaking in Portuguese, *"Olá belo anjo! Please forgive me for disturbing you, beautiful lady. You are a vision, your body is exquisite, a spectacular feast for my eyes as you lie here, completely exposed, on this secluded beach before me. I had to come up to you and see for myself if you were real and that I was not imagining you. Truly, you are not a mirage, but a gift sent to me from God in the middle of this magical lagoon. And, because I cannot believe that what I see can possibly be true, I offer you this sweet elixir as a sign of my penance for not believing such an angel exists here on earth. My name is José Cortez, and I wish for you to speak my name in your lovely voice, simply as JC."*

She quickly translated his sweet talk in her thoughts as he spoke in his very seductive voice.

Hearing his last sentence, and the name JC, she was taken by surprise! Without thought she pulled herself upright and sat up to face him directly, completely oblivious of her nakedness. She was greeted with lustful eyes that zoomed directly to her breasts and then lustfully violated the rest of her body. His was the smile of a Casanova which could've melted any other woman, but not her.

When she realized her nudity was obviously exciting him, she hastily covered herself with her towel and with deliberate sweetness, she said to him in Portuguese, *"Olá bondoso senhor. What a handsome name you have, JC. I am indeed very flattered with your beautiful words; but as you can see, I am a mere mortal on vacation like you, here in paradise on earth. I must confess—I desperately enjoy my solitude. I shall gladly accept your offer of this drink as your penance, for I am merciful; but I must insist that you leave me in peace. Unless, of course, you wish to feel the wrath of God!"*

As his smile faded, she added, *"If you do not wish to face this wrath, then I suggest to you, kind sir, please leave now. I am already in love with another man whose name you bear. I again thank you for your wonderful words, but I see another angel standing behind you. Your wife perhaps? Your girlfriend? As you know, heaven has no rage like love to hatred turned, nor hell a fury like a woman scorned!"*

She had taken the calculated risk that he was not alone, especially as he was clearly so far from his home country. At the mention of a wife or girlfriend, he reacted with unconscious worry, turning immediately to look behind him. Of course, there was no one there, but she had made her point very clearly. She simply wanted to be alone.

She took the drink, planted it next to her, and continued to enjoy the warmth of the sun on her back. Before he left her alone, she said, *"Não ouse falar sobre o amor para você não sabem nada dele."* She didn't brother translating it in her mind.

She drifted into a light sleep dreaming of Joe. He would be lying next to her in the privacy of this enchanted place if he was there, and they would make love all day, all night, and all weekend long. Her smiles deepened as she slept.

* * *

When Mercedes finally awakened, she was glad she had the morphine regulator in her hands. She greedily kept pushing the button whenever she heard the distinct beep that signaled another dosage was ready. It got to an uncontrollable and even comical point where she just completely ignored the beep, continually pushing on the button like an addict in desperate need of a fix, pressing it until she finally felt only discomfort, not pain, from the heavy pressure in her pelvic area.

Her distraction for a pain-numbing dosage was interrupted.

"Hi, beautiful." The voice was soothing and familiar.

She was drugged with morphine but aware of her surroundings. She was also being given three of the strongest antibiotics via IV drips. The bandages on her abdomen were bothersome and she felt very uncomfortable as she tried hard not to gag from a flexible tube that seemed to be inserted in her left nostril. She realized it was a nasogastric tube, or NG-tube. The NG-tube made speaking very difficult, and her voice was practically non-existent.

"Grant?" she whispered.

"Yes, it's me," he answered softly.

From the look on his well-shaven face, she knew it was excruciating for him to see her the way she looked. Her lustrous hair was disheveled, her face was very pale, her eyelids were swollen and her pouty lips were chapped. The sight of the NG-tube, the IV lines and her dried blood clinging to her hospital gown made his heart ache.

"Grant, I'm so glad you're here."

He was smiling. He said tenderly, "Me too."

Then he gestured to the nurse behind him and introduced her. "This is Cathy Bishop, your night nurse. She'll be here for you, should you need anything. I'll be here for you, okay?" The nurse was smiling sweetly at her. She had light brown hair worn short and layered and looked about five years older than she probably was.

"I spoke to Sydney earlier..."

"Is she here?"

"No, not right now. She was with you in the recovery room."

"I, I don't remember."

"It's okay, it's okay," he said. "She left soon after you were brought to your room. She had to check on the kids. She also said your parents are on their way here."

"Excuse me, I'm sorry to interrupt." the night nurse said in a soothing and kind voice. "Mercedes, on that panel on your left side, you'll find a red button. That's your call button. When you need anything, just press the red button and I'll come and check on you—all right? There must be full moon or something because each bed on the floor is filled, so if I'm not here right away—please be patient. If it's an emergency, there's a panic button on the panel too, okay? Any questions? Do you need anything right now?"

Her warm motherly voice was reassuring, and Mercedes didn't have any questions or any needs, so she shook her head as the nurse began checking her IV lines and then her vitals signs, noting her high-grade temperature on the chart.

While the nurse was busy with her patient routine, Mercedes and Grant continued their quiet conversation.

She could tell that Grant needed to remain detached with his emotions as he gently said with as much empathy as he could convey, "Mercedes, don't worry about anything. I looked at your chart. Trust me when I say you are doing fine."

She felt a tremendous need to apologize to him; she struggled for a voice that never came, so she whispered with tears welling in her eyes, "I'm sorry, Grant. I'm so very sorry."

Moved with her efforts to speak and understanding what she had meant, he said, "Mercedes, my angel, there's nothing to be sorry about. Everything is going to be fine. I'm here for you if you need me."

She was reassured, but when she noticed that two other doctors appeared outside the door of her private room, a frisson of fright passed through her body.

She looked at Grant with tears escaping from her eyes and mouthed, "Please tell me what's going on." Then she shifted her eyes back to the doctors who were patiently waiting to speak to her. He knew she suspected something wrong, and her fear clearly showed on her face and in her eyes.

His voice was still soothing, but he had shifted to his usual physician tone. "Drs. Finley and Wende are here. They'll be able to tell you more about your prognosis. As I said, everything is fine. It's going to be all right."

He was about to leave and give her privacy, but she took a firm hold of his hand and with a broken voice, pleaded, "Please don't leave! Please. I don't want to be alone—not right now."

Without letting go, he took a seat next to her bed before holding her hand to his lips, "I'm here, Mercedes. I'm always here for you." He turned to Cathy and asked her to get the doctors who were still outside the room talking quietly.

With tears rolling down her face, her voice completely gone, she mouthed the question, "My baby?" She could see it in his eyes. He couldn't hide it. The doctors came into her room and stood at the foot of her bed. They didn't have to utter a word. She already guessed the truth.

But Grant knew that she had no idea what other news they had for her. It was worse than she realized, so he lovingly gripped her hand, through which he projected all his strength and love to her.

Dr. Finley spoke to her first. He was a young tall surgeon, with blond thinning hair and kind blue eyes. His voice was low and soft when he said, "Mercedes, Dr. Larcher informs me that you are very aware of your medical anatomy. He also told us that you are well versed in surgical procedures. That will make it easier to explain your surgery, but please stop me if you have any questions."

She nodded and waited impatiently for his words.

He continued, "I performed a *Laparotomy*, which as you know is major abdominal surgery, much like a C-section. You'll discover after your bandages come off that you have a ten-inch surgical incision, right above your pubic line. It replaced the twin punctures from your previous *Laparoscopy*. When we opened you up, we discovered both your fallopian tubes were badly infected, so we performed a *bilateral salpingectomy*. Are you familiar with that procedure?"

She nodded, knowing both of her tubes were entirely removed; though she was alarmed, she continued to listen intently, for they clearly had more to tell her. She tightly squeezed Grant's hand, and he placed his other hand on top of hers. She braced herself for the rest of what they had to say.

Dr. Finley looked to Dr. Wende, who was standing next to him, to continue with the explanations.

Dr. Wende was from India. She discovered he was very soft-spoken and asked him to step closer. He did with a smile, speaking quickly in thickly accented British English, "Hello Mercedes, I'm Dr. Wende. I assisted Dr. Finley in your surgery. I was standing on the right-hand side of your torso. I was responsible for surgical procedures on that section of your body during the surgery. To continue on with Dr. Finley's explanation, after we promptly removed all the infected tissues from your abdominal cavity and suctioned out the infectious matter, I unfortunately discovered your small intestines, were also badly compromised with the infection. We removed eighteen inches of it, but please don't worry, there's plenty left in there. That procedure is a small bowel resection, as you know."

Then Dr. Finley spoke again, "Mercedes, it is with great sadness that we inform you that we were unable to save your pregnancy. I'm very sorry for your loss."

His sentiments were very sincere, and she had already suspected it, but hearing the words shocked her into a strangely stoic calm.

She was without a voice, though she had many questions for them. She turned to Grant and gestured for him to lean over so she could whisper in his ear. With great effort, she whispered her questions to him. He listened patiently, then he looked at his colleagues and began to ask, "She wants to know in plain medical terms why the baby did not survive? What was the gender of the baby? With the loss of her fertility, what are her options and chances for another pregnancy? What is her prognosis and how long must she stay in the hospital?"

The two doctors conferred before Dr. Finley answered, "Let me begin by answering the simplest question. I anticipate your stay in the hospital to be at least four weeks because of the severity of your infections. Contingent upon how well you respond to the medications, your stay may be shortened. I understand you are highly sensitive to medications, so you'll be monitored closely. Before I answer your other questions, Mercedes, I must apologize again."

She looked at him with a confused expression.

He added softly, "I am truly sorry. I didn't know you weren't aware that you were carrying twins—twin boys."

She gasped and sank deeper into the pillow. Her thoughts raced back in time. With her hectic European schedule, she had been unable to schedule an ultrasound appointment, but otherwise, she had been vigilant about keeping healthy. Because she had not wanted to know her baby's gender, she had never suspected she was pregnant with twins.

She had felt a false sense of security with her medical knowledge and background. She knew that after her first trimester, occurrences of miscarriage were greatly decreased, so rescheduling the ultrasound she had missed wasn't a great concern.

Devastated, she gestured for him to continue as she held tightly onto Grant's hand.

"May I ask if you knew when you were due?"
Nodding, she mouthed, "December 13th."
"You were well into your second trimester," he said. "The reason why your twins didn't survive was primarily because you suffered from *Placenta previa*, which is an abnormal placement of the placenta. It ruptured and..."
She simply didn't want to hear anymore. As Dr. Finley continued to speak, she covered her ears, and then with her eyes swollen in tears, she abruptly motioned for him to stop his explanations.

Both doctors empathized with her as much as they could. Being the bearer of bad news was an unfortunate task doctors had to complete. She respected their position and understood what they had to do, and so did Grant, who stood up and was about to accompany his two colleagues out of the room.

"Wait!" she screamed out with staggering effort. She managed to catch a piece of Grant's clothing before he walked away beyond her reach.

"Tell them to wait." Her sobs were almost uncontrollable.

"Please wait!" he called out to the other doctors for her. They stood at the doorway, waiting.

"What is it? What's wrong?"

"I want them blessed, please!"

"Yes, of course. I'll let the doctors know." Reassuring her, he said, "There should be a visiting priest in the hospital right now."

"Names, they need names." She whispered them to him.

He nodded, and kissed her on her forehead.

"Rest," he begged. "I'll be right back."

He joined the two doctors and told them of her request. After shaking their hands, he promptly sat next to her on the side of the bed. She was silently suffering against her pillow, in tears. She just wished she had not understood exactly what had happened. What had gone wrong?

Grant explained, "You barely survived with your life. Your fever was dangerously high and your infections were severe. Had you not gotten to surgery in time, the infection would've infiltrated into your bloodstream. And..."

"I would have been dead within hours."

"Yes."

"What about my fertility options? For a biological child?"

"In-vitro fertilization may be your best chance, but you'd still be at risk."

"I'll take that risk."

"Stubborn as always."

"If I had a choice between the life of my baby or mine, I would choose my baby's life."

"I'd choose for you to live in a heartbeat."

"I know," she said, looking away. All her thoughts focused on what she could have done differently; the missed ultrasound appointment plagued her. The ultrasound would have given many life-saving warnings to her doctor. It would have flagged her as high-risk for *Placenta previa*, and follow-up ultrasounds would have been helpful in admonishing the peril. She could've taken all the preventative measures and even stayed on complete bed rest if she had needed it. *It's all my fault. My arrogance was unforgivable! Why didn't I die with my sons? Karma... it's karma.*

All life drained out of her as she stared at the orange-red blooms of the

Kordes Floribunda Mercedes roses, sitting on the windowsill in her private room. Even after the petals had fallen, she refused to have them taken away. What once were a token of joy had now taken a dismal meaning for her. *Beautiful, now withered. Alive, now dead. So why am I still alive?*

It pained Grant to see her this way. When was she going to smile again? He knew that there was nothing that he could say or do to ease her suffering, and so he sat in vigil, holding her hand until her parents arrived.

"Sweetheart, how are you?" Her mother drew her gently into her arms.

"Mom," was all she could say. Then the sobs racked her, tearing at her throat. She clutched her and shook in the storm of her grief.

Aware of her father's presence, she whispered to her mother, in French, *"Please don't tell anyone, especially Daddy. Please."*

"Shh...." Her mother rocked her like she would have, when she was a little baby. Also in French, she said, *"Everything will be all right, dearest."*

"This hurts, Mom. This hurts. Make it stop!"

"Yes I know, I know and I promise the pain will disappear. You'll see."

"You must be so disappointed with me."

"Never, never. And I promise I won't tell a soul."

"Not a soul."

Her father, in stoic silence, waited for them to include him. Though he didn't understand the words, he knew they were sharing secrets. He leaned down and held her too. He wept. It was the first time she had heard her father weep and it broke her heart.

It left her with a dull ache in her center and an emptiness that would not go away.

They all shared a morose silence for hours. They all sat in vigil for she wouldn't speak; her tears just flowed. She kept hoping against hope for some miracle. She even fantasized about Joe walking in her hospital room; but she knew it was an impossible wish.

"Mom?" she said, when her father left the room.

"Yes, *iha?*"

"Is God punishing me?"

"No, my little one, no."

"Then why? Why would God take away such precious gifts before giving them a chance to live?"

"Oh, but they lived," she said with a loving smile, brushing her hair lightly, "Dearest, it's not the length of a life that matters, what matters is the impact that life has made. And a life lives on in the smallest of memories. It takes but a single word, a single thought, and your twins live again." And after a pause, her mother said to her, "Think well not on the tragedy but on the joy."

Her words did not make her grief less, but she gave her the strength to carry on.

In the days that followed, she received many visitors. There was a steady stream of family and friends. Even Myles came to visit her. Some of the surgical staff came up for an occasional hello as well.

"Hello, hello!"

"Raiden!" she exclaimed. "I can't believe you're here!"

"How's my beautiful sister?" Lucas greeted her with a careful hug.

"Could be better. I look like shit and feel worse," she said coolly, but suddenly felt insecure. "So how badly do I look?"

"You're always beautiful to me," he said, giving her a soft familial kiss on her forehead.

"That bad, huh?"

"Look at this place! Are you opening a flower shop?" He marveled at the flowers, balloons and stuffed animals that filled the room.

"Hey, I come bearing gifts!" He gave her a beautiful leather bound journal. "I know how much you love writing in these things. It could get boring."

"Thank you!"

"Something else too."

"My favorite chocolates and a wooden puzzle! Thank you," she said and blew a kiss. "How did you ever get away from Uncle Sam?"

"I've got some connections," he grinned." Hey, want to see my latest scar?"

"Want to see mine?" she challenged him, and carefully uncovered her bandage. He winced when he saw what was hidden there.

"Oww!" he exclaimed dramatically with a crumpled look on his face, deliberately turning silly.

"Stop it! My intestines are going to fall out!" She kept trying to control the grip of laughter that suddenly took hold of her.

"Did you see Mom and Dad?"

"They were here earlier. Grant drove them to my place to get some rest."

"Excellent, now I know where I'll crash. Who else dropped by?"

"You just missed Leonardo and Luccio by a matter of minutes. And I receive daily calls from Lázaro and Luis."

"Yeah, I heard Lázaro took the job at the FBI, and he's moving the family to D.C. What's up with Luis?"

"His dental practice is taking off."

"And Mason?" he asked carefully.

"I haven't seen him since it happened, but he calls often. He can't stand to see me in here so he's waiting until after I get discharged. He hates hospitals."

After a few of hours, there was a knock at the door.

"Yo, Drake! Thanks for taking care of my sister," he said and shook Grant's hand. "You're a good man, doc."

"Thanks, Raiden. No problem. Hate to do this to you but I've got to kick you out. Visiting hours were over an hour ago. Besides, the nurse is on her way with a sedative."

"Do what you must. Just get my sister back on her feet."

"That I can do."

* * *

Grant was ever present by her side. He would sit with her as she slept and even helped her bathe. He would insist that she kept up her breathing exercises, which were preventative measures to keep her from getting pneumonia while she was bed-bound.

Frustrated, she blew into a tube, trying to lift three small blue plastic balls to a certain height. Not one ball moved.

"Come on, you can do this," he coaxed.

"It hurts," she said like an angry little girl.

"Just one more time. Please," he said, "I promise it will get better everyday."

In between his shifts at the hospital and during every other free moment, he would be by her side. In effect, he became her personal doctor, alerting staff to fill her scripts and checking everything that was hooked up to her, even changing her urine bag.

"It's that time again," he said as he coaxed her to get out of her bed, and insisted that she start walking. She was reluctant, but he wouldn't take "no" for an answer. He attempted to lift her, but she got angry, refusing any help.

"Stop! I can do it!" her stubborn pride barked at him. "I can do this myself."

She held on tightly to her stomach, hanging on to a blue stand-up monitor and IV holders for support. The tug of pain was excruciating and uncomfortable. She rolled them slowly along the hallways while he accompanied her on her daily stroll.

An unexpected sneeze would send her screaming. A cough or laughing at his incessant jokes was worse.

"Here," he said, giving her a small hard pillow to hold on to as she braced herself for a cough.

"Thanks, Grant," she said with a grateful smile.

The day came when it was time to take her catheter and NG-tube out. It was a very interesting sensation as the nurse removed them both. Being able to visit the bathroom and showering became an adventure.

The unending sameness of the hospital food made her cringe, but eventually she was able to even laugh about it as she held on tightly to the pillow.

She smiled every day because of Grant. All he needed to do was flash his infectious smile and she would find herself smiling with him. He would also bring her wonderful little surprise gifts—they had no monetary value, but they were priceless in her eyes. And he sang to her often.

She watched silently as he lifted the spirits of her parents, especially her father who tried to offer words of comfort, but always managed to make her more depressed, though he never realized it. Finally, when her parents returned home to Florida, she was grateful that Grant drove them to the airport and saw them off.

A week before discharge her purse was stolen from her hospital room with Joe's coin and his card along with it. It happened while she was taken for a barium examination of her gastrointestinal tract in another part of the hospital. It was the final blow for her; it was truly the only tangible thing she had left of him, and with its loss she didn't wish to recover anymore. She took it as a terrible sign.

Her spirit started slowly dying, and she asked for all of her flowers to be distributed in the waiting room for the neonatal intensive care unit.

She didn't take any calls, refused meals, and she didn't want to see anyone.

On several occasions she'd wake up screaming and delirious, speaking rapidly switching from French to Latin, and finally to Modern English, "No! Tell me! Where am I? No!"

Grant would ask her about it, but she would change the subject seamlessly.

In her deepest melancholy, she received an unexpected gift. Grant came in one day with his hands behind his back, grinning, and said, "I've got a special friend here for you."

He quickly produced an odd-looking stuffed animal from behind his back. The doll was blue, covered with blue daisies and white patchwork hearts. He went on to say, "His name is Raphael. I'm still not exactly sure what he is, but my mom made him for me when I was eight years. I was very, very sick with pneumonia, and it was my first time in the hospital. She quickly sewed this little doll for me and the next day, I started to feel so much better. Well, last night, Raphael and I had a talk. I told him all about you. He insisted that he come with me to see you today. He wanted to ask if it would be okay for him to stay with you and keep you company until you are well."

She hugged the odd-looking doll like a child. She looked at it again and stared at it for a long time. She looked at Grant, who sat patiently next to her, trying not to intrude. With tears in her eyes, she said, "Raphael just told me you should give me a hug right now."

She opened her arms and her heart to Grant. It was at that moment that she fell in love with him. With newfound love she began to feel much better.

The day came when she was released from the hospital. She made a final decision that she would never tell Joe of their lost sons.

One by one, in private, she asked her closest friends who knew anything of the loss. Sydney promised without question; though Mason protested vehemently, he promised never to betray her confidence. Finally, there was Grant.

"Please? Not even whisper." Her lips twitched. "Nothing."

He was silent and expressionless. He opened his mouth as if to say more, but clearly reconsidering, he said, "I give you my word."

There was never a worry about his word. There was truly honor in it.

In no uncertain terms she vowed to take this secret to her grave.

Chapter 23

The Impossible Wish

Sadly, the secret started to strain many of her friendships, especially her friendship with Mason. He felt betrayed, but he wouldn't explain his feelings and distanced himself from her after she was discharged from the hospital. When their divorce was final, Mercedes chose to leave with what she brought into the relationship. To her, Mason's millions were his and she was not and had never been interested in his material wealth to begin with.

Mason demanded his legal team set up a special type of trust fund without her knowledge. He knew she would refuse it, so he arranged the paperwork so that she couldn't do so even if she tried. Knowing it was for Mason's own peace of mind, she loved him for his efforts, but she redirected the dividends to various charitable funds that were dear to her heart.

A few months later he had started to move on with his life and was able to find his soul mate and be truly happy. His happiness increased her own joy and Mercedes happily celebrated with him, dancing with him at his wedding.

"Will you be changing the name of the yacht?"

"I'm selling that piece of shit!"

"What?"

"Gotcha!"

"Mason!"

"I named that yacht after you. There's no changing it, ever. Besides it's a good luck charm for me."

"What about your new bride, Dee?"

"She hates the water. That's why I got her a car instead." They both laughed.

"I am happy for you and Dee!"

"Never thought lightning could strike twice."

"Well, you've got that kind of luck."

"You're a hard act to follow."

"Don't let Dee hear you say that!"

"Don't worry about it. I told her too."

"You've always been very blunt with everyone."

"Yeah, well, not much has changed except…"

"I know, Mason. I know."

"I promise I won't fuck *this* up," he vowed. She smiled, knowing he wouldn't. With his second chance in love, their friendship and love became an occasional friendly hello.

Her friendship with Sydney also suffered. Sydney's marital struggles with Patrick became even more maddening, and it became necessary for Sydney's psychiatrist to prescribe psychotropic drugs.

"Isn't Xanax addictive?" Mercedes asked, though she knew it was.

"I can handle it. Would you please stop worrying about me?"

"I am worried about you. I've been having nightmares that you got addicted to this stuff."

"Well, you're wrong."

She got off the phone praying that she was wrong, but sadly, she wasn't. Just as she had suspected, her friend became dependent on the drugs because of her low tolerance. Mercedes had to distance herself from her as it became impossible for Sydney to even maintain a coherent thought or a meaningful conversation. She was always drunk or stoned on prescription medication.

"Syd, is Cassie with you?"

"Cassie? Yes, no, I don't know, somewhere. Who? Wait, you said something?" Strangely, she began to laugh. "I'm sorry, what did you say again?"

"About Cassie…"

In a muffled voice, she called out, "Yo Cass—Cassie, you here?" A moment passed.

"She's not answering me. Wait, you're coming over with Cassie?"

"No, no," Mercedes replied, sighing, "Do you still want me to come over?"

"Huh? Yeah, come over. Sure, let's have a cook out. Swim a few laps around the pool. I know, let's have a sleepover. Yes, that would be great. Is Cassie here? Is that what you asked?" Sydney's speech was disturbingly slurred.

She drew in a sharp breath, frustrated with her efforts at the conversation. Sadly, Mercedes knew Sydney was self-medicating.

Even though she hadn't planned for it to happen, Sydney did succeed at infidelity. The affair began with the innocent rekindling of an old friendship with a former college boyfriend, Justin Thomas. Sydney bumped into him a few months after she gave birth to her third child, a daughter she named Theresa. After the birth, Sydney wanted to get back into shape, so she joined a muscle gym and started sculpting her physical appearance.

Justin was one of the personal trainers at the gym, and over time, she started getting very personalized and often intimate workouts during her private sessions.

"Merc, if Patrick calls you, tell him that I'm shopping with you. No, wait, tell him that we're catching a new independent film at the Ritz."

"Sydney, this is a dangerous game you are playing."

"Please, please, no lectures. Just do this for me, pretty please?"

"Okay, just this one time."

But it wasn't just that one time. It continued for months and Mercedes found that she had to be careful with her conversations with Patrick. She neither condoned nor condemned Sydney's actions. She simply understood them.

Sydney's life continued in a downward spiral, and during one very troubled encounter with Patrick, Sydney accidentally took too many Xanax. Frantically, she called Mercedes and poured her heart out about her angst over Justin and Patrick.

"You're drunk."

"Ding, ding, ding, ding—give the *manslayer* a fuckin' prize! Better yet, would someone give her a baby already!" she said flippantly. It was clear that Sydney had been drinking, but Mercedes didn't know about the pills.

"Oh God! I'm sorry. I didn't mean it. I'm so sorry…"

"It's okay, really—it's all right," she reassured her, though the sting of her words lingered.

"Are you sure?" she asked again, on the verge of tears. "I've been hurting everyone that I love lately! You're okay, right?"

"Yes, I'm fine, but what about you? Are you okay?"

"No, I'm fucked up! I don't know what to do. Justin wants me to leave Patrick! But I can't. I still love him—but I love Justin too. Is it possible to be in love with two people at the same time? Could it be possible? Tell me what to do… please, what should I do? Oh my God… help me… I can't live like this…" Her speech was slurred and frighteningly incoherent.

Suddenly, an uncomfortable silence passed between them. Mercedes pressed the phone closer to make sure she didn't hang up. She could still hear something, a whimper, but she was unsure. "Hello? Syd, talk to me. Sweetie, what's wrong? Sydney?"

There was no answer.

In terror, she asked again, "Sydney, what's wrong!"

Sydney almost didn't make it.

Every visit to see her at the hospital was excruciating for Mercedes. Worse, after that incident, Sydney was never the same person. Though she successfully purged the addiction out of her system, the old vibrant Sydney faded into obscurity. Patrick uprooted the whole family, moving them to somewhere in Arizona. She never knew whether the sudden move was because Patrick had discovered Sydney's affair or because he wanted a fresh start for all of them.

* * *

Mercedes tried to keep in touch with Sydney, but her own life made it impossible. Life threw her a series of unexpected menacing maladies, including a few scares with breast cancer.

Her work became increasingly demanding, both physically and mentally. She knew she needed to slow down, but she forged ahead with greater drive and ambition until it eventually all caught up to her, leading to her complete sense of exhaustion.

With Grant always present by her side, she managed to rescue herself from her darkest moments, striving to be strong-willed and optimistic, despite misfortunes.

Inside, her love for Joe remained intact. She tried very hard to have closure, so she could move on with her life, but her image of Joe as a flawless man made it difficult for her to do so or for Grant to wholly touch her heart.

In the years that followed, between December and May, Joe would manage to contact her. It would be brief, but nevertheless, he always made contact. She told him about the loss of his coin, but nothing more. He had immediately replaced the coin with another one, making sure it was a red coin, her personal color. She kept it guarded in her safe at home, only taking it out whenever she spoke with him.

Every time he made contact, she struggled to remain detached, but she never succeeded. For each time she heard his voice, she was propelled back into vividly reliving those four nights. And her phantasm would begin to haunt her again. More painfully, the wound in her soul's heart from the loss of their twins would reopen. Remembering that loss, she was constantly at war with herself, battling to keep from confessing about the loss to him, but her love for him wouldn't allow it. She bore the pain alone to spare him that anguish.

For a couple of years, she even managed to elude him for her own mental health; she had needed to keep her distance from him. There wasn't a moment unoccupied. When she had any downtime, she wrote prolifically about her inner turmoil.

Inevitably, she initiated a search for him when Grant asked her to marry him. She had accepted Grant's proposal and moved with him to Memphis when Grant received an offer from his father to go into private practice with him.

She gladly uprooted from Philadelphia to start life anew, wanting to take a chance at happiness and desperately needing to keep Joe in the past.

She hadn't agreed on a wedding date, because she had known that she would be unable to move forward with Grant until she faced her truths with Joe and told him exactly how she felt about him. After a self-imposed silence for two years, she found herself staring at his email address on her computer screen. She found it by simply doing an Internet search for him.

With great trepidation, she had finally typed,

"*Hello JC, write me back. Mercedes.*"

The following day, she was elated to find a response in her inbox, which read:

"*Absolutely incredibly glad to... Where are you? What are you doing? And why haven't I heard from you? Actually the answers don't matter, I'm just happy that you've decided to contact* me once again. I'm hoping you'll tell me that you're utterly happy and living on a deserted island in the South Pacific. I really had given up. So, now you must let me know."

The message also had his direct telephone extension on it, but she decided not to call him, not just yet. She wasn't ready to deal with the flood of emotions she knew she'd feel once she heard his voice. And since it was nearing his fortieth birthday, she decided to send him a special gift. It was an Aladdin Convention Casino Chip from the year they met. She ordered it and hoped that it would arrive on time for his birthday.

Then, on his birthday, she sent him a poem. She read it one last time before she clicked the "send" button:

"*Gentle Echo*

When next your lips touch another

let it be as sweet for it mingles

with mine unseen.

Reflections of moments in time

from a familiar smile, a look or

the warmth of another's embrace.

Let each word be a gentle echo

never fading so long

as beauty surrounds you

caressed with whispers that

this is not all for nothing.

As it will always be,

within thoughts eternal

there's none like any other truth

that in solitude

there I am beside you."

She tried to imagine his reactions to her gifts, wishing she could have given them in person. She had often thought what it would be like to see him again, but she had always dismissed the fantasy, remembering the promise she made to herself. *Never interfere, not unless we are both free in clear conscience.*

He had immediately written her back, and she smiled as she read,

"*From the bottom of my heart, thank you for remembering. I thought I lost you... I've missed you so much.*

Love,

JC"

She had left his email unanswered since she was on her way to the Big Apple to spend the New Year's holiday with Lucas.

When she returned a few days later, she checked her email messages and there was another one from Joe.

"I want (make that need) to hear your voice. Please call me."

While she debated to call him, her phone rang.

"Little one?"

"Hi Mom, how are you?"

"I'm fine, sweetheart. How was your flight back?"

"Uneventful and a little bumpy."

"Did you enjoy your visit with Lucas?"

"It was a somber experience."

"Oh?"

"We went to the site of the Twin Towers. They're calling it Ground Zero now. You and Daddy should come and see it too."

"It's too soon, dear. I still shake thinking about what had happened," her mother said, without masking the pain in her voice about the recent terrorist attack.

"Well, Lucas wanted us to go. He wanted to pay his respects to the victims of 9-11. He called Luccio to join us too."

"Did Kiley and Leandro come along?"

"Yes, and we stood in line for three hours just to get on a makeshift observation platform overlooking Ground Zero. And Mom, what really struck me was that everyone seemed kinder, more considerate and forgiving. Someone had inadvertently cut in line and I couldn't believe how polite people were. Normally, I would expect some verbal abuse, but not that day. The sidewalks were littered with makeshift shrines and I was so touched by it all."

"What happened made an impact in all our lives and I wish that it didn't take a tragedy to make us all realize how fragile life is. It's so important to reach out and let the people we love know that we do love them."

Her mother's words tugged at her heart. "I love you, Mom!"

"I love you too, dearest," she said. "How was little Leandro during this whole experience?"

"Well-behaved but very inquisitive. When we were on the Staten Island Ferry, he asked me if I'd have children of my own."

"What did you tell him?"

"I told him I would adopt after I got married again. He wasn't sure what adoption was, so after I explained it, he thought it was 'cool' that I would be saving a life," she said, smiling at the memory. "Mom, have you noticed how your grandson sounds so much older than eight years old!"

"Your father said he reminded him of his brother, Joseph, when he was the same age. And speaking of Joseph…" After a moment of hesitation, her mother said, "I got an unexpected call from a Joe Tristram just the other day."

"JC called you?" she said, stunned. "What did he say?"

"When I got the call, I was really taken aback. He wanted to know how to get a hold of you. I wasn't sure what to say. Remembering my promise, I told him that since I didn't know him, I would only convey his message to you, but I couldn't tell him anything else. I asked him to understand my position, which he did. Then I asked him to tell me about himself."

"Why?"

"Why not? I wanted to hear what this JC of yours had to say about himself."

"What more did he say?"

"He told me that he was an old friend of yours and that he flies planes for the Air Force. He said he was happily married and that they had a daughter and were living in Arizona. And from his voice, he sounded as if he was genuinely happy."

"That's so good to hear. I'm glad life is treating him well."

"He misses you."

"He told you?"

"No, I sensed it from his voice too."

"You got that from his voice?"

"A mother knows, sweetheart." Mercedes knew not to doubt her.

"Well, he left his phone numbers. He really wants you to get in touch with him. Now, it's not my place to say whether you should or not, but you know how I feel about it."

"You said he was in Arizona now? Did he say where?"

"He mentioned that he was stationed at Luke Air Force Base."

"Okay, got it."

"And little one?"

"Yes, Mom?"

"I'm here if you need me."

"I know," she said, nervously doodling in her journal. "And, Mom—thank you."

After her phone call with her mother, she continued debating about making the call to Joe. Finally, she nervously dialed his phone number. After a couple of rings, she decided to hang up, but when she heard his voice, there was no turning back.

From the first "hey there," it was as though time never passed between them.

She and Joe shared their successes and celebrations, as well as the mundane moments of their lives. She also shared most of the unfortunate dark episodes of her life with him. The urge to share her secret about their babies was strong, but she didn't. Her vow was one she held even more sacred than marriage.

With his next email he attached a few photos of himself. He also asked for a picture of her, preferably in a tropical theme. She reciprocated and his immediate response of "Oh my" was quite telling. She was equally pleased with his photos as he was with hers.

"Mercedes, I've got to tell you about this amazing coincidence."

"A coincidence? Now, why am I not surprised?"

"Did I ever mention my old friend, Frank—I call him Uncle Lloyd."

"Yes, wasn't he from Philly too?"

"That's him. He was the line chief I met at Nellis. Well, I lost touch with him until recently when we were both re-stationed here in Luke. He's a family man again with two more kids, Stef and Zak."

"Did you play poker?"

"Sure did! He invited me over for a game of poker just this past weekend. How did you know?"

"I didn't, just had to blurt it out. Strange, isn't it?"

"Like you said, why am I not surprised?"

"True."

"Well, when I got to Uncle Lloyd's place, I was drawn to a couple of pieces of art on his wall. He noticed how interested I was in his paintings, so he started telling me about them. He told me that his wife, Leela, forced him to go with her to this art show. He had never bought art before, but two things grabbed him: they were good and the artist was from Philadelphia. He said, 'I'll never forget her name. Mercedes—very classy, and so was she!' When I looked at the signature on the bottom of the painting and the initials were MPS, I knew he was talking about you!"

"That is an amazing coincidence! Which paintings were they?"

"One was of Marilyn Monroe and the other..."

"Was called 'Through my tired eyes', right?" she said, finishing his sentence. "Yes, I remember Uncle Lloyd. We talked for a while about the piece, and he also told me that he enjoyed how I opened the show."

"Yes, he mentioned that you shared an original poem with the audience. He also raved about how gorgeous you were to me. He had no idea how well I know you."

"Did you tell him?"

"No. I liked listening to him tell me about you. He said you were with some longhaired guy. Was that Grant?"

"Yes, it was Grant."

"Well, Uncle Lloyd was right. You are talented and beautiful. Your poetry is beautiful too. I loved my birthday poem."

"I'm glad."

"I saved every single one of your poems. I read them from time to time. How do you manage to get right on target with my feelings? It's as if you've peered into my mind and written down my thoughts, exactly as they are."

"Perhaps it's because I feel the same."

"You have no idea how many times I've fantasized about you over the years," he said sweetly. "I need to see you. I've missed you, Mercedes."

"I've missed you too."

A few moments later they hung up, and their phone contact continued to be one-way. He couldn't call her because of Grant and their promise that they wouldn't ever intentionally interfere with the other's life. And he had made it so that she could be in his life without having to face suspicions about his true feelings for her, never mentioning her name beyond acknowledging that they were old friends, which they truly were. They shared something more than a platonic relationship, but it was always unconditional and yet unrequited.

Mercedes wished it were true on her end too, but it was obviously impossible. It would have been ideal had the situation been truly different. She would not have hesitated to fly out to see him in the guise of an old college boyfriend. She would even have socialized with him openly and they would have been able to remain active in their lives. She had successfully kept her friendships with many men, especially those with whom she had been intimate. She cherished the love and friendship which remained, however distant, like with Mason.

*   *   *

Just before Valentine's Day Mercedes faced a crossroad. Her feelings for

Joe had seeped into her reality. It had happened gradually and without her noticing it.

Worse, she found six lumps in her breasts during self-examination. After undergoing a series of tests, she received devastating news: three of the lumps were cancerous, stage II/grade II breast cancer. She was scheduled for lumpectomies and a lymph node removal.

With Grant's medical reassurance she managed to set her initial panic aside. She became confident that her prognosis was very good—especially when he was brutally blunt in saying, "Mercedes, a diagnosis of breast cancer is not a death sentence! Please trust me."

Overall, her life had become too complex with the unexpected cancer diagnosis, Grant's marriage proposal, the 9-11 tragedy and reliving the past with Joe. All of those separate pressures sent her into an emotional frenzy. After many nights of soul-searching, and with a heavy heart two days before her surgery, she finally called Joe.

"You sound really tired or upset," he immediately said. He was alarmed when she began to cry over the phone. "What is it, Mercedes? What's the matter?"

"JC, I need you to listen to me, please!" Her tears flowed as she began to tell him of her unfortunate diagnosis. With indescribable anguish, she asked him, "Would you grant me a wish please, JC?"

"Of course I will. Anything."

"We must remain silent once again."

"What the hell does silent mean? I don't understand what it is you asking of me!"

With tears streaming down her face, she said softly, "No contact."

Already disarmed by her explanation of everything that had been going wrong in her life, he felt his frustration growing. It seemed that she was saying "no contact" with a finality that he simply was not going to accept.

"Okay, I can grant you that. I'll stop sending you email. I won't call you anymore, write you letters or even try to find you! But from time to time, you must drop me a note to let me know how you are doing. I want to know that you've beaten this cancer and that you have lived to be ninety-five! I want to know that you and Grant have gotten married and that you are happily living your lives. I want to know that you've tried in-vitro and that you've had tons of babies! Please, Mercedes, at least let me know about your health."

When he mentioned babies, she felt a pain as sure as if he had inadvertently shot an arrow into her, the same as he had on the night he confessed that his wife Eva was going to have a baby. He had inadvertently done it again, and this time, the arrow had instilled more pain than he could ever fathom!

Hearing his words, she prayed desperately that she would not betray herself and her vow not to reveal her secret. She was still weeping, but she controlled her voice, "No, JC. I meant no contact—forever."

"Don't you do this. You tell me right now that you don't mean any of this!"

Her voice broke and she choked out, "I'm sorry JC, but it must be this way. I'm very sorry." It sounded almost as if she was trying to convince herself.

"Stop being sorry! It doesn't have to be this way. We don't have to have this damned tragic ending! I have another happier ending in mind for us."

"Please, JC" was all she could say.

He inhaled sharply, fighting for control. He felt more frustrated than ever, "No. I can't and I won't agree to never contact you again. It's asinine to even expect me to grant you a wish like that. No contact forever. It is an impossible wish! The answer is no, Mercedes. No!"

Though his protest attested to his love for her, she couldn't yield to her heart. *I have no choice.* Just as in Las Vegas, she could not falter. She knew that no contact would be the best thing for them both. Just as she had vowed to herself years ago, she would go to her grave without ever seeing him, rather than having him hear and see her suffering. Importantly, she couldn't have him uncover the secret of their private loss. She couldn't allow it—ever!

Her sentimental old soul wouldn't allow it to happen either. She had to draw strength from her great love for him. It was a decision which wounded her heart deeply, but she had to do it. Tearfully, she begged, "JC, please try to understand, please."

"I'm trying to understand, but you're asking me for something—something I can't do! I won't do!" Finally, he said, "I'm in love with you, Mercedes."

She was about to say something when he said, "Hold on a second."

Moments later, he asked, "Tell me if you hear this." He shook something a few times. It had a distinct metallic sound.

"Did you hear that?"

"My puzzle," she whispered.

"I carry it with me, Mercedes. It's been with me since the night you gave it to me."

When she heard that, she cried even more profusely. She couldn't speak.

"Mercedes. Stop. You're making me want to crawl through the phone lines and just hold you, keep you safe. I never want to hurt you in any way. I don't want to put you in this negative frame of mind. I want you to be positive, especially now." He paused. "Oh God," he said in a low voice. "I can't do this."

She remained silent, waiting for him to go on.

Finally, he said, "Okay, I promise." He couldn't hide the reluctance or frustration in his tone.

When Mercedes heard him give his word, she knew it was time for her to fulfill another wish and let him know exactly how she felt for him.

She asked, "Would you bring up my picture on your computer?"

She was already looking at his picture on her computer. She had been staring at his face since before she made the phone call. In her hand, she gripped a red coin.

She could hear him typing. Finally, he said, "I'm looking at you now."

"Let me take you back in time, JC, to the Aladdin, during that very moment when you and I had to part. I want you to hold onto that moment when you gazed at me right before you closed the door to leave. It was the moment when I smiled at you for the very last time. Now, imagine that right after you saw my smile, you heard me say the words…" She almost couldn't say the words, but the words poured out of her. "I love you, JC."

"And I love you," he said instantly.

"I had promised not to tell you while—"

"And to finally hear you say you love me too is incredible," he said and continued tenderly, "People long for a love all their lives. Sometimes people live their whole lives dreaming, searching to have just one of the four nights we've had."

She found herself speaking in French, "*God has blessed our souls to reunite four nights long ago and for a few precious stolen moments through the years through words and our voices. The love we hold in our hearts is immortal, and it will endure.*" After she translated it for him, she hung up the phone, weeping. Her pain seemed unbearable. *I'll see you in my dreams, JC.*

She felt like she was back in that room in Vegas, sitting naked against the door, composing her poem. Except this time, she wrote a book about Joe.

The book started out as a poem, but it had evolved into the longest love letter that she had ever written. An emotional purging. Or was it an attempt to finally say goodbye? It sprang into an amorphous life of its own. Within it, she wrote her memories, her hopes, her fantasies... her secrets. Carefully, she wove truths within the fiction: 90% truth and 10% story.

* * *

"Mom, would you do me a favor?" Mercedes asked anxiously.
"Anything."
"Would you read something for me?"
"Yes, of course. What is it?"
"A manuscript."
After her mother read it, she received a call.
"Sweetheart, you should publish it. It's very good."
Concerned, she said, "It might be a Pandora's Box."
"Only to the guilty."
"I understand."
"Publish it," she said, firmly. "It's too beautiful of a story to be hidden away."
"Thanks, Mom. I love you."
"Love you too."

She submitted the manuscript to a few publishers. After a few rejections she finally received a notice for publication. She immediately thought of sharing the happy news with Joe.

Impulsively, she picked up her cell phone. She was scrolling through her electronic phonebook in search of his number. When she found it, she thought for a moment, *What am I doing?* Then quickly, she pushed the speed dial for Grant.

For her author's photograph, she chose a studio photo taken shortly after she found out she was pregnant. She felt it was appropriate to use since it mirrored the timeframe of the events in the book. Her heart still ached when she looked at it, though it no longer made her cry.

After her book was published, she promptly tucked her feelings for Joe deeply away in her heart once more. Compartmentalized, just as she imagined Joe must have had to do with her. And in the place of Joe, her illness consumed her. She had to endure four courses of chemotherapy, twelve weekly treatments of Taxol, and endless radiation therapies that took a heavy toll on her body. She experienced devastating chronic side effects, ranging from extreme fatigue to nausea and vomiting. Climbing the steps became a chore.

She often looked in the mirror and saw only a shadow of her former self. She barely recognized herself. Her hair... her smile was barely there. Sick and emaciated. There were many times that she wanted to reach out to Joe. She tried to imagine him and felt the horror of his reaction if he saw her in this state. She felt madness was descending upon her.

During her dark moments she wanted to slip away from existence, but life held on tightly to her. She slowly became a prisoner of her own body. The only way she could freely soar was within her mind, her imagination. She took solace in her writing and each day, she wrote Joe about her ordeal, but she never sent it. Instead, she hid them in her journal.

"How's my sunshine, doing?"

"Much better, thank you," she said. "I had a little relapse today, but I handled the situation. This sickness thing is what's really eating at me. Hey, how about a spin on the boat after your shift?"

"Great idea. Fresh air will do you some good. You need to be outside more instead of secluding yourself. Okay, I'll see you within the hour."

The cool evening air did wonders for her mentally. The water was calming and her mind was clear. She looked up at the sky and saw a plane go by. It was at that moment she finally decided on a wedding date.

"Valentine's Day," she said to Grant.

"What about Valentine's Day?"

"Let's get married on that day."

Speechless, he kissed her. "You won't regret it."

She smiled, and said, "Never."

"I love you."

"I love you too."

* * *

The following Valentine's Day, they had an elegant evening wedding in the Memphis Brooks Museum of Art; all of their immediate family members and closest friends were in attendance.

Both her mother and father walked her down the aisle, which was strewn with multi-colored petals. A string quartet serenaded them.

Wearing a custom-made silver tiara, her long ebony hair gently waved, flowing like a veil. Her whimsical wedding dress was based on her original design: a silver velvet brocade cloak over a delicate, shimmering white chiffon dress, with long cutaway sleeves. Gemstones were sewn onto her dress, trimming the silver embroidered bodice, long sleeves and a belt matching her cloak. She carried a bouquet of her favorite roses.

"Take good care of my only daughter," her father whispered before stepping back.

"Yes sir, I will."

Before they took their formal marriage vows, they surprised each other with their own words of love.

Grant nervously said, "I want nothing more than to love you without measure. If there is but one lifetime, my life is complete, for I have known the joy that is you. No spell shall ever break what binds us, we are our dreams fulfilled.

We are our own happiness." As his tears flowed unheeded, he continued, "With my eyes open, I see you clearly. You are my love without question."

Mercedes felt she couldn't speak for she too was tearful. Composing herself, she said, smiling, "You are my undying light in my darkest hours, my tower of strength, my laughter, my truth and my inspiration. You make each moment like a sweet flutter of a butterfly's kiss, awakening each day filled with renewed promise of all that is good. Your patience relentless... your heart pure, your strength unmatched and your laughter joyous. Our love is only what others dream of, lasting the winds of change. It is the envy of those who want to know what it's like to be in love with your best friend. Until my last breath, your name shall be on my lips, my heart eternally yours."

She turned to the celebrant before he could begin their wedding vows, "Wait, there's more I'd like to say." And to Grant, she began reciting a poem,

"Destined on this day of our joining

I breathe life once more from your lips

and, into your hands, you hold

my gift of my heart exposed

In your embrace, we kiss with passionate truths

With my hand in yours, I walk in trust alongside you

on this path I have never taken

I am immersed with your brilliant light

for you are

my radiant smiling angel

in disguise."

It was the first poem she had ever written especially for him. Joyfully and spontaneously, Grant began singing *a cappella My Angel*, the song which he composed and sang to her on the night he had proposed.

Later, Grant led her to one of the galleries, giving her a most unique wedding gift.

"My paintings!" she shrieked happily. They were hung alongside twentieth century artists Chaim Soutine, Georgia O'Keeffe and Thomas Hart Benton.

"You belong with the masters, my love."

They began to dance the waltz and continued dancing in Vienna, where they spent their honeymoon. And just as she wished, a year later they adopted their little girl, Carly Jane.

Chapter 24

The Larchers

"Hello, love! How was your day?" Grant greeted her as she walked into their family room and sat down next to him on the sofa.

Breaking into a smile, she responded, "Fine. How about you? How was your day with your new med-students?"

"Always an adventure! I taught them a thing or two about good old-fashion surgical techniques. I'd hate for them to rely completely on cutting-edge, micro-laser surgical instruments. I love their stamina! I could really use it with the bass tournament coming up."

He leaned over and gently kissed her cheek. When he smelled the sweet scent of her neck, a smile emerged on his face and he began a playful role-play. His voice dripped with sexy southern charm. "I've missed you, my pretty lady! I'm in need of your womanly charms, darlin'." He pulled her into a loving embrace.

She playfully drawled, "But, if you must—be gentle with me with those fine hands of yours, I'm feelin' a bit fragile."

They were jubilant with their role-playing but within minutes, she seemed aloof.

"You look a bit distracted. Everything all right?" Embracing her, he rested his head lightly on top of hers.

She grunted a reply.

"You sound like you could really use an all body pampering," he said, kissing her neck and tightening his embrace.

She pouted before saying with a frown, "Oh love, actually, a bath was more what I had in mind. Ugh! I can feel a wicked migraine coming on." Hating missed opportunities, her voice transitioned into a seductive one. "Don't think I won't take you up on that tantalizing offer soon!"

"Oh my poor love, let me try to make you feel better," he cooed and lovingly gave her "butterfly kisses" with his long lashes on her forehead.

"That feels so nice," she whispered, enjoying his pampering. She ran her hand through his hair. "I love the way your haircut turned out. It's much shorter than last time."

"I've noticed more gray hairs so I opted for a shorter trim."

"You're imagining those grays. I can't see any gray hairs," she said, inspecting the side of his head. "All I see is platinum blond hair and the sexy man attached to it," she said playfully, feeling the velvety softness of his newly cut hair that tickled her fingertips. She let her hands roam elsewhere and felt the contours of his physique, strong and fit. "Love, I meant to tell you that our treadmill is at its last leg."

A memory of an intimate moment they had after one of his workouts in their home gym seeped into his mind. Grinning, he said, "I'll take care of it."

"Thanks, love," she said, nuzzled in his arms, enjoying the weight of his head on top of hers again. She felt drained from her turbulent trip back in time.

"Joe called me today. He decided to fish the next tournament with me." He went on, but all Mercedes heard was "Joe."

"Oh, which reminds me, I took a call just before you came in. Your trainer wants to know if you're interested in the Breast Cancer Run next Sunday. If you are, your favorite cheering squad will be there. Carly and I always enjoy greeting you at the finish line. So are you running?"

When there was no answer, he asked again, "Are you listening?"

"Huh? Oh I'm sorry. You said something about your best friend... and Colleen called about a run?"

"You seem so far away right now," he noticed, "Care to share?"

She was silent for a second, not willing to tell him—not just yet.

"Love?"

"Just one of those days."

Tightening his embrace and shaking his body playfully, he said, "Shake it off!" Laughter soon ensued.

Their brief interlude was abruptly interrupted by a sweet young voice. "Okay, knock it off, you two! Get a room!" Carly was grinning as she joined them, greeting both of them with a huge bear hug and kisses on their cheeks. They were seated on the comfortable, linen-velvet sofa next to a love seat, chaise, club chairs and an upholstered bench. The seventeenth century pine-framed fireplace added more warmth in the room.

The family room was cozy with its seventeenth century period furniture. Pine paneling and cabinetry hid the family entertainment center and bookshelves. The deep red billiard cloth wall-coverings and a wool herringbone carpet projected a very warm feeling. Pine moldings, bisque draperies, amber candlesticks and Botero sculptures accentuated the room. Hardy plants were situated tastefully in every part of the space.

"How are my two most favorite people in the world?"

Running in behind Carly was Vangogh—a brown and grey tabby kitten they had recently rescued from the local animal shelter.

"How are you, *mia cara*?" Mercedes brushed away the stray dark tendrils of hair from her daughter's face.

Carly beamed, and replied, "I'm fine, Mom."

"How's your patient?" Mercedes was looking at the cat.

Carly smiled at her mother's teasing question, "Well, Mommy. Vangogh's prognosis remains hopeful. I've carefully administered his medications as prescribed. His sinuses are clearing up; the infection from his unfortunate castration is looking much better, except... there was an unexpected complication." She shifted her gaze to her father and asked, "Papa, did you tell Mom about it?"

Before Grant could say anything, Mercedes said, "CJ, how about if you break it to me gently?"

"Well, I took the precautionary measures to protect him from possible invading armies of fleas. So with the help of my aspiring veterinarian friends, I got a flea collar. By the way, Mom, it was the reason why I had to break our usual date at the museum today." She saw her mother nodding. "Anyway, I quickly found out that our little Vangogh was not fond of anything around his neck. He was wrestling with it, trying to get it off his neck, and in his determined struggle, the collar got stuck in his mouth. He panicked! I tried to free him, as is evident from my battle scars," she showed them her badly scratched arms, "I was unsuccessful. He got very bloody but, thankfully, the collar broke."

Quickly, she picked up the purring cat in her arms—he was playing with a grey toy rat that was twice his size. It was still stuck to his little claws when she picked him up. To illustrate her next point, she pried his mouth open and announced, "He is truly a Vangogh, for he is now missing a piece of his tongue!" Laughter filled the family room, and Vangogh got a lot of attention from the family of three.

Grant hugged his daughter, adding proudly, "What our little sundrop left out of her story was how she remained perfectly in control of the situation, remaining calm in this emergency. After administering to his wounds and hers, her little patient is doing great. Our star seedling here will make a fine doctor under fire."

For a few minutes they just sat there together, a family.

Carly enjoyed listening and watching her parents. Like her mother, she had the same build and matching smile, but she had always known she was adopted. It never made any difference in their lives as a family. They brought her home shortly after they had gotten married. She had been a four-year-old Amerasian orphan whose parents had been tragically killed in a car accident in California. The deep loving bonds they had developed made it difficult to tell that she wasn't their biological daughter.

It had been Carly's philosophy that there was no difference between biological and adoptive parents as long as deep familial love and respect existed. And there was plenty of love in their household. There was never a day she could remember when her parents fought or uttered an unkind word, and she even tolerated the cute, endearing pet names her parents gave her.

She felt very special and she just loved it! On her First Holy Communion her mother had given her lovely words along with her very first rosary beads. The rosary, made of fragrant crushed rose petals, was one her mother had brought home from the Vatican. When her mother had presented the rosary to her, she held her lovingly, tightly as she looked deeply into her eyes, saying with a smile, "Carly, *ma fille précieuse*. Before you were conceived, I wanted you. Before you were born, I loved you. Before you were an hour old, I would die for you. You are a special gift from God. We are blessed to have chosen each other."

Her mother's words of love moved her to tears, even at the tender, young age of eight. She had loved the idea of choice. She did choose them as her parents and thanked fate for having a hand on it. Her biological father, Owen, had been a good friend of her mother's. Her mother had shared the story of how she first met him in Vegas during a brief taxi ride. Even her name had a connection with her mother: Carly Jane meant *little merciful* in Latin and Hebrew.

"My name and your name mean the same thing, right Mommy?"

"Yes, *ma chérie*—how did you know?"

"Daddy told me," she replied and hugged her. "We really do belong together, Mommy!"

The coincidences meant a great deal to Carly, and it had been the main reason she hadn't been afraid when she first met her parents, and ultimately became their legally adopted daughter.

It saddened her greatly to think about other kids she knew who weren't as deliriously happy and loved. They often complained about how they hadn't had a choice when they were born into their own families. Sadly, they would even bitterly debase their own biological parents. She didn't and wouldn't. In fact, every birthday she insisted on hearing about the day they finally brought her home.

Every day there was laughter in their home, and singing, lots of singing! Their family life also included tons of art and poetry. Her mother had painted whimsical murals in her bedroom, and she had written a book of bedtime stories just for her. She had grown up with many close cousins, doting uncles, aunts and grandparents who tried to spoil her rotten! Though she admired her mother's multi-talents, she felt she was destined to be a physician like her father. Not a surgeon, but a forensic psychiatrist. Part of it came from having witnessed her mother's many spells, as she would call them. After one of them, she would manage to lift her mother's spirits immediately and consistently, even at her darkest spells. She was driven by an inherent need to heal people's broken spirits.

"You're a natural life saver, *ma fleur*," Mercedes had said, punctuating the compliment with a kiss on her forehead. Carly matched her smile, shaking off her thoughts.

When the grandfather clock chimed the hour, Mercedes announced, "It's getting late, I've got dinner to prepare." She quickly kissed Grant on the cheek.

She and Carly got up at the same time. Without her heels she was only three inches shorter than her daughter. They both giggled as they raced up the stairs to change and Grant went downstairs in the basement to take a look at the treadmill.

* * *

Mercedes was the first one back. Barefoot, wearing comfortable, black, side-zip twill pants and a crisp white poplin shirt with French cuffs, she went into the kitchen to start preparing dinner with opera by her favorite tenors playing softly in the background.

The kitchen was another one of her sanctuaries. It was one of the larger spaces in the house. Using her brother's architectural design, she had overseen the construction of the kitchen. Luccio had infused it with function as well as charm, and it was exquisitely detailed and elegantly finished, decorated with in an Old World European style.

Luccio had also ingeniously designed built-in storage cabinetry with the appearance of antique furniture. Wherever possible, he had incorporated appliances into walls or counters. The counters and backsplashes were blue granite from Italy, and the floors were laid with large red terracotta tiles. After the kitchen was completed in time for Halloween two years ago, she threw a huge dinner party for her entire family, both sides. The family reunion was a masquerade costume party. With her large family and Grant's, the entire house was full.

* * *

Mercedes was upstairs in Grant's study in search of the sword for his costume. Hearing a car pull up, she quickly ran to the closest window. Smiling with excitement, she hurriedly walked down a marble spiral staircase with wrought iron railings that led to a second floor overlook.

Neoclassical sconces flanked a golden mirror hanging above a side table that was directly in front of the staircase. The floor was also marble, and there was a beautiful thick, round Persian rug under a carved table in the center of the area. Huge impressionistic paintings in ornate golden frames were proximately displayed on the walls. The foyer looked almost like a lobby with its rounded, vaulted ceilings and grand palatial feeling. Except for the fact that it felt cozy and homelike, it could have been a museum with its fantastic furnishings. There were even fresh-cut sunflowers on a low table.

"Hi everyone!" Mercedes greeted her parents, Luccio and Kiley with excited waves of her right hand, trying not to drop the sword she held on her left. A happy smile looked like it was permanently sealed on her masked face.

"Hello, *iha*. How's my baby girl?" Her father greeted her with sniffing kisses. He was dressed as an imposing king in deep purple; he held a bejeweled mask and his wife stood next to him.

"I'm fine, my liege," Mercedes curtsied, smiling as she played the part. "And Mom, you're a gypsy!"

"You like it?" she smiled, "I even have a crystal ball. I shall tell fortunes tonight."

Nodding as she embraced her, "You look fantastic, Mom! I love the dangling earrings" and stepping back to look at them both, "I'm so glad you're all here!"

"Almost didn't make it. Your father thinks flying at his age will give him a heart attack," her mother said, flashing a silly look at him. "An anxiety attack is more like it."

He smiled, "But I'm old now, Momma."

Giggling, she said, "Lindor, I'm older than you!"

After a quick hug, her brother said, "Hey Merc, where's Grant? I want to show him my samurai sword."

"Why are men always so excited to show off their swords?" his lovely blonde wife teased, returning the welcome hug. Kiley grinned and said, "Can you tell I'm the geisha to entertain him?" She lifted her smiling geisha mask to her face.

Nodding, she said with a giggle escaping, "Love the mask! You look great in your outfit."

"Thanks," she said, breathing in deeply, "I can't wait to taste what you're cooking tonight. It smells great! And I love your floppy chef's hat—" Looking at her baggy red chef pants with a seafood print, she added, "Oh, those are so cute!"

Embracing her again, she said, "And before I forget, here's a hug from Leandro. He wanted to be here, but a big case came in and he's the lead prosecutor. You know how he is." After the hug, she said, "I can't believe my baby is almost thirty-five!"

"Amazing, isn't it? Life is truly less than a blink in time," Mercedes muttered.

"Just be friendly to yourself. Live as healthy and as long as you can. And make sure you leave your mark before it's too late. That's why we had six children!" A loud guffaw escaped from her father.

"Don't listen to your father, children. I think he's loosing his mind like his sight. Each moment is precious and new. And having as many children as possible is not the secret to immortality." She shifted her tone like a gypsy and continued, "To be remembered is to be truly immortal."

Her father peered through his thick glass, asking, "Who is that?"

"Daddy, that's Carly," Mercedes said, looking at the smiling Spanish flamenco dancer approaching them.

"I know my *nieta*, little one," he said, squinting again, "I meant behind her. Him!"

Mercedes glanced over her shoulder. She smiled at the masked knight in a red surcoat without armor, slow in his approach as he waited for his elderly parents, ambling slowly behind him.

"Grant, is that really you?"

"Yes, Sire," bowing reverently to the bewildered king. He smiled and cheerfully greeted him. "Great to see you, Pop! I'm glad you made it." Then quickly, he planted a kiss on the lovely gypsy's cheek. "You're a vision, Mom—what wonders will you predict for me tonight?" Mercedes handed him his sword as he made his way toward Luccio, thanking her with a kiss on the cheek.

"You guys look fantastic!" Carly loudly greeted them all as she approached with open arms. Turning to her grandfather, she said in fluent Castilian, "*I hope you're staying longer this time. I've missed you both very much!*"

With open delight, her grandfather said proudly, "You've been practicing! Your mother has taught you well, my beautiful *bailarín*." He flicked a glance at Grant, "*Now if we can only teach your father—my tongue won't twist so much!*" They both laughed heartily; Mercedes and her mother began giggling too.

"I know you're talking about me," Grant said, his voice had a hint of anxiety as the laughter continued. "Y'all got that same look whenever my wife and daughter talk about me in Italian."

"Oh don't worry, Grant. The same thing happens with me, but they do it in French!" Lindor said, trying to reassure him through his thickly accented, laughter-filled voice. Kiley commiserated with them too, and the laughter got louder.

"Granny, do you have a new riddle for me? What about a reading?"

"Yes, I do—enough for everyone. I'll wait until after dinner to start my fortune telling. Okay, little one?"

Finally, Grant's parents joined the group with warm smiles.

"We heard the laughter. What did we miss?"

"You look lovely in your oriental attire, Anne," Lindor said. After he kissed her hand, he shook hands with Arthur. "Number 3? Who is it?"

"Dale Earnhardt, Sr.—the professional race car driver."

"*Sí*, I remember that name. He was a good driver."

"Am I late?" A heavily cloaked, masked face peeked from the front door with a familiar deep voice disguised to a pitch lower than it seemed natural.

"Raiden!" Mercedes exclaimed and quickly gave him a tight embrace.

Lifting his mask up over his head, he asked, "How'd you know it was me?"

"I'd know you even if you were in pieces!" she said giggling. "Silly, you're the last one to arrive." Uncertain of his costume, she asked, "Who are you suppose to be?"

"A *phantom*," he said, wiggling his gloved hand at her like a hypnotist.

The word conjured up a memory that rendered her speechless for a moment. Finally, a laugh escaped and she mimicked him, "Oooo… a phantom." Laughing, she asked, "What? No date?"

"Still haven't found what I'm looking for."
"Wasn't that from a song?" she said, trying to remember.
"I think so," her brother shrugged and began saying his hellos to everyone.
"Come on, everybody! Let's join the rest of the family in the garden. Dinner will be ready soon."

They all walked through an arched door and down a long hallway to the family living room where the double French doors opened to the garden. Arched moldings crowned the path and antique side chairs were like silent sentinels along the walls. Light shimmered from crystal table lamps on several cherry side tables, and lining the corridors were the framed prints by Van Gogh, Pablo Picasso, Salvador Dali and Gustav Klimt, along with her own family's masterpieces.

After escorting everyone to the garden, Mercedes quickly ran into the kitchen to finish her presentation. Hiring a crew from a nearby caterer, she had carefully orchestrated the entire dinner. She had prepared a special meal and dessert for each family member, suiting their palate as well as their allergies. She considered cooking to be another creative venue for her artistic abilities; she fancily plated each of the courses herself.

One of her out-of-the-country birthday trips in Europe had been solely a gourmet experience. She had taken two memorable trips to Provence and Tuscany, where she learned many of her tasty secrets under the tutelage of French chefs and Tuscan masters. She often took gourmet travels solo, or sometimes with Carly or other family members, but her favorite traveling companion was her godmother, Veronica.

After the last plate was finished, she promptly rang a crystal dinner bell, which beckoned everyone to dinner outside in the garden where a long row of tables was set under a massive covered tent. When everyone was seated, Mercedes carried a crystal wineglass in her hand and walked to the front of the tables by the entranceway.

Glancing at her beautifully costumed family, she smiled, "Normally fate chooses our family and freewill chooses our friends. I am overwhelmed with joy in your presence for fate has conspired with freewill—for here we all are both as family and friends." Raising her glass, she said, "Here's to the best that fate and freewill brought together!"

Everyone raised their glasses and with another ring of the crystal bell, the servers emerged from beyond the tent, ornately dressed wearing powdered wigs. A collective gasp was heard, especially when the dinners were served.

Sadly, it was the very last time she would ever see her mother's beautiful face.

* * *

"Mom, do you need a personal *sous chef?*"
"Thank you. I do." Mercedes gladly took her daughter's thoughtful offer, still smiling at her memories. "Would you prep the spices and vegetables, either slice julienne style or dice them, which ever you'd like best."
"What's for dinner?"
"Tonight we're having bouillabaisse, clams *oreganato*, *homard au beurre*—lob-

ster with white butter—and an artichoke and mushroom salad."
"Yummy! And for dessert?"
"Tiramisu. Would you like to plate our dinner tonight?"
"Really?" she beamed, "Dessert too?"
"Yes, dessert too," she said matching her smile.
"But I'm not crazy creative with food like you, Mom."
"Just let your imagination go, CJ," she coaxed and turned up the volume when George Bizet's *Carmen* began to play. As the two of them busily cooked, they were lip-synching to the song. When the famous *Toreador* libretto started, they heard Grant singing on his way to the kitchen. And in a few seconds, she had him working with them as well, leaving him in charge of the messy lobster beheadings.

When the elegant dinner was ready, they paraded the food into the dining room and took their usual seats, joining hands to say grace before enjoying their feast. The spatial feeling of the room was achieved by the ceiling, which was devised to give the illusion of height. The Louis XVI mahogany dinner table and fabric-covered rollback chairs complemented the cream silk damask wall coverings.

After swallowing the last sweet bite of dessert, Carly looked at her mother and her father and shyly announced, "Dad, Mom—I have a date tonight."

Mercedes commented with gladness, "I was wondering why I had a most ravishing *sous chef* tonight who was wearing my stiletto boots!" She winked at her daughter and smiled knowingly.

"You know the drill: name, age, cell phone and license plate number," Grant said trying to be humorous. "Who is the young man? Your mystery date?"

Carly smiled, noting her father's protective shift. She said, "Well, when I was working out in the Friedman Center, a bunch of the guys from the wrestling team came in to work out. One of them whistled at me when I walked by. He's so cute! Anyway, I pretended not to be intrigued, but he was persistent. He insisted, so I let him help me spot my weights. When he heard my last name, he immediately asked about Mom. Of course, he only had great things to say. And Mom, he had signed up for your class, but he missed the last seat in your honors philosophy class! He would love to meet you sometime. I told him I was glad he was wooing me through you. He scored points on that remark alone—so I said 'yes' when he asked me out!"

Grant became uneasy as usual whenever his daughter wanted to go out on a date; he especially got nervous when she wanted to go out with an older guy. Actually, he got nervous when she wanted to go on any date with any guy! He still saw her as his four-year-old daddy's little girl. He looked toward Mercedes for some assistance.

Catching his worried glance, Mercedes asked, "What's his name and where is he taking you for your date? Also, what time are you coming home? Please put your dad's mind at ease."

Carly nodded, "His name is Joey Caton, but his friends call him 'JC'. He's picking me up at nine tonight. He has a car on campus and he's taking me to the Delta Lambda party." She quickly turned to her father and winced, gently placing her left hand on his arm when she said, "Papa, it's not as bad as it sounds. I'll be home no later than two in the morning. I promise."

Grant sternly interrupted, "One in the morning, Carly. Remember house rules. And Poppet, please keep your phone turned on at all times—for safety and emergency purposes, of course."

Hearing her father call her the endearing name of 'Poppet', she knew he was showing his tactful approval; she immediately got up, stood behind his chair and gave him a flood of kisses on both cheeks. He made funny faces, but it was clear he was thoroughly enjoying, her blatant show of affection.

She hugged him from behind, adding sweetly in a cute voice, "Yes, *Daddy*, I'll be home at 1:00 a.m. sharp and my phone will be on. I'll even have my GPS sensor on at all times. So, please, Papa, feel free to check on me. Deal?"

Grant gave her a kiss on the cheek and his approval. He easily yielded to his daughter's wishes and, more importantly, to his beautiful wife, whom he had been watching all night. When Carly looked at her mother, she noticed a familiar, yet disturbing expression on her smiling face. It forewarned her that her mother had entered one of her spells. Carly thought she was the only one who could detect it happening; the cues were very subtle, showing only in her eyes, which were hidden behind her glasses. She wondered what she had said that might have triggered her mother's spell.

Grant was wondering too, as he had already known something was amiss, sensing something was upsetting her.

All day Mercedes had felt herself being thrown off-guard by unsettling coincidences, and when Carly mentioned the name of her date, his name sent her head spinning. But she quickly collected her senses, "*Ma chérie*, would you mind if we added another young lady for dinner tomorrow?"

"Another guest? For our exclusive mother-daughter dinner?" she feigned disappointment, giving her mother a hard time before saying, "Of course not, Mom. I don't mind, at all. So—who is it? Anyone I know? More importantly, where are we going for dinner?"

Mercedes and Carly had an on-going Saturday night mother-daughter tradition. They would pick out a restaurant and dress up to experience new culinary tastes; it gave them a chance to catch up with each other on the previous week's activities, and an opportunity to bond closer together as they enjoyed the unique ambiance of each restaurant. Afterwards, they would catch a movie, a play, or just head home for a game of pool or backgammon or scrabble by the fireplace. It was a tradition they both loved, and rarely did they share their night with others, unless it was with someone special.

"Mom? Mommy, I'm waiting."

"Oh, her name is also Mercedes."

"Imagine that! Another Mercedes!" teasing her again, knowing how sensitive her mother was to coincidences.

Amused, Mercedes continued, "As a matter, she's a daughter of an old friend of mine. She's in my honors class, so she's a little older than you. Perhaps you can show her around town, since she just moved from Florida. I think you'll really like each other. As far as dinner, let's have it here."

"And our menu?"

Changing her tone, Mercedes pretended to be an Italian chef, "For starters, we'll have Portobello Mushroom Napoleon, with tomato and pasta salad with basil vinaigrette, accompanied with crab bisque. Finally, our main course will have all of your favorite ingredients on one plate: veal with artichokes, black olives, snow mushrooms and tons of garlic in white wine sauce on angel hair pasta." Switching her tone back to normal, she asked, "What do you say, *mia cara?*"

"On one condition."

"Name it."

"For a festive dessert, we're having white chocolate almond pudding fondue, garnished with fresh strawberries, butter pound-cake pieces and my ultimate sweet-tooth favorite, your killer homemade Philadelphia cheesecake!" In fluent Italian, Carly continued, "*E, cara madre bella, that's non-negotiable,*" then she winked at her mother.

"You are my daughter, indeed! You drive a hard bargain," she smiled with pride and leaned over to kiss her cheek.

Meanwhile, Grant had leaned back fully in his chair and was smiling lovingly at both of them, listening to the rhythm of their banter. His thoughts honed in on her remark about an old friend and he began to wonder about it. Looking at her inquisitively, he asked, "Which friend, love? Anybody, I know?"

She simply gave him an I'll-tell-you-all-about-it-later look. Understanding her meaning, he turned to look at Carly and quickly said, "Luckily, my little *honeoye*, I'll be fishing for that lunker in Alabama on Sunday. There'd be entirely too much estrogen for me to be here! *Y'all* have a great time!"

Hearing the inadvertent slip of his Memphis twang, they began laughing and playfully teasing each other with their individual respective drawls. They finished their dinner, filling the conversation with fishing anecdotes and excitement about the upcoming weekend adventures.

After dinner, they headed back in the family room where Vangogh joined them. Mercedes thoroughly enjoyed watching Grant and Carly playing with the brave little kitten. They continually teased Vangogh with a string of red yarn, moving it in colubrine motions. In the middle of a game of fetch with their cherished pet, the doorbell rang. Joey had finally arrived.

Carly ran down the long hallway and eagerly opened the door for her attractive date. She hurriedly led him back to the family room, shyly introducing him to her parents.

"Mom, Dad, this is Joey—JC."

"Joseph," Grant said with a slight smile, offering a firm handshake, noting he looked much older than a typical college senior.

"Hello, Dr. Larcher, sir," he said, his anxiety apparent. Grant simply nodded.

"Won't you sit down?" Mercedes said graciously, and Grant subtly grimaced at his daughter when the young man's back was turned. Carly instantly gave her father a silent plea to take it easy on her date with praying hands, mouthing "Please, Papa."

"Wow, Professor Larcher—I'm a great fan of yours," Joey said, vigorously nodding his head, his dark hair falling out of place. "I've read all your books."

As devoted parents, they performed their customary, yet subtle assessments of her nervous date. They welcomed him warmly, yet Grant remained a stoic while her mother smiled and patiently listened to Joey's nervous accolades about her celebrated reputation. Carly cringed at the agonizing sight.

After an awkward pause, Carly seized the opportunity to leave with her date. Before they headed back to the foyer, Joey reassured her father that he would bring her safely home on time. As he was stumbling for the appropriate sincere words, it was clear he was intimidated by her father's imposing presence, and that her father was not helping. Grant hadn't said a word the entire time except for his name.

Mercedes embraced her daughter, saying in Italian, *"Don't forget your phone, darling. Have a safe and fun time at the party."*

Carly appreciated her mother's discreet reminder about her phone, taking it out of her purse and turning it on, activating the GPS transmitter. Upon seeing her gesture, Grant smiled and kissed his daughter's cheeks, seeing them off with poised caution.

As the door closed behind them, Grant immediately pressed the toggle-button for the GPS option that was built in to their phone systems, quickly calibrating it to monitor Carly's phone coordinates. With his worries waning, he started to whistle as he stoked the embers of the fire and added more logs.

Needing a distraction for her troubled mind, Mercedes asked, "Nine-ball, chess, backgammon or scrabble?"

He pretended to think hard about the choices, but they both knew it was going to be chess. Seeing the same subtle look on her face that he had seen at dinner, he quickly changed his mind, "How about a friendly backgammon game?"

She lit up with excitement, "Well, my love—be prepared for a trouncing!" She always dominated the game when they played backgammon and he knew it.

After her second victory, he turned on his charm, rewarding her passionately as they made sweet love in front of the fireplace. It was the real distraction she needed, but she found that when she closed her eyes, her thoughts kept turning to the past. She could see the image of a face from the past, but she struggled to keep him out of her thoughts and focus on the present, on Grant's touch and his loving gaze. But when she heard Grant's guttural sounds from beneath her as she reached the threshold of a shattering climax, she felt a quaking intensity that she hadn't felt in a very long time.

* * *

In their master bedroom, an eighteenth century painted and gilded French *boiserie* defined the room. Hanging above the bed was her painting, *Archangel of the Lady*, which depicted Grant as the Archangel Gabriel during the visitation of the Virgin Mary. Over the two French marquetry commodes were her paintings of Carly. The muted hues and soft lighting of the room created a tranquil, enveloping environment.

Grant joined her under the covers; she was propped up against the pillows, writing as usual in her journal. He finally asked her, "Love, so which old friend is it?" She put her pen and journal down and said, "You would never believe it. But she's... she's JC's daughter."

"You've got to be kidding, right? Tell me you're joking," he said in disbelief, sitting upright to face her.

In a soft voice she said, "No, Grant. I am very serious."

"Oh, for crying out loud! What does this mean? Will he now be in our lives again? No, I won't let this happen. He's a source of pain for you—for us!" he saw her start to object, but he continued, "He should have been told, Mercedes! This is not going to happen ever again!" His voice was filled with anger, protest and concern.

She quickly offered an explanation. "I was completely taken by surprise when I found out who she was! I thought I was going to faint. My God, Grant—my signs are everywhere! Screaming at me! *Mon Dieu*, I've been inundated with *déjà vu* feelings all day! The final straw was finding out that my student who shares my name is really JC's daughter. Then later, hearing the name of CJ's date—what are the odds of that! I simply cannot ignore this! I need to follow this to its end. You know I have to. I MUST!"

Looking at him, she began to feel very sad. *Oh God, my sons would have been the same age as her right now.*

Suddenly she realized something was very wrong with the girl's birth date. *She couldn't possibly be JC's biological daughter! He was away on TDY at Nellis when his wife became pregnant!*

It was all very disturbing and she wondered if Joe had ever figured it out. Perhaps he already knew; but if he didn't, how she hoped he would never find out about Eva's deception.

She thought of her own secret and she began to say a silent prayer for him, projecting all of her good thoughts toward him. She hoped life was being truly kind to him and that he was just as happy as she was. Unable to help it, she began to cry softly, weeping for all the tragedies that had befallen both of them in their lives.

"Love, I trust your judgment implicitly. Without question! Know that I love you very much. So, let me leave it at that—all right, love?" Leaning over he gave her soft kisses on her cheeks, tasting her salty tears; he dried her tears with his fingers and snuggled up quietly against her, embracing her belly, which he knew would comfort them both. But his thoughts were racing and he desperately needed to sleep for a few hours before leaving to catch his early 7:00 a.m. flight.

Chapter 25

Bewitching Hours

Having succumbed to a bout of insomnia, Mercedes gingerly slipped out of bed. She pulled the covers over Grant, which he had managed to wriggle out of in his sleep. After lightly kissing him on his cheek, she found her way in the dark, guided by the many motion nightlights at every turn, to the sanctuary of her library.

There was a quiet, graceful pause between her art gallery and private library. The long yellow hall was broken up with white arched moldings. Adjacent to her library was her large and spacious artist's studio. It was the only place in the house where she allowed herself to have clutter and disarray.

She stood at the doorway to her studio and looked at all of her brushes, canvasses and paints which were scattered everywhere. Partially finished canvasses were against each of the four walls and rolls of unstretched linen canvass of different lengths leaned against the corners. There were stacks of dust-covered projects waiting for a few moments of her attention or inspiration. There were spatters of paint on the hardwood floors, the walls, and even the ceiling. Splashes of reds, blues, greens, umbers... they were everywhere. She had painted murals on every surface including the ceiling.

She had coated her studio with the brilliant colors of her palette, especially red. The smells of the mediums, solvents and drying paints bathed her as she looked up to look at her rendition of Michelangelo's *The Temptation of Eve*. It was a modern interpretation of the original in the Sistine Chapel.

For years she had wondered how the Florentine master felt as he had painted it, until a special out-of-the-country birthday trip. She was celebrating a milestone birthday and her official status as a *cancer survivor*.

As she had carefully planned, she had lain on her back on the hard cold floor, marveling at Michelangelo's *The Creation of Adam*.

After a short time, a smiling, brightly uniformed, stout, elderly Italian sentinel blocked her view. His nametag read Ugo Dianni, and he kindly asked her in broken English to please get up from the floor. She smiled in return and pleaded softly in Italian, *"Please, kind sir, I have traveled a long way to be here at this very moment. May I have please just another minute?"*

He was shaking his head and gestured for her to get up. She relented, *"Please, sir, please hear me out. I'm also an artist and I have longed to fulfill a lifelong dream. It's simply to be lying on this floor here in the Sistine Chapel and feel how Michelangelo felt when he celebrated many birthdays as he devotedly painted the ceiling, not for Pope Julius II, but for Almighty God. I'm also celebrating my fortieth birthday today. Would you be so kind and grant a weary pilgrim a birthday wish? A few more moments please—it's all I ask to pay my respects to Master Buonaroti."*

Upon hearing her words and seeing her smile, the sentinel simply hadn't been able to refuse, so he smiled and walked a few meters away, holding his stoic vigil, silently granting her birthday wish.

She took another deep breath and the different odors in her studio seemed to tickle her creativity. In every direction she looked, were easels of different sizes positioned haphazardly in the room. Only a few select pieces of well-worn furniture, like an old grey love seat and a beaten, creamy beige chaise were welcomed in the studio.

Brushes were plentiful, and some remained stiff with paint, lying where she had forgotten them on the floor. She picked up the closest brush from which she tried removing the dried burnt sienna acrylic paint on the bristles with her fingernails, but then flung it in her frustration.

There was no rhyme or reason in her studio. On occasion, she would pick a couple of sections in the room and set up her base camp. It would be very evident where she was working during those painting frenzies. A placement rug would be surrounded with her paint tubes, bottles, and gallons of Gesso paint in aluminum cans. She walked over and picked up a paint tube that was still open, left to harden with exposure.

She had studies, sketches and references, including photographs that were taped on the walls with masking tape or tacked up with multi-colored pins. She had portfolios and presentation cases everywhere, along with art supplies that were stacked next to her light tables. All of her calligraphy sets were open and quill pens were scattered on the top of her drafting tables, along with pieces of parchment. Sets of graphite pencils, charcoals, pastels and markers were strewn about without a care, lying where they had last been used.

It was a wonder how she could find anything, let alone create in such staggering chaos. When anyone asked if her studio mirrored her right-brain thinking, she would find herself laughing hysterically. She wasn't shy in sharing the fact that her creative mind was indeed more chaotic than in her studio.

Some evenings she would emerge from her studio, literally covered from head to toe in paint. She would then collapse from exhaustion, not having slept for days at a time, causing her to take her sick, personal and vacation days whenever she could so that she could recuperate. Yet, in the end her masterpieces were born, and she still managed to teach, write and function normally.

She sat on a high stool next to one of her easels and glanced around the studio. Aside from her tables, cameras and a projector, there was no hint of modern technology in the room. Not even a clock. She simply didn't need one when she was working. Time didn't exist in this part of her world, when she worked during her *bewitching hours*, after midnight well into the dawn. Perhaps it was a lunar effect. Perhaps it was the changing light. But she consistently painted prolifically after the sun set.

Many times her peers, students and fans had asked, "How do you paint so well? What do you see?"

She would just smile and say she was merely interpreting what was already a completed masterpiece, trying to explain how she saw things, using an analogy of a teacher using a projector.

"The way I see things relative to art is the same way as you see when you are first introduced to a photograph or a topic by a teacher or presenter using a projector as a tool to guide you in a class or a presentation. The picture or the presentation material has already been written and completed. For example, as a teacher lecturing on art appreciation, I wish to introduce to my students to the beautiful works of Vincent Van Gogh. Before I begin, I dim the lights. I place a photograph or a reproduction of one of Van Gogh's masterpieces on the projector. The image is projected onto the screen or the wall. Then I begin my lecture on his technique, his brush strokes and palette choices.

"That is exactly how I see my art, except I am no longer the teacher; but a person using the life force of the universe, or God. I am merely a student who sees beautiful images projected in my mind. For the very first time, the images are complete and perfect. Then I choose how to interpret it with my own palette and brush strokes. Hence, the masterpiece is uniquely mine. The initial suggestion of the masterpiece in my mind, in its perfect state, only serves as a guide for my interpretation, my creativity. That's what it's like for me. Pretty simple, isn't it?"

She would also explain that during her bewitching hours, her creativity peaked and reached its zenith. With her writing there was no set time of day or night when she might be writing; she would write whenever inspiration or a thought struck her. Any time, any place. She always carried several pens, because it wasn't unusual for her to run out of ink after only a day's use. She had filled dozens of journals and blank books with her ideas and thoughts.

For years she painted and had art exhibitions at least once a year. She had not painted with a feverish pitch of passion for what seemed like an eternity. Her muse had left her. Her paintings suffered. Right now, she was only able to recapture her fiery passion in her words, so she wrote constantly.

Her most prolific times as an author often coincided with the appearance of her *silent screaming signs*. She became a conduit for the whispers of the universe. Like her art, her words required no thought, no process. They were just there.

She never wrote with a particular storyline in mind, or from an outline with carefully planned characters and plots, as suggested in formal writing courses. She would simply start writing and the next thing she knew, the book had authored itself.

From her studio she made her way to the kitchen. After she prepared Grant's coffee and meal package, she rooted herself in the comfortable leather chair in her library—reading, writing, or simply in deep thought, staring out beyond the windows at the garden or the sky.

She stared at the shaped ceiling, barely noticing how the lowered cabinetry gave the room a wholly different architectural scale from the rest of the house. Her George III writing table held her Tiffany dragonfly lamp and the furniture was formally positioned: there were velvet pillows on the sofas, damask on bergeres. All four walls were delicate, hand-painted panels; but the mahogany bookcases dominated the room, complementing the mahogany crown moldings and large pocket doors. The books in her collection, many with leather spines, were hidden behind doors. Ivory fabric drapes and sheer curtains set off the dark mahogany casework and paneling.

Music made the ambiance complete. She listened to all types of music, depending on her moods and thoughts. As an aria finished, the next selection sent her to another level of contemplation, staring at the crystal chandelier in a trance.

She lit lavender-scented candles on her desk, deliciously infusing the air. She breathed in deeply and relaxed. Her thoughts were of a lost love, mixed with the sounds of Gregorian monks chanting.

"Oh fie!" she exclaimed when she heard the soft rap against her door.

* * *

Grant was up before the alarm clock went off at 5:00 a.m. He had slept restlessly and although he was very tired, he was looking forward to his four-day bass fishing tournament. He wasn't surprised to find that Mercedes was already out of bed. He wasn't concerned—he knew where to find her. He went through his morning ritual, excited with thoughts of his trip.

He followed the strong aroma of coffee to the kitchen; she had already readied a strong jolt of caffeine for his hour drive to the Syracuse airport. He smiled when he saw a small package on the counter. Behind it, he was surprised to find a Dominican cigar with a white ribbon neatly tied to it. After smelling the fragrant cigar, he opened the small package and the sweet scent of homemade cinnamon sticky-buns from an old Larcher recipe greeted him; it always reminded him of his feisty grandmother.

Inside the package he found a note from Mercedes written on one of his napkins. It was a caricature of her, one of many that she often used to express her love comically. In this one, she was wearing a hula skirt, bidding him good luck and an "I'm sorry" to explain the cigar. He cherished her little notes; she still kept surprising him with the originality of their hiding places. He would often find sticky notes in different colors with uplifting messages of "I love you" or simply saying "hello," with the note hidden in his tackle box, his medical bag or among his music sheets. His favorites were the messages he would find on the bathroom mirror when he emerged from the steam of the shower or when he was shaving.

The house was still silent. As he poured himself a cup of strong black coffee, he heard the aria from Puccini's *La Boheme* softly emanating from her private library. Hearing it, he began to worry, *Had she slept at all?*

After brewing a cup of her favorite tea—honey-vanilla chamomile, doused with more honey and lemon—and putting a couple of her favorite breakfast items on a china plate, he headed for her sanctuary.

"Would anyone in the house like a messy, cinnamon bagel? Some freshly squeezed orange juice? Ah, I see a beautiful lady in deep thought who might want some tea!"

He placed the tray on her desk and kissed her, saying, "Good morning, love—couldn't sleep?"

Even after all these years, he hadn't become accustomed to her eccentric behavior. He no longer protested, and when it bothered him to the point where he wanted to interrupt, he simply sighed deeply and tried to remember not to stand in the way of her creative flow. Yet he kept a watchful eye.

As always, his teasing greeting pried an excited smile and a little laugh from her, regardless of her mood. She responded to his greeting by kissing him and taking her hot tea and sipping its sweet taste, being careful not to burn her mouth. "No, I couldn't sleep. Too much was running around in my head, as you can well imagine."

"Should I be worried?"

Shaking her head, clearly distracted, she murmured, "Oh, love—what time will you be home on Wednesday?"

He looked at his watch and groaned, "I'm already late! I've got to run. I should be home Wednesday evening in time to tuck you in. If you need to reach me, everything's on the refrigerator door."

Though he was rushing, their goodbye lasted for another five minutes with constant hugs and light kisses. Finally, he was standing at the door ready to leave. "You are very beautiful. I love you, my angel!" He smiled and closed the door, giving her back her solace.

Grant tried not to worry about his wife, but his mind was racing as well. He was about to activate his phone, directing it to "dial home," but he didn't—instead the past seeped into his mind.

Chapter 26

Ad Infinitum

Waiting impatiently at the airport gate, Grant was relieved to finally see Mercedes. She was the last one to deplane and she looked nervous about something as she approached him.

"Hello, beautiful," Grant said, beaming with a wide smile, "Roses for my lady."

"They smell delicious. Thank you," she said, surprising him with a quick familial peck on his cheek.

"Did you notice what kind of roses you have in your hands?" he asked without hiding the disappointment in his voice.

"Oh yes, of course, my favorite roses, *Kordes Floribunda Mercedes*. I'm sorry I didn't notice right away," she said, sounding apologetic but offered guiltily, "I'm just exhausted, that's all."

"I hope not too exhausted for dinner. We've got reservations at Bookbinders."

Furrowing her forehead, she said, "Is it all right if we skipped dinner? I brought home this wicked migraine. Actually, I feel like my head is going to implode in my skull and I really just want a quiet evening."

"Sure, darlin', I'll take you home. It'll give me a chance to pamper you in private and celebrate our anniversary properly." He gave her a bear hug, whispering, "I've missed you so much, my angel."

She felt lifeless in his arms, though she returned the embrace rather weakly. He had sensed her distance. *Something is wrong.*

They had gone to the baggage claim area, and an uncomfortable silence passed between them. She seemed anxious and icy, not wanting to talk.

During the ride home, Grant tried again at a conversation as she glanced out the window toward the Philadelphia skyline.

"Chilly tonight, isn't it?"

"Yes, it is."

"I called your mom about the flowers."

"Uh-huh."

"The roses are from her garden. I had them flown in from Florida."

"That's great."

"Remember our one-year anniversary?"

"I got your card."

She nodded and seemed to pay attention to him as he spoke, but she was distracted. Grant controlled his growing irritation. When he took her hand and rubbed his thumb on her silky skin, the chill in her demeanor was palpable.

When they arrived at her townhouse, she immediately said, "We need to talk."

"I hate it when you start your sentences with that. It's never good news."

"I'm sorry, but we really need to talk."

"How's your migraine? Want me to get something for it? How about if I give you a massage."

"Grant, please! I need to talk to you!"

"Whoa! All right. Let's calm down and talk."

She blurted out, "I met someone in Las Vegas." Grant's face reddened in his shock.

"You what?"

"I met someone in Las Vegas," she repeated softly. The voice was weak, as if expecting the worse.

His eyes narrowed. His voice strong in tone, he demanded, "Who is he?"

"Does it matter?" she said, having difficulty meeting his gaze.

"Yes, of course, it matters! Now tell me—who is he?"

"His name is Joe."

"Joe What?"

"Joe Tristram."

"He's an engineer, too?"

"No, he's a fighter pilot."

His face tightened. "Did you have sex with this Joe?"

On the verge of tears, she lowered her eyes. Her silence gave him the answer, but he wanted to hear her say it. He repeated through gritted teeth, "Did you have sex with this Joe?"

"Yes."

Suddenly numb, he fell silent and watched the tears that finally fell from her eyes.

Once began, the tears would not stop and she stammered, "Grant, I'm so sorry but... but we need to stop seeing each other."

He stayed quiet.

"This might not sound rational, but it just happened. I just can't explain it," she said. "I just know that... that it wouldn't be right to keep seeing each other."

He took a long time to say anything.

"Was it a one-night stand? Or are you going to have a relationship with him?"

"That's irrelevant. This isn't really about him but me," she said, hating how she sounded like a cliché. "I don't want a relationship with anyone right now. I really just need to be alone."

"Oh no, you don't. You're not going to simply dismiss me. I want to know everything! Who is this guy?"

"I don't want to hurt you any more than I already have," she said tearfully. "Please, understand that we can't be together. Please, let me go, Grant."

"Damn it! I deserve to know the truth. I need to know! Now, tell me what you've done!"

She crumpled on the sofa by the fireplace. She began to sob uncontrollably. In between sobs she told him every detail about what had happened. Grant stood in silence, listening, each word hurting him immensely. He stared at her with varying emotions; the rage simmered within him, but he fought for control.

After listening as patiently as he could, he finally said, "How can you be so blind? Of all people, you should know that he's nothing but a snake in the grass—a damned married player!"

"My eyes are wide open."

"Continue believing in that lie."

She was about to speak, but he didn't allow her. "No, no, you had your turn. Now you sit there and listen to me." He was pacing back and forth, his face reddening as he tried to find the right words, the right approach.

"I'm having a hard time wrapping my mind around this 'fate' thing. If he were truly your soul mate, he would do anything to be with you right now. At whatever cost!"

He met her eyes, and continued, "I don't give a shit what situation he might be in. If it was truly fate, nothing could keep the both of you apart. Nothing... not even a wife or a baby." The words disgusted him.

"Please, Grant, I'm sorry! Please! I just want to be alone!"

"Don't worry, I'll leave you alone. But before I go," he said, feeling an ache in his heart, "know that I love you. Nothing is going to change that!"

She cried harder and foreign words quickly came out of her.

"Speak English!" he snapped in frustration.

Startled, her jaw dropped as if she didn't realize she spoke in another tongue. She quickly translated, "I didn't want to hurt you. Please believe me, please! I never wanted to hurt you, Grant. You're a good man. I don't deserve you... you don't deserve this!"

"Well you hurt me beyond words."

"Please forgive me."

Ignoring her words, he said sternly, "You talk about these damned silent signs—well, look at us! Open your eyes to the truth, we..." Suddenly, he stopped and pushed away the angry thoughts in his head. He took in a deep breath and simply looked at her.

She was curled up on the sofa with her head buried in her hands. She was still mumbling in words he couldn't understand. Her sobs stung him with greater pain than all the words he had heard earlier.

As suddenly as it had risen, his anger died. He sat down next to her, draping his arms around her tensed shoulders. She immediately retreated into his arms and cried harder whenever he attempted to talk.

We are soul mates. He wanted to say the words aloud but he didn't. He simply held her.

Grant left that night in utter disbelief, completely devastated. He never felt that type of pain in his life. He was outraged. He felt great respect for men and women in uniform; especially since his uncle, Peter, died in the service of his country in Vietnam. But what just happened with Mercedes caused him to engage in his own menacing phantom conversation. *What is going on here? Something isn't right. This isn't like her! What would make her act so irrationally? Who the fuck is this Joe?*

Though he tried his best in the days and months to follow, there was nothing he could say or do to change her mind, so he stayed away. He decided to attend his parent's fortieth wedding anniversary party. Instead of flying to Memphis, he rode the entire way on his motorcycle, stopping only when he needed to take a bathroom break, gas up or smoke. His mind raced faster than he could push his metal steed.

Shortly after he got in town, the Larcher Riders gathered for their usual romp through the woods nearby.

As he was getting his dirt bike off his best friend's truck, he finally talked about the sudden break-up.

"She ended it just like that?" Joe asked, genuinely surprised at the news. "A fucking asshole pilot with my first name. That's just fucked up, Drake!"

"Yeah, tell me about it," Grant said shaking his head, completely annoyed with the coincidence. "She's not with anyone else."

"No one that you know of."

"Bubba, that's not helping. Don't make me hurt you."

"Easy dude, but it does happen. She's vulnerable. You know—a classic damsel in distress and the next thing you know—"

"Not my Mercedes!" he snapped, but quickly offered an apology. "This was a freak circumstance."

"You're right," he said, nodding. "She's too much of a lady."

"I've never had my heart broken before," Grant confessed.

"That's because you've never been in love before!" he said, knowing his friend well. "Hurts like hell, huh?"

"I'd rather cut my heart out without anesthesia," he said, gesturing to his chest where a red dragon was emblazoned on his off-road V-neck jersey.

"Damn! Did she ask you to be her friend instead?"

"Yes, she insisted on it."

"I fucking hate that 'let's be friends' bullshit!" he said, shaking his head with his hands on his hips. Then, gesturing emotively, he said, "And that 'it's not you, it's me' is another line I can't fucking stand." Sighing deeply, he said, "I just don't understand women."

Grant was silent. He lit a cigarette and took a long drag from it. He grinned, knowing how Mercedes hated it. She called it a foul habit and wouldn't let him kiss her when he'd been smoking, but he felt he had nothing else left now except his vices. He took another deep drag, feeling the smoke in his lungs.

"You know what Drake? You'll get back together."

"What makes you say that?"

"A gut feeling. You two have that special kind of love—the kind I wish I had. I'm still looking for *Miss Right* but I seem to always run into *Miss Right Now* and—"

Grant shot him a look so Joe quickly said. "Not your sister, though. I swear nothing happened, especially when we were in Montana. She passed out. That girl can't hold her liquor. There are lines I would never cross; some things are not worth ruining a friendship over."

"I know—she told me," he said, smiling. "You're one of the good guys, Joe." He looked over to the rest of the Larcher Riders already waiting at the trail entrance. "You're one of us," but his smile quickly disappeared when he added, "unlike this—"

"Flying jock itch!" he offered with a laugh, but Grant wasn't laughing with him. "Like I said before, you'll get back together. It may hurt like a mother right now, but you'll see, things will get better."

Grant was again silent as he looked for his black helmet. Finding it on the tailgate, he flicked the cigarette butt away from the truck. He looked at the red flames emblazoned on its sides. Finally, he put on his helmet on.

Already on his dirt bike, Joe said, "Drake, nothing ever gets in the way of love. Nothing."

Nodding at his familiar words, Grant got on his dirt bike. "You ready?"
Joe nodded his response, his blue flamed helmet already on.
They started their bikes and side-by-side their engines hummed.
Finally, Grant yelled out, "Let's ride!"
Clouds of dust followed behind them as they entered the trail with the rest of their group.

Riding was something that Grant often did, especially when he needed to think. He was a champion racer and had broken or dislocated many of his bones several times. And when he wanted to be completely alone, he simply walked into a familiar stretch of woods, sometimes armed with a bow if it was turkey season. He enjoyed the solitude.

A week later, Grant had just finished his evening rounds when he received a call from a frantic Sydney. He was in terror.

Without waiting for the elevators, he flew down the stairs, practically running to the ER. Before he spoke to the ER staff about Mercedes' condition, he mentally shifted to his physician mode, and then he searched out Sydney and Mason.

He opened the door to the waiting room and Sydney rushed to greet him, but he found Mason distraught with a rage that he had not witnessed before. They had always remained cordial and pleasant, but Grant remembered when Mason had pulled him aside one day.

"I hear you're dating my wife."

"You heard right."

"I'll fuck you up if I ever find out youse hurt her, understand?"

"I'll do the same if you do," Grant answered his challenge, looking down to meet his glare.

"All right. As long as we understand each other."

"Perfectly," he grinned, getting the last word in.

In the waiting room, Grant and Mason shook hands.

"Yo, Grant."

"You all right, man?"

"Fuck no!" Mason snapped. "Sorry dude, nuthin' personal. This just fuckin' sucks. Nuthin' I can do but fuckin' wait here!"

"I know," he empathized. "Don't worry, Mason, she'll be fine. Temple's got the best surgeons on staff."

"Like you?"

"Yeah, like me."

"Youse better be fuckin' right." Mason fell silent, but his concern was clear.

"Grant, do you have any idea what's going on yet?" Sydney asked.

"No, not yet, but I will."

"I knew something wasn't right," she said. "But she convinced me it was just a reaction to the chocolate milk at dinner. I should've known she was—"

"This is bullshit! I'm out of here." Mason started walking away from them.

"Mason, why are you leaving?" Sydney called out. He kept walking away, ignoring her. She was stunned.

"Why is he leaving?" she asked, confused about his abrupt departure. "She's still in surgery. He can't just leave her…"

"Let him go. It'll be all right," Grant said. "Have you called her family?"

"Yes, I called her parents. They're taking the last flight out. Mason is sending his limo to pick them up at the airport."

Noting the time, he said, "Good, they should be here in time for visiting hours." His beeper went off.

"Sydney, I've got to run, but I'll be back as soon as I can."

After checking in on a patient, he quickly reverted to his worried thoughts of Mercedes. He used his hospital access to check up on her progress and before returning to the waiting room, he got two cups of strong black coffee.

"Sydney, it's taking longer than expected," he said, handing her a cup and sitting down beside her.

"Oh no, that can't be good," she said wearily, taking a sip of her coffee and preparing for a long vigil.

"Why don't you go home and get some rest?"

"I won't leave until I know she's safely out of surgery."

A few hours later, he was walking with her through the corridors to the recovery room when his pager went off again.

* * *

"We are now boarding all passengers."

When Grant heard it, he quickly got up and stood in line. Finally settling in his seat, his trip to the past continued.

He remembered the devastating ordeals he had seen her through, especially her breast cancer. He was with her during every waking moment he had at the hospital; and while she was getting radiation treatments, he was there to help her through the fierce side effects. She had to be hospitalized a few more times because of her hypersensitivity to the treatments and medications. Seeing her transform into an emaciated form devastated him, but he never faltered.

When she was in her self-imposed seclusions, he would see their friends and family more than she did. It always bothered him, having to dodge the questions of her whereabouts, especially at family functions. At his brother Daniel's autumn wedding it was especially difficult to explain her absence.

"Drake, where's Mercedes?" Joe asked, loosening his bowtie. Abigail was sitting next to him, sipping on second glass of wine.

"I took her home after the ceremony," Grant explained, tossing his own bowtie on the wedding party table.

The groom joined them and looked around, asking, "Hey, didn't I see Mercedes at the ceremony?"

"Stop worrying, y'all. She'll be all right. He's a doctor with access to any drug on this planet!" Abigail interjected and changed the subject. "Look how fine y'all are in your penguin suits."

Ignoring her, Daniel sighed, "Mercedes did look paler than usual."

"Where are you and Marie going for your honeymoon?"

"Aruba. Just acting like tourists, relaxing—"

"And having sex."

"Jet, would you please?"

"Well they are! They're no virgins!" she protested, sounding a bit like a little girl, "Quit being a big brother!"

"Here, Abby—have some more wine," Joe said, already pouring the wine in her glass. "You should know by now that shutting her up is *like trying to herd cats.*" His poorly imitated drawl made both Grant and Daniel cringe.

"You've been living here too long, man," Daniel commented chuckling.

"I just heard that the other day. Been dying to use it."

"Hey, Daniel, would you bring back me some good Cuban cigars?"

"Sure, Grant. How about you?"

Abigail answered, still pouting, "Nothing, unless you take me along,"

"I was talking to Joe."

She shot him a finger, spilling wine on her bridesmaid's dress. "Oh shit!"

"See what happens? Karma gets you!"

Ignoring Joe, she weakly tried to clean the stain and asked, "What'd you get Marie as a wedding present anyway?"

"A German Shepherd puppy."

"You got her a dog? Oh, how romantic," she said, rolling her eyes.

Directing his answer to Grant and Joe, he said, "Yeah, I wanted one, Marie did too."

"Y'all won't be able to enjoy that puppy. She'll be pregnant after the honeymoon. Then next thing y'all know, you'll have three kids, maybe six! It's in our genes, you know."

With her continued babbling in the background, Joe asked, "Does the puppy have a name yet?"

"We agreed on Maximus."

"A strong name, meaning great," Grant offered.

"Yeah, like a tight *gluteus maximus*," Joe said chuckling.

"Joe, you're a dog too!" Abigail exclaimed, glancing over her shoulder at him. Quickly turning to her brother, she continued, "You should've gotten her jewelry, more diamonds, or something like that—not a dog! It pisses all over the place, shits, whines, tears the furniture…"

Joe continued her sentence with, "It'll protect them, give them kisses, snuggle with them and…"

"Bite mean and drunk women," Daniel said jokingly. He and Joe gave each other a quick high five.

"I may pretend to have a *relaxed* brain, but I'm no fool! Y'all are making fun of me!" she shouted angrily. "Shit, y'all are boring me anyway—I'm goin' dancin'!"

She fell back on her chair. "I'm all right, I'm all right. I just forgot my date." Then quickly she said, glaring at Joe, "And I don't mean you." Grabbing the bottle within her reach, she turned around sharply with a loud "Humph!"

"Oh my, she's walking on a slant," Daniel chuckled. "Joe, would you—"

"Way ahead of you!" said Joe as he got up, leaving the table and catching up with her before she slipped on the dance floor.

"Hey, Brian's engaged to that girl he met in Montana."

"You mean, Kari? Well, good for him," he said.

"You know Dave met his wife, Jackie, during that same Montana trip."

"Yes, in that same bar."

A commotion on the dance floor got both their attention.

"A mosh pit!" Daniel laughed and yelled to their brothers who started it, and pointed to two unsuspecting friends. "Hugh! Leo! Toss Troll and Gary in!"

"Hey, who's that brunette with Caleb?"

"That's Linda. They met on the Internet."

"There you are!" A pretty blonde bride with girlish cadence in her voice beamed as she approached the table. The skirt flair of her white, sleeveless halter sweetheart gown brushed against the chairs as she maneuvered her way to them. Her veil draped her bare, tanned shoulders. The blue color of her eyes matched her groom's.

"Hey, baby." The newlyweds shared a quick kiss.

Straightening Daniel's bowtie, she turned to Grant, "Where's Mercedes?"

"Baby, she's not here. I asked him earlier."

"But I saw her as I was walking down the aisle—"

"Sweetie, she got terribly sick. Grant explained it all to me."

"Aww!" her forehead furrowing when she heard it. "Tell Mercedes I hope she feels better, but she's missing one hell of a party."

"She really wanted to be here, y'all," Grant said, feeling cornered.

"Mercedes made it to the ceremony, that's what really matters to me, to us," Daniel said as if to reassure his brother.

"Make sure you tell her that we missed her," Marie said sweetly. "Did Daniel tell you about our puppy?"

"Sweetie, he knows all about it."

"We'd like both of you to come over for dinner after we get back from Aruba so you can meet Maximus."

"Mercedes would like that," Grant said, still unsure.

"Now sweetie, come on and let's play nice with the rest of the guests—shall we?" he said, then turning to Grant, "Who knew I would marry a blonde!"

"And who knew I'd end up with an exotic woman!" Grant said with a grin, remembering how they both had expected to be with the opposite in their younger years.

"Yeah, interesting irony, isn't it?"

"Life seems to work out that way."

* * *

In their early years, Grant was stupefied to find Mercedes in such horrifying states, especially after she had been painting a series of paintings using Joe as the subject. Her clothes and face were splattered with paint, but her hair was protected with a bandana.

"Will you please stop bothering me!" she had sharply barked at him. "You know it breaks my creativity! Are you doing this intentionally? You are—aren't you?"

"Good grief, no. I'm not doing this intentionally—"

"Yes, you are!" she said accusingly.

He glanced at the canvasses without acknowledging her insensitive comments.

"You made that look," she said and motioned with her brush to the canvas in front of her. "It's about all of this, isn't it? Am I right?"

"It's actually a very good piece," he said and looked around, "They're all very good."

"Tell me—you're feeling insecure?" she pressed testily.

"It's three in the morning," he reminded her.

"And your point is?"

With an unmasked look of annoyance in his voice and face, he folded his arms in front of him. "We both know what happens when you don't sleep. It makes you sick. And I can't sleep when you're not in bed, love."

"Stop that!" she said abruptly.

"Stop what?"

"Stop being so nice. Get angry—damn it!" She continued pressing him, "Lose control—get *medieval* on my ass!"

"No," he said, a snicker escaping. "I don't want to get *medieval* on your beautiful ass. I'd rather do something else with it."

"Now you're making fun of me."

"No, I'm not. You said something funny," he said with a grin. "What's the use of my telling you how I feel when you don't listen, anyway? Hell, you don't listen to me even when I'm talking to you sometimes. Ignoring me—"

"Are you angry then?"

"I am angry but I'd rather not talk when I'm angry. It only makes matters worse," he said, sighing deeply. "Besides I'd rather be kissing you right now, being happy, honey pie."

She was silent, fiddling with her brush.

"I don't understand why you get so irritated with me. I simply wanted you to take a break, grab a bite to eat or drink, or sleep or take a short respite." He had also felt neglected and taken for granted.

"There—you're doing it again!"

"Doing what?"

"Being considerate and thoughtful!"

"Being me? Now what's wrong with being happy?"

"Damn it! It's not about that!" Admonishing him as she gestured emotively with her arms, "It's just—my muse has left the building! Hello? What about my artistic needs? What—"

Finally, he said sternly with his drawl escaping, "Enough, Mercedes. It's enough!" He was just as frustrated as she was.

As he had expected, she would sulk for days when her inspiration left her. Perhaps he had felt insecure when she was engrossed in her art or writing, especially when the subject was Joe, but he was more concerned about her health. Since her neglect for him occurred only during her artistic spurts, he had learned to walk away when he found her engrossed in her art, staring at a canvas crying or, more disturbingly, speaking in other tongues. He'd ride, write music or play a solitary game of 9-ball in the basement. Often, he would fall asleep in front of the TV with Carly before she would emerge from her studio or library.

A few years into their marriage, he had driven to Hilton Head, South Carolina, for the annual Larcher Golf Invitational, a family tradition he always attended. He brought Carly along so she could enjoy the company of her cousins.

"I wish you were here," Grant said. "I miss you."

"I miss you too. How's CJ?"

"Taking lots of pictures so you can see everything you're missing," he said, "How are you?"

"Fine. I just can't seem to catch up with the images in my head. I'm writing

right now, though. Just a quick break before I start another canvas."
"What are you writing about?" and before she could answer, he said, "Never mind."
After they returned home, he was distressed, finding her on the floor of her studio, asleep in front of the same untouched canvas.
All of her mysterious ravings seemed to coincide with the start of her phantasms. Even after they had married, the details of her night terrors remained unknown to him.
"Papa?"
"Yes, twinkle toes?"
"Is Mommy all right?"
"She'll be fine, Poppet. She's in her artistic mood right now—you understand."
"Yeah, she gets weird."
"You've noticed?"
"Uh-huh. Why is she like that? Like a totally different person," she said, full of concern. "Does she have split personality?"
"No, no," he said smiling a little, "it's nothing like that." He heard her sigh almost immediately with relief as she sat down on the chair.
Shifting to a playful British tone, he said, "Lady Twinkle Toes, can I tempt you with this delicious wild boar meat sandwich? Some dragon scales? And the fresh nectar of grape I squeezed with my own bare hands?" He offered her a ham sandwich, potato chips and a tall glass of grape juice.
"Oh yum! I'd love some stinky cheese with my wild boar please?" she answered flawlessly as a Brit, giggling along with him.
"Would you like a particular kind of stink, milady? We have stinky elephant or rhinoceros cheese in the fridge!"
"A stinky rhinoceros, if you please," she said, full of uncontrolled giggles. Suddenly, she stopped, frowning as she said seriously, "Is Mommy *bipolar?*"
"Now where'd you hear that word?"
"The Internet."
"Oh," he said, full of wonder, marveling at his ten-year old gift. "It could be, but I think it's another mood disorder called SAD, Seasonal Affective Disorder. The lack of sunlight affects her."
"But she's sad when the sun is shining too."
"Yes, you're right. Your mommy is a paradox."
"What's a paradox?"
"It's a big parrot inside of her and it doesn't know which direction to go," he teased.
"Mommy's a big parrot!" she exclaimed with a fit of laughter.
Later, Grant offered an official explanation, "Actually, sunshine, a paradox is something that seems both true and false."
"Oh," she said, taking a second to think about it. "Papa, who's the man on the paintings?"
"Why don't you ask your mom?" he answered quickly. He was thankful that his back was turned to grab the milk out of the refrigerator. He knew how perceptive his daughter was.
"Ask me what, love?" Mercedes said, entering the kitchen, surprising them both. After exchanging quick pecks, she repeated, "Ask me what?"

Not a flicker of expression touched his face, just a wide smile.

"You guys were talking about me. You're telling secrets, aren't you?" She cast a glance full of suspicion at him and Carly. She repeated her question in Italian, "*What were you going to ask me? You'll tell me won't you, sweetheart?*"

"Um..." Carly hesitated for a moment; a sweet smile crept on her face. Finally, Carly blurted out, "We wanted to ask you, if you'd like to join us for our grasshopper hunt in the garden!"

* * *

During that same year in December, Grant witnessed a side of Mercedes that he had never seen.

"Take a break," he said softly, peering over her shoulder at the painting, with an apple cupped on his extended hand.

She was in the midst of a deep artistic rapture, completely oblivious to his presence. Startled, she had hurled the apple against the wall almost as a reflex, and shrieked, "PLEASE LEAVE ME ALONE!"

Breaking down sobbing, she was unable to continue because her muse had simply gone again. He had not interrupted her since that incident, leaving her to paint uninterrupted with intensity and passion.

After that unexpected episode, she had straggled in to his study next to the bedroom and knelt astride him on the chaise.

Having recovered to a certain degree, he asked softly, "Are you done yelling at me?" Trying not to respond to her embrace, he cast his eyes up to his Medieval sword and battle shield collection on the wall.

"I am an awful person."

"Why?"

"Because I hurt the man I love."

"Me?"

"Yes, you," she said, resting her weary head on his shoulders. "Forgive me... *ad infinitum.*"

A tender kiss on her hair gave her his answer, and she whispered faintly, "I love you...Grant."

He sighed and loosed the tension in his body. "I love you in spite of yourself." She was already asleep.

He carried her into the bedroom and knelt gazing at her for a long while as she slept. As a doctor, he was worried about her overall physical and psychological health, and as her husband, he had worried about her emotionally.

They both knew that whenever Joe was her artistic subject, either on canvas or in words, she was her own nemesis. There was nothing he could do about it, except to be patient until she completed her painting or writing. At the end of her artistic madness, she would become her normal self again. She'd return as the beautiful, happy genius—his angel, his queen—whom he loved with his heart.

* * *

Grant finally let himself slip back into the present when he arrived at his hotel. He smiled looking at the family photo he had in his wallet.

"Love?" Grant thought he heard her pick up.

"Yes, love." Mercedes answered, sounding tired. "How was the flight?"

"Uneventful but you know how anxious I get when I fly."

"I know. I'm glad you're on dry land. Where in Alabama are you?"

"Eufaula," he said, barely pronouncing it properly.

"What a strange name," she said, letting out a soft little giggle at his attempt.

"It's very peaceful here. Wish you were with me."

"Ditto." It always bothered him whenever she said that. He suddenly felt irritated.

"About last night," he was about to make a point, but she interrupted him, "I understand your anger and you have every right to be worried. I was just overwhelmed after all these years because..."

"It feels like it was only yesterday," he read her mind.

"Yes," she said almost whispering. "I never thought that our paths would cross again!"

He was silent, trying not to let his frustrations get the best of him, but the anger still lingered from last night. He wished he didn't feel this way. She tried to explain, "I'm sorry for putting you in this situation again. Somehow I feel that it happened for a reason and I want to know what it all means. I really didn't mean to hurt you. I love you."

Acknowledging her, he said, "You did hurt me, Mercedes. I can't believe that we're here again. It's a bridge that I never thought I'd cross again. You've taken my feelings for granted. Am I always an afterthought whenever he appears in our lives? You never seem to include me in the equation when it comes to him."

"I'm sorry. I can't..."

"I don't want to feel like I'm second best every time his name is brought up. What pisses me off even more is that you knew this would hurt me, yet you ask me to accept everything without protest." He knew he was right and so did she.

Tearfully, she said, "I do want the past to stay in the past, but I don't know how to do that, especially now. The only thing I can think of to do is to be brutally honest with you and hope that you understand why I say or do the things that I do. Please understand that I can't help feeling the way I do. You've always known that when it comes to JC— nothing is rational. I'm confused!"

"Well, this needs to stop."

"You're right." She couldn't fight the tears that came.

It pained him to hear her cry. He sighed deeply, trying to find the right words to say. "Know that I love you more than you can imagine." He decided not to invest any more of the conversation in his thoughts about Joe; he shifted the conversation to something else that would lift up both of their spirits. He said softly, "Thanks for the note. It brought a smile to my face."

"I hoped it would. I just want you to focus on the tournament, have fun and win."

"Don't worry, I'll win." He meant it.

"Now speaking of fun, have fun with the ladies tonight. I'll be thinking of you."

"Me too."
"Kiss my little poppet for me. And, Mercedes..." he paused.
"Yes?"
"You are my love. I won't stand idly by anymore about this."
"I understand." Before she could say any more, she heard Carly entering the room, and quickly glanced away, wiping away her tears.
With a kiss on her cheek, Carly whispered, "Is it Papa?"
Mercedes nodded.
"Can I talk to him?"
"Love, your darling daughter wishes to talk to you," she said, smiling at Carly. "Have fun and don't worry about us. CJ and I will be fine. Kisses! Love you, bye." She quickly handed the phone to her daughter, who expertly hid her concern about her mother.

Chapter 27

Her Personal Collection

"CJ, please get the door and take our guest into the family room." Mercedes called on the intercom from the kitchen where she was preparing the crab bisque.
"Okay, Mom. We'll see you there in a sec," Carly answered from her bedroom intercom. Quickly, she slipped into her soft indigo sweater, tousled her hair, and put on a healthy dose of hairspray before she ran down the staircase to answer the door, wearing black straight leg twill chinos and low heeled leather boots.
"Hello, you must be Mercedes—I'm Carly. Welcome to our home and please come in," she greeted the young woman with a wide smile. "Let me take your coat."
"Hi, nice to meet you. Thanks!"
Joe's daughter stepped into the foyer, feeling like she was entering a time warp as she closed the heavy seventeenth century English wooden door to the foyer, which was filled with items from multiple centuries.
"Wow—something smells delicious!"
"I should forewarn you. When my mom cooks, she goes all out, so I hope you brought along your appetite!" After she hung the leather jacket in the coat closet next to the door, she led her guest into the family room.
Out in the kitchen, Mercedes took out a bottle of red wine from a wine refrigerator incorporated into the center island of the kitchen. She took out three crystal wineglasses and poured sparkling white grape juice into one and wine into the other two. She placed them on a dark wooden tray along with Brie sprinkled with toasted almonds, butter crackers, apple slices and a caramel dip. Taking off her apron off, she picked up the tray and carried it out to the young ladies.

Carly rose from the sofa, greeted her mom with a light kiss on the cheek and took the tray, setting it down on the coffee table. "Mom, you smell so sweet, and you've been in the kitchen for hours too."

"Thank you, *mia cara.*"

Their guest also got up from the sofa, greeting her with a wide smile. Mercedes smiled at her young guest, greeting her warmly, embracing her, touching her cheeks and lightly kissing the air. "I am so pleased you made it here safely. Welcome."

"Thank you for inviting me. I hope you don't mind my being a little early."

"Not at all. I'm happy you're here. It'll give you and Carly a chance to get acquainted before dinner. Oh how pretty you both look," she said, noticing the girls were similarly dressed except for the color of their sweaters, her guest was in red.

In the background, Carly was admiring her mother. *Mom looks better in that burgundy shirt than I do.* She noted her mother's ankle length, back-slit skirt matched her four-inch kidskin pumps, and a crimson lipstick gave a perfect line to her lips against her beautiful white smile. She wasn't wearing much make-up, nor was she wearing her glasses tonight. All in all, she looked very sophisticated with her hair pulled back in an elegant up-do. She tried to be as fashionable as her mother was, but she had yet to find her own personal style.

"I'd like to present a toast." She gave Carly the glass with white grape juice and offered her guest a glass of wine.

Raising her glass, she made a toast, "It has been said that wherever a beautiful soul has been, there is a trail of beautiful memories. Here's to all the beautiful memories!"

After they touched wineglasses to the toast, they sipped the cool liquids.

"I hope you brought along your fine book."

"Yes, Professor, I have the book with me." She took her prized book out of her black leather pocketbook and handed it to her.

She took the copy of her book and one of the calligraphy quill pens she kept in the family room table. Gingerly, she placed her wineglass on the end table and announced, "Ladies, it is time for the private book signing ceremony!"

Sitting down on the love seat, she signed the book:

"To my greatest fan, Mercedes D. Tristram

Dearest Mercedes,

Listen with your soul's heart to the whispers of the universe. For therein are the precious words you seek. Always write words in truth, yet speak with love. When you do—dreams always come true.

Continue to learn,

Mercedes P. Larcher"

Her young student was dumbfounded after reading the personal inscription. All she could say was, "I will treasure it always."

The young woman's familiar words struck her, reminding her of Joe and the small metal puzzle. Still stunned with the irony, she smiled and looked at the young ladies side by side with their own smiles. *Another beautiful generation brought together by fate.*

"Ladies, dinner will be served within the hour. Please excuse me—the kitchen beckons!" She was humming a familiar song from her memory as she walked towards the kitchen.

In the family room, the two young ladies became quickly acquainted, talking non-stop and enjoying the sweet caramel-dipped apples.

Carly enjoyed sharing family stories about the family pictures that were proudly displayed everywhere.

"You're a dancer?"

"Yes, I thought about being a ballerina or maybe even a choreographer."

"Why don't you?"

"Because my passion is medicine. And you?"

"It's always been about writing."

"Like my mom."

"Yes..." She paused, looking at a black-framed photograph on an end table. It was a photograph of a young couple. The longhaired blond man held a guitar in his hands. He was wearing dark sunglasses, a white mock shirt, and black leather jacket; he also had a small, dangling earring, a gold cross, next to a diamond stud on his left ear.

"Who's he?"

Smiling, she said, "That's my dad! Actually, that picture was taken on the night he proposed to my mom."

"Could you tell me about it?"

"Sure! It's one of my favorite stories to share. When I was a little kid, I always asked my parents to tell me the story about that night as a bedtime story. I remember my dad told me the story first. Anyway, he composed this song especially for her. He was performing at this place in Philadelphia called the Pontiac Grille. He made sure my mom stood right in the front row. Right after he sang *Walking in Memphis*—have you heard that song?"

"No, I don't think so."

"Well, it's pretty old, but a nice ballad. It's one of his favorite songs, since he's from Memphis, you know. Anyway, my mom knew he sang it for his finale. After he finished the song, he surprised her. He jumped down from the stage, got on his knees, guitar in hand; he started playing his guitar and sang to her this beautiful song he wrote about her. After he finished, he presented my granny's diamond ring with a new setting on it and asked her to marry him!" Sighing, she continued, "Of course, she was taken completely by surprise and with the spotlights on her, my mom cried while my dad held his breath because she didn't answer for what seemed like forever! He was sweating, thinking he'd be rejected, down on his knees in front of all these people! Finally, she answered with a resounding 'yes' to his proposal. That was when someone took their picture—that picture!"

"Wow, that's so romantic!"

"I hope when someone proposes to me, it's just as romantic."

"You and me both!" They smiled at each other.

The painting prominently displayed above the mantelpiece caught her interest, so she strolled over to closely inspect it.

"My mom calls this piece, *Epiphany*. It's another self-portrait of hers in acrylic. She painted it before she married my dad. It was her very last painting of the twentieth century."

It was just as Carly described it, a self-portrait of a younger professor in a kneeling pose with her eyes towards the heavens. It appeared to be in the Medieval era, and it showed her wearing a deep crimson robe and an ultramarine blue flowing cape held together with a beautifully detailed crimson-jeweled brooch. The background behind her showed heavy golden drapes that were sweeping and embroidered. The young woman held a long, delicate, white feather with both hands; and the way the drapes were arranged, it appeared as if wings—angel wings—were embedded within the golden folds of the drapes. Her face with its upward tilt held a resplendent smile and a familiar look of clarity, of knowing. The painting's details were very intricate.

"It reminds me of the way she looks up at us while she lectures during class. You should've seen her in class yesterday. She spoke of truths and epiphanies. In the middle of the lecture, she just broke out in Latin! And when she looked at us as she spoke in this dead language, she had that same look on her face. It's really moving to hear her speak. She has such fire in her eyes—so much passion in her voice."

Hearing the compliment, Carly beamed with pride. "That's my mom for you! She gets very deep, but you know, there's only one person I know that can snap her out of it."

"Who?"

"My dad."

"Really?"

"Yeah, and when it's just she and I together, it's like she's become a teenager again, especially when we all goof around. We don't take things in our lives too seriously. You should hear her when she's laughing hysterically!" She started to giggle when one particularly funny moment with her mom crept into her thoughts.

"I almost didn't get in her class," Mercedes shared. "Luckily, I got the last available seat."

"So you're the one."

"The one?"

"The one who bumped the guy I'm seeing for the last seat."

"Oops!" They laughed.

Looking at the painting again, Mercedes commented, "You said this is another self-portrait. Are there more?"

"Uh-huh, this is one of many. Hey, would you be interested in seeing more of her artwork?"

"Definitely! Would you also show me where your mother actually writes her books?"

"Sure. Her books and writing stuff are in her private library. We'd have to go through the art gallery on the way there anyway."

"Honestly, I've only read about her artistic talents from her author's bio; but I've never seen any of her artwork until tonight," she shifted her gaze back to the mantel. "I think that piece is unbelievably beautiful."

"Well then, you'll enjoy seeing what I'll show you next. Please follow my lead, Mercedes."

"Carly, I'd love it if you call me, Merc."

"Only if call me CJ, deal?"

"You got it, CJ."

They both took their drinks with them and Mercedes automatically grabbed her pocketbook. They chatted loudly down the hallway.

"CJ, this art gallery is amazing!"

"My uncle Caleb designed it. My dad had it built. It was his tenth wedding anniversary gift to my mom."

The art gallery housed and displayed her mother's personal collection. The room was rather large and the walls were bathed in muted colors so as not to detract from the mélange of colors in her mother's art. The muted walls were covered with framed paintings, and there were sculpture stands and display-cases with glass housings. The gallery featured selected works in chronological order, arranged by the type of media her mother had used. The one-dimensional works varied in size and ranged from oil paintings to lithographic prints, from charcoal and graphite sketches to her favorite medium, acrylics.

The room also displayed her sculptures in clay, plaster and ceramic, as well as wood and mixed media pieces. Above each of the framed paintings was an individual gallery spotlight, and the room was carefully monitored for a constant, ambient temperature since some of the pieces were very sensitive and fragile.

Mercedes moved over in front of a series of sculptures entitled *The Natural Progression of Life*. It depicted three white ceramic statues of the same female torso in the same loving pose, but at different stages of pregnancy. In the first, the woman appeared normal; in the second, the woman was at full-term; and in the last, the woman held a baby and her swollen belly was almost gone.

Moving to another piece, she called out, "This is really cool, CJ! What's this about?"

"Which one?"

"This one called *Journey of Soul Mates*," she replied, pointing at it. "It's a very interesting piece. It looks like one of awesome gardens I saw in France during my high school senior trip. Look at all this detail!"

The sculpture was protected by a glass casing where it sat on top of a lower display table, much like what an architect would use to display an architectural scale model of a building.

"You see that treasure chest in the middle of the garden labyrinth?"

"Yes," she nodded, looking at a bejeweled box that was slightly propped open.

"See the red coin inside the treasure chest?"

"Not really."

"You can barely see it right through here," she said, pointing to something from a different angle. "See it?"

Without leaning on the display, they both peered in it.

"Okay, I see it now. The red coin has markings in its center," Mercedes remarked, looking closer. "It has the King of Spades and the other one.... Hmm... I can't tell what the other one is, but it's another high card with a red heart on it," she said and thought, *That coin looks familiar to me.*

"I've never seen it up close. My mom considers it as one of her greatest personal treasures."

"Do you know it means?"

"I only know what it represents in the sculpture."

"So what's it about?"

"Metaphors. The labyrinth, the coins are all metaphors for the journey of soul mates. My mom explained that it represents the path soul mates must take in their search for each other in eternity."

"And the treasure chest?"

"It represents each of the crossroads where their paths cross and they finally find each other. It's the moment when life-altering decisions must be made."

"And the decisions are what? What are the choices?"

"Well, according to my mom, when the path of soul mates cross, the coin is the signpost; it triggers the whole process of recognition. You know, like a personal map which is always waiting for them to help in their search for each other. Ultimately, it helps them find their way out of the labyrinth. Anyway, my mom says that the recognition isn't always simple because of an important caveat."

"What is it? This caveat?"

"Well, you see, there are *other* souls in the labyrinth."

"Of course, like kindred spirits," she said almost involuntarily.

"Uh-huh. She told me that it could get very confusing because these other souls are so alike, twins almost. They're kindred spirits to each other, yet soul mates to others. That's where it gets tricky. You know, knowing the difference."

"I read somewhere that souls within the same circle of life always travel together in their perpetual journey."

"That makes sense. Now what was that Latin phrase she used?" She searched for the words, wiggling her fingers on her free hand. Immediately answering her own question, she said snapping her fingers, "'*Ad infinitum!*'"

"To infinity."

"That's right, forever. She told me that they—meaning the kindred spirits—also possess similar signs of recognition, except they'll only be able to figure out who's who if they really listen to the signs with their souls' minds and hearts. With freewill they can choose to ignore the signs or misinterpret them. Both soul mates and kindred spirits have to pay very close attention so that the signals don't get crossed. You know, wires are crossed, things go haywire and the correct signals are diverted elsewhere. The intended soul mate ends up going with another and so on. Anyway, when they finally get it all straightened out, the soul mates have to contend with another major hurdle at that same crossroad. They have to make more that just one decision."

She noticed how her new friend was completely absorbed with the coin and the center of the sculpture. After a moment, she continued, "Mom told me that if one of them decides to take the coin, or treasure, that person immediately falls into a state of forgetfulness, like amnesia, about the other again—which means they would part or separate, neither with a thought about the other. You know, like saying goodbye to a perfect stranger, or willingly with their freewill because of whatever circumstances they may be in. Then they would each continue their journey alone in the maze—hopelessly lost in their search for each other again while they find a way out of the labyrinth. Notice anything strange about the way she designed the maze?"

"Yes, I noticed that," she replied, putting her wineglass on the floor. She made a sweeping gesture with her arm and then gestured to the treasure chest in the center. "It always converges back to the center, back to the treasure chest. To the coin."

"You're right. And there's a good reason for the labyrinth's pattern. It mirrors what really happens in real life, forever actually. Soul mates always bump into each other and come back to the coin with the same choices again. It's really pretty clever, her design—don't you think?"

"It is. From a bird's eye view, the pattern of the labyrinth looks like the infinity symbol, except it's elongated with jutting, long winding paths; but overall, it's definitely the infinity symbol. And the little treasure chest is situated right smack dab in the center of the symbol so their paths always converge there."

"Excellent! You've got a good eye."

"Thanks," she smiled, "Though I didn't realize how complicated things can get when it comes to soul mates recognizing each other."

"Very complicated, I think."

"Hey, what about the other choice? To leave the coin behind?"

"Well, according to my Mom, when soul mates choose to leave the treasure behind, they're actually finding the real reward—the real treasure."

"Of course, the real treasure is each other!"

"Exactly! She explained that when they abandon the coin, they become fully aware that they're soul mates, which is the whole of point of the journey anyway, right?"

"I totally agree. Soul mates are a pair; they were destined to do it together. So while they search for an exit out of the garden maze, they would enjoy re-discovering each other, having nice respites and fun during their long travel together."

"Yes, but once they finally find the exit, they are faced with another crossroad."

"Another one?"

"Uh-huh. They could either ignore the crossroad and not make a decision at all or decide to walk out of the labyrinth and into the rest of the beautiful garden. When they decide to do that, they're actually journeying on a path that takes them home, to the Garden of Eden."

"Heaven."

"Exactly."

"Or because they're both curious, they might choose to journey back to search for the treasure and to try to solve the puzzle of the coin. If they do that and they finally figure out what it means, they can still walk hand-in-hand out of the labyrinth. If they don't, then it all begins again!"

"It's the ultimate puzzle."

"You know, this all sounds like your mom's lecture yesterday, especially about the Garden of Eden."

"Oops! Then, you'll hear it again because it's actually an extension of that soul mates lecture."

"Hey, thanks for the preview!" Winking at her, she grinned, "Don't worry about it. I promise, I won't tell." They smiled at each other. It was one of the many inside jokes they would share.

"Come on. Let's go to my mom's library."

"Lead the way," she said, picking up the wineglass where she had left it. After passing a series of dragon paintings, she commented, "Your mom sure likes red dragons."

"Here's a piece of trivia: whenever she paints dragons, they're always red—no other color."

"Really? I wonder why."

"It remains a mystery, but I think the red dragon is my dad."

Something Mercedes saw on the left wall, out of the corner of her eye, made her take a double glance to that direction. Without prompting, she strolled over to wall on the left, where the acrylic paintings hung. Instantly, she stopped in her tracks, unable to believe her eyes, almost dropping her wineglass.

Pointing at a painting, she exclaimed with delight, "Oh my God! CJ! That looks just like my dad!"

"Really?" she said, walking toward her. When she stood next to her, she explained, "The woman cradling the baby is my mom."

Stepping closer to examine the painting, Mercedes said insistently, "The man kissing her left hand looks just like my father."

Reading the title aloud, she said, "*Thirteenth Century, Devotion.*"

Moving on to the adjacent painting, she said, "This one, *Twentieth Century, Love Waits*, bears an uncanny resemblance to my dad too!" The painting depicted an imminent kiss between two lovers.

Carly had seen them since she was a little girl and her interest was piqued. "Really? Well there are five other ones a few paintings down from these. Remember, these paintings are hung in chronological order. Come, let me show you."

She had a hard time prying herself away from the painting, but she followed Carly to the other paintings, which showed scenes from later in the current century.

In amazement, Mercedes viewed the paintings while Carly stood there, pensive, very aware of her new friend's bewildered reactions.

Carly stood a few paces back to admire the paintings again. She was particularly fond of and drawn to these paintings with the mysterious man because they held personal meanings to her mother which were unknown to her. Her father never really took interest in them, except he felt that they should be displayed in a museum or a public gallery, like her other masterpieces. Since her mother never parted with them, it meant they held a special place in her heart, or they represented a significant moment in her life. She was immersed in thought. *I wonder if it's really her father. Hmmm, this opens up a whole new path to explore. But should I?*

She knew her mother preferred to draw from life and often used models when her time would allow it. Her mother would always tell her all about the models in her paintings, except she had never mentioned the man in these paintings. So, she had often wondered about his identity and why her mother had never shared any details about him. The only thing she could remember was a Freudian-like slip her mother had once made, saying something about him in her dreams. It had happened when she was just ten and Carly never forgot the night because it had been around St. Patrick's Day.

With that in mind, she decided to look at the paintings in a different perspective, which was something her mother insisted upon.

She began to silently remember something. *That's right. That's why I started calling her bouts of sadness "spells"—because of that night with her paintings. It was late, but I was thirsty. I got out of bed to get a glass of milk. When I heard the music playing in her studio, I knew she was up painting. When I peeked through her door, she was crying in front of these paintings. She was very despondent, lying on the floor and staring at them; she was in some kind of rapture, speaking in French and Latin. At first I thought it sounded incredible, but I started to sense it was really strange, and I was worried. I got very upset, because my beautiful mom was so sad and in tears. I kept wondering—what could possibly make her feel so sad like that? I just wanted to comfort her, so I ran into her studio and gave her lots of hugs and kisses. I remember how her eyes lit up when she saw me. She was so happy. She even pretended that everything was fine. Something got caught in her eye or whatever. I just kept drying her tears, and tickled her behind her ears. She laughed and I gave her such a tight squeeze. While she held me in her embrace, she said in English, "JC—I'll see you in my dreams."*

She paused to repeat it silently again. *I thought it was a dyslexic lapse—saying my name backwards, but...but she was looking at the paintings when she said "JC." Hmmm, I wonder.*

"By the way, Merc, what's his name?"

"Oh, my dad's name is Joe, Joe Tristram," she replied. "CJ, it's definitely my dad—no doubt about it."

Joe Tristram. Nope, that's not it. Only his first name fit in the initials.

"As a matter of fact, forget my words, let me show you instead," she said, taking her wallet out from her pocketbook. She showed Carly her family photos and a photo of him as a young pilot, standing in front of his plane.

Carly had initially thought the acronym wasn't a big deal anymore; but seeing the photos, her curiosity fueled her inquiring thoughts again.

Together they compared the painting with the younger version of her father to the paintings. They looked at the photo, then at the paintings, then back at the photo. They finally looked at each other with curious expressions and both said, "It is him!"

"You know, my dad told me that they were old friends."

"You're right, they are friends! My mom mentioned it yesterday. She said you were the daughter of an old friend, but I figured that she was referring to your mom, not your dad. Funny, she's never really mentioned your dad before; but I guess they were friends from way back, high school—maybe?"

"I don't know, but I know this much, my dad and your mom must've had a special friendship."

"You know, there's something very specific about these paintings. Come here for a second." They walked back to the first two paintings.

"Like this one for instance," she said, gesturing to the nude painting. "It's my mom's self-portrait."

"Wow, I love it!"

"It's called *Under a Spell* for a very personal reason. She told me she painted it during the darkest times of her life, which explains the vampire paintings too. See?"

Carly pointed out three paintings, depicting mystical creatures of the night that were catty-cornered on the wall next to the self-portrait. The paintings were dark and disturbing. It appeared as though the vampires would leap out of the painting, grab them, and haul them back into the canvas and into a frightening world beyond the wall. They both felt uncomfortable when they looked at the paintings.

"Creepy, aren't they, Merc?"

"Yes, very creepy."

"Anyway, my mom completed these disturbing paintings before she married my dad. My dad told me that she had a whole series of forty paintings dedicated to what she referred to as the lonely, misguided children of the night. She explained that they represented many lost souls who are wandering aimlessly or standing still in their search for answers, feeling abandoned and hopeless in the shadows. These are the souls who embraced the negative forces of life and have chosen to stay in the darkness. Anyway, for the first time in his life, my dad said he purposefully insisted that she stop painting such macabre subjects. He suggested happier subjects, like love for instance. So, instead, she painted those two paintings with the man who looks like your dad. See the dates under her signature?"

Mercedes looked at it closely and noted the year, comparing it to the other painting, which bore the same year. With a strange tone in her voice, she said, "This is really interesting. These two paintings of my dad were completed the same year I was born!" She walked back to the others and said, "But these paintings were painted when I was eight and nine. And..."

Before she could finish, Carly interrupted. "And then my mom stopped painting when I was ten."

They spontaneously looked at each other again with similar perplexed looks. They felt like they stumbled upon a puzzle that was just screaming to be solved. And they were both intrigued.

"My mom explained to me about how each one of her canvasses captures her feelings like a pictorial time capsule. You know—something that traps an emotion and suspends it in time forever. So, there's definitely a deep significance in each of them, but I don't exactly know what that is yet! Anyway, she painted *Epiphany*, the painting in the family room, soon after she did the first two paintings of your dad. She said it marked a significant turning point in her life. She even wrote about it in her third book about epiphanies. Have you read it?"

"Yes, I read the book. I hope it was purely fiction," she said, remembering. "It is fiction, right?"

"Why do you ask?"

"Because it speaks of horrific events: the rape of a pregnant woman who suffered a miscarriage because of it."

"It was based on a true story. Someone very close to her."

"God, I'm sorry to hear that." After a silent moment, she continued, "I wonder if your mom will tell us about these paintings."

"I don't know," she said. "My mom's pretty hush-hush about it. I mean she's great at changing the subject whenever I ask her, so I simply stopped asking about those paintings out of respect for her privacy. I don't like to pry really. I'm not one to force anyone when they don't want to share something—you know what I mean?"

"All too well."

"But I'm sure my mom would be glad to tell you if you asked her. I mean if it is your dad, I don't see why she wouldn't tell you."

"Hey, maybe my dad knows something about it. Perhaps he could tell us the story behind them, unless, of course, he hasn't seen them before. I mean the first two paintings. Oh, I don't know. I suppose that's possible." She paused to think some more about it.

"You know, I don't think my dad has seen these paintings," she said, still unsure.

Carly was also uncertain about something, but she was not sure what it was exactly. Whenever she was unable to figure something out, she would talk aloud so she could hear her thoughts. Sometimes she would write it down. It helped to sort out the facts for her. Sometimes, she would also brainstorm with a friend. She looked at her newfound friend. She thought that it would help her to complete her thoughts to their end, so she decided it was best to share her thoughts, which she had ruminated on for quite sometime.

"Merc, I'm curious about the other paintings. I mean, I was already ten, so I'd have remembered meeting your dad, but I don't. Unless—" She paused, and began rationalizing. "Well, of course—my mom's got a photographic memory. And I'm sure she has photos of him, though I never saw them." She paused again because she couldn't justify her next thought. All she said was, "Interesting."

"What's interesting?"

"I mean, why would she never say a single word about your dad after painting seven paintings of him? And the time frame they were painted doesn't make sense to me. You see, she would go on and on about her other paintings. Trust me, when she talks about her insights, especially when she has a lesson to teach you, you can't stop her! *But*, but when it came to discussing any paintings with your dad in them—nothing. Absolutely not one detail. Not a single mention of his name.

"You know, Merc, I remember asking her countless times about the man in those paintings, and what it all meant to her, but she would become uncomfortably silent. And then she would get a really cryptic look on her face." She paused, now looking intently at the paintings. Then she said thoughtfully, "But the expression wasn't in her face. It was in her eyes."

"What kind of look?"

"Well, it's hard to explain. It's was a look of…. I want to say *longing*, but that's not the word I'm searching for. It's more like—"

"Yearning," Mercedes blurted out, feeling the goose bumps forming on her arms.

"Yes, that's it! That's the word—*yearning*." Realizing the coincidence, she looked at Mercedes with a puzzled look, "Did you just read my mind or something? Why did you even say yearning?"

"I honestly don't know why I said it. It was the first thing that popped in my head." So they stared at each other for a few moments, taking big gulps of their drinks. A strange, inexplicable silence passed between them.

Carly broke the silence and continued sharing her thoughts. "Strangely enough, it would only happen in the winter. Then, other times of the year, my mom seemed ambivalent, yet it wouldn't be consistent because once winter set in, she would be thrown into a serious funk. Merc, with mom's mystical beliefs and genius status, as you can well imagine, she's any psychiatrist's prized case study! Anyway, it gets intensified only during one specific month out of the year consistently. It would be—"

"December," Mercedes blurted out, her heart pounding. *I know I'm right.*

Caught in mid-sentence, Carly almost spilled her juice on the floor. She exclaimed loudly again, her jaw dropping, "Yes, December! Right again! Hey, what made you say 'December'?"

"My dad and I were born in December, uncannily on the same day. I don't know why I feel this way, but I really sense that there's a connection with it. Do you feel it too?" She felt a bit light-headed when she thought about it.

Carly shook her head, except she really did feel it too. She wanted to admit it, but she didn't—not yet anyway. She replied, "I don't know. I'm starting to get confused. Actually, I'm a little freaked out about the whole thing."

"Me too."

"I think we need to stop this. I really don't even want to entertain any phantom conversations."

"What do you mean by a 'phantom conversation'?" She blinked in confusion.

It took a long time before Carly offered an answer. She reflected on the moment that her mother first raised the issue of phantom conversations. It was during high school when she was on the phone with her best friend, Denise, and they were caught up in a gossip about Beth, who was new in their circle of friends. Denise was questioning her sexual preferences and Carly was drawn into her queries, so she began sharing her own conclusions. When her mother overheard her side of the conversation, she broached the subject tactfully later that evening and Carly was given a valuable lesson about phantom conversations.

Finally, she shared, "A phantom conversation is the kind you have in your own head, asking questions and answering them at the same time, when it pertains to a decision or conclusion that you have to ultimately make. Sometimes you can have them with others, like the one we're having now."

"Mmph! You mean like tactical thinking? At least that's what my dad calls it. Strategy. He taught me to always anticipate the next move. As you might have guessed already, I was brought up around the military."

"No problem. I was brought up around medicine and art. When my mom first mentioned it, I immediately used medical terms like an assessment, a diagnosis. She told me that I was very close. It's not exactly how you and I understand it, even using all the synonyms for it. She explained that it is a very specific line of thinking, speculation or conjecture. Anyway, in her terms, it's known simple as a phantom conversation. Again, she reiterated that it's a specific type. Let me think, what were her exact words..."

"A guess?"

"Well, you're half right. A phantom conversation is an uneducated guess. It became clear to me, pretty self-explanatory really. My mom believes in simplicity, putting things in the simplest terms. In terms that I, or anyone else for that matter, can understand." She paused, thinking, *I don't think anything is really simple with Mom though she makes it seem simple.*

Continuing, she said, "My mom considers phantom conversations to be terribly menacing. Actually, she loathes them with a passion! She believes they are self-fulfilling prophecies. It is even more perilous when a conversation involves matters of the heart. It will significantly affect the lives of people, big time! You know, like the ripple effect!"

"Yes, of course. It'll eventually affect others."

"In my case, it'll affect everyone within the circle of my life. Someone I love will inevitably get hurt because of my actions. So basically, they produce life-altering changes on a grand scale!" She paused as if reflecting, then said, "You know, Merc, I've never known my mom to engage in a phantom conversation—not with me or my dad. I don't think she ever had one with anyone! She felt it never resolves anything completely to its end. She advised me that I would never get the absolute, honest truth out of phantom conversations. Unless, of course, I am having the conversation with the people I am supposed to have it with. She always stressed that the surest way out of phantom conversations and getting the correct answers—the truth—is simple. To explain, she uses analogies or metaphors. She loves to use analogies. With me, she used math. She asked me what I needed to make a straight line."

"That's easy, you just need two points."

"Right, that's what I said too. She asked me from whom I should get the answers if I couldn't figure out the math problem. I said the math teacher, of course! When I answered her question, I also found my answer about the surest way out of phantom conversations."

"Yes, of course! It makes sense. The surest way is the direct way: just ask the person who has the answers. In our case, it would be your mom and my dad!" *This is all very interesting. I'll have to talk to the Professor about her views on phantom conversations. She's probably going to bring up the subject up during class.* Suddenly, something dawned on her. "It's funny how your mom calls them 'phantom conversations'."

"What do you mean?"

"I find it interesting because my dad's call sign in the Air Force is *Phantom*. A coincidence?"

"I don't know, but you must know about coincidences, right?"

"Uh-huh. I also read your mom's book about coincidences. I'm always left bewildered whenever I encounter coincidences."

"Me too. But, you know, it's such a common occurrence in my life, so I've become a little immune to them. I find them fascinating. With my mom on the other hand, it's a completely different story. Anyway, speaking of asking the source, has your dad ever mentioned posing for my mom or ever seeing the earlier paintings? I mean, has he even talked to you about my mom, like how they met?"

After thinking back on many conversations with her father, she answered, "About the painting, not a word. Let me think. As far as how he met your mom, he wasn't very specific, plus I was too excited to even think or pay attention. I mean, just him knowing your mom blew me away! But now that I see these paintings, I am at a real loss. Actually, I'm stumped. But, I totally agree with you about the possible nature of their friendship. They must've been very close. That's pretty clear!" She gestured at the paintings.

"Again, your mom is right about the phantom conversation. I totally get it. An uneducated guess is like the blind men and the elephant—completely wrong about the conclusions! I hate to be wrong! But, before I ask your mom, I'll ask my dad first. I mean I'm sure he posed for those paintings. Maybe they had an artist-model relationship and that's how they became great friends. I'll also find out more about how they met and all that. Perhaps there's a really cool story about it. CJ, you'll definitely be the first to know, okay?"

"Outstanding! We really seem to think alike. I think you and I are kindred spirits."

"I feel like we've known each other before today."

"Yeah, like we've been here before."

"I'm really glad I met you. It means a lot, especially for a new girl in town. I don't even know where the malls are!"

"Don't worry. I'll drive you around town for the fifty-cent tour. Maybe my dad will let me borrow his classic Mercedes. And, I don't mean my mom!"

They started to laugh and were delighted to have stumbled onto a mystery. There were entirely too many coincidences. They suspected it was just the way that it was going to be with them too.

Mercedes finally finished her wine and took another moment to stare intently at the paintings with much closer scrutiny. Suddenly, she remembered a subtle look of something on her father's face and in his eyes during their last birthday dinner. She couldn't put her finger on it. Her thoughts raced. *He's very fond of Las Vegas. He would take trips there with his best friend from college. He always came home ecstatic, incessantly talking about great memories and bringing home many souvenirs for me. But there was one specific casino that he was fond of. Damn! I can't remember the name right now. Wait a sec. Come to think of it, I did see a look of something in the Professor's eyes when I talked to her yesterday about my dad. Hmmm, I wonder—*

"Hey, Merc, when you're done let me know and I'll take you to her library."

"Great, in a sec." Continuing with her thoughts, she strolled over to look at the self-portrait again. *He started telling me about the history of a specific hotel. He said it was an important Vegas landmark—Elvis got married there. When he talked about the original building being demolished, he got the same look again, except it was in his eyes, more distinct than when he gave me the book and the puzzle. It was a look of...*

She looked across the gallery to the labyrinth sculpture. She exclaimed in her head, *Of course! The same look CJ said about her mom! A yearning—a longing look! OH MY! That's it! And then he softly said my name, but oddly, he wasn't looking at me. He looked like he was in a daydream, obliviously staring out in space. When I answered him, he looked startled, then smiled, continuing on his tour of words without even skipping a beat, but he's like that anyway. Hard to tell what he's really feeling at times.*

She strained to remember more about the conversation and how the coin was made significant to her. There were also other occasions when she had noticed her father's dispositions and Freudian slips about the Professor. She felt all of it was very poignant to her current phantom conversation.

She looked at the paintings again and thought, *Like she said in class, looks can be deceiving. These paintings are more than what they seem to be*—*I just know it!* Then she found her thoughts were wandering back to the sculpture again, and especially to the coin in the bejeweled treasure chest. It looked so familiar to her.

Suddenly, a chiming sound from the down the hallway could be heard, but faintly.

"What was that?"

"The dinner bell. C'mon, dinner is ready!" she said, smiling. "I'll have to show you the library later, okay?"

"Okay—looking forward to it."

Finally, when they got to the dining room, they were greeted with an eye-popping feast.

"Are you hungry, ladies?"

In unison, the two answered, "I'm starving!" A burst of laughter followed.

Pleased with the sounds of laughter, Mercedes announced, "Tonight, I shall be your humble servant, your personal genie in a bottle. Your wish is my command."

All of the sudden, upon hearing her analogy, the young Mercedes' mind was erumpent. Many things collectively fell into place. She stared at her smiling Professor with feelings she couldn't describe.

Chapter 28

Heaven on Earth

It was the Friday prior to Cornell's 156th student May commencement. Shortly after lunch, Mercedes headed out to the Johnson Art Museum. It was her usual time of solitude to enjoy the new exhibits, write or sketch. With her upcoming art show, she was in her artistic mode. In this mode she had a different way of dressing. Her clothing palette consisted of primary colors with obvious feminine charm. She was dressed in red with an ankle-length, silk, front wrap-around dress with French cuffs. She had a distinct youthful appearance without her glasses. Her hair was wavy and a bit tousled; she wore her black suede mid-calf boots.

She brought along her sketchpad, but was still armed with her pen and journal. As usual, she planned on attending the fifteen-minute chimes concert—a Cornell campus tradition. When she wasn't at the concert, she would listen in open air. She felt the chimes sounded like they were coming from a distant foreign place. During the fall and spring semesters, the Cornell Chimesmasters performed three concerts each day, only when classes were in session. Aside from the entrancing music, it was the spectacular view of the campus from McGraw Tower that she truly enjoyed. It was breathtaking, although the 161 steps to climb the tower could take her breath away as well.

She glanced at her watch; she thought if she left now, she would make it to the tower before the door opened for the concert. And when she walked outside toward the grassy area, a very strong sense of *déjà vu* took hold of her. The sound of a plane overhead caused her to stop; she found a bench nearby to sit down. She put her things down and then looked up at the direction of the white trail path of a jet.

She tried to remember a similar moment when, suddenly, her trance was interrupted with a pair of strong hands covering her eyes from behind her. Startled, she was about to protest, when she heard a whisper in her ear, "There are places and moments in which one is so completely alone that one sees the world entire." A wide rapturous smile emerged, on her face. *It can't be.*

"JC," she gasped. When she turned to him, she exclaimed, "I can't believe it!"

Joe took his Aviator shades off, smiling as widely as she was. He said, "Hello beautiful. I've missed you!"

He held out his hands to pull her to her feet. She rose to meet him with a joyous smile. When he saw her smile, her beautiful smile, his hands pulled her waist spontaneously toward him. He lifted her up off her feet. They held each other for what seemed to be forever. When he kissed the nape of her neck, she sighed. *Don't wake me from this dream.*

"It's not a dream," he said, answering her silent prayer. He squeezed her tighter, enjoying the scent of her. He said, "Wish or no wish! I never doubted we would see each other again."

It was inevitable—their lips met. Passionate kisses rekindled emotions long buried, oblivious to where they were.

They held each other and felt as though they couldn't hold each other close enough. The urge to touch each other's bodies was undeniably strong; but they fell into capricious laughter of their reunion when they became fully aware of where they were.

Without taking their hands off one another, they sat down on the bench. For what seemed to be an eternity, they simply stared at each other, smiling. He held her hands in his and pressed them to his lips.

She took a deep breath, holding the moment forever in her memory and compartmentalizing it.

Finally, he spoke. "I am so incredibly happy to finally see your beautiful smile again. Time agrees with you."

She felt as though she couldn't speak, so she thanked him with a soft kiss. She said, smiling, "Joe, my Captain."

He laughed softly, "I just made Major General!"

"You look fantastic for a Major General. I see you've stayed vigilant about your workouts." She touched his hair and noted, "It's longer than I remembered and much lighter in the sun." He was casually dressed in a classic designer ensemble. He wore a pair of black lace-up shoes with an olive twill pants, a dress shirt with white French cuffs, and a black and cream sports coat.

"I've never seen you in the daylight," he remarked. "You're so beautiful."

"Thank you," she said blushing.

They were in the midst of the university campus, along with many other students sprawled on the grass enjoying the afternoon sun. They blended right in the campus landscape like a couple of college sweethearts mesmerized with each other. They were completely oblivious to everything around them.

"It feels like it was just yesterday," he said.

"It was only a moment ago, JC."

They sat there just talking; cramming over twenty years of their lives in a matter of minutes. Nothing had changed in their affectations. Nothing had changed in their affections, either—always touching as if to prove they were both really physically together.

He would take her hand, unconsciously rubbing his thumbs on her soft silky skin. Occasionally, he would reach over and brush the tendrils of her hair away from her face. While she would smile shyly, her eyes lit up in rapt attention when he spoke—listening and enjoying the sounds of his deep, sultry voice. She was so animated in her speech, unconsciously touching his legs, his arms. Her joy was clear. They would say things in unison, then laugh aloud at the coincidence.

He leaned over to whisper, "I want you, Mercedes. I want desperately to make love to you—right now!"

She smiled and swiftly answered him when she rose from the bench with her hand outstretched. Her actions were clear. He took her hand and led her down the path toward the parking lot.

He opened the passenger door of his fully restored, classic, black-on-black Porsche 911 SC. She smiled remembering how he had wanted to own it during their conversation at the Excalibur. She slid in gracefully and took out her sunglasses. He already had his on when he turned the ignition key to start the car.

She gave him directions to a nearby Victorian mansion that had been turned into a romantic inn just down the hill from the campus. She had never been there and felt it was appropriate for their intimate reunion. They checked into a quiet private suite with windows which overlooked the rooftops and church steeples.

The door shut and they were finally alone. There was no awkwardness, no discomfort and no guilt. And then, something phenomenal happened: their perceptions were altered, for in their minds, they were hurled back in time. It was as though the fabric of time was torn, and a portal opened for them to enter. They peeled the years like the layers of their clothing. Without their notice, they stood facing each other in their youth, back in the Aladdin when they first made love over twenty years ago. It was a replay of their actions and their emotions.

"Tell me, Mercedes. Do you want me as much as I want you?" He was stroking her face tenderly, feeling the silkiness of her skin against his fingertips. She smiled and said softly, "Yes, JC—with all my heart."

They could no longer contain their desire for each other, nor would they ever try again. They kissed deeply. He picked her up in his arms and laid her on a massive poster bed.

"Mercedes," he whispered. The warmth of his voice caused her to let out a soft moan.

The vision he had of her returned, as she was atop him, moaning in her dance and heightening his pleasures. Except this time the words which escaped his lips were, "I love you, Mercedes." She leaned forward and devoured his words.

Still thrusting into her, he rolled her over and faced her. He matched the rhythm of her force and passion. He pinned her wrists back to the bed and groaned with pleasure when he felt her tightening. Not wanting to race to that final release, he got on his knees and parted her thighs; his thrusts were steady and deep. She screamed deliriously, arching in her approval.

"I love you," he said again. In his mind, he begged, *I want to hear you say the words. Say it Mercedes!*

She confessed breathlessly, "I love you, JC."

Her feverish words broke his control. He kissed her hungrily, her taste as potent as a drug. And when the final moment of joining came, their bodies were on fire. They were the only two people in the world once again.

She snuggled against him, listening to his breathing, enjoying his scent. He gently stroked her hair and kissed her head, with only thoughts of how perfect this moment was. It was better than they had imagined in their fantasies over the years.

He shifted his body so he was behind her. He surprised her with his fervor, unlike what she had remembered. He began kissing the nape of her neck. His hand was on her breast, his grip tightening with each measured thrust. They began to slowly make love, again and again. Making up for lost time.

Exhaustion took its toll. And the curtain of time slowly pulled them back into the present. They were lying side-by-side in their repose. She was on her back while he was on his side with his right hand supporting his head. He was caressing her body lightly. He began his loving exploration of her profile. She still wore the delicate gold crucifix necklace. She smelled more fragrant than he remembered. He continued his path downward, and gently uncovered her. He noticed the ravaging results of her medical maladies: the injuries and the scars.

It saddened him terribly.

She was not shy to his soothing touch. Her skin tingled with each caress. She wondered how he would react to find her incisions. She gazed up at him. His eyes were affixed on her belly. He had a look she couldn't put into words. He was lightly tracing the path of her silvery lined scar, which formed like a shy smile. She could feel his fingertips but barely. The severed nerve endings never healed and remained numb to the touch.

Finally, he said softly, "I read every single one of your letters you sent me."

Elated, she said, "I never thought you received them, JC."

Before he spoke, he pressed his lips against her and she responded with tenderness. He looked at her lovingly; his hand positioned protectively against her stomach. She had seen that look before. She became greatly alarmed. With a soothing voice, he said softly, "Mercedes," he paused to sigh, then said, "I know about everything."

She was puzzled with his statement. She began to brace herself for anything, yet she felt vulnerable. Anything she could think of. Her lips tremulous, she asked, "What do you mean everything, JC?"

"Our sons."

She gasped in terror. She was mortified! Her heartbeat became very erratic. She thought she was going to hyperventilate. She pulled herself upright, with her hands against her face. Again, he had caught her unaware. In her mind, she screamed, *Impossible! No one would ever betray me this way! No one!*

He immediately sat up with her, trying to calm her spirits down. She took deep breaths. She mustered a nervous smile and asked a barrage of questions. She said, "I don't understand. But, but how? Who told you? When did you find out? How long have you known? Why haven't you said a thing? WHY?"

Her disbelief turned into anger at the last question. She was trembling as she waited impatiently for the answers. Then, she became overwhelmed with emotion. The tears came, and she was not going to hold in her feelings any longer. Not anymore.

He tightened his hold on her dainty hands and said, "Mercedes, please, please calm down. I don't mean to upset you like this." He held her while she clutched at him and sobbed. He said softly, "It tore me up when I heard you cry on the phone, asking me, begging me for an impossible wish. And now, after so many long years, we're finally together in the flesh. Seeing you cry now kills me!" He kissed her wherever his lips could touch. Still holding her, he asked, "Now, please, I'd like you to listen to me, okay?"

She nodded, still trembling with tears flowing beyond her control. She listened intently while in his embrace. His voice deepened, but filled with tenderness. He said, "I just found out about our sons." She pulled away and was about to interject, but he raised his finger to her lips and said, "Shh... let me speak, my love." The tears kept escaping, from her eyes, though she kept her composure. She wanted to look at his eyes, his face.

Without looking away from her gaze, he said, "I received a letter from a lawyer on my last birthday. I was in terror when I saw a familiar name on it. I thought something unspeakable had happened to you—do you understand?"

She nodded again and lowered her head, her eyes affixed on their entwined fingers. He continued to say, "I brought the letter with me and I want you to read it. Then we can continue talking about it—if you wish." With that, he got up from the bed naked, picked up his sports coat from atop their clothing, strewn on the floor, and produced a legal sized certified letter. He slipped back under the satiny covers and kissed her gently on her forehead before he handed her the letter.

Her tears were flowing uncontrollably. She took the letter from his hand. She turned it over and noted the address of the legal firm. She knew the attorney well; they were classmates in high school. She took the letter out of its envelope and looked up at him, as if to gather the courage to finally read what was written within the pages. He smiled with encouragement. His hands were unconsciously squeezing and caressing her. He had his left hand outstretched, embracing her shoulders.

She saw a very familiar handwriting. She cried even harder. She fought for composure and began to focus on the words, which read,

"*To Mr. Joe Tristram...*

I am writing you because of my daughter's great love for you. I made a solemn promise to my youngest and only daughter never to reveal a life-altering secret while I lived and breathed in this life. I never promised to keep this secret beyond the grave. Since this concerns you, I must now reveal to you a truth.

You and my daughter have suffered the tremendous and painful loss of each other in your unrequited love. A love which I understand all too well. Timing is key for soul mates in life. Alas, I am sorry this is not to be for you both.

With great sorrow, I must write you of another loss, born out of your unrequited love. Shortly after you parted with each other many years ago, you and my precious daughter had twins. They were twin boys, Joe. Sadly, they did not survive to be born. It wasn't meant to be, just as your love and need to be together in this lifetime. I am truly very sorry for this. I really am.

Now you know the great burden of truth that my daughter willingly imposed upon herself, and, yes—on me. It is up to you, Joe, to decide the right path for this truth.

I know my daughter will inevitably read this letter. Let me say to you, dearest little one, please forgive me, my precious child. I know you understand why I have written this to your JC, don't you? It is simply because I love you, dearest.

Remember 1 Corinthians 13:1-7. "Love bears all things, believes all things, hopes all things, and endures all things." Never forget what I have taught you, my beautiful daughter.

For you, Joe, choose wisely. Speak the truth with love and you will know what you must do. Find peace in knowing—love never falters. It's really that simple.

I remain,

Mercédès Ruiz-Donato"

She stared at the letter, and read it over and over again. Finally, she clutched the letter to her heart and sobbed. She kept saying incessantly, "I'm so sorry. I'm so sorry. I should've told you."

He coddled her in his embrace and let her cry. He kept kissing her forehead, her hair and her face. He dried her tears, which kept coming in waves. He couldn't stand to see her this way. There were no words he could say to comfort her at that moment. He kept holding her and waited patiently until she finally stopped crying.

Then, speaking as tenderly as he could, he said, "Mercedes, please know this—" He paused to gently lift her chin up, so her eyes would meet his gaze and give her a lingering kiss on her lips. "Know that I love you. I have always loved you. I've wanted to tell you this while looking into your eyes for a very long time. I wanted to tell you how I wished I was with you when you went through the hell of loss. I wish so many things for us, Mercedes. But I didn't know. I didn't know the cross you bore for us. Had I known, I wouldn't have let you suffer alone. I wish I'd known so many things, so many other things." He had to stop himself, because he needed to regain his resolve from the deluge of emotions threatening his grip of control.

He glanced up to the sky beyond the windows and then looked at her face. Even with tears and agony on her face, she remained beautiful to him. He took a deep sigh. His heart was pounding. He finally said, "For there is more. My daughter is not mine. I had suspected it, but denied it for a very long time. Remember the vow I made to myself?"

She nodded, looking drained.

"Well, it blinded me to the truth. I convinced myself that I was happy with the life I built with Eva. A life without you! I couldn't allow the few days we had to seep into my reality. I had to build a wall around me. But you remained a part of me. Alive in my dreams and fantasies. I was so hell-bent to not turn out like my parents that I chose to live a lie! Until I received your mother's letter and I decided that I needed to finally face many painful truths. So, I finally confronted Eva with what I already knew in my heart. She couldn't deny it any longer. In turn, I told her exactly how I felt toward you."

"No," she said in disbelief. She was now looking away, but he took both of his hands to her cheeks and held her gaze.

"There's no room for any more secrets in our lives."

"But our daughters—"

"What beautiful irony," he said. "Remember you once said that 'the most important thing that a father can do for his children is to love their mother.' God help me, but it was the child that kept me tethered to my vows—not my wife! And my love for you—"

"Your love for me? Is it rooted in reality or fantasy?"

He met her teary eyes and answered, "You are my reality." After a soft kiss, he asked, "Remember writing about your only regret?"

Her eyes closed when she nodded. Finally, she took his hands from her face and kissed them both. After a deep sigh, she looked up into his eyes and said softly, almost in a whisper, "Life without the distractions or noise of uncertainty and longing. A beautiful life together, living our lives with unconditional love." After a pause, she said, "Then, have you figured it out yet?"

"Yes, I have—I've figured it out."

They kissed and embraced tightly. They fell back against the pillows, just holding on to each other. Then, the sounds of the nearby church bells struck the hour of five. She immediately panicked and exclaimed, "*Oh, mon Dieu!* I forgot CJ!" She looked at him with frantic eyes and said, "I must go! I'm sorry, but we must leave. I've got to get back to the museum. I must meet my daughter at five-thirty. I'm never late!"

"It's okay, it's okay. We'll get there in plenty of time. I promise you."

They quickly got dressed and before they left the room, they embraced. She stood behind him as he turned the doorknob to open the door. He looked back at her, took hold of her hand and together, they walked out the door. With hands entwined in a lover's knot, they walked down the hallway and outside to his car.

Not one red light stopped them during the drive back to campus. They made it back in less than a half hour. He helped her out of the car and carried her sketchbook for her.

While they were walking toward the museum, they could see the outlines of two young ladies sitting on the steps, waving furiously at them. They slowed their steps when they saw the sight of them rushing to meet them halfway down the path.

Her thoughts were invaded. *The hurt of letting him go again will be scathingly unbearable, but the hurt to the innocent lives in the fallout will be worse.*

Mercedes said finally, "I think we need to stop this—" Her gaze shifted to the smiling young ladies walking briskly toward them. "Oh God, JC—we have no choice." She felt she couldn't trust her voice.

With a frustrated look on his face, Joe was about to speak, but he was interrupted by the sounds of joyful laughter. They were familiar tones of happy voices.

"*Cara madre bella!*"

"Hey, Dad!"

The laughter grew louder as the young friends drew closer to them. They were walking hurriedly alongside each other, which quickly transitioned to a slow jog to race toward them.

Ecstatic at how their young daughters were acting toward each other, each greeted their daughter with hugs and kisses.

In her mother's embrace, Carly whispered in Italian, "*Everything all right, Mom? Allergies again?*"

"*No, my darling, but I'm all right. Thank you for asking.*"

"Hi, Mr. Tristram."

"Hello, CJ."

"We were so worried that you weren't going to find my mom," then, in unison, the girls said, "I'm so glad you found each other!" They shrieked at the coincidence and their laughter was infectious.

"We've planned this forever!"

"I thought it would never happen since he had some silly Air Force war games somewhere in Vegas! So glad you were able to make it, Dad."

Joe turned to gaze at Mercedes and, with love in his eyes, he said, "I wouldn't want to miss it for the world." To his daughter, he said with a grin, "I simply couldn't resist your charms."

She grabbed her father's waist and squeezed him tightly. "I learned from the best!"

"That's my girl," he said, smiling proudly.

"We both thought how great it would be to surprise you! You know, a long awaited reunion between the artist and her model."

"Friends together, at last! Isn't it great, Mom?" Carly clutched her heart and began miming the painting action on an invisible canvas while her friend posed as the model, acting out different, classic poses. It appeared well-rehearsed. Again, the laughter ensued.

Both Joe and Mercedes looked at each other, tickled with their playful charade. They shared their own private moment of laughter. These two young ladies acted like they had known each other all their lives. Mercedes took it as a sign.

"Mom, have you officially invited Mr. Tristram to your art show tomorrow?" Without waiting for a response, she immediately asked, "You are going to be there, right Mr. Tristram? I mean, General Tristram, sir. And Mrs. Tristram too? You won't be disappointed!"

Before he answered, he looked at Mercedes for any signs of reluctance, but found none. Instead, he found her beautiful smile of assent. "Of course, I'll be there. We will all be there."

"Excellent! It's settled then. I'll call Mom and tell her that she should wear her black outfit, not the purple one. Oh, I'm sorry Dad, but she already gave us the thumbs-up," she said with a sweet look and a darling voice which melted his heart. He was shaking his head, but was smiling widely.

"Ladies, are you hungry?" and then, again in unison, the girls answered, "I'm famished!"

Again, Joe and Mercedes shared a private laugh as they began to walk alongside their own daughters with a hand draped over their young shoulders.

With phones in their hands, they called their spouses, telling them where they were going to be. They were heading toward Willard Straight Hall to eat dinner at the Ivy Room. They talked as they walked and noticed how their eyes would constantly lock, smiling whenever it happened. They had become oblivious to something they should've noticed. The two young friends were also sharing private thoughts. On occasion, their eyes would also meet—knowing looks and smiles appeared again and again.

* * *

A few weeks earlier, young Mercedes asked Carly if they could put their heads together about a reunion between her dad and the Professor. They relied heavily on her unchanging teaching schedule and habits. So, she briefed her father on Mercedes' Friday ritual.

Friday had arrived, and the planned reunion was set in motion. Once her father left the apartments, she kept in constant communication with Carly via cell phone. They began converging to a previously agreed upon location. They had planned to meet so they could join them shortly after their happy reunion.

When they got to their designated meeting place, the young friends were excitedly engaged in a frenzied conversation about how to broach the questions regarding the paintings. When they finally decided to join them, they had already gone. They wandered around campus in their search.

"The phone!" Carly exclaimed. "My mom always has her GPS sensor activated."

"That's great!"

"Hey, they're heading to town."

"They must be going to a restaurant. Let's go."

"Here, you keep an eye on the signal while I drive."

They followed the signal to a section of town with restaurants and an inn within a mile radius. She was about to turn toward the restaurants when her friend quickly said, "Wait, the signal is closer to the inn."

"Are you sure?"

"See for yourself."

"Maybe there's a restaurant in that inn."

"I don't know. Let's find out."

With their excitement heightened, they drove to the location, uncertain of where they would find them.

When they arrived at the coordinates, they saw them unmistakably heading toward the inn. Then, they saw them in an embrace, but when they saw them kissing deeply before they entered the inn, the girls both gasped.

They were sitting inconspicuously in another classic car, hidden behind a grand old oak. Their initial reactions were of sudden shock. They were stunned and speechless!

Together, they sat silently; they waited to feel horrible and humiliated about what they had just witnessed.

"What are we going to do?" Carly broke the silence.

"I don't know."

"It's strange, but I don't feel angry or—"

"Betrayed or disgusted… It doesn't make sense to feel this way. To—"

"Understand completely?"

"Yeah."

"It's as if I knew it all along."

"I know exactly what you mean."

"What should we do?"

"Say nothing?"

"It may be for the best."

In unison, they said, "Just between us."

They gave each other a knowing look, mirroring each other's thoughts. *Who am I to fight fate?*

Finally, Carly said, "Let's get out of here."

"Yeah, we'll need the time to come up with a game plan."

Sitting on the steps of the museum, they became cohorts and carefully orchestrated their reactions and explanations in preparation of their parents' return.

* * *

Fueled with the irony of meeting Joe's daughter, in a few short months, Mercedes began to paint with a passion. She managed to complete twenty-one acrylic paintings.

In between her classes and writings, she would sketch endlessly. She also molded clay into art. She had a sculpture's studio with a kiln in the garage area. She included doll-making in her repertoire as well. She created ten one-of-a-kind porcelain portrait dolls for the show. The name of her doll series was *Generations of Love*.

But, she was still stumped on the crown of her show, the one masterpiece that she used for the customary unveiling ceremony. She had picked out a piece which she felt would suffice, but she wasn't completely satisfied with it.

It wasn't until after her reunion with Joe that her muse presented her with her true masterpiece. She had sketched a study of it as soon as they parted company at the Ivy Room.

During her bewitching hours, she painted furiously, completing it before the break of dawn. After she emerged from her studio covered with paint, she was deliriously happy. She promptly collapsed in bed with exhaustion, physically, mentally and emotionally.

* * *

A longtime colleague, Professor Quinn Farrell, played host to the opening of the art show at the Johnson Art Museum. The show was aptly known as *Unveiled*. It was her first exhibition in over two years at the museum since she tenured in Cornell.

At 7:00 p.m. Professor Farrell held out his crystal wineglass and tapped it lightly with his pen. It signaled everyone to attention, and the volume of the music was turned down.

"Ladies and gentlemen, welcome! I am thrilled to join you in experiencing a rapture of senses from the new paintings created by one of our own. Without further adieu, I am honored to present to you our very own artist extraordinaire, Professor Mercedes Larcher!"

A burst of applause welcomed Mercedes to the front of her invited guests. She was very nervous, especially with Joe and his family in the room. She was stunning in a long dress version of a formal classic—a deep burgundy, halter tuxedo dress— with wrap-front satin lapels. It dipped low in the back with a bias-cut skirt, giving her an incredibly slim A-line shape. She was wearing her red, snake leather, four-inch cuff pumps, and her hair was swept up to a classy up-do. With diamonds and blood red lips, her presence was majestic. It was made more dazzling when she flashed everyone her confident feminine smile.

Everyone in the room was also sharply dressed for the occasion. *Beautiful people surrounded with beautiful paintings*, she thought. She scanned the room and finally her eyes rested on Joe, standing in the back of the room. She smiled directly at him, and he smiled lovingly in return. Then she turned to Grant and Carly, and at last addressed everyone.

"Tonight is very special for me," she said, looking at Joe again. It was as though she spoke directly to him. "I thought I lost my muse, but I was mistaken. For my muse returned, bearing many gifts—very precious gifts. I reluctantly accepted these blessings; but finally, these gifts touched me, moved me." She took her eyes off of him and looked around the room at her rapt audience. She continued, "It urged me to create the beautiful paintings and sculptures you will enjoy tonight. Yet, I must confess there was this one extraordinary gift bestowed upon me, a truly unique masterpiece that is hidden under this veil of silk."

She turned her gaze to the covered canvas on a golden artist's easel next to her. It was draped with a thick white silk veil that shimmered under the lights. Again, she looked at her audience and said, "Ladies and gentlemen, respected colleagues, my students, dearest friends, and my precious family—I was doubly blessed! For this one particular gift was even more special than I could have ever imagined it would be! I am pleased to share with you, tonight—*Heaven on Earth*."

With that, she unveiled her masterpiece. Applause erupted that pleased her immensely.

Heaven on Earth was a 72" x 60" acrylic painting on canvas. It depicted Carly and Mercedes as pre-pubescent little girls, and eight-year old twin boys, enjoying each other's company in fun. They were on a white sandy beach near a lagoon building sandcastles, fortresses against the waves lapping on the shore, with their hair blowing in the gentle breeze in their timeless frolic. Shadows of two people, a woman with long, windswept hair and a man with broad shoulders, were cast over the children like a loving, protective shade. It was a pristine moment—a serene loving scene forever captured in the timeless vessel of her painting.

Grant was first to embrace Mercedes and kiss her lightly on her lips. Carly followed along with others in the audience. They were extending their congratulatory sentiments. She received praises and accolades. The music turned up and the festivities officially began.

Mercedes and her family stood in light conversation when another family of three joined them, Joe and his family. It was a surreal moment. It was the first time Grant ever met Joe and Mercedes, Eva.

"Fantastic show, Professor," her young protégé greeted her, kissing both cheeks lightly in the air.

"Thank you, Mercedes." She noticed Eva's eyes were on her and she didn't have the slightest intention of looking away. Nevertheless, she looked her up and down because she couldn't help it, and because she was different than what she had imagined her to be. She hoped Eva wasn't staring at her with hatred.

"Hello Mr. and Mrs. Tristram," Carly said politely, and greeted her friend, "Hey Merc. Great to see you!"

"Hi CJ. You look great!" her friend smiled and turned to her mother beside her, "Mom, may I introduce to you my mentor, Professor Mercedes Larcher."

"Hello, Mercédès," Eva said, pronouncing her name with a hint of Spanish accent, no more. She was a lovely Latina woman, who just turned sixty, with dark hair and her eyes, in spite of the fine wrinkles around them, were dark and intense. She was dressed in a flowing silhouetted black dress with fluted sleeves and sling-back high-heeled shoes. She was taller than Mercedes was. The attractive features on her face were taut with stress.

"Wonderful to finally meet you, Eva," she said, her voice sounding inadequate to her. She had not rehearsed what she was going to say.

"I'm glad you came to the show."

"I couldn't say 'no,'" Eva looked at her daughter when she answered and added with a strained smile, "Lovely show."

"It's a terrific show," Joe said, trying to soften the awkwardness. "I especially enjoyed the unveiling."

"Thank you," she said smiling, though she could barely muster it because she was trembling inside. She was glad to feel Grant's protective hand on her back.

Turning to her husband, she said, "This is Joe Tristram and his wife, Eva."

"A pleasure to meet you, Eva," he said charmingly and shook her hand lightly. With Joe, he offered a firm handshake and a silent nod.

Both men took a hard appraising look at each other. They stood eye-to-eye and their unrestrained stares spoke volumes. They were dressed in dark suits. Grant wore a red tie and Joe, blue. For a brief moment, they were poised like two knights on a battlefield, but quickly withdrew for the sake of decorum.

"Where are you staying?" Mercedes directed the question to Eva.

"In one of the apartments in the north campus."

"How do you like the area?"

"Charming but I couldn't live here" was her terse but ladylike reply.

For a long time, the ladies exchanged polite conversation while the men remained silent. The tension was palpable.

"Let's have a drink, Grant." Joe's invitation broke the long note of silence between the two men. The invitation was more of a declaration that neither one of them had a choice but to talk.

"All right," Grant said and turned to the ladies, "Would you excuse us?"

At the bar area Joe motioned the bartender for two shots of whiskey. The order was promptly filled and placed in front of him.

"Always wanted to learn how to fly."

"You should. It's liberating."

"Never had the time. Always at the hospital."

"That's right. Mercedes told me you're a surgeon."

"Yes, I am," he said. "And you're JC."

"She told you."

"Everything," Grant replied, and looked steadily at him. "I love her more than you can ever imagine."

So do I, Joe thought but said, "I know, Grant."

"Then you know what has to be done."

"Yes, I do," he said, quickly swallowing the shot of whiskey, feeling the heat of it in his mouth. He placed a shot in front of Grant.

"I do have a lot of respect for fighter pilots like you."

"Thank you."

He stepped closer. "But you as a man, Joe—I have no respect for you."

Holding his gaze, Grant took his index finger, slid the shot glass back to him—untouched. He grinned and walked away.

On the other side of the room, four ladies were loosely grouped together.

"Congratulations on your Magna Cum Laude, my dear," Mercedes said endearingly to her young student.

"Way to go, Merc," Carly congratulated her friend with a wide smile.

"Thanks, I don't know what to say." she beamed, blushing, with her mother beside her.

"You must be very proud of your daughter."

"Yes, Joe and I are very proud of our Mercédès," Eva replied. It sounded like a cue; Mercedes got the drift.

"Mom, did you notice how one of the girls in the painting looked like me when I was ten or eleven?"

"Yes, I did notice," Eva said, clear that the resemblance did not escape her. Directing her question to the artist, she asked, "Who are the children in the painting?"

"Carly and as you guessed, your daughter," she shared.

"And the twins?"

"Children from my imagination." Mercedes felt invaded.

"Interesting" was all Eva said. A silence passed between them.

"Mom, taste the mini stuffed mushrooms—they're delicious. Here," Carly tempted her with a sample, offered on silver platters which the tuxedoed servers doled out around the room.

"No, thank you, *mia cara*," she declined sweetly, noticing that Eva wasn't eating either.

"My daughter tells me you speak several languages."

"Yes, I do."

"Spanish?"

Mercedes nodded.

Another tuxedoed server came and flirted idly with the women, offering wine. Three of them took a glass. Tactfully, they commented on the food, the music and the guests.

"I'm going to the ladies room," the young Mercedes said, giving her friend a stealthy wink.

"Me, too," Carly quickly said, "Would you please excuse us?" The girls left giving both mothers the privacy to talk.

"Certainly," the two women said in unison, surprising them both.

Mercedes broke the ice. "You have a gifted daughter."

"Yes, I know." Eva smiled suddenly, but the smile vanished as quickly as it had come. "I know she told you why she decided to transfer here."

Mercedes felt her sourness, her disappointment. She said nothing, yet kept eye contact.

"Until recently, I didn't know why my husband insisted on naming our daughter, Mercédès," she said in flawless Spanish. She tried to say it without feeling, but her eyes could not hide her glaring anger and pain.

"I've forgiven him. And now it seems you've taken the two loves of my life," Eva said, with total and disarming candor, and there was great restraint. Pride ran deep within her. Finally, she said, "*Haz el bien sin mirar a quién.*"

Her words had the effect of a well-aimed dagger. Mercedes was stunned into perfect silence. *Haz el bien sin mirar a quién. Do what is right, come what may.* Words her mother had lived by.

Before she could utter a word, Eva had walked away without looking back.

Suddenly Mercedes felt a tap on her shoulder. She almost dropped her drink.

"Sorry to startle you." The elderly gentleman seemed anxious.

"It's all right," she said, concealing her distress. "What is it Quinn?"

"A buyer is interested in the painting, *Heaven on Earth.*"

"But you know I'm not selling it."

"I realize that, but he was quite persuasive. Will you reconsider?"

"Well, it's just that the painting is—"

"Priceless," the voice behind her finished her sentence.

"JC, you're the buyer?" sounding pleased.

"Yes, of course, I know the artist and I'd like to support her."

"Quinn, would you please excuse us?" she said politely to her colleague.

Joe offered her a fresh glass of Merlot. They walked through the crowd, talking and smiling, and consciously avoiding their spouses until they found themselves standing directly in front of the unveiled painting.

There was no one near them. He studied the painting and said, "The two shadows are—"

"Us," she completed his sentence, feeling safe to tell him.

"Beautiful painting. Like you," he said, looking at her. His eyes were fixed and devotedly on hers. "You never cease to amaze me."

"It's yours. I painted it for you," she said. "There's a poem to go along with it."

"Why didn't you recite it tonight?"

"Too personal," she confessed with a small frown. "It was only meant for you."

She produced a small sealed envelope addressed simply "JC" and for a moment she hesitated before handing it to him. He placed it in his jacket pocket.

Looking at the painting again, she said, speaking quietly, "I named our sons Ethan and Gabriel, for they both mean strength."

"They're beautiful names." He was pensive. *Now whenever... wherever life takes us, we'll be able to call them by name.*

There was a morose silence between them.

"Love?" A voice behind her asked.

"Yes, love," she replied somewhat startled, turning to his direction.

"Time to say goodbye," Grant said while he looked at Joe intently. Joe felt a rush of nauseous jealousy.

"Yes, you're right. It is time," she said softly, and took the lovingly outstretched hand offered, and gracefully walked away. She stole one last look at him and smiled, a very beautiful and sweet smile, like the one she gave him in Vegas. It made Joe feel uneasy.

"Dad?"

Joe quickly turned. "Hey there princess. Where's your mom?"

"In the ladies room," she said, now looking at the painting.

"The resemblance is really uncanny," she observed. "It's like I posed for her at that age."

"She's very talented."

"I wonder who the twins really are. Did she tell you?"

Feeling the envelope in his pocket, he replied, "Only that they're very precious... just like you."

* * *

Later that evening, sitting on the bench where they had reunited, Joe opened the envelope, expecting to find her poem, but instead it read:

"My dearest JC,

I am asking once again for that impossible wish you granted to me years ago. No contact forever. Perhaps it's meant to be this way, so let's blame fate for all this agony. Perhaps it's all our own doing and we've made the wrong choices all along. Then sadly, we only have ourselves to blame. Fate or freewill? I have yet to find an answer. Perhaps you will.

You are forever a part of me, as I am forever a part you. Above all, Ethan and Gabriel will forever be a part of us. Revisit us often where we will always be, in Heaven on Earth.

Goodbye, Joe my Captain.

Mercedes"

"No!" His strong voice echoed in the vastness of the campus. He sat back and looked at the stars for what seemed to be hours. He could scarcely believe it had come to this.

Fate or freewill? The question echoed, lingering with his frustrations.

He stared at the word "Goodbye".

His composure wavered. *No! You can't mean this!*

He read the letter over and over again, as if to make the words untrue. He felt lifeless. *Yes, you're right, this needs to stop.*

Finally, he crumpled it in his fist and made a wish. An impossible wish.

A rush of beautiful memories flooded his mind. He couldn't get her smile out of his head. He couldn't bear the image and wished it to vanish. All of it.

He heard a sweet faint whisper behind him.

"I'm here."

He smiled, thinking, *No wish is impossible. Not with us.*

"I love you," he said. He felt relieved.

"I love you, too."

Finally, he turned around to face her. *It can't be.*

It was Eva standing there.

Chapter 29

Valentine's Day

Grant's white Queen had just taken her black knight, and Mercedes only had her black King left. He had his two pieces, the white King and Queen. She looked intently at the board and remarked sweetly, "Love, the Queen may be the most powerful piece in chess, but it cannot by itself mate my King. This may be a stalemate."

"Go ahead, love. Let me show you how I'll deliver a checkmate when both the King and Queen work together. Much like we do," he leaned over with a smile and kissed her gently on the lips.

With the first of his mates, Grant's white King controlled three of the squares to which her black King might otherwise retreat. With his second mate, his white King and Queen shared that responsibility and more.

After she made another hasty retreat, it was inevitable he was going to have her in checkmate in just one move. She looked at the board again and shook her head, then bowed in reverent surrender, "I stand corrected, your Highness. I have just received a trouncing from an incredible powerhouse of a couple!"

He smiled at her gesture and commanded, "Rise my Queen. I shall now show you how your King celebrates victory!" he stood up, took her hand and kissed it. She got up and embraced him tenderly and said, "Happy anniversary, love."

In the midst of their private moment, the phone rang.

"Hello, Papa!"

"Hello, Poppet! Let me put you on videophone," Grant said, gesturing for Mercedes to come closer.

"Happy anniversary to the best parents in the world!"

Her parents beamed with responses of, "Thank you, Butterbee!" and *"Grazie, mia cara!"*

"How does it feel to be married for a quarter of a century?"

"Ready for the next quarter!" Mercedes responded happily and Grant instinctively kissed her.

"Okay, you two! This is a videophone, you know," she giggled. "Are we all ready for our fishing trip?"

"I've got everything ready for us!" Grant answered excitedly. After retirement, he had convinced Mercedes to move to an area near Lake Tohopekaliga, popularly known as Lake Toho, in Central Florida.

"Will the weather cooperate, Papa?"

"Great weather! Bring your sunblock."

"And the photos from our Lisbon trip, *ma chérie*."

"I will, Mom." She had forgotten and was thankful for the reminder.

"Any thoughts on where we'll go for your sixty-fifth birthday this year?"

"I'm thinking France."

"Again?"

"And guess what?"

"Tell me!"

"This time, we'll have another guest," she said, smiling at Grant. "Your father is joining us."

"Strange, but true," he said.

"That's incredible! Hope you can handle all the estrogen for an entire week, Papa!" she teased. "Speaking of incredible, is the rumor true? Uncle Joe convinced Aunt Abigail to come along?"

"Yes, I got a call from your Uncle Joe earlier today to confirm," he replied with a smile, thinking of his best friend and his sister. After two failed marriages, Joe and Abigail had finally gotten married and had honeymoon babies, Jacob and Belle. Jacob just made them grandparents while Belle, like Carly, was a career-oriented free spirit who was too busy to settle down.

"He had to promise your godmother that for the entire trip, he'd take the fish off and bait her hook for her!" He chuckled.

"That is just like Aunt Abigail!" she said, giggling.

"Now, now, you two," Mercedes interjected, laughing along with them.

"How's your book about karma, Mom?"

"Just finished the first draft," she happily reported. She was devoting her time completely to writing metaphysical books.

"I can't wait to read it! Oh, did you get Merc's new book?"

"Yes, I received it yesterday."

Her protégé's newly published book of poetry delighted her greatly. It was entitled *A Marriage of Art and Poetry*, and the inscription was simple:

"To my dearest Professor Larcher,

As promised, I have continued to learn.

Love,

Mercedes Tristram-Bradley"

A year after graduating from Cornell, she had gotten married to one of her classmates, Adam, and Carly was her maid of honor. They kept their friendship alive, visiting each other often.

Once in a great while, Joe's daughter would update Mercedes about her parents in her emails, which were plentiful, or Carly would mention something about the Tristrams in one of her phone calls, but she never pressed for more details; instead, she would seamlessly change the subject.

"They just moved to Binghamton and Merc is expecting her first baby! She's due on St. Patrick's Day. She wants me to be the godmother."

"That's happy news! Would you let me know of their new address? I'd like to send them a gift," she said, barely listening as her daughter went on. "Now, what about your flight?"

"I got someone to cover my patients so I can take an earlier flight in the morning," she said excitedly. "I'm really enjoying Temple Hospital. Glad I made the choice of having my psychiatric residency here."

"That's fantastic, Poppet! Call us right before you leave for the airport."

"I will, Papa. Oh I almost forgot—Happy Valentine's Day!"

"Happy Valentine's Day to you too! We love you!"

They were blowing kisses before the call ended.

* * *

As Mercedes stood beside the chessboard, she turned and opened the cherry-stained, pine double French doors that led to the swimming pool. The paved terrace framed the pool, which was built into a swale with existing stone outcroppings that were augmented by granite boulders. The terrace was lined with custom-made balustrades that her late father had created as a trademark that showed her family lineage, much like a crest celebrating the family name.

She remembered how busy her father had been, becoming an intrepid world traveler after her mother passed away. When he was a young architect, he had made a promise to himself that he would visit every single architectural marvel his favorite architect, Frank Lloyd Wright, had created worldwide. She had accompanied him once on one pilgrimage to Arizona. He had been like a child! At the age of ninety-two, he possessed the unbelievable vitality to tour the world twice over, trying to fulfill his constant need to be immortal. Immortality, she had discovered, was the reason he had wanted to have many children.

She thought about her sage mother, still wishing to rival her wisdom someday. *Oh Mom, Dad still hasn't figured out the secret to immortality. Just as you said, "To be remembered is to be truly immortal."* She drew in a deep breath and smiled. *Just like you, Mom. Immortal.*

Although it was early evening, the stars were blazing in the night sky and mist from the water gave a surrealistic feeling to the terrace. She mused at its enchantment, looking up at the heavens. After about ten minutes, Grant joined her, covering her shoulders with her indigo shawl of blue, cashmere silk. There was a chill in the air.

As they looked at their view of the water, Mercedes sat on a chaise while he sat on the ottoman facing her. She shifted her gaze back at the stars.

"I've got a little something for you, love," Grant said, piquing her interest.

"What is it?" She perked and smiled.

"We have to get back inside. I'll ask you to close your eyes before you get in the study—don't open them until I tell you."

They walked hand-in-hand back toward the house. She closed her eyes before entering the study and Grant carefully led her into the room. Impatient in her eagerness, she feigned a young voice, asking, "Can I please open my eyes now?"

"In a moment, love. Not just yet."

As she entered the study, she was greeted with a wonderful fragrance. It was the distinct smell of Stargazer Lilies, and their sweet aroma filled the air. She sensed the room was brightly lit, and then the soft sounds of Mozart flooded the room. Finally, he said, "You can open your eyes now, love."

She did and gasped, instinctively bringing both her hands up, covering her mouth.

The room was filled with fragrant lilies and lit candles were flickering everywhere. He took her hand and walked with her toward the hand-carved wooden mahogany table where they had sat for their game of chess. Two filled wineglasses sat next to a beautiful red, embroidered, Oriental silk scarf. There was something hidden underneath it. She couldn't tell from the outline what was hidden and she was excited, eager to find out what it would be. As they were approaching the table, she noticed there was something else hidden in the shadows.

She turned to him with a sweet smile, as though she was asking his permission to find out more about the hidden gifts. She loved his surprises.

And he felt wonderful seeing her so excited. He smiled back at her as he bent down and reached under the table, taking out a wicker basket tied with a big red bow.

Sitting in the middle of the basket was a small, six-week old, brown and grey tabby kitten with a red heart and bell. The message on the heart read, "Hello, Mommy! My name is Mozart. Be my Valentine. I love you!"

She let out a scream of delight, gingerly taking the kitten and snuggled it close to her cheek. The soft purring of the kitten filled her with happiness. She kissed its furry little cheeks and held him close to her face. "Grant! Thank you, Grant! He looks just like our little Vangogh!"

Grant answered, quite seriously, "You know, love, little Mozart was Vangogh in his past life."

They began to laugh and as they embraced, she could hardly stop her giggling as it escalated to uncontrollable laughter. When she finally stopped laughing and was just enjoying snuggling the kitten, Grant announced, "Ah, but there's more!"

He handed her a glass of Merlot, offering a simple toast, "To my beautiful wife, and my Queen."

To which she responded with, "To my handsome King."

They toasted each other with their glasses and sipped the wine. He stepped closer and kissed her. She loved the taste of the wine on his lips and their warmth against his.

He then said, "Love, please lift the silk scarf and discover a treasure."

She gladly obliged, first placing Mozart back in his basket where he started to play with the red bow. She felt the smooth silk of the scarf with her fingertips, and then she gently lifted it away to uncover its hidden treasure. Her eyes widened when she discovered that the treasure was a beautiful violin with the bow lying across it. Again, she gasped.

Her very first acrylic painting done forty years ago was a violin. She had never learned how to play the violin, so she had painted it instead, calling it, *Artist's Life*, because the music sheets behind the violin depicted Strauss' music of the same title. The original painting hung in the permanent collection of a Philadelphia gallery, and prints of the painting were popular with violinists and other music lovers.

She was speechless. All she could say was, "Oh Grant. It's so beautiful. But neither of us knows how to play the violin. I must—"

Grant interrupted her with a simple action. He swiftly took the violin and the bow in his hands. Then, he began to serenade her with Mozart's *Violin Concerto, K216: Allegro*. She was mesmerized by how expertly he was playing. She slowly lowered herself onto the sofa in utter disbelief. She had not known that he had ever taken a violin lesson, much less played with such feeling and beauty.

Suddenly, she realized he had not only given her a gift of Vangogh's twin, he had found a natural talent for music that celebrated her very first painting. She simply sat there, listening and marveling at him. He had given very special gifts, one for each of her five senses, and she loved him for who he was and for what they shared.

From that evening on, her dreams of the thirteenth century stopped and the phantoms finally vanished.

Chapter 30

The Masquerade Ball

It was five years later when they arrived at the Philadelphia Museum of Art to enjoy a night of elegance at the annual Masquerade Ball, a custom they had kept since they were married. They would faithfully migrate back to Philadelphia every year to attend the gala event every Halloween.

Mercedes was wearing a high-waisted, bell-sleeved Renaissance dress: an elegance of luxurious, deep dark-wine satin, with double puffed sleeves and a square, gold-trimmed neckline. She also wore a beautiful stand-up headpiece in a matching color. It was attached with white tulle on the headband, trimmed with plum and gold braid at the headpiece's base, and topped with pearls. Her veil reached six-inches below her shoulders.

Grant escorted her as an intimidating U.S. Marshal with the familiar silver star pinned on the breast of his long sleeved, creamy beige shirt. He had a cowboy hat, boots with the silver spurs, and small fringes on the side of his leather pants, along with a replica of Billy the Kid's gun in his leather holster.

Accompanying them at the ball was Carly. She had just accepted a position with the Philadelphia Bureau of Investigations as their lead Forensic profiler in the sex crimes unit. Whenever she could, she would tag along with them. She came as the Greek Goddess, Athena, dressed in a simple Greek peplos tunic and himation cloak. Her date, Sean Fitzpatrick, was a tall, dashing gentleman, who worked as an Intelligence Analyst with the U.S. National Security Agency, or NSA, in Washington, D.C. He was dressed as an imposing Brigadier General. They met while Carly was serving as a consultant for the NSA, providing assistance in profiling and evaluating the terrorist mind. They hadn't been going out very long.

They were seated in the east balcony overlooking the orchestra and dance area in the East Stair Hall. The orchestra began its harmonious melodies of Johann Strauss' *Blue Danube*, inviting everyone to dance the waltz. Grant stood up, took hold of Mercedes' hand, and asked with his usual southern charm, "May I have the honor of this dance, purdy lady?"

"Why I would be delighted, Marshal Larcher," she said, mimicking his drawl And smiling lovingly at him as she gracefully slid out of her seat. They passed Augustus Saint-Gaudens' *Diana* at the top of the stairs. While they walked down the stairs, they admired Alexander Calder's mobile *Ghost*, which seemed to float above the Great Stair Hall.

When they began to dance, she was filled with inexplicable joy. Her whole life, it would seem, was an incredible journey. A journey which had led her to this very moment, dancing to music she adored in the sanctuary of her favorite museum where she met Grant so many, many moons ago. Grant spun her for a precocious kiss, then surprised her when he dipped her; she was full of laughter. It felt like they were in Vienna again. It had been one of her memorable trips, along with Florence and Paris.

As another Strauss waltz, *Artist's Life*, began its melody, she glanced up at Carly and Sean, who were seated by the edge of the balcony. They had been furtively watching them in their Viennese waltz; then they returned to gaze into each other's eyes. On occasion, she would be shyly smiling at him. They would laugh and talk, oblivious to the gaiety around them. They did make a wonderful couple, and Mercedes knew they would soon take their relationship to a higher level. She smiled at the thought as she looked at Carly lovingly. With a content smile, she turned her gaze to Grant. She said a silent prayer of thanksgiving for all of her blessings. She was enjoying herself in another dance, to *The Merry Widow* from the Viennese operetta.

Suddenly, she became light-headed, perhaps from the rush of blood, when she tilted over. The room was swaying. She thought it was from the passionate kiss and giddiness of the moment. She was no longer young in body, though she remained young in spirit. She dismissed it as part of her blissful euphoria from her happiness. It was merely the rapture of a perfect moment, because she was filled with immense joy, just dancing in what seemed to be paradise to her. She was surrounded with beauty and thought, *What more could I ask for now?*

As she completed her thought, she felt a darkness descending upon her. It happened so quickly. She had fallen to the ground in Grant's arms. Carly ran down the stairs in terror. She had immediately rushed to her side. Sean had already grabbed his phone, calling 9-1-1. There was panic in the room and the music abruptly stopped. But Grant was adamant—he urged the orchestra to continue playing. There was reluctance which tried his infinite patience. He never let his anger show or his rage to even be felt, but tonight he was in rare form, and out-leashed the heights of its manifestations in tactical control. The maestro simply could not refuse him. The orchestra began to play Mozart. Once the music began again, it did not take long for his stoic demeanor to return. He knew how music calmed the spirit, and he needed all the serenity he could muster, especially with his beloved's life on the line. He was glad to see Carly at her mother's side, checking her vitals signs while Sean took control of the growing crowd around them. The ambulance was on its way.

She was going in and out of consciousness, and she stopped breathing. Both Grant and Carly were in their detached medical modes and were administering emergency measures. When they had successfully revived her, Mercedes gasped desperately for oxygen. She felt strangely calm and serene. She looked into Grant's eyes, whose image was slowly fading from her vision. The sounds of Mozart enveloped her, but it, too, was fading. Her senses were becoming dull and she began to feel cold, yet it was a very familiar and comfortable feeling. The closest feeling she could liken it to was that common phenomenon when she would find herself in between wakefulness and stages of sleep, where her mind would struggle to keep awake in spite of the fact that her body had already fallen asleep. When she didn't realize it was happening, it frightened her and caused her to panic, making her fight hard against it. But when she finally understood that she needed to join her mind and her body in the natural course of sleep, she would calm down, ultimately succumbing to a deep, restful night sleep. It was ultimately not frightful, simply natural.

As she felt the impending sleep approaching, she smiled, understanding exactly what was happening to her. It was time.

But it was when she looked at Grant that she began to miss him already, beyond any words she could utter. And she wanted so desperately to speak. Grant knew she was fading away, but kept refusing its truth. Carly was now in Sean's embrace, fighting against the tears which came uncontrollably.

Grant pressed his cheeks against hers as he held her in a tight embrace. He kept saying words of reassurance in his usual soothing tone, and told her repeatedly how much he loved her. Tears were rolling down his cheeks and falling on her face. Finally, she said in a faint whisper, "Grant—my love." He brought her closer to him, so he could hear her. He managed to muster a smile when she opened her eyes, now filled with resigned understanding. With tears in his eyes, his voice breaking, he gently and tenderly whispered to her, "Yes, my love—I'm here. I'm here and I love you so much. Everything is fine, love. Please. Please hold on to me. Please." He began to silently sing to her as he usually would, during her darkest of spells.

She struggled for the words, trying to speak in between gasps. Finally, she said, "You... you've made me very happy..." Her tears flowed. She felt her breathing ebbing away but she smiled, full of love, "I... I love you... Grant..."

Her eyes fluttered one last time. Her lungs stopped heaving and her smile faded.

Her eyes were now fully dilated, with an affixed peaceful gaze at Grant.

He was in stunned disbelief. He was completely engulfed with an overwhelming surge of sadness. A sorrow so deep he could not even begin to acknowledge it.

"NO! MERCEDES—DON'T GO! NO!" The strong echo of his voice resonated above the music of Mozart. With a fierce and contumacious determination, he administered CPR again and again. Carly had to struggle to stop her father, who was persistent in his efforts.

She was gone.

Chapter 31

Journey Home

A vacuum-like force was pulling Mercedes upward. She turned to look and she saw herself in Grant's arms. He had scooped up her limp body and he was holding her close to him. Carly was holding both of them in her embrace, and they were both sobbing. Sean was directing the emergency medical technicians to her as the crowd of men and women in beautiful costumes surrounded them. The music played on. Suddenly, everything vanished.

She felt like she was soaring on a current of light that was bathing her and welcoming her in a joyful embrace. It was a solace she had known, and she felt free and peaceful.

Extraordinarily, she began to hear whispers, voices familiar in tone. She felt rather odd, yet again it was a very familiar sensation. She could feel herself smiling. She was stretching in catlike movements, when she shifted her body. The whispers grew louder, more audible.

As she turned her head from side to side, she heard a very distinct female voice filled with bursting delight. The voice had the same tone as that of her beautiful mother. "*My dearest, how fare'st thou?*"

She was utterly confused, uncertain whether she heard what she had just heard. Then the soothing motherly voice became insistent, yet gleeful. "*My child, thou art awakening! Oh joyous day! Nurse! Nurse! Rapidement! Quickly!*"

She heard footsteps, many footsteps. Was she in the phantasm once again? If so, why was this different? She took a deep breath, expecting to smell the scent of burnt candles, but to her delight she smelled the fragrant lavender blooms, and oddly, a mixture of spices. She shifted slightly, feeling the texture of linen on her fingertips.

A deep timbre sound, that of an elderly man, resonated with joy, "*Didst thou sayest awaked? Hark! My son doth arrive in the most opportune time.*"

She smiled with her eyes still closed. She recognized the speech patterns, the dialect, and the meaning of the words. Her thoughts were in more Modern English. She had expected vespers, but she heard none. Instead, she heard a man's voice in song, as footsteps from a staircase grew louder.

The doors slammed opened and the voice was one which she had heard all of her life.

"*How now, father?*"

"*God save you, my good son. How dost thou?*"

"*I did ride most swift after receiving word from my squire—my wife, in final hours of birth's travail. Pray how fare'st my wife?*"

"*Freed from her delirium!*" said the lady with her mother's voice. "*'Twas of grave concern in thine absence. After a most difficult birth, she took to a deep slumber. In our vigil, we feared death hath but ta'en her. Alas, thy lady fair now awake. Faith thou art here and thy babes await ye both for thy welcome! 'Tis a happy hour!*"

"*Happy news, indeed, sweet lady!*" His voice sounded even more joyful, "*Forsooth! Didst thou sayest babes? How fare'st they?*"

"*Healthy, thank the heavens! Awaiting ye for thy kisses! Pray pardon me; I must away to fetch thy babes. The nurse she tarries.*"

His father beseeched him, "*Go to thy wife, Tristram.*"

Tristram!? Mercedes willed herself to open her eyes, bracing herself for what she would see. Finally, her lids lifted. Her vision was clearer and all her senses were sharp. She looked around the room, in awe of what she saw.

She was in a great chamber of a château; she knew it was the solar on the upper floor, in a separate wing at the *dais* end of the hall. She called on her memories of Medieval life—the chamber was usually located over a storeroom, matched at the other end over the buttery and pantry, by a chamber for the family, for guests or for the steward.

She looked for the source of lighting and she found rushlights, candles of tallow, impaled on both vertical spikes and on iron candlesticks with a tripod base. Along the walls the rushlights were on iron candelabra and wall brackets. Oil lamps in bowl form were suspended in a ring to provide better illumination. Even flares hung from iron rings in the wall.

She was lying on a great bed with a heavy wooden frame, overlaid with a feather mattress, sheets, quilts, fur coverlets and massive pillows. The linen hangings of her curtained bed, which were normally pulled back in the daytime, were closed to give her privacy and protection from the window drafts. The hangings on her left side were being pulled back as she awakened.

From where she was lying, she could see most of the room. Squinting and peering through the linen hangings of her bed, she glanced at the windows, floors and doors. The windows, glazed with greenish glass, were covered by wooden shutters and secured by an iron bar. Glancing at the floor, she expected to see carpet, but it was strewn with rushes mixed with herbs. Massive wood-carved chairs were near an arched fireplace. A wall with a funnel shape collected and controlled the smoke.

Silently, she complained, *Oh fie! I can't see his face*. Her mysterious beloved was hidden from view. He stood just behind the post of the bed, his back turned toward her, his long blonde hair streaming below his shoulders

She was startled when she heard the door open again. She peered through the hangings and saw a beautiful elderly woman enter. She was carrying bundles in her arms, and she greeted a well-dressed man who appeared to be of the same age. She happily announced to this man with her mother's voice, "*Our precious little grandchildren, my lord!*"

"*Such strong voices on these poppets!*"

The loud cries of babies pierced her ears. She thought, still in a daze, *Not just a baby, but babies? What's going on here? This isn't how it usually goes*. She had silently braced for the pain, which would now overwhelm her at this moment, but there was no pain. She could feel her womb, which was raw and sensitive, tender to the touch with discomfort, but there was no piercing pain.

This is so strange. Where's the pain? She waited, but several minutes had passed. *Okay, any minute now. Any minute.* But the pain never came. She was very intrigued, so she sat upright with ease and leaned back against the massive pillows on the bed. She pulled away the sheets covering her and looked down at her clothes.

She was wearing the same off-white chemise she always wore during these flashbacks. She inspected it closely, looking for the bloodstains, which had always been there in previous flashbacks, but she found none. No bloodstains. She was astonished! She also looked at how young her hands were and she felt her face. She even looked at her breasts under the chemise just to make sure. She was very young—a teenager—but she couldn't be certain.

In her mind's voice, she shrieked, *Holy Mother of God! This is unbelievable!* The long tendrils of her hair that were draped over her breasts were blonde. Feeling the texture of it on her fingertips, she gently yanked on it, grimacing when she felt the pain of her tug. *This is too real! Stay calm—just stay calm. You'll soon wake up.*

Quickly, she covered herself when she heard the rustling of a skirt approaching her. She looked up and saw the radiant smiling faces of two very familiar people. A beautiful matronly woman sat down on the bed beside her, leaning over and kissing her gently on her forehead, saying tenderly, "*My dearest child, thou wert then in peril. I be one as well if thou did not awake!*"

"Was I in a coma?"

"*Aye, a deep slumber, my sweeting.*"

"How long ago?"

"*'Twas seven days past.*"

"A coma for seven days…" she said, a note of anxiety, perhaps even wonder in her voice.

The woman wore an empire waist, regal purple velvet dress. Standing beside this lovely woman was a distinguished, handsome gentleman about five years her senior. He was wearing a hunter green vest, waist length in back, open in the front, with buttons at the bottom. He also wore an open black coat, trimmed in gold. He gave her a warm embrace and said, "*I share thy mother's joy to find thou art most well.*"

Behind them, she saw him slowly approaching the foot of her bed. She felt herself smiling, the beating of her heart increasing to a crescendo as he got closer. His battle-hardened face bore a joyous smile and he carefully held a baby in each of his strong arms, kissing their cheeks as he got closer. The couple next to her had moved aside to let him through and silently, they left the room to give them privacy.

Combing her hair nervously with her fingers, she thought, *I'll finally see his face in the light.*

She was so excited in her anticipation of seeing him clearly, that she began to cry. She also set aside her interpretations, logic, and theories about what was happening to her. She no longer cared if she was going to be jolted out of this different version of her phantasm. She just wanted to look upon his face. Finally, there he stood before her, with babies in his arms, smiling in his joy. At last, her beloved was revealed.

When the knight stepped into the light, she didn't recognize him. It alarmed her greatly, but the sight of the babies distracted her. Her heart was overwhelmed.

Lowering the babies into her arms, against her chest, he said, "*Our poppets, my lady.*" He sat on the bed beside her and gently placed a kiss on her hand, his blond beard tickling her.

She held his gaze and noticed a red embroidered scarf tied around his arm. *My favor?*

She began wondering who she was and what her name was. She tried to make sense of it all. The little voice in her head whispered, *Nothing is, as it seems.* She wondered when she had heard those words.

After she placed gentle kisses on the babies' foreheads, her emotions overwhelmed her and she began sobbing.

Reaching to lift her chin up, he wiped away her tears. "*Thou art most beauteous fair, my Joséphine.*" After a soft kiss, he said tenderly, "*O fair Jo—*"

I'm Joséphine! she shrieked in her mind, but out loud, she said calmly, "Tristram."

"*Thou speakest my name so sweetly as if thou heard it for the very first time,*" he said teasingly.

She opened her mouth, yet no words came out.

His brows knitted in thought and finally said, "*I had a most disturbing vision that, that distressed me since our parting. Every night it plagued my dreams. A nightly terror and truly strange. 'Twas—*" He paused.

It was what? Don't stop now. What was it about? She hadn't dared to voice it out loud. Instead, her bewildered eyes urged him to continue. Finally, he said, as if he heard her silent plea, "*Un chevalier du ciel.*"

"A knight of the sky!" She repeated the words in shock, her skin tingling. "In your vision, were you…" her voice faltered to a stop.

"*In a fierce battle, unlike one mine eyes e'er seen. The battle was…*" he looked deeply into her eyes, dazed and dark green like the gemstone and whispered, "*'Twas for thee. The battle—for thee.*" His voice then rose triumphantly, "*And by God's wounds, my love prevailed! For thou art here, awaked—with me.*" He was smiling widely.

Finally, her eyes fell on the heraldic arms, emblazoned on the chest of his surcoat. *A red dragon crest!* Wide-eyed and smiling warily, she stared at him, her jaws dropping, and then back on the familiar crest. *My paintings!*

All of a sudden, the surge of her adrenaline increased; her heart began pounding harder than ever and her breathing became erratic. She tugged her babies closer to her in her shock as though they would vanish at that moment. She cried out, "Please, dear God! Don't wake me now, not right now!"

"*What art thou saying?*" The look on the young knight's face shifted to one of worry and concern.

"I'm not really sure, but I'm frightened," she said, tears falling unheeded. She tried to calm herself, repeating in her mind, *Breathe—be calm. Everything is fine.*

"*Shh,*" he said as he drew her into his arms, placing soft kisses on her head. His whispered voice soothing, his words filled with love. "*Do not be afraid. Thou art with me, my love.*"

Pulling gently from her, he kissed her eyelids, tasting her warm salty tears, before drying them gently. Staring into her eyes, he repeated, "*Thou art with me for all eternity."*

She looked into his eyes, light and honey-brown like autumn leaves. They were filled with the timeless love and devotion she had known all her existence. A strange and wonderful calm came over her. Suddenly, a phantom conversation began, unlike one she had ever experienced before.

So he is...
Yes, the truth hiding in plain sight.
But he called me Joséphine... that doesn't make any sense... unless...
Eve in search of her Adam also finds—herself!
So this is... this is... but is it?
Yes it is.
Seven days...seven ages... seventy years.
"For a thousand years in thy sight are but as yesterday when it is past, and as a watch in the night."
Psalms... Yes, yes, of course! But Mercedes and Joe...
Means merciful, forgiving and God shall increase.
Increase what? Pain and suffering?
It is not the answer that is important—it is the question.

At last, she understood.

There was no mistake about his heart, his soul and who he really was.

"Love dost prevail, even all deaths," she said, without noticing the phenomena, her thoughts and speech had smoothly transitioned from Modern English to her native French.

"Aye, my love." His kiss brushed her lips and then her eyelids. "*I love thee verily with my life, my lady fair.*"

"And I love thee, my lord Tristram."

"'Tis time we give titles to our sweet poppets."

He carefully picked up the baby clad in swaddling bands of blue and proclaimed proudly, "*I shall name our son Victor—a strong name, meanest conqueror. For, he shall be most victorious in his day. Like father, like son!*"

"Aye, like father like son," she repeated lovingly, matching his smile. She looked at her daughter's tiny little wide-eye face, into her cupid mouth. After thinking of her own journey, she breathed deeply and said, "*I shall name our daughter Devin—for her name meanest poet. I know 'tis true in my heart—words, beautiful words of prose shall well be in her future!*" Then, she predicted, "*She shall touch the hearts of men with her most profound words, and she shall speak them with truth and love in her soul.*"

Their lips met with a kiss filled with joy—a most passionate kiss with eyes closed, holding their twins together into their loving embrace.

Outside the window, she heard the loveliest sounds, and with a soft smile of understanding, she whispered softly, "*Home.*"

As she listened to the melodious distant sounds from beyond the curtained walls of Château Larcher, her memories of modern times slowly disappeared and finally vanished.

In the distance, bell ringers were filling the thirteenth century Poitou-Charentes, between Bordeaux and the Loire Valley of the French western coast, with their final evening chimes, orchestrating, welcoming the dusk of *Lady's Day.*

Author's Note

This book evolved into something more than the inspired romantic love story that I had set out to write. Instead, the story took a life of its own and became more mystical than I had anticipated. And much like the reader, I didn't discover the "twist" of the story until I wrote the very last page.

Through the process of editing, the real story unfolded within the language of romance. It offered many epiphanies to me (hopefully to you, as well) about fate, freewill, truth and especially love.

The quote from Samuel Taylor Coleridge in the epigraph (before the start of the book) beautifully sums up the whole point of this story. Here's a secret: I didn't find the quote until *after* I finished writing this book. Serendipity, right? Well, I actually had three quotes to choose from.

Like the main character, I enjoy puzzles, especially ancient ones; but they sometimes tend to be biblical. And yes, I did indeed endure twelve long years of Catholic school—not that there's anything wrong with it, mind you; but consequently, you might have to suffer valiantly as I share my second choice for the epigraph, and see if you can figure it out:

"*9 The thing that hath been, it is that which shall be; and that which is done is that which shall be done; and there is no new thing under the sun.*

10 Is there anything whereof it may be said, See, this is new? It hath been already of old time, which was before us.

11 There is no remembrance of former things; neither shall there be any remembrance of things that are to come with those that shall come after.

-*Ecclesiastes 1:9-11*"

Perhaps, I should have opted for the third quote from Chuang Tzu or Zhuang-zi:

"*Once upon a time… I dreamt I was a butterfly, fluttering hither and thither, to all intents and purposes, a butterfly. I was conscious only of following my fancies as a butterfly, and was unconscious of my individuality as a man.*

Suddenly, I awoke, and there I lay, myself again.

Now I do not know whether I was then a man dreaming I was a butterfly, or whether I am now a butterfly dreaming I am a man."

No matter. Whether it's from new age thinking, religion, or philosophy, it's all about the same simple question: What does your awakening mean to you? This question may drive you to madness, but that's the book I'll be writing next.

Finally, I couldn't resist the opportunity for another puzzle—actually a word scramble. Within the two chapters where the main character is teaching class, take the first letter of each student's name, thirty of them, and unscramble them to discover a message (hint: it has five words). A shameless ploy to make you read it again? Of course!

Enjoy and live in love.

Printed in the United States
53752LVS00002B/55-66